An
UNHAPPY
MEDIUM

KATE DAKIN

First published in Australia by Aurora House
www.aurorahouse.com.au

This edition published 2024
Copyright © Kate Dakin 2024

Typesetting and e-book design: Amit Dey (amitdey2528@gmail.com)
Cover design: Donika Mishineva (www.artofdonika.com)

The right of Kate Dakin to be identified as Author of the Work has been asserted in accordance with the Copyright, Designs and Patents Act 1988.

 A catalogue record for this book is available from the National Library of Australia

ISBN number: 978-1-7635726-4-5 (paperback)

Distributed by: Ingram Content: www.ingramcontent.com
Australia: phone +613 9765 4800 | email lsiaustralia@ingramcontent.com
Milton Keynes UK: phone +44 (0)845 121 4567 | email enquiries@ingramcontent.com
La Vergne, TN USA: phone +1 800 509 4156 | email inquiry@lightningsource.com

DEDICATION

To my mother, Deborah, whose sage advice has always been a great inspiration to me and without whom this book would not exist.

ACKNOWLEDGEMENTS

A huge debt of gratitude is owed to my family, Lyndon, Debbie, Aaron and Jared, who hoisted me up when I was falling, as well as all my friends and my boyfriend, Ben, whose encouragement kept me going despite my wavering confidence. And, of course, my cat, Columbus, the best writing partner I could ask for.

I'd also like to thank Aurora House, whose acceptance of my manuscript was a huge honour. The team has been an absolute joy to work with, including my lovely editor Anne Lawton, whose advice and guidance encouraged and sustained me throughout the writing process.

All of these wonderful people helped to give life to this, my first novel, and I could never have done it without them. They have my sincere thanks and gratitude for helping my dream along its way.

Thanks also to Highfield House, a beautiful homestead in Stanley, Tasmania, whose deep history greatly influenced and inspired my writing and the central plot for this book. I'd also like to acknowledge Clarendon House and Woolmers Estate – pieces of Tasmanian history whose settings and surrounds provided inspiration for the dwellings and, in particular, the Archer Estate where much of *An Unhappy Medium* is set.

The main inspiration for my writing style must be credited to such literary works as *Coraline* by Neil Gaiman, *The Haunting of Hill House* by Shirley Jackson and *The Beasts of Clawstone Castle* by Eva Ibbotson, all of which were a driving force behind my desire to create a book of my own.

CONTENTS

PRELUDE

It's true what they say about forks in the road. A simple choice as to whether to go this way or that can have life-changing effects. It can mean the difference between life and death. Between happiness and unhappiness. Between having a bright future and being stuck in the past.

Let's face it ... everyone thinks I'm more than a little strange. I don't have any friends to speak of. Apart from the ones my little quirk attracts, of course. Dead ones. Life for me is a calamitous contrast between despairing loneliness and being bombarded by the spirits of tormented souls looking for answers. In fact, everyone except my brother, Will, thinks I'm so crazy that I've virtually been cast out of the town where I grew up.

Yet this house ... this dark old, crumbling house, crouched in the woods just a stone's throw from my back fence, could be my saviour. Or not. I can feel the pull. I can sense the mysteries surrounding it. There are ghosts here, of that I'm certain.

I take a deep breath. I enter.

0 | THE FOOL

People talk to the dead all the time. It isn't an exclusive talent and it isn't difficult to do. It can confidently be said that most people in the world have spoken to the dead at least once in their lives, whether knowingly or, more often, unknowingly. On birthdays. Death days. Special occasions. Perhaps just to pass the time on a calm, sunny day. Or on a dreary, rainy day when their spirits are flagging and they feel weighed down enough to indulge in a reminiscent ramble. Speaking to the dead is, in fact, quite normal.

However, it's quite a different matter – and makes for a rather lonely, depressing existence – when all or most of the people you *know* are dead. Conversation with them can get maudlin, and the act of communicating with them can look a little strange to spectating strangers. Isadora's particular ability is not something she necessarily wanted or cultivated, nor is it something she can control. Her situation is more of a 'make the most of your circumstances' type thing. Only she's not very good at it. Death makes her uncomfortable in ways she can't even begin to describe, so conversing with these 'friends' is awkward. Mostly from Isadora's perspective, as the dead generally don't listen to her anyway, too engrossed as they are in their tearful soliloquies to notice her uncomfortable lip-chewing and half-hearted hums. She tends to shuffle on the spot before slowly inching away, hoping to escape with nothing stuck to the sole of her shoe. If only she could be so lucky.

Isadora had never been what one would consider a normal girl. Quite simply, she was strange. Her strangeness mostly stemmed from the deep-seated, inescapable loneliness that was a direct result of her 'gift'. You see, not all deaths are violent; therefore, not all dead people *looked* dead to Isadora. Speaking to a random stranger on the street was akin to a guessing game. Does this person have a caved-in skull? No, they must be alive then … only, SURPRISE! Turns out they had died in their sleep and hadn't been able to find their way into the great beyond without their glasses. Consequently, when venturing out, Isadora tended to walk with her head down, gaze fixed firmly on the pavement. If she didn't speak to anyone, she dramatically reduced the chances of accidentally conversing with dead people. It was an almost foolproof tactic – if a bit of an isolating one.

Normal, ALIVE friends were a foreign concept to Isadora, even at school, because although schoolyards were rarely a magnet for wandering spirits, the inevitable had eventually happened. Isadora couldn't quite fathom why the poor ex-student who had accidentally fallen from the top of the science block and broken his neck had resurrected himself. But apparently he was still too anxious about the fact he had an exam the next morning to realise that, because he was now but a mere imprint of a human, he no longer needed to be concerned about his grades. Isadora and the departed classmate had spoken for a full minute before the ghost's head had bobbled loosely on its neck and fallen onto its shoulder, revealing the true nature of its form.

Regardless of the reason, Isadora could safely – albeit unhappily – say she had very few friends, a situation that continued well past high school and into that strange in-between time when no one really knows what they're doing, only that money is suddenly the number one priority.

It would be a lot easier to find a job if everywhere I went wasn't filled with dead people, Isadora mutters sourly under her breath after her third unsuccessful interview. There had been a blistered, melting man garbling some form of English at her the whole time. Unfortunately, the interviewer had thought Isadora's look of disgust had been directed at her and had cut the whole thing short with a "Sorry, but I don't think you're quite what this company is looking for".

Melting Man meanders along beside her as she walks home, mouth still moving but, with only stringy flesh for lips and half a charred tongue, unable to produce any meaningful chatter.

"I don't understand why you're following me!" Isadora yells, rounding on him. Her outburst causes a little old lady across the road to trip and fall into her walker, which then begins to roll down the street, leaving a full bag of groceries spilled on the sidewalk. Isadora cringes and hurries over, grabbing the walker before it can escape entirely.

"Sorry. I didn't mean to frighten you." She hefts the old lady up and adjusts the walker. All this earns her is a stormy scowl and a rather rough jerk when she tries to hand the gathered groceries back.

"People like you shouldn't be wandering the streets without a carer!" the shrivelled old prune snaps before she waddles off. Melting Man gargles unhappily and shakes a blistered fist in the old lady's direction, which Isadora feels almost makes up for his intrusion into her interview. He rolls a singular eye in her direction and part of his spotted face lowers in what she supposes is meant to be a show of sympathy. Given he doesn't have any eyebrows – or really, any facial features at all – the effect is mostly lost, although Isadora appreciates the gesture all the same.

"It's okay, happens all the time."

And that was the whole problem. Crazy doesn't have to mean 'bad', but despite Isadora not actually *being* crazy, it was difficult at times for other people to differentiate between the two. Isadora shakes her head, hoists her bag higher on her shoulder and continues on her way, Melting Man dogging her heels and making off-putting squelching sounds with every crooked step. Isadora sighs resignedly. She already has quite a collection of wayward spirits at home, but she doesn't doubt they'd all be excited to meet someone new.

No one else stares or snaps at her on her way home; in fact, they cross the street to get away from her, as if she is contagious with some awful disease. Painful as this is, Isadora can understand it. In truth, the air is often a little colder around her, and occasionally the smell of rot emanates from the spirits surrounding her. Melting Man lays a sticky, commiserating hand on her shoulder as she nears her house. It takes a few seconds for him to pull loose, as the skin is tacked onto the fabric of her shirt and needs significant force to be ripped free. Isadora huffs when she notices some of his skin remains embedded in the fabric. Another shirt ruined. "Thanks," she mutters and brushes her hand across her shoulder, trying in vain to wipe it away. Melting Man gurgles happily in response.

Isadora finally stops at a rather ordinary house at the end of a very ordinary cul-de-sac and walks despondently up the neatly lined path to the front door. One of her parents will be at work, and the other is most likely in the backyard, so there is no need to worry about running into them and having to face their disappointment. Her mother is convinced Isadora simply has hallucinations – very vivid ones, but nothing more than that. Isadora can understand why her mum is then frustrated at the lack of her job success, considering there are medications that can help this condition – medications Isadora steadfastly refuses to be prescribed. She has already tried most of the treatments available. They have never worked, which is not surprising. She has known from a very young age what she was seeing – and they aren't hallucinations.

Wandering inside, she finds no one hanging about in the living room, so continues on to her bedroom. Here, there appears to be a meeting going on. Things, spirits, beings – whatever you prefer to call them – are gathered in every corner and on every surface. Groaning, Isadora forces her way through the crowd to her bed and flops down onto the mattress.

"Hard day?" A spectral hand places itself delicately on her head. Isadora bats it away with a grunt.

"Not really in the mood for a debrief. If you could all continue your meeting somewhere else that would be much appreciated," she mumbles into her pillow. An eerie murmur reverberates around the room as, one by one, each shadow shifts. Like wind blowing through a leafless tree, it sends familiar shivers up her spine.

"Well, where can we go?" one of the shadows responds. "We can't very well use the *LIVING* room, can we?" Isadora nearly snorts in amusement but keeps her reaction to a slight lifting of the lips.

"I don't much care where you go, so long as it's not here," she replies flatly. From the back of the room, there is a garbled howl, eliciting a wince from Isadora as she remembers they have extra company today.

"Also, I'd like you all to meet …" she pauses, realising she has no idea what Melting Man's name is. She can hardly introduce him as such. Ghosts don't appreciate fun being made of their deaths. Makes it awkward. "Him," is all Isadora can come up with in the moment. She gestures vaguely in his direction, as precisely as she can with her head still hidden in her pillow, and listens to the resultant greetings. Only a couple of her guests are fully capable of words and sentences; the others are mostly content to hover and glare, screaming every so often if they manage to muster enough energy to remember where they were and why.

"Now that's over, can you please get out?" she asks, pulling the edges of the pillow up more tightly and pressing it against her eyes to avoid even a glimpse of the huge crowd as she feels them moving around her. Her skin is tingling with the energy contained within the small room; it is making her very uncomfortable. There is a brief moment as the spirits hover, waiting and watching, then, suddenly, her door swings open to reveal a silhouette that Isadora, turning her head slightly, sees does not belong in her ghostly and rather miserable entourage.

"How'd the interview go?" Isadora only just manages to hear her brother ask over the hissing whispers that float around the room. She groans and slowly lifts her face, immediately singling out her brother as the only substantial figure in the doorway. He is leaning casually against the doorframe, eyes on his phone despite his direct question to her.

"Not well," she says flatly. Her brother tears his eyes from his phone and looks at her.

"Elaborate?" he probes, not moving from the doorway. Isadora huffs and sits up, crossing her legs on top of her bedcovers so her ankles won't be exposed to the under-the-bed area. She can hear something crawling about down there and catches a brief glimpse of scuttling gnarled hands.

"Don't really feel like it, to be honest with you," she replies dourly. Will shrugs.

"Had a visitor?" he pokes, slipping his phone into his pocket. Great, now he is paying attention.

"Apparently the company's fire safety procedures were not up to par," Isadora says, throwing a very obvious glance in Melting Man's direction. He notices and shambles closer, gargling loudly against the melted skin stuck in the back of his blood-clogged throat. Isadora flinches and shrinks back, drawing her legs up closer to her chest to make her limbs less available to touch.

Will watches her passively. "This guy follow you home? Guess he's looking like a used candle, wax burned down to the wick?"

Isadora nods, then lowers her head into her hands.

"What am I going to tell Mum and Dad?"

Will squints. "Sorry, Dora, couldn't hear you behind your hands." He leans closer. "Go again."

"You did hear me. How about you try helping me out instead of being a dick!" She doesn't remove her hands, but she hears Will sigh. She feels his presence slide closer, sees his mismatched socks plant themselves on the carpet in front of her, just near enough to the bed for those snatching hands to extend from under it and attempt to grasp at his exposed ankles. She sees small goosebumps rise on his skin, but there is nothing else. No other reaction to being ghost-groped.

"It doesn't have to be a production. Just explain that they said they'll get back to you, then in a couple days tell them you missed out." Damn him and his calm, sound logic. "Or you could tell them the truth."

Isadora snorts. "And rediscover how much worse psych hospitals are than regular hospitals?"

"At least you get breakfast in bed. And a pair of grippy socks."

Isadora watches Will's socked feet move away, the white hands beneath her bed snatching and clawing unsuccessfully, eventually balling into fists before retreating back into the endless darkness. Lifting her head fractionally, Isadora peeks between her fingers as Will stops briefly in the doorway.

"Dinner's in half an hour if you've stopped wallowing."

And he leaves.

Isadora slumps, her hands leaving small red trails on her skin as she drags them away from her face. As much as she sometimes dislikes her brother, he is the only living person who believes her when she shares her other-worldly experiences. She had once told him about a man, covered in leaves, dirt and nasty scratches, who informed her that he'd spied Will's lost football in a wombat burrow in among the pine trees that grew in the deep gully behind their house. Will found it exactly where the man had said and didn't press her for more information. If she tells him she sees shadows hovering in her peripheral vision, or a woman with a bent neck waving at her from outside the neighbour's house, then that is that. He believes her. But that doesn't mean he understands her (although brothers rarely understand their sisters anyway, so that isn't particularly surprising or upsetting). To him, her description is a pale, water-coloured version of the real thing – but at least he believes her.

Isadora doesn't stop wallowing until well after dinner. Neither her mum nor her dad comes looking for her, and for this she is thankful. Sitting through dinner with her parents asking questions, being careful not to say anything that might upset her, would have been maddening. Even more maddening than lying in bed with spirits gathered around her tugging at her clothes and stroking insubstantial hands through her hair. Weird as that sensation is, she is more comfortable with it than having to deal with her parents' awkwardness around her.

As she lies cocooned in her blankets in that childish way people adopt when they're attempting to hide from the monster under the bed, she begins to drift towards sleep. But no matter how she tries to conceal herself, 'they' always find her eventually. Dreams replace reality. She sees hands, wispy and glowing. Fingers that twist and twine in her hair in a strange semblance of affection. They dance around her face, stroke along her collarbone and, eventually, drift into the billowing fog. Bodies replace the hands – faceless, expressionless. She sees figures – tall, thin, short, dismembered – dressed in clothing that doesn't belong in her lifetime. Crinolines and bonnets. Fine hats, wine-stained shirts. A cyclist whose Lycra is torn away, ribs plastered with road rash. A grey, wrinkled face pushes its way through the mob and everything else fades away. Isadora sleeps on.

Isadora wakes sometime later feeling odd. She pushes her way up through the darkness, managing to open her eyes and look around the room. She feels heavy, weighed down, as if something is pressing her into the mattress. She can't lift her head or arms, can only lie there, eyes flicking from left to right. There is no one around her and the room feels HUGE. Cathedralesque. Grand. Open. *Empty.* Perhaps the ghosts have all become bored and wandered away, as they are apt to do on occasion when tormenting her loses its appeal. Isadora manages to flick her eyes to glance out the window. The moon hangs low in the sky, shrouded by clouds. She's slept well into the evening. As soon as she can move her limbs, she'll check the time.

In her periphery she catches sight of the bedroom door moving. Her eyes dart in that direction. The door is being gently pushed open and is slowly swinging inwards. Through the open doorway Isadora can see into a perfectly dark hallway that seems to stretch on and on. She squints. Suddenly, hallway lights burst into life, candelabras flaring and casting small globes of white and yellow along striped wallpaper. *Neither of which belong in her house. Where is she?* None of the houses around Isadora's neighbourhood are old enough to have these features. She can see dark-panelled doors lining one wall of the hallway. One of them is open, an ethereal blue light shining from within. The light gets brighter as someone passes through the open doorway and turns to amble down the hall towards the room where Isadora is. She can only lie and watch as the figure gets closer.

In the light spilling from the hallway, Isadora sees an elderly woman approach, dressed in a long, white, lacy nightgown. She is hunched over, wobbling a little as she leans on a walking stick. She stops just short of the bed and stands staring at Isadora through glazed eyes. She takes a hesitant step closer and moonlight catches her dark, papery-looking skin, throwing raised veins and liver spots into relief. But she doesn't appear scary. Not in the slightest. If anything, she appears confused. Her furrowed brow crinkles in a frown and the corners of her mouth droop.

"Is this it then?" she asks, voice rasping in the silence. Isadora raises her own brow as much as she can while still apparently partially paralysed. "This is the end? No chorus of angels or big bright light to herald me into the pearly gates?" Creeping closer, her slippered feet shuffling on the carpet, the old lady leans over Isadora and peers at her expectantly. "Well?"

Isadora opens her mouth, momentarily elated she can move more than just her eyes and eyebrows. "Sorry?" she says gently, not really sure what else to say. The old lady sniffs, looks right, then left. An awkward silence envelops them. Isadora mentally shrugs. She's not very good at this, but she may as well give it a stab. "What's your name?" she asks, semi-kindly. Old Lady peers at her again, her gaze now more than a little shrewd.

"Iris." She sniffs again. "And who might you be?"

"No last name?" Isadora presses. It can be difficult to appease a wandering spirit if you don't know their last name. How is she supposed to help them rest if she can't find them? Not that she's very good at that, either, considering the still-growing size of her spectral entourage.

"Not for the likes of you," Iris replies. "And you didn't answer my question." Iris leans on her walking stick, pinning Isadora with suddenly laser-sharp eyes.

"Isadora," Isadora says. Still no feeling in her body from the neck down.

Iris 'harrumphs'. "A ridiculous name," she declares.

Isadora rolls her eyes.

"Now that introductions are over, might you be able to get me to where I need to be?" Iris asks haughtily.

Isadora smirks. She does enjoy the next part of the procedure with some of the ghosts, especially if they're not particularly nice. Case in point, Iris.

"Sorry, Iris, no can do," Isadora replies, with no small amount of smugness. Even if she does get stuck with the old bat, this is rather satisfying.

Iris glares at her. "Excuse me, young lady?"

Isadora grins. "If you're here with me, it means there *is* no moving on. You're stuck here for the time being. Maybe forever. I'm not entirely sure how it works. Sorry." She isn't sorry, not at all.

Iris gapes at her, false teeth teetering on the edge. She manages to gather herself together enough to be affronted and demands, "Why? Why am I stuck here?"

Isadora wishes she could shrug her shoulders. Instead, she sighs and admits, "Can't tell you that. Only you would know or can discover what it is that's tethering you to life and, by extension, to me." Iris does not look pleased with her answer. Isadora doesn't have it in herself to feel particularly sympathetic though. It's been so many years of telling spirits the same thing that all her sympathy has dried up.

"Why have I been drawn to you if you can't help me? What am I supposed to do?" Iris asks, seemingly genuinely upset by the situation.

Isadora ignores her forlorn expression and closes her eyes.

"I can't tell you that, either," she responds, "but you're welcome to join my parade if you like." Isadora can't see past her closed lids, therefore isn't sure whether Iris is agreeable to this suggestion or not. It won't make much difference, regardless. As Isadora waits for the answer she feels a cold shift in the air – enough to make her open her eyes again. Iris is leaning heavily on her walking stick, one arm extended towards her.

"Better than staying here, I suppose," Iris mutters, brows still lowered grumpily. She shuffles forward and places a hand on Isadora's arm, which subsequently burns icy-cold. The cold spreads through her flesh, into her very blood vessels. She feels it rush up her arm and into her chest. It throbs in time with her heart until, gradually, the feeling extends to the rest of her torso and limbs. Behind Iris, the hallway appears to be shrinking, sort of sliding towards them, making it appear shorter and shorter. Darkness follows it, swallowing the small orbs of light. Iris looks back and shifts uncertainly. Isadora doesn't share her concern, but she does wince as the darkness gets closer. Experience tells her this is going to be very unpleasant.

Finally, the hallway slams right into the bedroom doorway. Darkness flies into the room, swelling and sticking to every corner, engulfing both Iris and Isadora. Frigid air howls through the pitch-black space and Isadora feels a strange snapping sensation, like a rubber band breaking. She feels herself being flung back into her body so suddenly that she physically flies out of the bed and into a wall, cracking both the plaster and her head. Finding herself on solid ground, Isadora doesn't open her eyes until she hears a dry, withered voice saying her name. She feels something knocking against her leg and decides she should probably take a look.

She is slumped on the floor of her own bedroom with Iris standing, hunched and questioning, directly in front of her, her walking cane tapping rhythmically against Isadora's shin.

"Are you alright, dear?" Iris asks.

Isadora is thrown by the abrupt change in demeanour. She blinks.

"Yes. I've done it before. Normally hurts a bit, but I'll recover." Isadora rubs at the back of her head. Her hand comes away wet with blood. Damn, it's sore! And her limbs are all tingly, pricking with freezing pins and needles that will remain for days – and no matter how much clothing she wears, or how close she gets to the wood fire in the living room, she won't be able to warm up.

"And what is it you do on a frequent basis?" Iris probes, leaning forward curiously. Isadora grabs onto Iris's walking cane and uses it to help haul herself to her feet. Iris pulls back, mildly offended, looking suddenly ridiculous in her ancient nightgown. Isadora can't help but chuckle drunkenly. She probably has a concussion. Iris whacks her on the shin, leaving the bone vibrating painfully as Isadora doubles over.

"Ow! You didn't have to hit me, you old bat," Isadora mutters through gritted teeth, chuckles fading as the pain radiates up to her knee. Iris doesn't appear to care.

"Then answer my questions, insolent child."

Isadora notices all the other spirits gathering again, a conglomerate of sneering, wailing energy. They, too, seem interested in Isadora's answer, particularly the newer subscribers to the 'Spook Troupe' (Isadora spends half her waking life coming up with various names for the group of ghosts, bereft as they are of an official collective title). She hobbles to her bed and sits down, mindful to keep her voice low. If her parents wake and walk in to find her nattering away to thin air, as they see it, it will go down like a lead balloon.

"Sometimes when people die, they call out to me in a spiritual sense. It doesn't happen all the time." Isadora gestures to some of the spirits who have followed her home from wherever it was they'd been haunting. She can separate them all quite easily now. "But other times, I connect to new spirits. I don't know why. I don't even know how, only that it always happens in my sleep. And those ghosts tend to be ones with unfinished business that only a living being can complete for them."

She meets Iris's gaze. "So, Grandma, that means something in your life has been left undone, and you have unknowingly called out to me on your death day for help." Iris wilts imperceptibly but straightens again in a moment (as much as she can with a permanent dowager's hump, anyway).

"Then why are some of these still here?" Iris asks, gesturing to the gathering – more specifically the spirits who had called out to Isadora as she had, recognisable in their mutual unfinished energy. "Why haven't you completed their business for them?" Some of the newer ghosts grumble in agreement, while the older ones, the ones Isadora has known since early childhood, stay silent. They already know. Isadora smiles humourlessly.

"Because this is my life. Not yours. I want to do my own thing, not wander aimlessly trying to get all these lazy ghosts to move on. If they didn't complete it in their lifetime, why should I have to? They had their time. I've got mine. I'm going to do whatever I want, you selfish creeps!"

A sudden shifting is audible from a few rooms away. Isadora winces. Maybe that last bit, clearly a sore spot, had been a bit loud. But it got the point across. Isadora turns back to Iris, glaring hotly.

"So back off, you old crone. I'm not doing anything for the greater good of these insubstantial imprints."

She wraps herself in a blanket and buries herself back in bed, closing her eyes and counting her breaths to focus her attention away from the moaning crowd. Eventually, she hears the echoing thump of Iris's cane growing fainter and fainter, and the rest of the group fading away as she falls into uneasy sleep.

1 | THE MAGICIAN

Grouchy Granny is just that the next day. And it's wearing thin. Isadora is home with Will today, each keeping to their respective areas of the house. It's been an awkward breakfast, with Isadora confessing to her parents she didn't think the interview had gone very well, sans any mention of exactly why. Her parents had been disappointed (*Ha, told you so, Will!*), but more on her behalf than in Isadora herself. And now, she is alone-but-not-alone once again in her room with the blinds closed and a book open on her lap. She is trying hard to read, but it becomes difficult when Bloody Betsy leans over her shoulder and opens up the wound in her throat. Now her book is covered in blood that only she can see and feel.

"That's disgusting." Isadora looks up at Betsy, who probably isn't actually named Betsy but, due to her obscenely slit throat, is unable to talk to tell Isadora otherwise. Betsy clutches at her gaping wound, face stretching in everlasting pain and anguish, eyes popping, streams of scarlet dribbling down her chest. Isadora wrinkles her nose and snaps her book closed. No point trying to read if the pages are going to be continually smeared with blood. They'll all be ruined, stained rusty brown, the paper stiff and unyielding. Maybe her mother will be able to enjoy the book instead.

Wandering over to the bookcase, Isadora dodges past the soldier with the blown-off limbs who is army-crawling towards the couch, and swerves past the strange woman-maybe-man whose bald head shines in the sunshine. Sunlight and ghosts are an interesting combination, Isadora thinks, for how can something as morose as a wandering, tortured imprint possibly exist when exposed to something as bright and joyful as the rays of the sun? Ghosts are by nature cold, a mere memory of what once was, a drifting shadow attracted to the mustiest, dampest places to wallow away their infinite half existence. Sunlight provides heat, a bone-deep warmth that leaves a lovely 'swaddled' feeling and obliterates the murky thoughts that slink around in the darkest parts of the human brain. Musty, damp places don't exist in sunlight. Yet these ghosts who are living rent free in Isadora's bedroom can lounge in the sunlight all they want. Jerks.

She hops over Army Man and places her book back on the shelf, grimacing as the cover leaves streaks of blood on the white shelving. At least no one can see it but her. A hand paws at her shoulder and she swipes it away impatiently. If she can't read, what else is there to do? Perhaps she can go for a walk? But half the troupe would follow her, ambling, shuffling and scuttling in her wake. Making things annoying and far less peaceful than she would like. She hears a whooping coming from the other end of the house, followed by a long string of creative insults. Will must be playing a video game. Most likely online, with other people who enjoy whiling away the hours screaming and swearing at each other. It creates the kind of serene ambience (not!) Isadora is already far too used to. Another hand tangles itself in her hair.

"Ugh!" She rounds on the guilty spirit and slaps its mutilated hand away. "Keep touching me and I'll break your remaining fingers!" she threatens, raising a hand as if she means to snatch its arm and do just that. The spirit backs away, crying morosely. It is quickly swallowed into the ever-expanding crowd, all vying to get close to the only medium in the vicinity. Exasperated, Isadora throws her hands into the air and storms off, sliding the back door open with far too much force and slamming it behind her as if the glass will provide a suitable barrier to keep everyone at bay.

The backyard stretches invitingly before her, bathed in midday sun, with small white flowers speckled among the lush green grass. Isadora feels herself relax a little. The yard backs onto the woods, packed tight with seasonal pines and strange, twisting trees whose names she doesn't know. A foreign plantation, but a welcome one. Isadora walks towards the back fence, ignoring the body lying face down in the pool (he's always so dramatic!) and climbs carefully over the wooden palings, escaping into the embrace of the dense forest. If anyone tries to follow her, she'll be partially obscured by the tightly packed trees and sun-speckled shadows.

She wanders on deeper into the canopy, crunching over the fallen pine needles and underbrush, enjoying the scent – so different from the usual whiff of something sweetly rotten, decaying in the deep recesses of the forgotten. Okay, so that isn't a scent she can put a name to, but it's one she can easily identify – and one morticians and grave robbers would instinctually know but not be able to describe. She takes a deep breath and allows herself a small, unguarded smile. There is no moaning, groaning or crying. No crackling breaths, garbled words or repeated phrases so morbid and clandestine she can't listen to without either shrinking in on herself or laughing inappropriately. This change of scene is exactly what she needs.

Until she trips over a half-hidden tree root and face-plants in the dirt.

"Watch your step, dear." A walking stick 'clumphs' down in the earth beside her head. Isadora curses loudly. "And watch your language, too, you're not a sailor," Iris reprimands her sharply, accompanied by a tap to the head with her damn stick. Isadora is tempted to reach out and tug it sharply enough that the old lady will topple and eat dirt herself. Unfortunately, all this would do is put her in an even fouler mood, and she wouldn't even have any lasting injuries! So unfair.

Isadora pushes herself up and brushes off her clothes. Her white jumper is covered with dirt and pine needles. Her mum will be annoyed. And she'll ask questions, though none are likely to be accusatory. Her jeans have a hole in the knee, too, and she can feel the cool air brushing against her skin. This she is not so worried about. Jeans with holes at the knee can easily be passed off as fashionable. The only drawback is the small bloodstain near the edge of the tear. But if no one sees it then no one will ask any questions or find any more reasons to find her strange. Not that anyone *will* ask … she has no living friends, after all. Not even an acquaintance.

"You'll need to mend your pants and wash that jumper now." Iris moves around to inspect the damage, squinting and adjusting her glasses. Wait, when did she get glasses? And where from? As far as Isadora knows there's no such thing as ghost-shops or ghost-optometrists. Shaking the thought away, but not disregarding it entirely, Isadora continues walking, but with far more spatial awareness and eyes constantly flicking to the ground to ensure her route is clear.

"I won't bother. It'd be a waste of fabric and time. Rips are in style at the moment."

Iris is flabbergasted. "Ridiculous! Rips are never fashionable!" she squawks, hobbling along unsteadily to keep pace. Isadora brushes aside a low-hanging branch.

"You died in this century. It can't be that ridiculous," Isadora says flatly, eyes scanning her surroundings. She knows there's an old barn or something up ahead, and there's definitely an old house hiding up behind the tree line. It was condemned some years ago and has been drastically overtaken by nature, but it's still there. Isadora enjoys finding places like that, and certainly isn't as scared as her peers might be to investigate. After all, the worst that can happen is that it's haunted – and Isadora, while not particularly hoping for this, isn't bothered by the prospect. She herself is haunted. They won't hurt her.

"I lived in this century, yes, but that doesn't mean I enjoyed every aspect of it," Iris responds, mildly affronted Isadora doesn't seem to respect the fact she may not like speaking of her departure. Isadora barely notices anymore that ghosts are sometimes offended by her referencing of the events leading to their death, and if she does, she doesn't much care.

"Oh, right. Not a fan of all the modern things then, I guess, phones and such. Did you enjoy aspects of the time when you were younger?" Isadora asks, a small part of her genuinely interested, the other part waiting for an opening for an acerbic comment.

Iris nods, mouth tugging upwards into a nostalgic grin.

"The clothing. The dancing. The music! All sorts of things." She appears enraptured in fond memories. Isadora casts her a sidelong glance, a sharp rejoinder on the tip of her tongue, but she decides she'll let Iris have this moment and remains walking in silence.

"Music was organic, I suppose you could say, only instruments and voices. You could really sense when someone had actual talent."

"I'm supposing it's 'different these days'," Isadora mocks her in an old-lady voice and hunches over, mimicking Iris's posture. Iris doesn't appreciate the humour and merely sniffs in a haughtily disapproving manner. Isadora snorts and jumps over a fallen branch. Birdsong rings out in the air. She lets the conversation fall away as Iris makes no move to reply and listens instead to the sweet melodic chirping that echoes all around her. Isadora spins in a circle to follow the bird's position, only vaguely noticing the congregation of grey spirits surrounding her. Abruptly, the bird stops singing.

Isadora frowns and looks over her shoulder, thinking it must be the ghosts that disturbed the bird. But they stare right back, as innocently as one can when in varying degrees of decay. Turning back, Isadora examines the undergrowth ahead. It's thinning out, and shafts of sunlight are beaming down, turning the dirt motes to gold. Isadora pushes through the last of the shrubbery and emerges into a clearing that is almost completely smothered in weeds. Small yellow flowers poke through the grassy mounds and shine in the light. The meadow stretches out towards a large, crumbling timber structure that looks as though it's being swallowed by lichen and ivy. The corrugated iron roof is rusting away, leaving great holes for the rain to get through and erode the long-forgotten farming equipment below to almost complete disintegration.

Isadora eagerly walks around the old barn till she catches sight of the house beyond. It's huge, double storey at least. Made of sturdy, sand-coloured brick, the building sits placidly in the middle of the open field, a large 'CONDEMNED' sign hanging over the once-grand front door. Some of the unbroken windows are bare of curtains and give the impression of large, empty eyes peering out at the new blood.

It isn't difficult to see why it's condemned. Isadora already knows the back of the house is crumbling into the earth, the bricks made wet and unstable from years of seasonal torrential rain. The concrete back steps are almost completely swallowed by mud and are likely irreparable. Isadora loves the house, imperfections and all. If you run round to the back, you can see the driveway making its way through the dense trees, circling around to eventually taper off near the front door. Isadora knows the road the driveway leads to, remembers staring up it as they passed by on car trips back from the city. If you look really hard and know exactly where to focus you can also see the hole-ridden roof from the highway, brick chimneys standing steady and proud among the towering tree boughs.

"A magnificent building, reduced to something so pitiful," Iris shakes her head. "Terribly sad it had to come to this." For the first time, Isadora agrees with her.

"Haunted too, probably," Isadora says casually. Iris, shockingly, barks a loud laugh, causing Isadora to stare at her, nonplussed.

"Everywhere is haunted once *you* head inside," Iris laughs.

Isadora allows herself a breathy chuckle. Never a truer word was spoken! Iris settles herself on the grass, legs stretched out, varicose veins on display. Isadora tracks the muted blue paths and journeys squiggling along under papery skin. To see a person's deteriorated body moving around is disgusting, Isadora thinks; only occasionally is there something fascinating to study.

"Ow!" Isadora cries out and clutches at her arm, a round, stinging welt already growing on the upper bicep. She whips round and spots Will ambling out of the bushes, a shit-eating grin on his face. Isadora's eyes narrow into a glare, but Will only laughs. He moves casually around her and stoops down to grab the tennis ball he'd pegged at her. Isadora knows if he'd been aiming properly, he would have hit her directly on the side of the head.

"Sorry, Dora," Will drawls, tossing the ball with one hand. "I thought you were meant to be able to sense when that kind of stuff was going to happen." He stands just off to the side, arms moving in a demonstration of some cricket bowling technique.

"I can't see the future. I'm not psychic," Isadora mumbles, still rubbing at her reddened skin. "Idiot!" she adds as an afterthought. Iris is sniggering next to her, false teeth clattering away. Will frowns at her.

"Who woulda thought spending every waking moment surrounded by death is guaranteed to make you at least a little bit insane?"

He turns back to his bowling display, right arm swinging gracefully in a wide arc over his head. It takes a moment for his remark to sink in and, when it does, Isadora stares at her brother incredulously, trying to decide whether it was an intentional slight or whether he really is that dense. She settles for giving him the benefit of the doubt.

"I think the word you're searching for is 'psycho', moron. What are you doing out here, anyway?" She flicks her middle finger up at Iris, who is still snickering away until she spots the gesture and settles for a more offended visage that pulls at the corner of her nose. Will knows none of this, caught in the obliviousness of the fully living. And that of the older brother.

"Wanted to practice my bowling skills without risking smashing a window," he replies, and with the next elegant arc lobs the tennis ball at the side of the barn, hitting it head on. The ball bounces back towards them and rolls along the thick tufts of grass, settling a few feet away. Isadora watches the feat with equal parts disinterest and suspicion.

"Of course you did. Did you know I was going to be here?" she asks pointedly. Will shrugs.

"No. I don't know where you are most days, and I don't give a shit either." He wanders over to collect his ball and tosses it neatly to Isadora.

She catches it (only fumbling slightly) and doesn't relinquish it when Will gestures for her to toss it back.

"Really?" she asks. Will gestures again for her to throw it to him. She doesn't. Speckled opalescent eyes stare up, innocently-guilty brown. The standoff carries on for well over a minute until Will caves – and this time Isadora might just be psychic because she knew he would. Will can't lie to save himself. He's far too transparent. He huffs a sigh and sits down, cross-legged, opposite her.

"It wasn't hard to follow you. There's a broken branch back there that you definitely tripped over. Did you go A over T?" He's grinning widely, dimple popping in his right cheek. Isadora scowls darkly.

"Of course I did! You already know I did."

"It was the faceprint in the dirt that gave you away," Will supplies helpfully, gesturing again for Isadora to give him his ball back. She relents and tosses it underarm. Will snatches it out of the air and tucks it away in a pocket he somehow conjured from nowhere. The siblings sit in silence for a moment. Isadora's eyes wander over the landscape, flitting from the gently swaying tree branches to the occasional bird hopping along on the hunt for worms. Eventually, she settles for studying the house, the cracked windows and grappling ivy-stricken walls, until suddenly something catches her attention. There's a figure standing in the top-centre window. One moment it wasn't there, the next it is, clear as anything. Ephemeral, smoky-grey, one hand splayed on the glass windowpane, which is whole and clear rather than foggy and shattered like the others. It's staring right down at her and Will, despite having no discernible eyes or other facial features.

Goosebumps rise on Isadora's skin, and she balls her hands into tight fists. She stares, unblinking, at the figure until it vanishes. She doesn't actually see it vanish. Doesn't see it wisp away into nothing. Simply, one moment it's there and the next it's not. The window is back to its neglected state and there's nothing else in the clearing. All the ghosts have gone, leaving only herself and Will sitting on the grass. Isadora shudders, her whole being suddenly very cold. The chill has erupted from somewhere deep within the centre of her body. A 'so cold it's burning hot' feeling spreads through her chest and down into her extremities until her entire body is trembling.

She vaguely registers Will grabbing hold of her arm and asking her a question, but she can't hear him. All she can understand is the cold, and the sharp, deep-rooted, never-ending anguish that accompanies it. A blackness has seeped into her soul and is refusing to let go. A hopelessness so encompassing nothing else can live alongside it. The sky is inky, despite it being only early afternoon, and she can see nothing but darkness except for tiny specks of light flickering behind the windows.

Then, suddenly, a ghostly glow appears on the front steps of the house. A woman with long, flowing dark hair is standing there looking out towards the barn. She doesn't acknowledge Isadora, kneeling empty and bloodless on the dew-speckled grass. The cold leaches through Isadora's mud-streaked dress and into her knees.

Filth.

Filth that cannot be cleaned away.

She is dirty. She needs to wash it out. But the dark-haired woman assures her she can never do so. *You can never be clean. Never. What has been ruined, made rotten from the inside, will never be whole, can never be the same.* She does deserve this. She doesn't deserve this. But perhaps she does. A pale hand stretches out to meet her across the grass. She can't be touched now, not by a living hand. Eyes stare sightlessly into the starry sky. Reflected there is a future so close to grasping it scares her. Scares her terribly.

"Isadora!" Her eyes snap open as her body shakes violently, head lolling against her shoulder. Will's face blurs in and out of focus. He looks concerned, scared even. Frighteningly scared. Isadora brings a shaking hand to her forehead and squeezes her eyes shut, brain flashing foreign images.

Will's hand on her arm is grounding, painful even, but she doesn't want him to let go. She might get lost if he does, might become untethered and end up floating in the endless expanse of subconscious space.

"Are you okay?" he asks. Isadora can hear the tremor in his voice.

"No." She may as well answer honestly. "Can we go, please?" she adds in a weak whisper. Will nods and hauls her to her feet. Shuffling footsteps give way to Iris, whose wizened eyes are studying her carefully, her dark, wrinkled face creased in concern. The other ghosts part to make way as Will leads her back through the trees and over the fence without a single stumble. Isadora's head thuds in time with her heart.

"Are you going to be able to sleep without pain relief?" Will sits her down at the kitchen bench as he scours the cupboards. Isadora lays her head on the cool surface and fights against the nausea that is crawling lethargically up her throat. She doesn't remember coming inside.

"Nope. Grab the good stuff, please," she says hoarsely. Will rustles through the medicine box, hand emerging triumphantly with a packet of strong pain relief tablets. He hands them to her and she dry-swallows them without hesitation. One of the tablets gets stuck halfway down her throat. Irritated, she rises from her seat to get a glass of water as her brother watches her carefully.

"I'll be in the living room if you need anything," Will murmurs and leaves her leaning against the counter. The caring sibling quota has apparently been sufficiently used up for today. Isadora shudders, tears welling up in her eyes. Her one and only safe-ish haven has been destroyed. She will now always associate that house, that wide open clearing, with a searing sense of hopelessness. A clogged, nauseating sensation would now always settle in her chest when she even thinks of the place. Isadora begins to cry. There is nowhere for her to escape to now, nowhere she can run to. An alien despondency has taken up residence in her mind – hers now and no-one else's.

A strangled wail breaks from her throat. She presses her pinched face into the bench, her cry echoing across the hard surfaces in the kitchen. A curtain of hair obscures her face as she chokes it back down to an anguished mewl. Soft, barely-there hands settle on her shoulders; another hand alights on her head, yet another on her spine – a troupe of spirits gathering in a claustrophobic tight circle around her slumped body. A head lays itself on one of her shoulders and a whisper wafts across her ear.

"Feelings this vibrant are for the living. Embrace it all while you can."

The smell is nice. Nicer than her mum's floral candle, anyway. Isadora watches the fumes as they twist and dance up towards the ceiling. She grips her bunch of sage tightly and waves it around the 'empty' corners of her room, trying to ignore the guilty pit in her stomach as the spirits hiss, wail and dissipate mournfully into nothing. Considering her once-safe space has been completely spoiled, Isadora has set about creating one to replace it. In her haste, she hasn't done much in the way of solid research – she's relied mostly on her own speculation and old, hokey Victorian pictures of what mediums may have done to protect them-selves. The sage seems to be working well so far, although whether it's a long-term solution or merely a temporary, flimsy Band-Aid is up in the air. Time would tell.

Iris had vanished before she'd lifted the sage out of her shopping bag, and Isadora doubts she'll see her again – at least until Iris wants something from her. The old woman still hadn't determined what it was that tethered her here, but she hadn't actually made much effort to dis-cover the reason. Rather, she had taken to complaining every moment, thoroughly annoying both Isadora and all the loitering spirits into yell-ing at her to be quiet. It had been the first and only show of solidarity between both planes of existence. A moment for the history books, if there ever was one.

"If you have something good, you should share it." Will appears behind her. Isadora jumps and rounds on him furiously.

"Don't sneak up on me!" She whacks him with the still-smoking sage. "And don't make drug jokes, especially when it looks incriminating for me. Mum has enough reason to be disappointed in me at the moment." She hustles Will out of her room and shuts the door firmly behind them. The air is much clearer in the hallway and Isadora feels the fogginess melt away a little. She hadn't realised how smoky it was getting in the bedroom. It had felt so cleansing.

"That's what happens when you aren't the 'pink eye'," Will teases. "Family disappointment." He walks past her into the kitchen. Isadora follows, blowing on her burning sage before tossing it in the compost bin.

"Yes, I'm fully aware Mum and Dad love you more than me. What do you want?" she snarks, arms folded defensively. Will ignores her as he pulls some orange juice from the fridge and proceeds to chug the entire thing directly from the bottle.

"That's disgusting," Isadora adds.

Will shrugs and tosses the bottle into the recycling.

"Avoidance doesn't count as 'dealing with things', you know that?" he asks and, despite realising the question is rhetorical, Isadora answers.

"I *am* dealing with it. By banishment. All problems solved." She wanders back through the hallway and to the murky air in her room, where she inhales deeply. Inside and out, the sage is making things significantly better.

Until …

"Has someone burnt something?" Her mum's voice rings through the house as the telltale thump of a handbag on the counter announces both her arrival and her displeasure. Isadora cringes. Hopefully she can shut her door and hide in the safety of her bedroom without her absence being noticed.

"Isadora?"

Damn.

Isadora spins, socked feet gliding on the timber floor. "Hello!" It sounds forced, and her smile looks forced, too. Isadora's mother notices. People in space would probably notice.

"Hello ..." Her mum walks a little closer, peering into Isadora's room, eyes lingering over the very obvious fog hovering near the ceiling. "What's all this?" she asks. Isadora swallows and considers telling her it's completely recreational and not something she needs to be bothered about, but that excuse is undeniably worse than the truth, so ...

"I'm burning sage," she says evenly, trying not to fidget.

"Sage?" Her mum is confused. That's fair enough. Isadora would be, too, if she was a mother and had no idea of the scope of the things her child sees and experiences.

"It's cleansing," Isadora elaborates. "Cleans the air ... and the room. Spiritually." She could be a New Age person, after all; there are lots of them around. It would be better that way for her mum, more plausible. Her mum's eyes widen a little.

"Spiritually?" Her face pinches. "Okay. Why do you need to *spiritually* clean the room?"

Isadora attempts to contain her frustration. "Because I want to?" It's a question more than a statement, which gives an opening for her mum to prod further.

"Not an answer."

Okay, now Isadora's annoyed, and she can't contain the hot rise of her anger. She knows it's unfair of her to take this out on her mum. But after the day she's had, Isadora can't control how she feels. It's uncontrollable in a way that blinds, suffocates and possesses her, surging upwards and onwards into her face, flushing her cheeks and neck red.

"You don't need an answer! I don't have to explain it to you. I don't *want* to explain it to you!" Isadora leans forward. "As if you actually want to hear it, anyway. If it doesn't affect you it doesn't matter, right?"

Embarrassingly, prickly tears gather in the corners of her eyes. "Why start now?" Isadora waits for the inevitable explosion from her mum, which will typically lead to a yelling match that ends only when Isadora storms away to mope sullenly in her room. Until the guilt creeps in and eats at her insides, forcing her to shuffle mulishly back to apologise.

Only, Isadora's mum doesn't do any of that. Rather, she stands perfectly still, face an elegant mask before responding, "That's a fair statement, Isadora."

Her voice is so soft, so forgiving, that Isadora almost allows her jaw to drop in astonishment. Her mum adopts a considering façade. "Please keep the fumes to your room and the hallway." She begins to walk away, but not before an overwhelming wave of shame flushes Isadora's anger away.

"Mum!" she calls down the hallway, feet planted to the floor. Her mum half turns. Isadora swallows painfully. She opens her mouth but nary a croak escapes. Her shame flushes her cheeks and she lowers her head, hoping her hair will cover the guilt that's painted plainly on her features. Her mum offers a small smile.

"It's okay, honey." And she vanishes, her high heels clicking smartly along the floorboards, changing to a sharp clacking as she crosses the kitchen tiles. Eventually, the sound muffles as the carpet takes over.

Isadora is left, foolish, alone and crying in her bedroom doorway, backlit by the sun streaming through her window, which is uncovered for the first time in months. And there are no ghosts to distract her, other than her own personal ones. The effort it takes to uproot her feet and slink back into her room is colossal. With a finite snick the door closes behind her and she sits heavily on the edge of her bed.

Isadora is prone to being low in mood. Everyone knows it. But this … this is a new personal low. A disgustingly self-pitying low. A low born from a misguided assumption that no one can possibly understand her or get close to her. From the insurmountably wide chasm separating her from the world. Her naivety, of course, arises from the same lack of life experience that afflicts every other new adult. Her foolishness has never felt quite so tangible before and, rather than cry as she may once have, this time she accepts her misgivings and the wrongness of assuming her situation is impossible for others to grasp. It is not.

She grows in that moment, although she doesn't know it. She grows infinitesimally, a tiny bud inching closer to the topsoil. Unseen, but soon to be.

⌒⸱⸱⸱૭

Isadora sighs, the sage fumes still filtering around her brain and fogging everything up. A soft knock precedes her brother as he inches around the door and stands on the threshold of her space.

"All good now?" he asks. Isadora can't look at him. "Yelled all the problems out?" He doesn't move closer but remains standing in the doorway with his arms crossed, looking every bit the image of the 'footy player' so many young men aspire to be.

"Funny how that works," she manages to croak out, still hidden behind her hair.

"You don't need to apologise. If that makes you feel better."

Isadora can't answer that because it really doesn't make her feel better at all. Apologising would at least assure her overthinking brain that the matter was fully put to rest. Leaving it open-ended leaves room for intrusive negotiations to the contrary.

"It doesn't. To you, maybe."

Everything about this conversation is stilted, uncomfortable. Brothers are meant to inflict torture, not attempt to offer comfort.

"Turn your brain off from that way of thinking. Or let it sit until it doesn't upset you anymore. Or you could get Mum in a headlock and demand she listen to your apology. That works a treat sometimes."

And it would for Will. Have a bust up, find a solution. Typical Will problem-solving technique. To be fair, it did work well when he did it. Isadora would end up hurting herself more than anyone else. She preferred words to actions, anyway.

"Considering your brain is barely ever active, I'll give you a pass for thinking I can turn mine off," she replies, returning somewhat to her usual acidic self. Will appears to appreciate the return, a smug grin scrawled on his thin face.

"Well, now that you're into all this New Age stuff, have you thought about meditating?" Will uncoils from his arm-locked stance and reverts to leaning casually against the doorframe. Isadora rubs at her cheek, pushes a wad of thick hair behind her ear and, for the first time, looks him in the eye.

"What do you know about meditating? Wouldn't have thought anything like that would be up your avenue." She leans forward, planting both elbows on her knees. Will snorts.

"Apparently I'm more world-wise than you thought."

He doesn't stick around after that, apparently content that Isadora is in a more positive state of mind (relatively speaking), and wanders off to find his headphones. Minutes later, Isadora can hear the faint thudding of his basketball on the concrete paving of the driveway. It was enough to plant the seed, however, and Isadora, amid the heady scent of sage, considers it carefully.

She knows the sage is only a temporary solution, one she now isn't so certain she wants to continue with if it's going to cause emotional upheaval in the mother-daughter bond. She doubts meditation would solve the problem though. At most it would serve as another Band-Aid among the myriad solutions she has already tried. But it could help with other issues – ones more deeply rooted in scientific study than the paranormal. It would, at the very least, allow her mind to relax slightly.

One thing at a time.

Isadora jumps up from her bed and heads outside, hoping some fresh air will improve her mood. She passes her mother who sits reading a book, pointedly ignoring Isadora on her way out the back door. Nor does Isadora acknowledge her mother as she floats past, carefully avoiding any chance of eye contact.

The backyard is overcast. An iron-clad blanket of clouds obscures the sky, leaving the swimming pool a rippling mass of grey. It's empty today. No waterlogged body floating serenely, pushed and pulled by the tiny currents. It feels bare, somehow, almost wrong. Isadora decides not to dwell on it too much. However, she feels almost keenly the loss of Iris and Melting Man, who are no longer dogging her every move making snide comments or gurgling epithets at her decisions, or lack thereof. They had somehow achieved an acquaintanceship of sorts, and their absence has left a bereft hole in the very centre of her being, penetrating deeper than skin and muscle into a different dimension entirely.

She opens the pool gate, enters the enclosure and sits down on the grass. She decides she will give meditation a go. Just as soon as she figures out the best way to do it. It can't be that hard, surely? She remembers her mum used to do yoga and that's kind of similar, isn't it? She just won't have to do all the strange stretches and moves. Isadora crosses her legs and looks out over the yard towards the fence whose presence blocks the path to the old house.

She shudders involuntarily, unconsciously uncrossing her legs and curling them closer to her chest as she pushes the image of the house firmly out of her mind. Instead, she focuses on the gently swaying tree boughs, the sound of the wind rustling the leaves and shaking bark loose. She breathes in deeply, inhaling the scent of nature, and on releasing the breath exhales her clambering thoughts. With each inhale and exhale her mind begins to feel calmer, quieter. But vague anxieties insistently push their way in, interrupting the ebb and flow of calmness that is beginning to take root and threatening to become a stream of noisy thought traffic.

What if this doesn't work?

What if the thoughts and the ghosts all come scrambling back?

I can't keep living surrounded by death. It scares me, unsettles me. This isn't working. I did quite enjoy having Iris around though.

Melting Man, what's he up to now?

That house, why did I see what I saw?

Frustrated, Isadora thumps a closed fist on the ground. She can't stop thinking. Her mind is a carousel, never halting, always spinning. Each thought is a neon-painted horse, bearing a bobbing passenger who shouts sentences at her, sending her own voice echoing back. She tries to shove them down, keep them at bay, but it only increases their strength and frenetic pace.

"Why don't you try letting them be?"

Isadora jumps and whirls around. Iris is seated next to her, her form glowing gently and looking quite phantasmic.

"How on earth?" Isadora wonders aloud.

Iris smiles.

"You're far too strong a force to shut us out with herbs, dearie." Iris settles, walking stick placed primly along her lap. "You should take my advice this time around."

Isadora scrunches her nose. "Just let the thoughts happen?"

There isn't much sense in that, at least Isadora doesn't think so. Surely if she did that she would be overwhelmed, unable to avoid getting swept away.

Iris shakes her head. "Let them exist. If you let them exist, you'll become accustomed to them and the thoughts will seem less overpowering."

Isadora frowns, her brows pinching together as she tries to make sense of that sentence … visualise what it might look like. Perhaps like being caught in a giant wave, trapped and pinned underwater where all that can be done is wait until the frothing settles to come up for air. Let it take you … and relax. A gurgle of assent bubbles up next to her as Melting Man takes a seat on her other side. Isadora stifles a groan. The sage has worn off much more quickly than she expected. Soon the whole circus would be gathered around her. She releases a heavy breath.

"Okay."

She looks back at Iris, whose lined face is set expectantly, one eyebrow cocked.

"I'll try it your way."

Iris smiles, wrinkles deepening.

"Good girl."

And she settles into the grass, her already hunched spine curling further. Melting Man reaches out and places a sticky hand on Isadora's shoulder. When he pulls away, he leaves blackened blobs of skin that start oozing into her jumper. Isadora smiles at him all the same, in a strained kind of way. He can't help his disfigured appearance, after all.

Isadora resumes her cross-legged position. She closes her eyes and allows her body to feel every bump in the grassy ground. Feels every vertebra in her spine, stacked on top of each other. Feels the air flowing in and out of her lungs, automatically swelling and deflating. She can feel the slight stir of breeze and smell the earth. There's a splash to her right as the drowned man gleefully throws himself back into the water (or simply reappears as the sage evaporates from her brain). She senses rather than hears the rest of her macabre troupe gather around. Smells the iron of blood and the sickly-sweet whiff of decay that accompanies them. Instead of cringing away she simply inhales it. Allows it to sink in, but not overwhelm her senses.

Isadora begins to count her breaths. The exercise steadies her considerably and, eventually, without her even noticing, the external stimulus begins to melt into the background. The cluttered road in her head still brims with traffic, but now she simply watches impassively as it rolls by. The thoughts continue but are more muted. Made less, just as Iris said they would be. Isadora can feel something else as well … something building cautiously in her midriff. It feels familiar, as if she has known it before and always will. Warmth, tranquil and fragile, spreads along her extremities. The dark behind her eyelids glows with gold …

And then, shockingly, a sharp sting of pain yanks her right out of it.

Eyes snapping open, Isadora jerks back, left hand coming up to clutch at her cheek, now wet and dribbling with a thin stream of blood. Iris has made a noise of horrified protest and Melting Man has risen to his charred feet, one arm raised as if to strike. Isadora seeks out the cause of the disturbance and is aghast. A thin, crooked figure is looming over her, its features shadowy apart from a cracked and frightening imitation of a smile. Its stick-like limbs are long and covered with thorn-like prickles, and one of its hands is streaked with blood. Isadora rises to her feet, body crackling with annoyance. This 'thing' – because that's the only way she can describe it – horrific-looking as it is, doesn't scare her; it infuriates her. How dare it interrupt her just as she was making progress!

"What the hell do you want?" she hisses. The creature makes no move, so Isadora makes the first. She lunges towards the creature and grabs its arm. pulling it forward so they're face to face.

"I asked you a question." Her voice is low now, filled with steel. The creature flinches and lets out what sounds like a pathetic mewl. Isadora halts her gathered assault, allows it to slide back down her throat and stares, dumbstruck. The creature is cowering, whimpering, dark head lowered and body trembling. Isadora throws a confused look at Iris, who can only shrug. Isadora opens the query up to all the other phantoms with the same result. They don't know what's going on. Isadora releases her grip on the thin, prickly arm and allows the creature to back away, still bowed over and crying.

"Um …" Isadora trails off, feeling wrong-footed, "Are … are you okay?" she finally ventures. A pair of white-coloured eyes rise to meet her own and the thing slowly shakes its horned head.

"O-kay …" Isadora says slowly, moving closer to lay a tentative hand on its back. "What are you doing here?"

Best to get some background before attempting to counsel whatever it was. The creature's ribcage shudders, then expands and an ethereal voice replies, "You called me. I answered."

The voice quivers as it hangs in the air, resonating around the back-yard. It's not at all like anything Isadora was expecting. It's akin to a high note played on a piano, accompanied by a spine-chilling cadence that has goose bumps rising on her arms, or perhaps a discordant violin being played in an empty cathedral. Isadora winces at the noise and then gapes as she absorbs the answer.

"I'm sorry?" She rears back as the creature bats its head into her open palm like a demented cat.

"You called. I answered."

Apparently, whatever it is knows only these concrete facts. Isadora keeps a careful eye on the creature as she scans the rest of the group; they all seem content to be sticking to the outskirts of the circle. Whatever this being is, it isn't well-liked by the other inhabitants of Isadora's second sight. She swallows and focuses back on the stick-like body.

"*How* did I call you?" she settles for asking, genuinely curious.

Its head perks up, white eyes glinting. It whines and sways forward a little. Isadora's face pinches into a quizzical frown.

"How did I call you?" she repeats, but again, the creature only whines animalistically back.

"Why aren't you talking now?" she presses.

The creature simply shakes its head once and settles back on its haunches. Apparently talking is off the agenda for the moment. Instead, it raises one oily-looking black limb and points, first to Iris, then at Isadora. Isadora frowns, not connecting the dots immediately – and even when she does, they don't quite match up. But she has plenty of pent-up emotion at the sudden arrival of whatever it is sitting before her, so Isadora does what she does best and rounds on Iris.

"I knew you had it in for me!" she yells. The circle widens as the group moves back a little. Iris stares, dumbstruck, at her, cane tapping the ground.

"What on earth are you on about, child?" she asks, astonished. Isadora stalks towards her.

"That meditation rubbish has called forth whatever *this* thing is ..." she gestures wildly at the spindly mass of black and spines, which has now lowered itself to all fours and is swaying rhythmically back and forth, shrinking as it does so until it is about the same size as a domestic cat. Iris wrinkles her nose as her gaze settles on its form. "... as revenge for not helping you find the light to whatever!" Isadora finishes.

"I most certainly have no idea what that creature is," Iris sniffs, insulted. "Let alone how to conjure one. And I have no idea how to get you to 'send me into the light'!" Iris jabs her cane at Isadora's hip. "Don't be throwing about accusations until you have the facts rather than complete fiction."

Isadora flushes, eyes boring into Iris's, eventually dropping as reason takes over. They dart, instead, to the ground and eventually trail to the creature's tail as it flicks, all sinew and tiny spines. Like a horned snake slithering through the grass. Iris stands still and waits patiently until Isadora musters up the strength to apologise.

"Sorry," she says. "I didn't think about that." She raises her eyes and meets Iris's level gaze. "It's just making me uncomfortable. And …" she swallows thickly, "… I'm scared that *I've* managed to do this. If I can do this, then what else can I do that I don't know about?" It takes a lot to admit this, as Isadora usually tries very hard to avoid revealing chinks in her dented armour – especially when that weakness is fear.

Ghosts thrive on fear more than anything else.

Iris, to her credit, does not make a meal of Isadora's admission and simply nods firmly. "I can understand that. Apology accepted."

The creature whines and rubs against Isadora's leg, head bumping her roughly as it glides around her. It raises its eyes and stares unblinkingly, white lenses gleaming. The small ridges on its coat catch on her jeans and pierce through the material to prick the flesh beneath. Isabella feels a freezing sensation, so cold it burns through her skin and penetrates into her bones. Isadora wants to banish the creature back to wherever it came from, but she instinctively knows that hoping it would be that easy is incredibly foolish. Defeated, she sighs and asks if the thing has a name, not really expecting an answer. A smile stretches across its face, revealing a crescent moon of at least three rows of pointed incisors that recede into an inky well of throat.

"Bee."

Isadora blinks. The surrounding company share glances and rumbled words too low or incoherent for Isadora to catch.

"Your name is Bee?" she confirms, voice rising in confusion. 'Bee' nods and slides up against her again, head resting against her midriff, one spindly arm wrapping around her leg.

"Bee," it repeats confidently.

Isadora chucks a look at Melting Man, who shrugs one blistered shoulder, then Iris, who also shrugs.

"If that's its name then let it be," Iris advises.

So Isadora does. She even pats Bee on the head, shuddering only minutely.

"Okay, Bee, welcome to the club. Unfortunately, I'm all out of new member packs so you'll have to go without."

It sounds reluctant at best and downright disappointed at worst, but Bee doesn't seem to understand emotion very well and continues climbing up Isadora's body, eventually managing to find a momentary perch on her shoulders. Isadora pushes it off immediately, to much discontented whining.

"What's going on out here?" Will meanders across the grass, bouncing a tennis ball ahead of him casually, stopping only when he notices Isadora's crumpled posture as Bee tries again to grapple its way up. Isadora sways beneath its weight. Will frowns, seeing nothing but his sister acting as though she has a large, very heavy bird perched atop her head. Isadora grins thinly and offers a thumbs-up.

"All good!" she calls, ghostly choir chuckling and moaning theatrically on the sidelines. Will isn't reassured.

"You sure? You look like you've got a hanger-on." He wanders closer, ball now held tightly in his fist. He doesn't appear to like the fact that Isadora is being visibly affected by her otherwise invisible company.

"It'll learn eventually," Isadora huffs as she once again pulls Bee free and settles it roughly on the grass. Bee turns to Will and purrs, bounding forward with tail held high. Will stands still, none the wiser to the approaching companion. Much like an excitable Labrador, Bee gathers its hind legs and leaps when it gets to within a metre of Will. Isadora honestly has no idea what to expect as none of her regular ghosts have ever been able to touch anyone – other than her, of course. But this time feels different, Bee seems committed in a way that just screams trouble. She shouts out just as Bee launches.

"Will, look out!"

Which sounds ridiculous. What is he supposed to look out for? He can't see the mass of midnight-coloured spines and moon-bright eyes. Will opens his mouth to speak, but never gets the chance as he's knocked flat by an invisible foe. He shouts out in alarm and throws his arms up to shield his face (typical, always going to protect his face, absolute drama queen!) sending the tennis ball flying into the pool. He rolls on the grass, legs kicking at whatever it is keeping him pinned, brown eyes wide with shock. Isadora swears loudly and runs into the fray. To its credit, Bee is doing nothing more than playfully swatting at Will's wildly attacking arms, pointed face stretched wide with glee.

"Bee, get off him!" Isadora grabs the back of its neck, finding (much to her surprise) a kind of scruff of reptilian skin, and tugs sharply. Bee gives a high-pitched yelp and goes flying, clearly not expecting this amount of force. It skids along the ground, rapidly gathers itself to its clawed feet and watches as Isadora pulls Will up, still shaking with the sudden rush of adrenaline. He's panting harshly, hands still half raised, the very picture of the phrase 'poised for battle'.

"What in the hell was that?" he finally manages to get out. Isadora examines his pale face. She turns to Bee who appears to be slinking forward, head lowered and eyes raised in submissive apology. So it can understand some form of human emotion, after all. Will grabs her arm and gives her a shake.

"Isadora!" She startles. "What was it that just attacked me?"

Will looks half mad in that moment, frightened beyond belief by something he could neither see nor defend himself from. Isadora shrinks back.

"It said its name was Bee?"

Will stares. Then splutters, then laughs a deranged laugh. One arm comes up and he runs a hand through his dishevelled hair.

"Bee," he wheezes. Isadora backs away a little more.

Bee bumps against her leg and croons, eyes on Will.

"I think it's sorry," she adds weakly.

Will, still laughing, lowers his hand from his head. He looks to be calming down a little. Isadora allows his laugh to peter out to a mildly delirious chuckle before asking gently.

"Are you okay?"

Will brushes the back of one hand across his suspiciously shiny eyes, but answers her query all the same.

"I think so." His eyes roam over the empty spot beside Isadora's legs, as if he can almost make out Bee's crouched form. "I'm just a bit scared, I guess."

Isadora's stomach drops. If Will is finally scared of her and of what she can do, that's it. That's the end of her. Will's eyes widen, clearly seeing his sister's horrified expression. "Not of *you*, Dora," he assures, slapping her on the shoulder. "Of whatever just happened."

"But what if it happens again?" Isadora cries out. "Will you be scared of *me* then? What if you get hurt? What if …" she stops. She's crying now. Bee croons again and wraps itself securely around her legs, tail and all. Will looks a little ashamed.

"I didn't mean it like that," he says quietly. One arm makes an aborted motion to gently grab her hand. It drops back to his side. They stand like that, Isadora sniffing, trying desperately to keep from sobbing, held in a tightly wound spiral of other-worldly creature and surrounded by a semicircle of deceased people, with Will an awkward metre away, watching her.

"I'm not scared of you," he tries again. "You've never scared me. Unsettled me, absolutely. Annoy me, all the time." He grins a watery, wobbly smile. "You're too small to scare me. Too timid."

Isadora sniffles, rubs at her eyes and nose with a fist but doesn't reply, feeling far more like a child than a woman in her early twenties.

Will sways from side to side contemplating where to go next. He isn't particularly well versed in tender moments and has a tendency to put his foot in his mouth. Maybe letting the silence sit is better than trying further reassurance.

"Thanks, Will." It comes from nowhere and everywhere at the same time. Will relaxes fractionally.

"No worries."

Isadora turns to Iris. "Meditation was such a bad idea."

Will barks a genuine laugh and takes a small step forward. "At least now you know." He takes the final step and pulls her into a headlock.

"Ow! Will!" Isadora shoves at him fruitlessly. "Let go!"

"And at least now you know you can set your guard dog on me whenever you want." Will lets her go and walks towards the pool, groaning when he sees his tennis ball floating aimlessly in the centre.

"Only if I can train it to come back when I want it to," Isadora grumbles, accepting his well-intentioned, albeit slightly bent, olive branch.

"That's the thing about people," Will grunts as he kneels at the edge of the pool, stretching to the tips of his fingers in an attempt to grab the ball. It bobs along the surface, spinning gently in the current, tauntingly out of reach. Will winces and stretches just that tiny bit more; his fingers skim the furred surface of the ball and it goes sailing towards the other side.

"People can do anything if they really want to. And if they try hard enough."

Isadora frowns and walks over to the pool gate. She places her forearms on the top of the fence and rests her head against them. "I can't fly if I want to, Will. Even *if* I try hard enough." She closes her eyes. "Sometimes the confines of human capacity are enough to stunt anyone, regardless of any special abilities they may have. And as far as I know I'm the only one who can talk to the dead. Thinking we can do *anything* is silly. 'Anything' amounts to whatever humanity will allow. In reality, that isn't much."

A splashing sound almost has her opening her eyes. She resists. If Will falls in, she'll know soon enough.

"That's maudlin thinking. Although you always have been glass-half-empty."

Isadora nods against her arms. "If the glass is half empty, I won't be so disappointed when it's *completely* empty," she reasons. "Never get your hopes too high and you won't be let down when things don't work out."

"So you plan to live in perpetual disappointment?" Will's feet are making a wet, slapping sound on the pool tiles. So he did fall in then.

"It'll make the good things seem even better when they do happen. Expect the worst and be prepared or be incredibly, happily surprised." The gate shifts under her weight and Isadora opens her eyes. Will is staring back at her from under heavily saturated curls. Isadora steps aside, allowing him to exit the pool enclosure. His clothes are dragging, pulled down by the weight of the water. He shakes his head, sprinkling her with tiny, cold droplets. Bee hisses and hides behind her legs. She'd almost forgotten it was there.

"Sounds like a sour existence," is all Will can say to that, tossing the tennis ball into the air and catching it neatly. "But it's your life." And he heads back inside, shoulders tensed.

Isadora heaves a deep breath, ignoring the glances of her troupe, and goes to head inside, too, but just as she does so, a figure steps in front of her. Isadora looks up to see the shaking head of a young woman dressed entirely too nicely for the current century. One side of her face is missing, treacle-like blood sliding in neat lines down the other side of her otherwise pleasant countenance.

"Leave him to it, Miss," she whispers. Isadora shifts her depth perception and peers through the woman as Will walks through the back door.

"I didn't mean to upset him," Isadora says softly. The woman offers her a kind smile.

"We never do."

She's travelling. She doesn't know where to, but she can feel the movement of wheels beneath her, all the bumps and notches in the road as they drive along.

There's someone next to her. She knows them very well and yet somehow not at all.

Lights flicker past every so often, spilling bright and yellow across their faces. Between one light and the next she has her hands on the wheel. Warm from where his hands had been mere moments ago.

It takes one second.

One.

The ditch rushes up to greet them …

II | THE HIGH PRIESTESS

She's sleeping when it happens. Bee has decided the end of her bed is a grand place to curl up and has taken to migrating right into the middle of it throughout the night. Isadora has been trying to ignore it and failing miserably. Her last few weeks have been slow. Slow in the metaphorical sense, as she seems to be on eggshells around her mother and father and instantly feels an awkward blanket engulf the room when even attempting to be in the same room as Will. She and her mum have reached a kind of peaceful impasse. Isadora found a pack of Tarot cards on her pillow one afternoon, along with a small heartfelt note. It touched her just as much as it irked her. But everything else has settled into a mildly prickly atmosphere of calm.

Tonight, though, is different. Everything is sharper, bristling with electricity. Isadora had dreaded going to sleep as she is familiar with this feeling.

A newcomer is on the way.

The familiarity of the paralysis had done nothing to settle her nerves, nor had the impending sensation of being stretched up and away from her body, a metaphorical rubber band pulled gradually until it was so taut it felt like a hook tugging at the back of her stomach. Now darkness rings around her, bleeding into the corners of her room and beyond. There are no stars outside the window, no lights twinkling beyond the glass. A cold, dark something is breathing around her creating a steady whoosh of air that suddenly increases sharply and blows her bedroom door open to reveal a tarmac road lined with tall, imposing pine trees that sigh and dance with the breeze.

Isadora wants to sit up. The hook tugs painfully in her stomach, but the will to sit is stronger than anything she's felt before. When she rises, she is no longer in her bedroom, despite the fact she is still resting in her bed. Rather than being inside the house, she is on a road. The road she had seen through her bedroom door.

A car is wrapped tenderly around one of the pine tree's trunks, hazard lights blinking innocuously as smoke drifts in swirling streams from under the bonnet. It travels lazily upwards until it is completely swallowed by the inky night.

There is a body in the front seat. The driver's seat. Only one. They had been driving alone. Terrible happenings, car accidents. They don't discriminate.

Isadora wants to stand. Her sleep-warm feet hurt as the frigid surface of the tarmac hits them. She takes a step, silk pyjama pants rustling as she follows one step with another. She hesitates on the threshold of the scene, unwilling to venture further. A figure appears next to the car, swathed in shadow. She hadn't seen him appear, hadn't seen him move. One moment the space is vacant, the next it's occupied – simple as that. He is tall. Thin. One shoulder is soaked in red, and she can see a shockingly protruding lump on his neck that clearly indicates the cause of death.

The result of not wearing a seatbelt, most likely. Foolish, but not unusual in young people. For he is young. Younger than anyone would ever want to see snatched away by something as silly and preventable as a car accident.

He doesn't come any closer and, unlike most of the other fresh spirits she's encountered, he does not immediately ask her anything. He simply watches, scrutinises and concludes. A trembling breath rents the air. Isadora can't move. She wants to. Wants to run. But it seems she is paralysed by this alter reality.

"Dora?"

She clamps her eyes shut, lifts her leaden hands and presses them over her closed eyes to block it all out. Unconsciously she begins to whisper a frantic mantra. Her heart is thudding a horse's thunderous gallop, so loud it drowns out everything else. It sets her limbs quaking, hands trembling, body shuddering as sheer horror sweeps her away. A sob of despair starts at her feet and rises up, flooding her midriff, her gullet and escapes out of her mouth.

Not him, not him, not him! That side can't have him!

Something inside her burns hot as a brand.

She cannot hear him as he approaches, only feels the sudden grasp, the blazing touch on her forearm, and whatever it is inside her locks violently into place.

The snap back from her altered reality is so intense she feels herself physically falling as she is thrown from her bed across the room. When she opens her eyes, the darkened tarmac is nowhere to be seen. The moonlit road has vanished, along with him.

She scrambles to her feet and lurches along the hallway, tears streaming, making no effort to be quiet so as not to wake her parents. She slams her brother's door open and gawks at the empty bed, the empty room. Cold and stark.

He's not there.

Her knees hit the carpet as she leans forward, retching, hair hanging in a thick curtain around her pallid face. She doesn't register the arrival of her parents, doesn't feel them grip her shoulders to pull her upright, doesn't hear past the hollering in her head the questions they ask her in a language she can no longer comprehend. The presence of her ghosts grows stronger in her grief, becoming thicker and livelier as they feel her emotion. After all, every one of them has felt it before – stronger than any living person is capable of. Like an icy-cold wash, it revitalises them, giving their deadened hearts cause to mimic a beat. For them, it is as glorious as it is horrendous, as euphoric as it is depressing.

Isadora's mum draws her into a tight hug, pressing her face into Isadora's hair as she shushes her. Her dad is dumbstruck, unsure of what to do. Gingerly, he places a hand on her shoulder and squeezes as he asks what's wrong. Isadora can't tell them. She just can't. It's breaking her heart to know and to have seen. The images are burned into the backs of her eyelids and with every tear-laden blink she can see flashes of the scene flit across her vision. Her mind will not allow itself to imagine what her parents will feel when they find out. When they learn they have outlived that which should never be outlived. To know the beginning, middle and end of what should have surpassed them.

They should never have to feel this grief.

Sick to the pit of her stomach, Isadora vomits all over the carpet.

Their reaction, quite naturally, is to want to whisk her off to hospital, but she vehemently refuses, pushing against their grasping hands and concerned insistence. As they at last relinquish their hold, her ghosts gather around her, glowing, reaching and pleading with every false breath for her tears to continue, desperate to feel again that euphoric rush of emotion. In Isadora's mind, they meld together into a hazy veil that eventually dispels into an effervescent grey smoke screen as she angrily wills them away.

She doesn't remember much else about that night. Not the light-bulbs blowing or all the glassware in the house exploding, when she had first awoken from her vision. She doesn't remember her parents being there after she had calmed and become silent. Nor does she even clearly remember the ghosts gathering greedily around her. Isadora can only remember the pain, the overwhelming well of grief that swallows all the light she's managed to hoard, sucking it away and leaving a black hole in its wake. In her mind's eye, she can see the flashing red and blue lights. Hear the heavy knock at the door. See as if in a fishbowl, minimised and unreal, the two policemen, hats in hand, like parodies of themselves. "We're so sorry for your loss …" Her mother's screams of denial as she slumps against her father, white-faced with shock.

Isadora floats through it all.

She remains stuck between her two worlds for days afterwards. On one side of the divide are her parents – living, breathing, cloaked in a thick layer of loss. On the other side is a very dead, no-longer-breathing brother who nevertheless still very much exists in another form, despite not appearing to her since the night of the accident. She wonders reluctantly when he will present himself to her.

Isadora can feel her feet planted firmly on both sides of reality, one amongst the dead, the other with the living. She has never felt her psychicness as clearly as she does now. Whatever lid she has firmly placed over the well of her gift has been blown open to reveal a vulnerable, gaping wound.

It has always been like this, she muses. Like a heartbeat, constantly ticking away, a pulse that throbs unchangingly. You know it's there, but you aren't consciously aware of it. Only now, it thuds so forcefully she can't possibly ignore it. If anything, she can only focus on how strong, how heightened, it has become. The division between her and the rest of the world has never been clearer, nor more heartbreaking.

Isadora helps her mother organise Will's funeral, but doesn't attend. She can't, despite her parents' pleas. Instead, she sits in the back garden and gazes up at the trees, mesmerised by the way they sway in the breeze, almost like bits of seaweed pulled and eddied by the ocean's current. In her state of disconnection, she feels like that, too – floating, drifting, tugged this way and that by her own private current. The world does not do her the decency of allowing her to sink.

It's a bright, sunny day when Will is laid to rest in a carefully dug-out pit at the local cemetery. A few clouds make an effort to block out the sun, but eventually they drift almost apologetically out of sight, leaving the beaming rays to shine on, a rude contrast with the black mood. Isadora cries to create some rain, just for herself. She doesn't appear for the wake, either. No one will ask after her. In the past, she's made a point of vanishing for any kind of gathering, familial or otherwise. Her absence will be seen as normal. Just another Isadora thing.

Even if it is her brother who has died.

She is alone, her only company the myriad dead. Strangely, they appear to be mourning with her. It's almost nice to know they understand her grief.

"My funeral wasn't half as nice as your brother's." One sweet old man tries to make her feel better. "The funeral director was so dull, and the speeches were entirely ridiculous. Didn't speak about me once, recited a heap of disconnected poems that had half the crowd bored to tears." His grey eyes gleam sympathetically. "They sent your brother off nicely, dear, don't you worry about that."

As gratifying as it is that they are trying – for more ghosts have sidled closer to regale her with their own tales (and all their funerals seem to have been put together by half-brained amoebas with no common sense to rub together) – Isadora isn't terribly concerned about Will's funeral. She's kept her eyes peeled ever since she'd been tugged to that road and connected with that strange psychic something within. A connection that still burns and refuses to fade. But there's been no sign of him yet. Which is odd, although not entirely unwelcome. Isadora *doesn't* want to see him just as much as she *does*. She's scared to see him. If he never appears at all she might cry with simultaneous joy and despair.

Her parents sit her down to talk the day after the funeral. The conversation becomes a bizarre interrogation that leaves more than one party in tears. Isadora belatedly realises she should have seen it coming.

"It's alright if you see him," her dad begins flatly. "Just make sure you tell us, okay?"

"I'm not a telephone," Isadora replies, voice monotonous. Already her parents are looking nervous. Her dad is of the opinion they should have this discussion quickly, rip everything off like a Band-Aid and get it over with. Her mum is twisting her hands together while anxiety oozes from every pore, seemingly more willing to step carefully lest the conversation crack and become messy, splattered with words that can't be taken back.

"We still find it ... difficult to believe," her mum says. She's staring at the table. Isadora takes a deep breath and clenches her hands into fists.

"I know," she replies shortly.

Her mum lifts mournful eyes and meets her daughter's gaze. Her eyes are brown. Just like Will's. "But if you did see him, you would tell us. Wouldn't you?"

"Wouldn't that make things worse?" Isadora asks hesitantly. Although she herself doesn't experience mourning in the normal sense of the word, her intuition tells her that knowing their son is so close but so far away will only serve to drive them mad. Living creatures die; that is the law of the world. People are not meant to be able to peel back the veil and upset that balance to converse with their lost loved ones. Death is a natural part of life, and so is moving on.

"You think we'd have an easier time if we didn't attempt to speak to him?" her dad finally ventures. Isadora nods. The ghosts around her shift. They don't share this philosophy and spend most of their unending days moping around wishing for their loved ones to contact them. Selfish is what they are, in Isadora's rather biased opinion.

"Moving on is important," Isadora says. "You know … to move through those stages of grief and come out the other side a well-balanced, at-peace individual."

Her parents do not look convinced.

"He's our son," her mum whispers hoarsely. "I need to be able to see him."

"No," Isadora refutes firmly. "You don't *need*, you want. You don't need to see him to be able to love him." Lots of people can't seem to understand that fundamental fact of life, Isadora thinks. Love is transcendent. She knows this.

"And …" she pauses, wondering whether she should really go where she's about to. Ah, screw it! "I don't need my parents to be crazy, too." Isadora is self-aware enough to realise she could technically be considered insane. Her parents have never said it, but they have thought it – of that she is certain. "Seeing him in front of you, but knowing logically he's dead, would drive you mad. Please trust me on this."

"That's not fair," her mum spits. "He's my *child*! Please, Isadora, just let me speak to him!"

"Saying 'please' doesn't change anything." Isadora can feel herself getting angry as her skin starts tingling. "I'm not doing this. Anyway, I haven't seen him yet, either – although I know I will! And …" she leans across the table, "the fact that you're only choosing to believe me now there's a benefit in it for you isn't something I'm going to ignore." It hits like a slap in the face and both her parents rear back, utterly shocked. Her mum's face reddens in anger.

"You can't use that. You can't!"

"I can." Isadora cuts her off. "You think this is easy for me?" Without realising what she's doing, Isadora rises from her chair. "That I might get to see him every day for the rest of my life?" She scrubs furiously at the tears beginning to build on her lashes. "I get to wake up every morning and remember that my brother is dead! I get to stare into his dead face and remember that he's gone! That he can't live his life, that he's going to be stuck wandering around with only me to talk to! That I might eventually witness him go completely bonkers like the rest of them!" She's shaking. "I'll never get over it. I'll never be able to think back on him fondly. All I'll be able to think and see is that he's dead! And you, the both of you," she gestures wildly at her seated, silenced parents, "can get on with your lives more than I ever will!" She breaks off, panting for breath, and runs a shaky hand across her watery eyes. Her breath hitches. "So be fucking grateful I'm not doing what you want."

Isadora runs from the room. Flees the heavy silence, the emotional havoc she's wreaked upon her parents, with ghosts in tow. She stumbles out the back door and makes a beeline for her car, flinging herself into the driver's seat. She's going. She's driving while sobbing like a toddler. She throws the car into gear and peels away from the driveway, taking off down the street. Her sobs continue well into her journey as she speeds down the highway. At some point the crying becomes a sort of shaky laughter, more incredulous than anything. She teeters between desperately upset and utterly disbelieving, and for some reason this translates into sob-infused giggles. She doesn't know where she's going. She's just driving. Eventually, both the weeping and the giggling die down leaving a painful, empty chasm in the centre of her chest.

"So, what's the plan here?"

Isadora shrieks and swerves, nearly running herself off the road, but manages in the nick of time to pull over to a skidding stop on the shoulder of the road, gravel flying. She glances sideways and bile rises in her throat. Will is sitting in the passenger seat, looking ridiculously normal. She looks away again quickly and squeezes her eyes shut. Despite the glimpse lasting less than a second the image is scorched in her brain. She can see it clearly in high definition. She presses her head against the steering wheel, heart racing, fists clenched. A curtain of hair keeps Will hidden from view. She takes a few tremulous breaths, allows herself a few precious moments to gather herself, then swipes the wetness from her cheeks. Checking the road is clear, she pulls back out and continues on as if Will's interruption had never happened.

"Lucky you didn't crash."

Unbelievable.

Isadora turns up the volume of the car radio until music drowns out her brother's voice. She elects to ignore the tasteless joke, keeping her eyes fixed firmly on the road. Will shifts in his seat and, although his body makes no sound, Isadora catches the movement in her peripheral vision. Her eyes sting and she twists the volume button even further until the music is thumping and she can feel it vibrating in her bones.

She drives on, desperately trying to ignore the apparition at her side, alternating between tears and hysterical laughter at the predicament they're both trapped in. He doesn't speak again, merely sits silently in the passenger seat as quiet streets lined with small shops give way to hills and valleys spread with sheep-scattered fields and dotted with dusty old farmhouses. Eventually, the road evens out and the countryside becomes scrubby, trees turning to toughened bushes and gravel shifting gradually into sand. Isadora rolls down the window and lets her hair fly in the breeze. She can smell the salt in the air, hear the shrieking seagulls. She senses the change in Will's demeanour as he realises where they are heading. As the open sky widens further and there in front of them is the shimmering blue blanket of ocean, speckled with sun and frothing as it rushes into the sand, her mood lifts as well.

Despite being sunny, it's a cold day, and there's no one on the beach. She chugs the car into the empty car park, stops and switches the ignition off. In the silence that follows, she sits for a moment, enraptured by the view and calmed by the endless push and pull of the rushing tide. The horizon stretches out, infinite.

"You came to the ocean." Will's voice breaks through the haze and Isadora blinks back to reality.

"Yeah," she responds softly. "Guess I did." She pops open her door and climbs out. She doesn't bother stretching her back, instead striding to the concrete ramp that takes her down to the white sand. She hadn't stopped to grab shoes. The sand squeaks beneath her bare feet. It feels warm against her soles, imbued with the heat of the sun. It becomes firmer the closer she gets to the water. Will follows at a distance. Isadora isn't sure if the rest of her posse have followed; she's not sure if saltwater is good for them, if it will keep them at arm's length. Salt, she knows, can be a deterrent, much like the sage she'd tried before. Spirits don't like its purity.

Her feet reach the tideline. Small waves of icy water rush in, barely brushing at her toes, the white, frothy edges kissing them tenderly, bubbles expanding and breaking as the ocean pulls back out again. It's so peaceful. A smooth, constant rhythm. Her chest swells and a surge of unexpected grief wells in her throat. She claps a hand to her mouth and clutches her stomach with the other. She hunches over and sobs quietly. Will is watching from a few feet away. She can sense him.

He steps hesitantly towards her, feet making no imprint in the sand, and stands at her shoulder. Apparently saltwater isn't as pure as she had thought.

Isadora struggles to reel the emotion back in, managing eventually to wipe her tears away and swallow the rest.

"I sometimes ..." she swallows again, sniffs, " ... sometimes used to look out over the ocean and imagine myself walking into it." A small hitch in her breath. "I'd keep walking, feet on the bottom until the water was over my head. It blocked out any sound, any smells, any sight. It was cold but calm. And I'd breathe in. Just let everything slip away." She hugs herself. "It was such a nice way to imagine myself going. No pain, no sound. Just floating away." She shivers in the salty breeze.

Will shifts. They allow the sounds to settle around them. Crashing waves, the occasional bird cry. He moves again.

"Do you imagine that now? Looking at it?"

"No," Isadora murmurs. "Because I'd just wake up here, standing on the sand realising that I'd always be imagining the same thing with the same outcome, wishing that I'd be able to let everything go dark without waking up again. And that it will never happen. Not for me. It wouldn't be the escape I would wish it to be."

There's nothing else to be said after that. Isadora knows that no matter what, she will always be. She will always have a spot on earth that can never be erased. She will live on. No escape. No ending. Eventually, it will drive her insane. The real kind of insane. Maybe she'd have Will, maybe she wouldn't. Regardless, it would be a terrifying thing.

Isadora sits, eyes never straying from the tumbling waves. Crossing her legs, she rests an elbow on one knee and settles in, outwardly calm but thoughts still raging inside. A blurred movement to her left signifies that Will is sitting next to her – not so close that she can actually see him, but just near enough for her to catch a greyish form on the fringe of her peripheral. As much as his presence is painful, the fact he doesn't disappear provides a small measure of warmth and comfort. The mix of feelings is an odd one.

They stay there long enough to be bathed in the rays of the sunset, as the seagulls glide overhead seeking shelter for the night. Only one set of footprints leads away from the ocean, yet Isadora is far from alone.

III | THE EMPRESS

She is lying in bed, staring at the window, the sheer curtains allowing streams of light to bathe her face. Isadora feels her mattress dip; a hand resting on her shoulder. Her mum is talking quietly. Following her tantrum and flight to the beach, it all sounds … empty. Irrelevant. Her mum presses a kiss to her cheek, squeezes her shoulder one more time and leaves. There has been no discussion, no yelling match following Isadora's quiet return post-meltdown. Small mercies, she supposes bleakly.

Isadora curls deeper beneath her duvet. The shadow of a tall, familiar figure falls over her. Iris has been watching her for the last couple of days, concern etched in the lines of her face. Melting Man has also been keeping an eye out, mumbling and gurgling gently if Isadora starts to cry. Bee has been helpful in a way Isadora never expected. It stays close, occasionally nudging its face against her cheek, and has kept up a steady stream of purrs. The deep rumbling is therapeutic on nights when sleep evades her. Bee's companionship acts as a kind of security blanket. Warmth in the cold world of suddenly being an only child.

Not that her parents haven't tried to appease things, almost making an apology in their own wordless way. Isadora would have to be completely blind to miss their attempts. But that's all it is to her. *Attempts* to provide a support Isadora can lean on. Quite simply, Isadora can't rely on their support because of its fragility. One fully weighted discussion and it would shatter, send her plummeting. How can they possibly give her what she needs when they don't understand?

Bee snuggles closer as Isadora sinks deeper into her pillow and closes her eyes. It's under the covers, obscured by the sheets and pressed tightly up against her stomach, perfectly curled in the space her foetal position creates, nose cold and wet against her knees.

"Dora." The voice grates jarringly. Isadora winces and feels heat rising behind her eyelids. "Would you please look at me?" It's such a desperate plea that Isadora can't refuse. She'd been unable to face him on the long drive home, keeping her music blaring, desperate to drown him out. She hesitantly cracks one eye open and peers at him through a distorted haze. His face swims in the reflection of her tears. Bee shifts. Sensing her trepidation, it shivers in response.

"I'm sorry," he says. Isadora swallows, eyes darting away to stare, unseeing, at the curtains and the world beyond. "Isadora, I'm sorry." His voice cracks on the last word and Isadora lifts her head to look at him properly for the first time. The streaks of flaking blood are too hard to look at, so she focuses instead on his eyes. They're exactly the same. Dark brown and so overflowing with emotion it hurts. She hasn't let him apologise so far. Every attempt he's made she's refused, ignored, certain that if she allows him to do so it will hurt too badly, cut too deeply to ever recover.

Isadora sucks in a deep breath. She opens her mouth to speak – for the first time since the scene on the beach – and can't. Her dry throat catches and can only produce a forlorn croak. She tries again, pushing against her reluctance to have this conversation. "You don't have to say it, Will. I can see it myself." Her voice breaks. Bee croons.

"You shouldn't have to," Will says softly. This is the most despairing Isadora has ever seen him. And this, she thinks, is far more painful than seeing him dead. To see her brother – who to her knowledge has only ever broken down in private – cracking in front of her. It makes her chest stutter. It's hard to watch.

"You should have worn your seatbelt," Isadora eventually says emptily. "Why weren't you wearing a seatbelt?"

Will buries his face in his hands. His back shudders, shoulders shaking. Isadora realises she's made him cry.

"I'm sorry," she whispers. Will takes a moment to surface and when he does his demeanour has changed, become slightly defiant even.

"Apology not accepted. It wasn't warranted," he retorts hoarsely.

Isadora turns her face away. She doesn't want Will to know her sadness is quickly deviating into fury. How dare he do this to himself? How dare he do this to *her*, when he knows—? Why wasn't he wearing his fucking seatbelt?!

In the heat of her anger, she completely forgets the opening of her dream, the sense of something wrong and the unbidden jerk of the wheel in hands that had not been her brother's.

Her clenched fists tremble. Bee mewls and shifts away, sensing a thunderstorm approaching. Isadora is propping herself up ready to let loose when a small poke in her back prompts her to turn. A small child is standing behind her, a large crater in the middle of his head, forcing one eye to protrude obscenely. The eye stares at her now through enlarged, reddened capillaries. Isadora raises an eyebrow. The little boy laces his hands together and begins to speak in a high, slightly lisping voice.

"You will forgive him, won't you miss?" he asks innocently. Isadora is floored for a second, unsure exactly why this child's spirit is even talking to her when she's never noticed him as part of her entourage before. Quite sad, really. But then again, they do all eventually tend to morph together into one conglomerate of despairing howls. She sputters, then catches sight of Will's face.

Cheeky asshole.

"Is this your doing?" she asks, gesturing at the diminutive ghost. Will shrugs, watery grin stuck in place.

"They've taken to me," he answers, hands deep in his pockets, head slightly ducked, feigning an innocence Isadora does not buy.

She turns back to the child and is taken aback when he giggles brightly and ducks his own disfigured head, bulging eye wobbling dangerously. Will's smile broadens slightly, juxtaposed by the tears still welling in his eyes. The child has broken the ice between them, however, and flickers away to appear next to Will, hugging his legs. Will pats him on the head (another thing Isadora has never really noticed before, how the spirits physically interact with each other) and the boy vanishes back into the bordering crowd.

"They've taken to you?" Isadora asks quietly. Will nods.

"I don't really know why, but …" he pauses, "… I think it's because of you?" He finishes hesitantly, voice rising in pitch at the end. Isadora nods, dumbstruck.

"Maybe because they've seen you alive and know who you are," she says. "But they take to most other ghosts that follow me home," she adds.

"Right. But they seem to, I dunno, really like me?" Will replies, shrugging again. "I think they knew how angry you'd be." He hides his face once more. "At me."

"Yeah, no shit, Will!" Isadora surges forward, her anger revived. "You don't wear a seatbelt, even though you know how important it is, and manage to drive your car into a ditch! And then I have to live with the fact that I'm going to be followed around for the rest of my life by my dead brother!"

Silence. Absolute, suffocating silence blankets everything.

Isadora claps her hands to her mouth and stares, horrified, at her wilted brother. The poignant anger dissipates until not a wisp is left, replaced instead by guilt so strong Isadora buckles over, hands still clasped over her mouth. Because she isn't nearly as angry at the prospect of Will still being around as she is making out.

"Wow," is all Will manages to come up with.

Bee, who has been sitting sedately on the sidelines, meanders over to Isadora and forces itself onto her lap, mewling softly. It doesn't like the way its human is feeling, doesn't much like the way the human's brother's imprint feels either. It pushes its face up to nudge at Isadora's hands. Isadora tries to shove Bee away, but Bee doesn't shift. Instead, it sits firmly in Isadora's lap, head twisted like an owl's to look at Will. Will baulks at the sudden milky, white-eyed attention.

"Why make each other this way?" Bee whines, tail swishing. Will jumps sky-high and gapes, making Isadora snort despite being uncomfortable with Bee speaking. She doubts she'll ever get used to it. If it continues to speak, that is.

"Err, why make each other … upset?" Will guesses. Isadora runs a hand absently down Bee's back, which makes it arch up sharply. Bee grins, Cheshire-cat face gleaming, apparently pleased Will was able to understand, and nods once.

"Well, if Will hadn't totalled his car, I wouldn't be sad," Isadora says shortly, even as the words ring falsely in her ears.

"I don't even know how it happened. It could have happened to anyone, Dora!"

"Yeah, it could have!" she starts up again, eyes blazing. "But it wasn't anyone, Will! It was you! Just accept the fact that you killed yourself in a stupid accident that you could have prevented if you had used even ten percent of the brain God gifted you with!" Bee's sharp claws knead her leg and Isadora hisses as pain spreads in hot, stinging strings up her thigh.

"I will if you will." Her brother's flat response catches her off guard. Maybe – and she forces herself to admit it to herself – he's right in a roundabout way. It's a little too much to unpack right this minute, so Isadora squashes it into a box in the back of her mind.

"There's no point arguing over it," she decides, diverting the conversation, which she is quite sure Will notices but does not comment on. "We're still stuck in the same situation." She gestures at Will's transparent body. "You're dead. I can see you." Pause. "It sucks." Isadora's hands settle back in her lap and, consequently, on Bee's spiny body. It's very warm now, a small dark furnace purring away in her lap. Will's gaze follows and he studies Bee.

"Is that the thing that attacked me in the yard that day?" he asks finally.

"Beautiful, isn't it?" Isadora asks, grinning sarcastically.

"*Bee*autiful," Bee whines in what could be construed as a 'happy' voice. Isadora isn't entirely certain Bee feels human emotions. Or perhaps it feels emotions humans have no access to. Will raises his eyebrows and the siblings swap matching looks.

"And has it been this attached to you ever since, or just now that I'm dead?" Will asks curiously. Bee is watching him, large silver-dollar eyes following his every move, like a snake ultimately drawn to and hypnotised by the charmer. Isadora runs a hand down Bee's back, eliciting a warbling purr.

"Ever since," she hums thoughtfully. "I think I accidentally conjured it from the other side."

"Accidentally?" Will asks, moving slowly from left to right, Bee's head bobbing to follow.

"Yeah. I didn't mean to. How could I? I don't even know what it is." Isadora shrugs. "Is it a demon? A kind of … warped ghost? A familiar even?" She shakes her head, hand still gently patting along Bee's bone-ridged spine. "I have no idea." She stands up and Bee clambers onto her shoulder.

Will stops his strange dance and stands still, eyes locked with Bee's.

"I'm not sure if it likes me or not," he admits in a dramatic whisper. Bee trills and lurches forward, nose jutting out to mirror Will's. They stand, face to face, nose to nose for one heart-stopping moment. Bee makes a low grumbling noise in its throat and goes to strike. Isadora tries to grab its oil-slick body, but her hands simply scrabble uselessly at its bumpy sides. Her heart leaps into her throat and she shrieks as Bee, slick as a snake, …

… licks Will's nose.

Wait, what?

Isadora, heart thumping loudly, watches in astonishment as Bee cheerfully slurps a long stripe up Will's pointed nose. Will, shocked, jerks back in disgust and swipes frantically at the string of saliva caught between them.

"That's gross! What the hell?" he protests as Bee settles back on Isadora's lap, long, prickly tail curling neatly around its lean body. Isadora has a hand on her chest and, now that everything is calming down, has a sudden, inappropriate urge to burst into laughter. It bubbles up, fizzing in her throat until the compulsion is overwhelming. She allows a squeak and the trickle leads to a flood until she is howling – oblivious to the fact that the ghosts around her are now glowing as they feel warmth akin to afternoon sunlight shining on their heads – a bit like a clapped-out lightbulb finding new life as the breaker box surges.

Even Will, so new to being dead, feels this strange sensation. A smile lifts his cheeks and dimples his skin. His body feels lighter than it ever did in life. In that moment, he realises his death doesn't have to be a sad occasion. Perhaps there can be some semblance of happiness to be found in his passing.

"Why didn't you laugh like that at my funeral?"

IV | THE EMPEROR

Isadora shuffles her Tarot cards and sets them in front of Will.

"Choose wisely," she says, deadpan expression making it difficult for either of them to take it too seriously. Will rolls his eyes and picks three cards from the stack.

"You know this is hocus, yeah?" he asks, setting them face down on the carpet. Isadora scowls.

"I'm a medium, excuse you," she sits up primly. "I'm a master of the Arcane Arts."

And quickly rifles through her *Introduction to Tarot* book, eyebrows pinching together thoughtfully. Truth be told, Tarot makes no sense to her. She has only vaguely heard of it. She has gathered from the internet that each card represents either a figure or situation, and that each combination of cards holds a different message – but that's the extent of her knowledge. She also guesses she probably isn't using the pack correctly.

Her 'troupe' lie around watching, showing various levels of interest ranging from intense (a small, immaculately dressed woman in a flouncy dress) to utterly bored (a one-legged man in Army garb who has pulled his way across the floor and draped his torso over Isadora's legs). Bee has decided Will is in more need of comfort than Isadora and is observing proceedings from a perch on Will's broad shoulders.

"So … 'Master of the Arcane Arts' … have you finished reading the instructions yet?" Will drawls, leaning back on his hands and causing Bee to wobble precariously for a moment.

"Hmm, what a load of absolute hogwash this is." Iris is firmly in the disinterested camp, as she peers distastefully over Isadora's shoulder.

Isadora snaps the book closed and leans over the deck of cards to inspect the three Will has chosen and haphazardly lined up face-down.

"These are your three?" she asks. Will nods. "Okay." Isadora's hand hovers over the one furthest to the left. "This is your past …" She points to the middle one "… your present … and your future."

"Bit redundant, that one," Will comments, grinning.

Isadora smirks. It's nice to be able to make jokes around Will's unfortunate situation, and he appears to be settling reasonably well into his next existence. Her parents haven't mentioned anything about Will for a while now (they're probably avoiding bringing him up, considering how she had blown up at them before) – which has been a bit confusing as she'd been certain they would come to her again to try and have translated conversations with him. Pushing thoughts of her parents away, Isadora focuses on the cards. Their midnight-blue backs shine with gold filigree detailing and they seem to stare right back at her.

What are you waiting for?

"Let's flip the first one and see how we go," she says. She turns the first card over. "Reversed Fool," she declares.

"Which means?" Will prompts when she doesn't elaborate. Isadora grumbles and reaches for her book, flipping it open and scanning quickly.

"So, apparently it means …" her face scrunches up a bit. "Recklessness and risk taking."

Will nods sagely. "The accident."

"Not wearing your bloody seatbelt," Isadora adds helpfully, to which Will rolls his eyes.

"We're not having *that* argument again."

Isadora holds her hands up innocently. "I wasn't starting an argument. I was making a statement."

"Next card."

She rolls her own eyes and flips the next card. "Upright Tower." Another perusal of the instructions. "Sudden change, upheaval and awakening," she declares.

"I'm honestly surprised I didn't get the Death card," Will comments, raising an eyebrow. Isadora groans.

"The Death card doesn't symbolise death, idiot. I think it means transformation or change, something along those lines."

Will frowns. "That still would have made sense, though."

"But you didn't get it, so it doesn't matter." Isadora dismisses him and gestures at the last card. "And finally, future. Turn it over."

Will reaches forward, Bee jostling with the movement, and lifts the final card. Death stares right back at them. The ghosts surrounding them all begin muttering and murmuring, grey shadows rippling in the background. Isadora blinks in disbelief.

"Well, that can't be right." Lifting up the book, she consults the paragraph on Death. "So, at some point in your practically non-existent future you will experience change, transformation and transition," she reads and looks back up at her brother, who doesn't look at all confused.

"Cool," was the answer she was given.

"Why are you so unbothered?" Isadora asks, setting her book aside. Will shrugs again.

"If it's what the Tarot says, then it is what it is."

"Don't 'it is what it is' me!" Isadora replies grumpily. Will plucks Bee off his shoulders and hands it back to Isadora.

"No need to get grumpy over it." He sits up and stretches. "It's a card game. And you're not a psychic. For all you know the cards mean nothing. Don't worry about it."

"I'm a medium," she retorts, standing up so she can put her hands on her hips. "And I'm not worried about it. I'm just confused."

"Not so different from any other time then." Will stands up, too, and wanders to stand by the window in the sunlight, although he can feel no warmth.

"Alright, fine. Can you get out of my room, please?" Isadora asks the room at large. Will plants his hands in his pockets and leaves without argument. Most of the others, as usual completely ignoring her, stay. Once her brother has left, Isadora closes the door and presses her forehead against the timber. Although Will doesn't know it, the final card has unsettled her.

"When are you going to tell him?" Iris reappears over her shoulder.

"I don't know," Isadora replies, eyes tightly shut.

Will has no idea that the manner in which he has appeared to Isadora means something. That he is different to the others, different even to Iris. Isadora isn't quite sure what exactly it does mean, having not been given a handbook along with her abilities. And she isn't sure if he is here to stay or if there's something else to it. Still, it doesn't change the fact that nothing scares her more than losing her brother for good.

Iris nods wisely. "Do you think you'll do it for him?"

In all honesty, Isadora doesn't know what Iris is talking about, but she nods vaguely to avoid having to have another in-depth, possibly argumentative conversation with the old woman. She can worry about it later, she decides. Leave it as a problem for future Isadora.

Isadora walks out of her room. She suddenly needs to be anywhere else but here. Absorbed as she is in her thoughts, Isadora crashes into her mother as she is leaving the kitchen, nearly sending them both tumbling to the floor.

"Sorry!" Isadora grabs her mother's forearms to steady herself. "Didn't see you there."

Her mum offers a strained, waterlogged smile. "It's okay, sweetie. I'm a bit distracted myself." She clears her throat. Isadora's stomach clenches painfully. Her mum is a strong woman. She barely cries at anything. It's hard to see her so upset.

"Actually, I wanted to give you something," her mum continues, voice clearer.

"Okay," Isadora says softly.

Her mum smiles thinly and leads her into her bedroom where a small, wrapped package is sitting on her chest of drawers. She picks it up tentatively and presents it to Isadora.

"I know it's been difficult for you," she begins. "And I know that with Will gone, it must feel like you have no one left who you can talk to about your gift." She swallows uncomfortably. "So I wanted to make sure you had something that can protect you when things get dark."

Isadora takes the package and unwraps it carefully, gently prying the sticky tape open so as not to tear the paper. A small Amethyst pendant lies nestled in pastel pink tissue.

"I read that Amethyst has special qualities. One of them is protection from dark energy." It's clear her mother is sceptical, even if Isadora is not. "And that it can enhance special abilities. Like yours."

Isadora strokes a finger along the gemstone's smooth surface, taking in the deep violet colour and the rivers of palest purple and white streaming elegantly under the surface. It is warm in her palm, weighted with the kind of affection Isadora has seldom received from her parents. She knows what her mum is trying to say, can clearly recognise the olive branch she is extending. She chokes up.

"Thank you," is all she can summon.

Her mother reaches out and pulls her into a tentative hug, which tightens when Isadora wholeheartedly hugs her back. Isadora revels in the embrace until they eventually separate. Her mum, peering at her through new eyes, opens her mouth and draws in a fractured breath.

"Can you tell him 'hello' when you see him next?" she asks tearily. "And that we love him very much?" Her voice cracks midway through the sentence.

Isadora nods. "Of course I can."

She hesitates, then reaches out and touches her mum's arm.

"He already knows. He's here every day."

She isn't sure whether it's entirely wise to bring this up considering the rather heated argument they'd had only days beforehand, and when her mum's grief-stricken face twists even further she almost regrets it. But her mum offers a tremulous smile, and the shaking hand she places against Isadora's cheek reassures her that she has found comfort in her statement. Her mum gives her one last watery smile and brushes her hand over Isadora's shoulder as they part ways.

Isadora watches as she heads down the hall and waits for the front door to open and close as she knows it will. Her mum is like her – or perhaps she should say she is like her mum. They both rely on being close to nature to clear their heads.

Turning her attention to the pendant, Isadora studies the delicate gold chain, the way it dangles from her hand with the Amethyst a steady, comforting weight at the end of it. She undoes the clasp it and fastens the pendant around her neck. The stone sits neatly against her upper chest, and she knows the warmth she feels from it has more to do with the giving of it rather than the stone itself.

Isadora lingers in the hall for a moment admiring her gift in the mirror, before remembering she has a message to pass on to Will, who has no doubt hidden himself in his room. His door is closed, of course. Isadora knows her mum won't have been able to stomach the sight of his room yet. Won't have been able to face the haunting emptiness of it. Or the treasured belongings she and Isadora's dad have yet to sort through.

Isadora knocks quietly and slips inside. She almost expects there to a small gathering of spirits around him when she enters, the ones Will says are attached to him and trail his every move (a fact Isadora is not altogether unhappy about, given that it means they leave her alone). The room smells stale, and a fine layer of dust coats every piece of furniture.

Will is sitting despondently on his bed, although his demeanour falsely brightens when he sees her – a common reaction the past few days. Isadora doesn't blame him. Having only her to interact with can't be easy. She knows she can be incredibly maudlin a lot of the time.

"Calmed down?" Will asks, stretching his legs out as if he hadn't just been pretzeled up, knees to chest, face hidden.

"Yes." Isadora didn't bother reigniting their brief argument. "Mum gave me a present." She displays the pendant to Will who, as most brothers would, gives it a cursory glance before commenting it looks 'nice'. Isadora lets the pendant go, the Amethyst bumping against her chest as it settles back in place. "She also wanted me to tell you something."

Will snaps to attention, dark eyes wide.

"A message for me?" he asks breathlessly. Isadora nods.

"It isn't anything you don't already know, but …" Isadora shuffles awkwardly. "She wanted to say hello, and that she and dad love you. And miss you very much." Although her mum didn't say that last bit, Isadora knows they do. She watches Will as it sinks in. He slumps and smiles a weak 'thank you'. Isadora knows in that moment she is about to overstay her welcome and beats a hasty retreat, carefully closing the door behind her.

She turns and is immediately met with a horde of curious spirits.

"I'm giving him some space," she points her thumb at the door behind her. The ghosts watch her. "To cry," she clarifies. "Why are you all gathered here, anyway?"

"You seemed distressed," one ghost answers, a small pale woman with a very broken neck. It's a wonder she manages to speak at all.

"We wanted to make sure you were okay," another chimes in, this time a mousy teen with a peppering of gunshots on his chest and neck.

Isadora blinks. "You've never done this before," she mutters, mostly to herself. The ghosts all hear her anyway, of course.

"Everything is amplified," the broken-necked woman explains. "As if we can feel everything you can."

"Can you always feel it?" Isadora asks nervously, thinking she doesn't want the ghosts to be able to feel all her emotions. That has the potential to be incredibly embarrassing. The gunshot-riddled boy nods.

"It's normally a lot fainter. Until recently, of course." His pale eyes roam over to Will's bedroom door.

Oh. Right. They must mean her epic freak-out the night Will died.

"You guys felt that?" she asks, genuinely shocked. The ghosts nod as one.

"And now we can feel everything, almost intuitively. Much stronger than we could before." A harsh, rasping voice cuts over the ghostly muttering that has started up in response to Isadora's query.

"It's been amplified," the broken-necked woman says again. "We feel much more connected to you than before."

And damn – if that doesn't freak Isadora out a little. Granted she is more tolerant of them now than she has been in the past – over-exposure and all that – but that doesn't mean she wants to be close to them. The living should never have anything to do with the dead; they should stay completely separate. And okay, yes, that was pretty impossible for Isadora – but she *is* trying to keep her boundaries in place, dammit!

"Fantastic," she mutters darkly.

"This could be a good thing, young lady." Iris hobbles forward. "Now you have a chance to really help these people." One gnarled hand gestures to the translucent group. "You can do your job."

A firecracker of anger goes off inside her chest and Isadora opens her mouth to release a tirade when a sudden thought halts her. It's completely off-tangent, completely out of the blue … yet completely relevant at the same time.

Job.

A job she can do.

A job that could actually be easy and one that only she can really do and do well! She mulls it over silently. The only thing that stalls her slightly is Will. And yet despite all the tragedy, despite all the dark nights and dismal days, two things are not going to change. Will is always going to be dead and life will be determined to go on.

And Isadora really needs a job. That fact has not changed. And here it is, sitting right on the edge of her brain just waiting to get started. She needs to shelve the whole Will thing for a while. Put it on the back-burner. It's not like it's going anywhere. *Compartmentalise Isadora, it's what mentally ill people do best.*

And it won't be difficult to get it all set up, surely. And there will almost certainly be a market for it. Yeah, she can absolutely make it work! With a little bit of planning, of course.

Isadora looks at Iris, mind settled, and smiles.

"You might just be a genius, Iris."

Iris snorts. "Of course I am, child."

V | THE HIEROPHANT

Isadora peers down at her hastily scribbled outline, notebook at an angle as she quickly jots down a couple more sentences. Iris is reading over her shoulder, face pinched as her lips mouth along. Melting Man is hunched just behind her other shoulder, steadily dripping waxy flesh onto her jumper. Luckily it's not a jumper she particularly loves and, luckier still, other humans can't see the ectoplasmic residue and so won't flinch when she goes out in public with her shoulder covered in gloopy red and yellow stains. But *she* knows it's there and doesn't appreciate the fact she'll have to wash it, as she does with lots of her clothes every day so she doesn't have to see (or smell) any bodily fluids. *Who knew when you died horribly you continued to leak in the afterlife?* The rotting smell has long since ceased to cause her distress. Not so Will. He is struggling with his new-found state of death far more than Isadora would have expected.

Usually, Will took things in his stride with nary a complaint. This experience has broken the trend, and it's been nothing but complaints so far. After she'd allowed him his solitude for the first few weeks, he'd come back disgruntled. It's beginning to grate on Isadora's already shredded nerves. Hog-tied as she is by not wanting to snap at him – considering he's dead – Isadora has taken to smiling thinly, being overly saccharine, and humming whenever he grouches to contain the acerbic outburst bubbling at the back of her throat.

"Is that everything you've got so far?" Speak of the moping devil. Will leant past Iris, sticking his nose right into Isadora's great game plan: *How to set up a mobile medium business on a very limited budget because this will be my first job*.

"I'm still working on the small details, obviously." Isadora scrunches up her nose, "But I think I've mostly got it mapped out." She taps her pen against the table, re-reading her dot notes and scrutinising for any possible weak point. Will reaches over her shoulder, causing a shiver when his ghostly arm goes straight through her. His finger points at the one item Isadora is consciously aware of and equally concerned about.

"'*Businesses need funding*'. Good point. Something, might I remind you, you don't have."

Isadora waves an arm aggressively in his direction, dissipating his hand in a cloud of milky white ectoplasm. "Not all backyard businesses have a multi-million-dollar budget to work with. Sometimes people have to get creative, which hopefully the general public will appreciate more."

Will sinks back into himself, arms crossed.

Isadora groans. "Come on, Will! You're meant to be the positive one in this scenario! Where's your irrepressible bright side?"

"Dead," he deadpans. Isadora's sense of humour decides right there and then that she is going to hell (purgatory is probably more likely), because there is no way she isn't going to laugh at that. She forces herself to swallow down a giggle and composes herself.

"Fair enough."

Something sharp begins to claw its way up Isadora's leg. She jerks back at the intrusion. Bee's moon-white eyes peer back, an unnerving smile stretching across its face. Its jagged edges catch on her skin at every movement and small red spots are beginning to bloom along the length of her leg. Finally, Bee is fully settled, prickles and all, in her lap. Isadora runs an absent hand over the small streams of blood, wondering how she'll explain the marks away if her parents notice.

"Thanks, Bee," she mumbles sourly. Bee purrs and nestles in, whipping tail calming to curl tightly against its spiny, surprisingly warm body.

A small furnace completely ensconced in inky darkness, Bee's white eyes close to slivers as its purrs rumble away.

"Back to the important points," Will continues. "Are you going to be a charity case? What's your great business scheme? Are you going to busk in the mall to raise money?"

Isadora grins. "Something like that. And don't discount my singing voice. Remember the night I whooped your arse at karaoke?"

Will scoffs. "Whatever! You deliberately chose a song that was out of my range."

Isadora smirks. "All I'm hearing are excuses. But we're getting side-tracked. You haven't sussed out what my great plan is. Go on, have a guess."

Will considers her carefully, dark eyes tracking her face as she waits impatiently. It shouldn't take him long. She only really has one special skill to utilise, after all. Will squints as his brain continues to whir away, long enough for Isadora to be concerned he hasn't got it yet.

"Will … seriously, have your brain cells necrotised?" Exasperated, Isadora swings round to fully face him. Will's eyebrows quirk.

"In a word: yes, my brain cells have in fact necrotised," he answers, a tinge of a dark inflection making a home in his voice. "But my final guess is that you're going to read palms for a living."

"Final guess is incorrect – but close enough that I'm tempted to give it to you, anyway," Isadora snorts, swivelling back to her meagre plan, sketched roughly in spidery cursive. She taps her pen thoughtfully on the table again, heart nervously swelling in her throat as she re-reads what she's written. Sure, many people won't be interested; but humans thrive on the unknown, on curiosity. She's certain there will be some takers. Look at all the famously fake mediums that are featured on daytime talk shows. They had to have started somewhere! Plus, she had the actual medium factor at her disposal.

"I'll start with Tarot cards, given my recently strengthened spirituality," Isadora indicates the first dot point, "then move on to contacting deceased relatives, and from there I'll begin the closure part." Bee shifts on her lap. "People love the idea of closure. Feed them some lost loved one's final words and they should be lapping it up enough to pay me something."

"You'll get minimum wage at best," Will adds unhelpfully. Isadora shrugs her narrow shoulders, despite her apprehension at hearing Will's words.

"Minimum wage is better than no wage," she replies, snapping her journal closed and tucking it in her bag. Brushing her long hair out of her eyes, she catches sight of Will's single dimple as a tiny grin peeks at the corner of his mouth. Her heart leaps at the minuscule victory.

"I suppose you'll want our help?" Iris intervenes after a beat of thick silence. Melting Man hums wetly, face twisted into what could be construed as interest if he were under a decent light source. Isadora nods, one arm propped on the back of her chair, Bee keeping the rest of her body planted to the seat.

"I think so, to begin with. Eventually, other ghosts should surface and then I won't have to rely on you as much."

Iris's already crinkled face sinks into a concerned grimace. "Are you sure about all this?"

Iris, unlike some of the other hangers-on, had noticed quite quickly Isadora's dislike of their presence. Living in a state of constant cold, surrounded by those who were gone (but not) was unhealthy in every sense – physical, mental and spiritual – and Iris has clearly seen that Isadora is an unsettled being. She tolerates the spirits around her because she has no choice. Perhaps her prolonged exposure has lessened the animosity a little, Iris isn't sure. But the question remains: will Isadora be happy to increase her exposure?

Isadora's eyes flash briefly with some complex emotion, but she nods all the same. "I need to be able to do something. Something that's productive at least." *Something to keep her going forward as opposed to stagnating, rotting away in her room wreathed in a haze of grief.*

Iris sighs a non-existent breath and concedes, "We'll help you, dear. All of us."

A faint grey glow pulses through the gathered crowd in Isadora's room, a veritable sardine tin packed tightly as possible. Isadora smiles thinly at their agreement and returns her attention to her morose brother. On realising he's unwittingly recaptured her attention, Will cracks a fake smile.

"Let's do this thing."

Bee trills in agreement and rubs a rough head beneath Isadora's chin.

"Ugh! Bee! I'm bleeding all over the place now!

VI | THE LOVERS

It starts off slowly. Isadora has to face the scariest part far too early: applying for a licence to 'busk' in the mall. However, she does make it perfectly clear that she won't actually be busking and, thankfully, the ageing, dusty receptionist appears mildly intrigued at her proposal.

"About time we had some entertainment other than mediocre musicians," she croaks, extending a shaking pen in Isadora's direction. Isadora smiles brightly, thanks the crone and fills out her form in relative silence, pointedly ignoring the excited whines from the ghost pack, all of whom are squished tightly into the narrow reception area. A few newbies have been drawn in and are now peering over Isadora's shoulder. The hair of one is long enough to drape onto the receptionist's desk, and Isadora watches aghast as ghostly lice crawl across the plastic surface. She tries not to cringe when they scuttle over her hand.

Once the bureaucracy has been completed, stamped and properly signed, Isadora goes about gathering supplies to create her workspace. Walking quickly through town, she tries to avoid the stares of the many wandering spirits who are caught in their own unfortunate loops, carrying out what would have been their normal daily business, aware but unwilling to accept they are dead. A few heads follow her progress, one notable one spinning 180 degrees to keep her in sight. Isadora tries not to let her eyebrows rise and reveal how reluctantly impressed she is at this feat.

Will skulks along at her side, hands in pockets, face downturned. His dark curls hang lankly across his forehead, not quite long enough to obscure his eyes, as if that would draw any kind of attention away from his depressed aura. Isadora attempts to distract him by making quiet comments, some pleasant, some snide, as they pass people, houses and pets. One lady strolling by looks almost exactly like her overweight bulldog, which does get an amused twitch out of him, but not much else.

Business gets off to a slow start. After setting up her stall, Isadora places her Tarot cards on the table and settles in to wait. Saturdays are bound to be busy, right? The mall is sure to be filled with people wandering back and forth, bored eyes scanning the shopfronts they've seen hundreds of times before. Something new is sure to stir up some interest! Bee, sensing her mood in its wickedly alert way, mewls and settles directly on her sneakered feet, tail curling around her ankles as awkwardness sets in. Regardless of her legitimate skills, there is one obstacle that Isadora is going to struggle with. Showmanship.

She's not a naturally bright, bubbly person. How can she be, shrouded in death as she is? She doesn't make people feel at ease with a single smile, can't charm her way through small talk or create instant rapport. She's not an open book, happy for the world to read and enjoy. But neither can she be described as plain or boring. There is such a quality as 'otherworldliness' and this Isadora carries in spades. It can be off-putting, she knows this well, but it can also be alluring, and it is this appeal she hopes will draw people in. That and basic human curiosity, the best and most dangerous trait for any prospective customer to have.

It's slow going initially. Will hovers mulishly behind her. Iris and Melting Man have set themselves down at either end of her table and are making quiet comments as the crowds pass by. The rest of her entourage are milling about the mall, noticed by the living only in the way they suddenly clutch their coats tighter and frown at the abrupt temperature change, looking this way and that for wherever that chill breeze has sprung from.

After a series of mildly interested glances but no actual customers, Isadora is all but ready to declare failure when a small woman cautiously shuffles over.

"Excuse me?" she asks, timid voice squeaking and breaking through Isadora's staredown with the floor. Isadora looks up, fully expecting to be asked to 'please exit the mall, you're clearly not worth it' (or something along those lines) and curiously regards the hunched person standing tensely before her table.

"Hello," Isadora musters up a warm smile. "How can I help you today?"

The woman scuffs her feet nervously. "Would you be happy to read my cards?" She gestures at the pack of Tarot. "I've always wanted to have my cards read," she adds quietly. Isadora falters, then nods enthusiastically, determined not to be caught off guard by a real live customer, and gestures for the woman to take the seat opposite her.

"Please ..." Isadora waits until the woman has settled herself tensely on the very edge of the seat then fans out her deck. "It's $10 for a full reading. Cash only." She gestures to her makeshift sign and holds out the small crystal dish she'd managed to snag in the local op shop to accept her payment. It had looked mystical enough, and Will had given her the thumbs up when she'd picked it out of the eclectic 'BARGAINS!' box. Good enough. It would certainly serve its purpose.

The woman pulls out a ten dollar note and places it carefully in the bowl, which Isadora quickly removes from sight in case her customer tries to take it back after her session. Shaking her hair behind her shoulders, Isadora straightens herself up and attempts to look as wise as possible, despite her youthful face.

"Please pick any three cards from the deck."

A small, shaky hand demurely selects three cards and places them off to the side. With a flourish that looks and feels entirely too stylised, Isadora sweeps the remaining cards into a neat pile. At least she didn't scatter them everywhere. Thank God for small mercies.

"Now, set them down in a row," Isadora instructs. Once the lady has done this, she sits on the very edge of her chair, hands tightly clasped in her lap, close-set eyes flickering from the cards to Isadora's carefully composed face. Isadora places a finger on the first card and meets the woman's nervous gaze.

"Your past," she smoothly moves to the next card. "Your present," and on to the last card … "Your future." Her voice trails off into a dramatic whisper, while a snide voice speaks up beside her.

"Stop being so dramatic and get on with it!" Iris raps her cane against the table leg. Isadora barely manages to conceal her annoyed hiss. The tiny lady draws back a little, now looking more uncomfortable than hesitant. Isadora smiles apologetically.

"My apologies. The spirits are being exceptionally noisy today." There can be no mistaking who among the dead she is referring to. Iris scoffs and adjusts her glasses snootily. Isadora draws herself back to the present and faces the mousy woman once more.

"Are you ready to confront your cards?" she asks gently. The lady's hands fumble in her lap as she nods sharply. Isadora plays with the corner of the first card, attempting to build the anticipation. "Very well." She flips the card.

"The Fool in reverse …" Isadora runs her finger along The Fool's profile and thinks hard. To the outside world, it appears to be an enigmatic face, twisted with knowledge and all the powers that come along with it. To Will, it appears that Isadora is thinking hard, trying to remember what the instruction booklet had said the card meant.

Just as the pause is beginning to enter the awkward stage, Isadora straightens and taps gently on the card. "The symbol of Foolishness, risk taking and recklessness." She looks up at the woman and cocks her head. "Does this sound familiar?" Most people would relate to having a period of recklessness and bad decision-making in their past. It's the perfect card for coincidental recognition. The woman jerks her head in a rough nod, hands clutched tightly in her lap. Isadora nods smoothly in tandem and moves on.

"Your present." She gracefully flips the middle card, ignoring the shifting in her peripheral as a new spirit creeps closer, its cold energy raising goosebumps on her exposed arms. "The High Priestess, also in reverse." Isadora studies the card. "A symbol of secrets, withdrawal and silence. It can even mean a blockage in some circumstances."

Something feels off here. Isadora's dark brow furrows as she glances up. The woman is visibly shaking in her seat, face downcast and thin lips pursed. An uncomfortable tightness gathers in Isadora's stomach as the spirits began to murmur. Bee's tail whips around her ankles and squeezes, tiny spines prickling her skin.

"And finally … your future." Isadora traces the outline of the card, attention laser-focused on reading the woman's face. The sense of 'something is wrong' only grows, expanding tangibly outwards until the two of them are contained in a bubble of unease. Trying to conceal her trembling fingers Isadora flips the card and stares down at the graphic figure printed delicately on the black background, title embossed near the bottom in gold print.

"Justice …" Isadora whispers. Three Major Arcana cards. While not unusual, it's most certainly something to take note of and acknowledge. The spirit who has joined them creeps closer still, his face becoming clearer. The woman sucks in a sharp breath, hands now shaking violently. Isadora draws back, stomach in knots. Suddenly a single tear drops onto the face of the final card. Isadora seeks out the spectre, now standing right over the woman's narrow shoulders.

A child, no more than five years of age, is reaching out, trying to get a grip on the woman's arm. His fingers brush across the drab, brown fabric of her coat and pass, unseen and unfelt, right through to the other side. His face pinches in sorrow and he opens his mouth to cry, only for a stream of water to come bubbling out. It pours from his blue-tinged nose and lips, floods down his pyjama-clad body and onto the concrete floor.

"This card symbolises fairness. And truth," Isadora intones softly, eyes never straying from the poor, dead child. A picture forms in her head and recognition strikes seconds later. "I'm so sorry," she murmurs to the boy, who locks onto her and refuses to look away. They share a moment just staring at each other until the boy places a delicate hand on his mother's shoulder. The woman shoots abruptly from her chair and stares at Isadora through red-rimmed eyes.

"You are very good," she says breathily, chest hitching and twitching with contained sobs. "But you got my future wrong. There is no justice." And she turns, swaying as she begins to scurry away. Isadora watches the small child begin to reach, arms stretched and screaming, for his mother past the frothy water filling his mouth – for she can be no one else – and Isadora knows she can't just let her walk away.

"Wait!" she calls, rising rapidly and hurrying around her table before the woman can disappear into the crowd. "Please wait!" Her posse watches her, hovering curiously.

The woman stops but doesn't turn to face her.

"Your son," Isadora says. The ghost boy swivels and zeroes in on her once more, incredulous. Isadora meets his desperate stare. The woman twitches, head sinking into her shoulders, fists tightening. A small crowd of living onlookers stop to observe. "It was your son, wasn't it?" Isadora continues tentatively.

The woman gives a short sharp nod but remains in place. Isadora walks hesitantly forward and pauses just by the little boy's side, fully aware that what she is about to do is only going to make her look even crazier. But she can't let this little boy go on like this, or his mother.

"What's your name?" she asks, so softly it is barely audible. His eyes widen almost comically, jaw dropping as more water trickles over the edge of his lips.

"Timothy," he replies, in a voice so small, wet and innocent Isadora nearly staggers.

"Your son, Timothy!" Isadora calls to the woman, who turns so sharply Isadora retreats a few steps, suddenly scared she has misread the situation. The woman's eyes, so similar to her son's, widen and she clasps her hands to her chest.

Isadora continues hastily. "He was drowned. And they never charged the person who did it." This was entirely guesswork, although Isadora figures there is no other way the boy could have perished. No other marks on his young body (that she can see) and it certainly makes the narrative the cards revealed seem accurate. The water beneath The Fool's cliff and at the High Priestess's temple comes to mind.

The woman crumples in on herself, a slew of tears sliding down her pasty face. It is then that Isadora notices she is wearing clothes that cover her entire body, bar her face. As one of her sleeves slips back from her twiggy wrist, Isadora catches sight of a fading green-and-yellow mark.

Isadora's throat closes up. There is nothing more she can say, as it all slots together. Nothing except ... "I'm sorry."

The woman shakes her head and strides forward, the most purposeful movement Isadora has seen from her. She reaches out and clasps Isadora's shaking hands in her own before speaking thickly.

"You've seen my boy?" she asks, her voice clogged with tears. Isadora glances over at the child, who has scurried closer now that his mother is in reach. He wraps his immaterial arms around her legs and presses his head against her waist. Isadora nods.

"Can you ..." the woman breaks off and swallows painfully. "Can you tell him I love him? That I miss him?" She appears to be gathering her courage for the next sentence. "And that I'm sorry. For abandoning him the way I did. For leaving him because I was too weak to do anything else." She squeezes Isadora's hands so hard they begin to go white.

"I can tell him everything," Isadora replies shakily. The woman bows her head and whispers a thank you. One last squeeze and she bobs her head back up.

"Thank you." She releases her grip, stumbling back and righting her clothing self-consciously, aware of the eyes of the onlooking crowd, curious in the same way a bird might be curious about an injured lizard. Isadora makes a face, confused as to why she should be thanked for bringing up undoubtedly horrific memories. The mousy woman notices and elaborates. "If you can really see the future, you've given me something to look forward to. I haven't had that in a long time." She sounds wistful and truthful. Isadora crosses her arms and shrinks back, head lowering enough for her hair to swing over her shoulders and partially cover her face.

"You're welcome."

She watches as the woman finally retreats. The child's eyes follow her, his little face crinkled in hurt – a hurt Isadora is sure he is not old enough to recognise and understand as grief. Grief for himself and for the loss of his living mother as he watches her disappear into the mall, into the crowds of people who have stopped to gawk at the unfolding drama. Isadora turns away, catching only the barest glimpse of him from the corner of her eye as he races to catch up with his oblivious mother. She will never see him again; but that becomes an easy enough concept once you've made peace with it. And he will, hopefully, in time.

In the echoing silence, Isadora floats back to her table. The hovering spirits part swiftly, creating a kind of catwalk for her to navigate, until she falls back into her seat. A cold hand touches one of her slumped shoulders, and Iris's wrinkled grin slides into view.

"Very nicely done, my dear," she appraises. Smiling thinly in thanks, Isadora's gaze moves to Will. He is stock still, no smile, looking every bit the confused, wandering spirit she so desperately hopes he will not become. Her heart sinks a little.

"Will?" she enquires gently. He twitches and faces her with a blank look. Isadora is just opening her mouth to ask if he is okay (purely rhetorical at this point, but worth a shot) when a rapping on her table interrupts. Isadora spins to face a well-dressed older man, whose glinting eyes rove up and down, over her Tarot cards and further to rake along her face. One of Isadora's hands unconsciously moves up to clutch at her throat.

"That was a good show you put on there!" he exclaims loudly in a boisterous voice. It's an 'I want that, too' voice. Isadora hesitates. She's already drained – and she's only seen one customer. A small nudge to her shin from Bee has her stitching on a smile. Money is a strong motivator when it comes down to it.

"Would you like a reading?"

VII | THE CHARIOT

The line had been extensive and when Isadora finally stumbles home that afternoon, her head is throbbing, her eyes are itching, and her chakra is all out of energy. Her mum offers her a small smile when she clatters through the front door, and her dad extends a hand and runs it across her dishevelled head.

Isadora shuffles to her room, shuts the door and collapses face down on the bed, groaning into the covers. Her headache is worsening.

"You did good today." Something cold is nudging her leg and, even in her exhausted haze, Isadora recognises the first words her brother has spoken all day. Still laden with melancholy, but tinged with something else. Isadora kicks back and feels her foot pass through a wave of frigid air.

"Thanks," she mumbles in reply. "I only traumatised an abused ex-mother whose child died a horrible death, and now she has to live knowing her son's spirit is hanging around forever tethered to the earth due to the violent nature of his demise until she eventually dies and doesn't reunite with him in whatever afterlife there is that exists – if it even does exist!" She slams a fist down on the bed, causing her body to bounce with the contact. A cold shift in the air near her feet lets her know Will is now sitting at the end of the bed. A tutting voice and rapping cane next to her head distract her.

"Negative thinking never got anyone anywhere and *you*, missy, are the harbinger of negativity," Iris scolds. Isadora can imagine the wrinkled, wagging finger and pushes her head further into the bedcovers.

A grumble of discontent and a heavy, prickly weight on her back demand her attention. Bee paddles roughly and settles in, rumbling unhappily. Isadora's chest tightens. She can see that the spirits could be right about this. Who knew more about this kind of thing than them? If the ghosts truly believe she has assisted that poor, lonely child then maybe she should give them that. Outwardly, anyway. Inside, Isadora will probably doubt her handling of the situation for the rest of her morbid life.

"Okay, fine," she concedes, rolling over to talk to the ghosts properly. "I'll admit it all went better than I expected, and there were some positives to the experience." She traces her patterned bedsheet with her index finger. "And I did make some money."

"Good money," Iris corrects. "You made more than a little. You're well on your way to establishing yourself as a legitimate medium worthy of charging a higher fee."

Bee kneads its paws against her leg, grumbles gradually transitioning to contented purrs. Will's mouth ticks up in a tiny smile. Isadora feels the tightness in her chest recede, replaced by a warmth that expands and spreads outwards. With the prospect of actually making something of herself – finally! – within grabbing reach, her hope can only grow, chasing her habitual negativity into non-existence. Almost.

"Same time tomorrow then, I guess." She brushes a strand of her long hair behind one ear.

"It can only go up from here, Dora."

"What? 'Cos I was at rock bottom?"

"Pretty much."

"Rude. But fair."

VIII | STRENGTH

W ill isn't often wrong, a trait Isadora both despises and admires in equal parts. Her small business does, in fact, 'go up'. A steady stream of customers consistently lines up or hangs around her small table. People gather to watch, curious to know if she is smoke and mirrors or the real deal, placing their money in her 'Funds' tin when they aren't content to just observe. She sometimes cops abuse from sceptics or the strictly religious, who see her as either a con-woman or a witch. It makes her invisible entourage laugh when they pipe up, preaching about Heaven and the peace souls find in the Lord's garden of afterlife.

"Angels must have been off duty when I tried to get in," one of them mumbles, chest a scrambled mess of guts and minced flesh. Isadora contains her snort, ignoring the fact she is interacting naturally, perhaps even amicably, with the dead. Her Amethyst necklace remains fastened around her neck, and she often finds herself rubbing a thumb or forefinger against the stone when doing a reading. She has been asked by a few customers if it is for a particular purpose, to which she has responded that it 'assists in opening her third eye'. Iris gets a real kick out of that one.

Bee stays by her feet at every reading, tail wrapped firmly around her calves, keeping her grounded and being far better behaved than when it met Will for the first time.

Isadora can't deny, business is good. Better than good. And to top it off, she is becoming increasingly proficient with her 'mediumship' skills.

She's performing the Tarot readings more confidently – probably due to her memory improving – and her ability to connect the souls of the living to spirit souls is getting stronger every day. The links are more pronounced, the lost loved ones glowing more brightly when a family member, spouse or friend comes for a reading. Her headaches are not nearly as intense as they used to be, and her reaction – once so adverse – to seeing decomposing ghosts wandering off with their oblivious loved ones is becoming more mellow.

She is almost proud of herself.

But today is busy. Busier than usual. Isadora has a long line-up and is trying to keep her mysterious aura from being tainted by the compounding stress coiling in her chest. Each card reading flies past her; every sorrowful spirit floating off is more irrelevant than the last. All she can focus on is the crowd of people. In truth it's making her breathing more laborious. Is this anxiety showing its unwelcome face? Most likely. Unfortunately, her surrounding pack is also beginning to feel the stress, in spite of her efforts to contain it. Bee has been lashing its tail violently almost the entire morning, and Will has not stopped grinding his teeth as he keeps his arms tightly crossed against his chest. Even Iris is tapping her cane irregularly on the concrete, sounding an uneven tempo that is grating on Isadora's nerves. Considering she's been working this spot in the mall for the past six months, Isadora chastises herself for not handling the crowds better in the face of her spiking stress. The tension only continues to balloon until Isadora can feel it in the air, one breath away from bursting.

Her next client steps up and takes a seat as Isadora waves her hand. He holds himself stiffly, so tense every muscle in his jaw is clearly visible beneath his olive skin. Isadora instantly knows this one is different to all the others. He's not here for the showmanship, to ask whether he's going to get that promotion or whether his future is filled with riches. He reminds her of her first customer, the sad, mousy little woman.

"How can I help you today?" And for the first time since she started this morning, Isadora means it. She leans forward and places her hands gently over the cards, brow pinched in empathy. The ghosts around her quieten, their forms shifting to become opaque, still and silent.

The young man swallows thickly, loaded dark eyes peering up at her, as intense as the man himself. Isadora, of course, can see more than what's on the surface. They reveal a dark well of despair, with no light in sight – an emotion Isadora herself knows intimately.

"I don't need my cards read," he answers, his low voice rough and pebbled. "I just need to know if my sister is here." His eyes drift to the tabletop, hands clenching the fabric of his jeans. Isadora pauses. She carefully sweeps the cards aside into a neat pile and rests the backs of her hands on the table, palms up. Her fingers are trembling.

"Isadora?" Will's voice seems to come from miles away, soft and echoing, outside the bubble she has unknowingly created. There is no sound inside it. Only the existence of one grieving soul and a helping hand. Isadora can't see Will, can't see the puckered frown, the teeth digging into his bottom lip or the clenched fists and troubled sideways glances.

"How long ago?" Isadora asks gently, her voice as soothing as velvet as the young man places his shaking hands in her own.

"Two days."

Isadora nods once and closes her eyes. She has never voluntarily done this before, but it feels natural enough. At this very moment, in fact, it feels right to willingly search out a spirit to drag back to the living plane – considering that much of the time their passing happened accidentally. She pushes through the darkness behind her eyes, reaching past the soft, wavering curtains and into a blackness that seems too intense for any human to witness without being driven completely mad. She dives down into this strange, deep well rooted inside her centre. There are things hidden here, in the all-consuming nothing, things that don't breathe but pulse, that beat so gently they are almost inaudible. Each one is different. Each has a name that Isadora can sense. Most have shifted further away, eager to remain peaceful in the black expanse. Some drift closer, curious.

Swaying tendrils of jellyfish limbs stretch, brushing tentatively against her consciousness until, finally, she feels a pulse stronger than the others. A tinge of light begins to glow. Its amber gleam shines urgently. A thread connecting the light to Isadora's palms strengthens and Isadora, without knowing exactly how, tugs smartly and feels it pull from the well right in the middle of her body. A bungee-like snap and Isadora's eyes fly open.

A teenage girl is standing behind the client's back. Her face streaked with tears, arms slit from wrist to elbow, she stares at the back of her brother's head, eyes wide with yearning.

"Andrew," she whispers forlornly, placing a hand on his shoulder. Andrew shivers, fingers tightening their grip on Isadora's. "I'm sorry."

Andrew, dumbstruck, gapes at Isadora. "Is she here? She is, right? I can feel her hand on my shoulder." His breathing quickens. "Is she here?" Isadora answers his desperate plea with a slight nod.

"She says she's sorry," Isadora murmurs. Andrew's face crumples, and then a small smile begins to bloom at the corner of his mouth.

"She doesn't have to apologise." He glances up, moisture gathering in his eyes. Isadora's face twists in confusion.

"But it was her fault!" It comes out before she can think about it, genuinely unable to understand why Andrew isn't more incensed than he is at the manner of his sister's passing. He tilts his head back down and stares at the table, not caring about the tears that are streaming down his face.

"If anything, it was my family's fault," he responds simply. Now he is confused. "We were more ready to see her as a problem rather than see ourselves as a possible solution. We let her do this to herself. That's worse. *We* should be apologising to *her*!" He tightens his grip on Isadora's trembling hands, his eyes tracing her features far too intensely for Isadora's liking. She feels very exposed now, a raw nerve cringing, trying desperately to find a safe place to hide. She shifts uncomfortably.

"Someone close to you died recently," Andrew deduces.

"Car accident," Isadora chokes out. Why is she revealing all this? Andrew's sister is watching her now, too, eyes soft with sympathy. Isadora hates it.

"The way you're talking it doesn't sound like you think it was an accident," Andrew states, looking at her curiously, probing for more.

Isadora's eyes narrow. "He wasn't wearing a seatbelt. It was his fault." Something stabs and writhes deep in her chest as she recognises the falseness in her words.

"Hey! Can you hurry this up? I want my future read!" A belligerent bark bursts their bubble and Isadora comes crashing back to earth.

She peers over Andrew's tensed shoulder, venom burning in her eyes as she yells back, "Wait your turn, asshole!"

It all happens very quickly after that. Bee, who's been sitting on Isadora's feet all this time and is already strung-out from the anxiety crackling around Isadora, growls low in its throat and leaps. Long talons clattering, it streaks across the concrete floor of the shopping mall and pounces at the culprit.

"Bee, stop!" Isadora rips her hands from Andrew's and launches herself out of her seat. Bee ignores her. It sinks its claws into the unsuspecting heckler and rakes. The large, middle-aged woman screams as a long, large, deep slice appears in her upper thigh, Bee's claws having cut right through her jeans. Blood spurts everywhere. Another wound manifests on her shin; three jagged cuts arranged suspiciously like claw marks open up and begin to add to the blood pooling on the ground at her feet. The woman is in hysterics, hands up, mouth open as she wails and tries to clumsily flee from her unseen attacker. A hand raises and points accusatorially at Isadora.

"You freak!" she screeches, before falling backwards onto her fat rear. The horrified crowd turn to an even more horrified Isadora, who can only stand, frozen like a statue, mouth parted and utterly dumbstruck as Bee crab-walks back to her side, spine raised into pointy black barbs, tail whipping dangerously. Its white eyes are slits, and its long fangs are bared as other-worldly snarls ring out through the thickened air.

"You attacked me!" the woman screeches, several bystanders now kneeling at her side. One of them has a phone to their ear, no doubt calling an ambulance. Others begin to crowd in on Isadora, hands raised threateningly as they shout and yell. One faceless man grabs her wrist and tugs her close, shouting at the others as they all try to apprehend her. If the police get here before she can escape, it's over.

Isadora panics, lashing out with her foot and kicking her captor viciously in the shin. She hears him yelp as she rips her hand free, shoving against the onslaught of shocked, hysterical people. The injured woman is still howling in the background.

"Isadora!" Will is suddenly right beside her, abruptly pulled into focus as he yanks on her arm. *Touching her arm.* Since when could he actually touch her? "You need to go, now!"

Isadora nods. Spinning around, she pushes her way back to her table. In a frantic daze she gathers up her cards and money tin, then books it, bumping into several people as she wiggles her way through the quickly closing gaps. Andrew gets lost in the crowd behind her as she sprints away and down the main corridor, dodging agilely around several onlookers who stop and stare instead of moving out of her way. She crashes into a couple of innocent bystanders, sending one sprawling, confused between the spirits and the living as they create one intangible mass around her. She doesn't stop to help them up. Her one thought is to get to safety. Eventually, she bursts out of the mall and runs into the street outside. Her pace doesn't slow. Bee is galloping along beside her, tail between its legs.

Isadora finally begins to slow to a stressed jog, which then turns to a strange speed-walk slash hop, constantly checking over her shoulder to make sure there's no angry mob following her. Her breath is coming out in sharp pants, and her chest is heaving as she tries to catch her breath, beads of sweat trickling down her forehead and neck. Her hair is a long, tangled, sweaty mess. She looks insane and she vaguely realises this. But there's more to freak out over than her stupid hair.

"Isadora!" She startles as a categorically tangible hand grabs her bicep. Spinning round, Isadora finds herself face-to-face with her brother, his pulled into a myriad of animated – but mainly worried – expressions. She's almost happy to see the show of feelings, as opposed to the blank nothingness he's been toting recently. But time for that later, she realises as he begins rapidly talking. "Where are you going? What's the plan here?" he demands.

Isadora shakes her head, still dazed. "I don't know what happened," she gasps breathlessly. "I hurt someone!"

"No." Will stops her before she can spiral. "It wasn't your fault." He glances around the quiet street. "We'll have time for the freakout later, okay? We need to get somewhere safe first."

"I can't go home!" Isadora says faintly. "I can't take the witch hunt there …" Her eyes flick up to meet Will's beseechingly. "Mum and Dad only just stopped hating me!"

"They never hated you." Will responds exasperatedly, rolling his eyes.

Isadora shakes her head frantically. "Even so, I can't lead a mob of angry people straight to them. They'll never be left alone! They'll become like me, a social pariah!" Her hands gesticulate wildly. "Will …" her voice cracks. "What am I supposed to do?!"

"You're going to calm down for a start," Iris barks, limping up and tapping her cane loudly on the sidewalk to get Isadora's attention. "Stop panicking and start planning." Her steely grey gaze pierces effectively through the miasma of panic. Isadora gulps in a deep breath, followed by another. Her hummingbird heartbeat begins to slow a little.

"Okay," she gasps. "Okay." She wipes her face, pushes back her tangled hair and takes a final deep breath. "Okay. Game plan." Isadora thinks. "I need a place to hide. Somewhere that won't cost heaps of money, considering I have next to no savings."

She thinks of her back jeans pocket where the stashed money tin resides, rattling comfortingly with every step. "So, I need to find an empty place to squat." Her eyes widen. "And there's only one place nearby I know that will be empty, where barely anyone goes." She shudders. "I really don't want to go anywhere near that place after last time."

The vision flashes through her brain. "But I don't really have a choice," she sighs reluctantly.

"It doesn't matter what you do and don't want to do at this point, missy," Iris cuts in snippily. "It's a decent place to hide. You have to make the best of this bad situation."

Isadora scowls. "Why do I get the feeling I'm going to hear that a lot from now on?"

"Because it's the harsh, honest truth," Will replies softly. Isadora shifts her weight from foot to foot, attempting to convince herself it's the only option. She knows she needs to make a move – and soon, before the crowds find her and attempt to make a citizen's arrest or something equally alarming.

She groans. "Alright. Fine. Good. Let's go." She turns and stalks off. The spirits dutifully follow, legs moving but feet never touching the ground. With every step she takes, Isadora's shoulders tense higher and higher until they're nearly touching her ears. Eventually, the sidewalk falls away to a grassy gutter and, further on, to dirty paths that lead out of the suburbs towards a long dirt-and-gravel road lined by tall, domineering pine trees. Pine needles litter the earth beneath her feet, and the protruding roots of the trees almost trip her up with every second step. Heavily laden branches stretch right across the width of the road, brushing against each other to create a ceiling of swaying greenery. Isadora breathes in the piney scent, her entire body thrumming with anxiety.

Will walks a step behind, head turning this way and that to examine the old wire fences that separate the road from the fields, dilapidated and sunken with age and neglect. Beyond the pine trees, the fields stretch away, overgrown with weeds and bereft of livestock. On one side, the field dips about halfway across, sloping down to a riverbank, where sparkling water flows serenely along.

Isadora's pace slows imperceptibly, and she crosses one arm across her body to grasp the opposite wrist. She isn't fond of this path. A pair of crumbling white chimneys peek over the tree line as the road narrows to a path that forks and twists around a single towering pine tree, older and knottier than the rest. The branches reach high into the bright blue sky, casting long-drawn shadows at Isadora's feet. She heads left. Her journey comes to a halt at a pair of intricate, rusted iron gates, which have been padlocked shut and display a large metal 'DO NOT ENTER' sign. Her posse closes in, flanking her and boxing her in against the fence. None of them speak. Isadora rolls her shoulders to psych herself up to pass across the threshold, then stops, head cocking to the side. The air is 'off'. Pitched sideways, diverging from normality and freezing in her lungs.

Will steps alongside her. He appears more … substantial than before. She can't see through his torso to the trees behind him, and he is almost glowing in the shadow of the monster pine tree.

"Will?" she asks, her voice hushed. There's no birdsong here, she notes idly.

"I never realised until now," he murmurs quietly, "what you must have felt when we snuck there before."

"It's never felt like this," Isadora refutes quietly. She and Will lock eyes. Isadora gathers up her waning courage and cracks a strained smile. "Let's get trespassing."

Tackling the gate is hard. Her hands touch the pitted rust, settling heavily on top of the gate as she determines just how she's going to get over it. It's taller than her. The gaps aren't big enough for her to squeeze through. And the pointy spikes adorning the top don't endear themselves to the idea of climbing over. But what other choice does she have? Or maybe … Isadora wanders along the fence line adjoining the gate. There has to be a weak spot in the neglected iron railing. A loose paling perhaps. As she walks, she tugs on each post to check. Her feet crunch through the fallen pine needles until one yank proves successful. The post pulls easily from the ground, and Isadora pushes it to the side to create a gap substantial enough for her to squeeze through. Strangely, her deathly parade follows her, carefully manipulating themselves through the gap and into the mansion's grounds. Isadora, baffled at first, suddenly remembers that ghosts can't touch iron. It's too pure an element to be touched by the damned.

Bee, meanwhile, leaps gracefully over the wrought iron fence and touches down on the other side.

Isadora waits until they are all present and accounted for before continuing on. The dirt path has given way to an overgrown driveway that cuts through the weed-ridden lawn and sweeps magnificently up to the house. Large silver birch trees line the avenue, less intimidating than the pine trees. They give Isadora a strange sense of calm. Eventually, the birch trees peter out to reveal a large, stained fountain, adorned with cracked cherubs and worn detailed stonework, and surrounded by a loop of concrete. The whole thing is overgrown with grass and spattered and stained with smears of rusty red. Isadora can't help shuddering as she peers past the fountain to the towering mansion – windowless, empty and haunting.

Isadora stands and stares for what seems an age, before Will prods her in the shoulder. Hesitantly, she shuffles forward, hands clenched tightly by her sides. A crumbling set of stairs leads up to a concrete landing, then split to continue heading up left and right. Isadora chooses right, her steps echoing hollowly on the aged stone as the stairs even out onto a wide front verandah. Isadora suppresses a shiver. A large, peeling green door stares at her, flanked by two windows, one on either side and boarded up messily. Almost as if it had been done as hastily as possible before the workman ran screaming from the grounds, she muses.

She brushes one hand along the tarnished brass door knocker and down to the equally tarnished door handle situated in the direct centre of the door. Isadora pushes half-heartedly, waiting for the moment she can turn and announce, "The door is locked, there's no way in … too bad, guys". To her shock, the door swings open easily, hinges barely whispering, as it gives way to admit her to the foyer. Goosebumps have erupted all over Isadora's arms, legs and neck. Her skin is prickling so badly she wants to peel it off like a jumpsuit and throw it as far away as possible. Pushing past the uncomfortable sensation, Isadora carries on.

"What the actual fuck?"

Her words echo across the immaculately tidy foyer. The polished floorboards gleam in the early afternoon light. There are two rooms branching off from the spacious entrance, and Isadora can see all the way through the house to the back door. The perfectly intact back door. The hint of a staircase peeks out from behind a wall on both the left and right sides of the house. A large, ornate crystal chandelier hangs from the ceiling, surrounded by an intricate ceiling rose that gleams with gold-leaf detailing.

Isadora's jaw drops. She whips around, stalks through the group of stunned spectres and pokes her head outside. The garden is horrifically overgrown. The fountain is still stained suspiciously red. Isadora retreats back inside, trying not to gape too much at the grandiose décor, and heads into the room on the right. It's a living space decorated lavishly with plush floral sofas and large oil paintings of grim-looking people in fancy clothes. She actually does gape as she looks out the perfectly pristine window, which is framed with luscious rich-red curtains. Isadora presses her nose against the glass. It is very tangible – cool to the touch and completely clear of grime or stains. The garden outside is immaculate. Large, sweeping lawns of perfect emerald green are dotted with healthy-looking, immaculately groomed trees and hedges. A gleaming white fountain stands in the centre of the turning circle, clear water spraying from the spotless cherub's perfectly puckered mouth.

Isadora backs away from the window, heart beating frantically as her brain struggles to comprehend this second most shocking revelation of the day.

"You're seeing the same thing I am, yeah?" Her voice is shaking so badly each vowel trembles on the clear air. There's not a dust mite to be seen in this picture-perfect room, its view plucked right from the scenes of an oil painting.

But when she looks at Will, all she can see is a bemused crinkle between his brows. "All I'm seeing is a gross, dirty house," he replies carefully. Isadora's tiny 'Huh?' of confusion is almost lost when, suddenly,

Will cracks a huge grin. "Nah … I do see what you're seeing." He glances around. "Who would have thought this was possible?"

Isadora punches her brother vindictively on the arm, so hard that if he were alive, it would be black and blue.

"Ow!" Will grabs at his arm, smirk still dancing around his stupid dimple.

"You asshole!" Isadora yells, furious. "If you weren't already dead, I'd strangle you!"

Will only laughs. "How could I resist the chance, Dora? It's like you don't know me at all."

"Yeah? Weren't you depressed just this morning and for the past few months? Go back to being silent and sad," she retorts waspishly. She folds her arms defensively across her chest, her cheeks flaming red. Will's face falls, and Isadora immediately unfolds, anger rapidly fading to regret flavoured with guilt. "Oh my God, Will, I'm sorry." She reaches out and presses a tentative hand to the spot she'd walloped just moments ago. "I didn't mean that."

Will shrugs her off and shakes his head, dark curls bouncing.

"Nah, don't worry about it," he replies. "I shouldn't have messed with you. You're dealing with a bit right now. It was insensitive."

Isadora halts, screwing up her nose. "Since when did *you* learn the word 'insensitive'?"

Will gasps in mock offence. "How dare you?" He shakes his hair back. "I've always known that word. It's a regular part of my vernacular."

Isadora smirks. "The same vernacular that once forgot the word ambulance?"

"Hey," Will snaps. "I was concussed at the time. You can't blame me for that!"

"Well, that's what happens when you head-butt people's knees."

The gathered ghosts watch the spirited back and forth much like spectators at a tennis match, with undisguised interest and a keen amount of anticipation for each response. Eventually, the siblings dissolve into chuckles and turn their separate ways, Isadora hiding her smile of delight, despite the still unique and terrifying situation.

Speaking of which, Isadora completes a small circle, a hand running tentatively along the back of one floral couch. "How …" she mumbles, eyes tracing the picturesque surrounds, " … is this happening?"

An abrupt scratching sounds pulls her from her trance. Isadora spins around to see Bee, back arched and dramatically clawed paws digging into the fine fabric of one arm of the couch, its scratching leaving deep holes for the couch stuffing to poke through.

"Bee!" Isadora exclaims, shooing it away. "Don't do that. This is nice furniture!" Bee bounds away, spine-laden tail high in the air. Isadora huffs and goes back to examine the damage, finding to her shock that the holes are no longer there. The couch is as it was when she first entered the room. Flawless.

"O-kay …" Isadora faces her gathering, internally quivering but realising that, if any group of beings are qualified to present their theories about this 'ghost house', it's this one. "Does anyone have any idea what's going on here?"

A number of spectral hands fly into the air. Isadora scans the crowd for the one most likely to be able to talk cleanly without spilling any blood or perhaps losing their jaw completely. Eventually, she settles on a pale-faced middle-aged woman. She has no visible injuries and – for an endlessly wandering spirit tethered to the astral plane by a deep-rooted desire for either revenge or peace – reasonably clear eyes.

"Yes?" Isadora points to her. "You with no visible injuries, middle-aged woman."

The woman's face lights up and she hustles to the front of the group.

"My name is Danielle." Her voice is pleasantly normal so Isadora gestures for her to continue, trying to ignore the other spectres that have crept closer. "I think we're stuck in a ghost house," Danielle continues.

Isadora almost interrupts her to say, "Yes, Danielle, I think we've all gathered that, thank you!", but decides to let her keep going in case she provides something more informative. "It feels like the house is stuck in the year in which something terrible happened." Danielle's eyes cloud over. "Like it's reliving a time prior to that event on the inside. Maybe the spirits here want to preserve the time before whatever it was happened, rather than acknowledge the horror that came after." Danielle drifts back into the group, eyes now shadowed with a feeling Isadora neither understands nor desires to.

A brief silence follows before Isadora clears her throat. "Right. Thank you, Danielle." And then Isadora immediately reverts to ignoring the crowd of spirits once more.

"It's not the worst place you could be hiding," Will says softly, coming to stand beside her. Isadora can accept his point of view. She can understand why he would say this. The house is beautiful on the inside, an ideal place to remain hidden from the world. No one would consider that anyone could survive in a house that, from the outside, appears to be nothing more than an abandoned, mould-infested skeleton of a building. A condemned one, at that – too dangerous for any normal living thing to sustainably exist for longer than a couple of hours. Nobody would think of looking here.

And yet, Isadora is not sure. She can't wipe the vision from months earlier out of her mind. This place had either warned her of something, or accidentally let slip what had transpired here before the homestead was abandoned. The sheer violence and unrest made Isadora uncomfortable right down to her core. None of the ghosts, not even Will, could understand that. They were part of that horrific world themselves, and when you're part of something, it's almost impossible to view the situation from an outside perspective. Isadora walks a line in between, gifted with the ability to see both sides objectively (or perhaps she means *subjectively*. She always forgets which is which). But they are right in the thick of it.

Something gives, in spite of the fact her spine is still tingling with the echoes of the vision she'd had not so long ago, and Isadora reluctantly admits to herself that Will is right.

"I hate when you make sense," she mumbles, stalking off before he can respond. Her footsteps echo grandly in the expansive entryway. The chandelier overhead sparkles in a shard of afternoon sunlight, casting jewel-bright colours onto the pale wallpapered walls. "Guess I'd better find the bedrooms and claim one," Isadora says to herself, setting off up the right-hand staircase. A plush red rug runs up the centre of the steep, wide oak stairs, held in place by thin golden rungs at the base of each step. The dark timber banister is completely bereft of dust and cool to the touch.

Isadora climbs slowly, passing a window on the landing as she turns to head up to the next storey. Tree branches sway calmly in what appears to be a pleasant breeze. Isadora's skin breaks out in goosebumps. The unnaturalness of this place grates on that place inside her, the one that feels like a dark well just begging to be explored but far too frightening for her to contemplate. One hand drifts up to clutch at her Amethyst necklace and the feeling settles slightly.

Doors run along the stretch of hallway, each framed in dark oak like the staircase. Isadora walks along it, feet thudding softly against the same red carpet. Each door is slightly ajar. Everything in the house appears to be simply resting, as though human hands had only just left, and it could easily have been inhabited only moments ago. The sensation that she might bump into someone around each corner adds to her uneasiness.

Isadora pokes her head warily around each door, hands inching around the edges to open them. Each door reveals a different, but perfect, room. Three are bedrooms, decorated in their own monochromatic themes. There's a small library. Two are bathrooms (sadly, these too are true to the era). Then there is what appears to be a nursery complete with the mandatory array of creepy porcelain dolls. Isadora doesn't linger in that one. The last door opens into an empty space. This room smells mustier than the rest of the house and sets Isadora's spine tingling unpleasantly. She beats a hasty retreat. The corridor ends at another staircase that Isadora assumes is the left-hand one from the entryway.

She heads back along the hallway to choose her room, leaving the ghosts to mingle. They finally have an actual house to haunt, and most of them appear to be reasonably intrigued or excited. Isadora isn't sure which.

Only Will, Iris and Bee stay by her side. Melting Man has long ago faded into the general group. Isadora has all but forgotten him.

"Ugh, why are they all so cold?" Isadora asks, as she hunts for the best room, carefully avoiding the nursery.

"These old homes have no heating source other than the fireplaces." Iris is waddling along close behind, tapping her ghostly cane on the hardwood floors, deliberately ignoring the carpet so she can make as much authoritative noise as she can. Isadora grits her teeth and decides to ignore it in favour of continuing her search.

"I have no idea how to light a fire, so that's going to be perfect," Isadora gripes as she heads into the green bedroom. Adorned with silks, velvets and a fancy-looking screen set in front of the fireplace, it's a little too gaudy for her. "But it's not too late to learn either, I guess. Who knows, I might even have a knack for it, become a pyromaniac."

Will, hands in pockets, responds flatly, "Yeah, you would. Plus, you're the only one who's going to have that problem. Ghosts can't feel anything *but* cold."

"Thanks, Will, that's so helpful."

The next room is all decked out in light blue apparel, and everything appears to have either frills or lace adorning each edge. "Too busy," Isadora decides, and prays that the next and final bedroom in the otherwise enormous house isn't going to give her a headache. It seems that luck might finally have given her a break, because the next room is painted in a lovely shade of lavender. And pleasingly plain in decoration.

"It'll have to do," Isadora declares, walking further into the bedroom to explore the furnishings. She can see no frills, no lace, no decadent embellishments. There's a four-poster bed, the same as in the other rooms, an armchair, a dresser and a desk complete with gilded mirror. It's the only outwardly fancy piece, not including the gold-leaf chandelier that is hanging daintily from the ornate ceiling rose. Isadora sits lightly on the edge of the bed, and the goosebumps begin receding from her arms. The thing inside her appears mollified, at least for the moment.

"Okay …" Isadora takes a deep breath, brushes her hair back and glances up at Will, whose ghostly hand is dusting over the mantlepiece, fingers toying with a petal from a large bunch of brightly coloured flowers that are spilling over the edge of a dainty porcelain vase. He's touching it. She is *allowing* him to touch it. Up until now, the ghosts could only pass through things. Yes, they did make some sounds – like Iris tapping her cane on the ground – and some ghosts were able to create noises that echoed those they made in life, although Isadora isn't sure how. But one constant has been the ghosts' inability to fully interact with the living world. If they attempted to touch a person, they would move through them, leaving only a faint trace of cold in their wake. Not anymore.

"Am I allowed to freak out now?" Isadora asks shakily.

Will's brows rise in question. "About?"

"Will!" she bursts out. "As if you don't know what about! Did we not experience the same thing back in the mall?" Her hands fly to her messy hair. "Bee attacked someone!"

Will shrugs. "It's not the first time it's done that. Remember me?"

"He didn't slice you open like a Christmas ham!" Isadora retorts. "And that's not the only thing. You grabbed my arm!" She points at her bicep. "You grabbed me, physically grabbed me! How did you do that?"

"I don't know, Dora!" Will yells back. "How am I supposed to explain? It was like I was suddenly lit up, filled with some weird adrenaline-type thing, and all I knew was that all of a sudden I was more than what I am … more solid. And it wasn't me, it was *you* that caused it, right?"

"I-I think so. But Will," Isadora leans forward, desperate, "what am I supposed to do with this? I can barely deal with a bunch of ghosts who float around moaning and crying, let alone a bunch who can suddenly go all poltergeist and touch people!" She plants her elbows on her knees and tries to slow her breathing. Will doesn't approach her, but she hears him clearly enough over her freak-out.

"You look to be dealing just fine to me."

Isadora chokes back an incredulous bark of laughter. "Oh, so my lungs collapsing in on me is fine, huh?" she wheezes.

"No. Back in the foyer – heck, even back in the forest – you didn't seem to be dealing badly. Have you ever thought that your aversion to ghosts is just you psyching yourself out? Making a mountain out of a molehill?"

"I'm a high-functioning freak, Will," Isadora bites back. "Just because I look okay outwardly …" she gestures to herself, "… doesn't mean diddly about how I feel inwardly. I'm in a constant state of crisis."

"Only because you make everything a crisis," he replies evenly. "Don't look at me like that. You only hate me because I'm serving you home truths."

"Maybe now that you can touch things means I can punch you in the head to make you shut up," Isadora snarls, clenching a fist.

"Alright, children, that's enough of that." Iris, who had been eavesdropping unapologetically, steps between the two as Will makes a face that clearly screams 'try me'. "Fighting only ever leads to violence and, while sometimes entertaining, it's going to solve nothing." Iris turns her withering gaze on Isadora. "And you've had your little freak-out so suck it up and make a plan, missy. Turn your worries into motivation to make the best of your situation."

"Such a poet, aren't you Iris!" Isadora drags her hands over her pinched face.

"If you aren't going to help me or any of the others with their problems, at least help yourself." Iris is unfazed by Isadora's grouching, leaning casually on her cane and looking infuriatingly calm. "You are capable of it, you know."

"I don't need your pep talk, Iris." Isadora stands swiftly so as to tower over the crooked old lady. Iris is unimpressed.

"No. At this rate you need a smack up the earhole. But I know you are better than that, so start acting like it." Iris turns and hobbles away. Isadora's fists squeeze shut so tightly her knuckles go white and her nails cut into her skin. The door, untouched by any hands living or otherwise, swings and slams shut behind Iris with such force the windows rattle in their frames.

Isadora sways as the anger drains away leaving her an empty, de-energised husk of a body to work with. She falls back and plops right on the edge of the mattress, which creaks quietly in response. An uncomfortable silence blankets the room and its two remaining occupants. Neither breaks it as Will slowly approaches and settles on the bed beside his sister. She hears him draw in breath and braces for it, but what he says catches her off guard.

"I think you picked this room because it reminds you of Mum."

Isadora's head pops up sharply, inquisitive eyes studying Will's face. He isn't looking at her. He appears to be studying the dark hardwood floors at their feet. The remaining anger and distress in her stomach smooths and softens as she catches sight of the wetness along his lash-line.

"It's the purple, isn't it?" she says softly. Will nods.

"Reminds me of that drapey plant that runs around the verandah back home." He begins picking at his shorts, uncomfortable in his vulnerability.

"The wisteria," Isadora supplies. Her mum was so proud of herself when it finally started to grow. She'd been gifted a cutting from her own mother and hadn't expected it to flourish, so was subsequently thrilled when it proved her wrong.

"Yeah, that one." Will huffs a small laugh. He rubs a hand roughly over his face. "God, this is all so messed up, Dora," he admits, waving a hand haphazardly in the air. "This place. The mall. My car crash." He ducks his head. "It's all felt like a crazy fever dream. None of it felt real. Like I was walking through fog, caught between everything. It didn't feel real until earlier today." He meets Isadora's eyes. "When you made us corporeal."

Isadora gapes a little, then rapidly closes her mouth when she realises what he's saying. "I didn't know you knew what that word meant," she blurts. It isn't what she had wanted to say. But then again, Isadora isn't sure she has words enough to reply with any kind of depth or substance.

Will chuckles. Isadora echoes it. They let the sound fall back into silence. Eventually, Will punches her in the shoulder and roughs up her already messy hair, garnering an annoyed grunt as Isadora attempts the detangle it.

"Get some sleep." With that as his parting advice, Will leaves Isadora alone, closing the door carefully on his way out. For the first time in a long time, Isadora is left completely alone with her thoughts, sitting on a surprisingly soft mattress in a huge, haunted house.

What a crazy day.

IX | THE HERMIT

The next day is just like the first in this strange, time-trapped house. Streams of sunlight filter through clear windows, not a piece of furniture out of place. Tall, healthy trees sway gently in the breeze outside and beyond. It makes Isadora queasy.

Traipsing down the stairs and into the main foyer, Isadora realises she needs to find a way to get food – and quickly. Considering she is the only one who actually has to eat to survive makes it easier in one way. It means she can go and grab whatever she wants without having to take others into consideration, and the amount she'll need will be relatively little. The main difficulty is how she's supposed to get food when showing her face in town is an absolute no-go. At least until she can't smell fire and brimstone in the air around town or see the tips of pitchforks waving among the houses.

Isadora wanders over to the room on the left-hand side of the entrance this time and finds herself in a rather spectacular dining room. She gazes around in wonder, then spots her money tin exactly where she must have placed it the night before, sitting on the edge of the glossy dining table. The shock of discovering the dilapidated mansion's secret interior had, admittedly, overridden all her other concerns, and she must have unconsciously placed it here while exploring last night, although she doesn't remember doing so. Then again, she had been rather hung up on her brief but fiery fight with Will and must have blacked out pretty much everything else.

She drums her fingers thoughtfully on the tin, which rattles away against the timber dining table, which stretches for at least two metres down the centre of the room and is laden with shining silver tableware. Isadora counts at least six sets of cutlery for each delicately decorated plate, bowl and cup. There is even a large silver tureen in the centre, set on a white lace doily. The walls are painted a moody purple and adorned with sombre oil paintings. There is the obligatory ornate candelabra chandelier, holstering far too many candles to be safe when lit.

Isadora taps a small tune on the money tin and tries to brainstorm some food-procuring ideas, most of which conclude that 'maybe a food delivery service wouldn't be too mad if they had to deliver out here?'. But then, wouldn't that give her hiding place away? She hasn't checked her phone since early this morning when she texted their parents to let them know she was alive, so she can't even be sure if she is still in delivery range. As she is mulling over this problem, Bee patters into the room, tail held high in a question mark over its back and rumbling away as its moon-white eyes travel around the room. Isadora has yet to forgive the demon creature for its vicious performance yesterday – and for tearing up the couch in the living room like some kind of demented cat.

"Don't you come in here looking for forgiveness," Isadora reprimands sternly as Bee moves closer. "Not after your actions at the mall yesterday."

Bee mewls and trots over to rub up against her legs, its unpleasant reptilian skin brushing along her jeans and catching at her exposed knees. Bee's spines open up a series of long, razor-thin cuts on her kneecaps, which instantly begin to bleed.

"Dammit, Bee!"

A host of spirits meander into the room, some through the open doorway and a few seemingly gliding directly through the walls. It really is becoming a typical haunted mansion. Just not the fun kind. If there actually is a fun kind.

"What's the fuss?" Will materialises beside her. Isadora almost flinches but covers it by folding her arms tightly across her chest and glaring at Bee, who now sits innocently on the floor, head tipped slightly back and strange ear-horns canted forward. If it had pupils Isadora is sure they'd be blown to create the patented: 'I'm not innocent but I'd like you to think I am' look that pets of every description have mastered.

"I'm trying to think of ways to get food and other supplies without being immediately recognised in town." Isadora leans back against the table edge and crosses her ankles neatly. Her arms remain firmly folded. Will screws up his eyes and strokes at his chin comically.

"Gee, I don't know Dora. Isn't there a house at the edge of the forest that connects to a certain backyard?"

"No." Isadora shuts him down instantly. "I haven't even considered it, but the answer is no."

Will seems genuinely shocked. "Why not?"

Isadora huffs through her nose. "It's too risky. I don't want Mum and Dad to get caught in the crossfire."

"More like you're avoiding them," Will counters, mirroring her stance. Isadora tugs at the loose ponytail she'd scrunched that morning, a rare hairstyle for her as she's usually keen to hide her face from the world. But today she can't stand the rat's nest her hair has become in all the chaos. She'll just have to leave it up, at least until she figures out how to heat the water to take a decent bath in the clawfoot tub she's found, tucked in the corner of the bathroom at the back of the first floor.

"Would it be so bad?" she asks softly. "That I would rather they think I ran away than have them know where I am and have them hovering constantly? They'd draw attention to themselves *and* me. I don't want to be lynched."

"You could at least text them, you moron. And you're not going to be lynched!" Will groans, astounded at his sister's stupidity. Isadora's eyes narrow.

"You think I'm an idiot? Rhetorical," she adds quickly, as Will opens his mouth to reply. "I texted them this morning to let them know I'm safe – but not where I am." She slips her phone from her back pocket and waves it at her brother. "And to tell them that I love them both very much. And that you love them both very much as well."

Will is mollified by this and relents a little. "Fine. Okay. So, what's the plan? I mean you're not that conspicuous. You just have to wear your hair up and expose your face for a change. It's not like people actually know what your face looks like, as you never show it."

"Should I chuck on some makeup, too? Really lean into it?" Isadora jokes. She can't deny her brother is speaking some truths. She never has shown her face, not really. Only glimpses. And she's never worn makeup before – at least, not enough that if she slapped it on thickly anyone would recognise her. She has to admit, sometimes it helps to have a plain face.

"You'll have to wear sunglasses, though," Will says seriously, sliding his hands into his pockets. "No offence, but your eyes are creepy."

Isadora rolls said eyes. "I know. You've told me before. It's like looking into a mirror that knows exactly when and how you'll die. I've heard it all before." She frowns. "Did you have yours with you when you bit it?" she asks bluntly. There's something she wants to try.

Will glares at her. "Yes, I did, they're in my back pocket." He retrieves them and goes to hand them to her, then hesitates, "Wait, am I even going to be able to give them to you?"

Isadora shrugs. "I don't know, but if you can interact with the living and their things, and I can interact with the dead, theoretically I should be able to interact with your things." She holds out an impatient hand, fingers wiggling in the universal 'give it to me' motion. Will relents and passes his sunglasses over. They fall solidly into Isadora's palm.

"Success." Isadora places the glasses on her face and smiles at Will. "Looks like your afterlife is going to get interesting."

Will grins. "Too bad you don't have enough money to buy me a gaming system. It's going to be so boring here."

Isadora snorts and reaches up to pull out her hair tie so she can redo it. She gathers her hair and pulls it tightly up into a high, neat ponytail. "Yeah. What a shame."

Adjusting the sunglasses, she wanders out into the hall in search of a mirror. Spotting one on the far wall she hurries over to inspect her reflection.

"I look stupid," she groans, whipping off the glasses and fiddling with the arms.

Will snorts. "You don't have to look good. You just have to not look like you. The worse you look the more likely people are to avoid you," he points out logically.

Isadora pouts. "What about my pride? I don't want to look like a homeless person." She props the glasses on top of her head and fold her arms. She knows she's being petulant but wonders all the same if Will realises what it is she's subconsciously doing.

"You kind of are homeless," Will argues. "Would you just put the glasses on and go to the supermarket?"

"Fine," Isadora relents and perches the glasses on her nose. "Think I should buy some hair dye? Really change it up?"

"Would you stop stalling and just go already!"

Isadora huffs. "Rude," she mutters and makes her way to the front door. It's as far as she gets. She bounces back and forth, swaying from side to side and muttering a litany of inspirational words before groaning and throwing her hands in the air. "I can't do this!" She kicks frustratedly at the ground. "I can't go!"

"What's stopping you?" Will wanders up beside her. Isadora shrugs hopelessly.

"I just can't."

"No," Will shakes his head. "That's not it." He pokes her shoulder. "Be honest."

"I'm scared!" Isadora bursts out. "I'm scared and anxious and I can't go out there without wanting to collapse into tears. It's stupid and silly and weak, but I can't do it, Will! I don't want to be attacked. I don't want to," she breaks off, gulping back tears. "I don't want to be committed to a mental hospital because they think I'm crazy or dangerous," she admits hoarsely. "I don't want them to experiment on me. I've seen enough movies and documentaries about it." Isadora shudders.

Will's face softens. He places a tentative hand on her shoulder. "Just walk and act like you're meant to be there and people won't even look twice. Be confident in yourself."

A cold head bumps against her leg. Isadora looks down and smiles weakly when Bee settles at her feet, inquisitive face tilted upwards, tail curling protectively around her ankles. She supposes it's all in support of her, a final push in the right direction to keep her from stalling any longer. Society is exhausting enough as a regular person; it's worse when you already have an anxiety complex. This really will be a challenge. Isadora steels herself, resigns herself to the knowledge she really does need to do this, and straightens up.

"Fine."

The first step is the worst, the second not much better, like walking through wet cement. Isadora drags herself over the threshold and down the wide steps, oblivious to the incandescent, ghostly eyes watching her back as they peer through windows and gather in the doorway behind Will and Bee. None of them attempt to follow her, feeling far safer and more content in their new sanctuary. Until Isadora hears the tell-tale thump of Iris's walking cane.

"What are you doing?" Isadora asks through clenched teeth as she reaches the bottom of the steps. Iris hums.

"Moral support."

She ambles on, comfortably keeping pace as they begin to wander down the driveway. Isadora would prefer to avoid walking back along the abandoned road, instead cutting through the woods and into her parents' backyard as she normally would, but she can't afford to let them catch a glimpse of her. Not until everything has settled down, at least. The last thing she wants is the police finding her there, and to possibly be arrested in front of her parents. She's embarrassed them enough for this lifetime.

Isadora listens to the crinkling grass beneath her feet, the gentle birdsong drifting on the air. She glances back at the mansion only to see nothing other than a decaying mess once more. Her brow creases with thought. It's a puzzle she is fully aware is probably unsolvable. The 'why' behind the metaphysics of the house. The world, her world, is like that more often than not – simply too difficult to fully comprehend.

As she wanders nervously down the empty country road, Isadora feels oddly lonely without her usual ever-present posse. Something must have flickered across her face, and Iris spoke up.

"A troubled thought, my dear?"

Isadora shakes her head even as a halting half-admission tumbles from her lips. "Just a bit of an empty feeling." She chews it over in her mind and smiles ruefully. "I suddenly feel weirdly lonely without them." She casts an eye around beneath Will's sunglasses. "Which is silly, because I feel just as lonely when they're with me!" Isadora utters a confused laugh and allows it to trail off into silence. Iris hobbles along beside her still, wrinkles arranged into an expression Isadora has never seen before. She's about to mention it when Iris speaks.

"It's your soul that hungers for company. Not your body. Not your mind." She says it matter-of-factly, as if this answers everything. "It's the same for all of us who feel lonely in a crowded room."

Isadora casts a sideways glance at her companion but can offer no response. The words trail off into the damp breeze, the crackling of dead and dying leaves beneath Isadora's sneakered feet their only ambiance. Inside, however, Isadora's mind is a tumultuous storm of noise. Her thoughts are bouncing back and forth relentlessly, and it continues this way for the entire walk into town. Once her feet hit pavement instead of the springy forest floor, Isadora consciously holds her head higher and walks with more purpose than she's ever felt worthy of before. Will's words emerge from the confuddled fog of internal noise and ring suddenly clear in her mind. 'Act as if you're meant to be there. No one will look twice.' She holds the thought close, like a comforting blanket.

Isadora barely remembers the rest of the journey. Barely remembers seeing any other humans. Grabbing food items from the shelves. Paying for them. She enters that kind of zoned-out state of mind people experience when they arrive home from work and find themselves parked in the driveway with no recollection of how they got there. Isadora feels that enigmatic shift and blinks several times as she realises the pavement has given way to a gravel-lined road littered with fallen leaves. Red, gold and brown, wet from the light misting rain and making satisfying mulchy squelches when she walks over them. Two plastic bags dangle from her white-knuckled fists, swinging and banging rhythmically against her legs. Iris wanders sedately at her side, wrinkled lips pursed in a grin that Isadora would almost call proud if she didn't already know the older lady semi-well.

Slipping back through the gap she'd created in the rusty iron fence the day before is easy enough. The plastic bags go first, and she follows. Iris joins her again as they trek their way back through that strange sideways air, as if the rusty gates have given way to an entirely different world. Isadora reels a little, feeling that dizzying shift of time seep into her skin. The house rises, gleaming and new, on the horizon. Death giving way, opening up to reveal tainted life. Isadora wrinkles her nose but says nothing.

Will is there to greet her as Isadora hurries up the slick stone stairs and inside, feet squeaking on the polished floorboards and leaving dirty footprints in her wake.

"Successful?" He shuts the door smartly and whirls to face his sister, who removes the sunglasses and tosses them to him. Will catches them neatly and stows them away in his pocket again. Isadora tugs her hair from its ponytail and gives it a shake, allowing it to fall in curtains of shimmering blonde. Isadora immediately feels comfort wash warmly down her back as she is cloaked in the familiarity of being able to hide.

"I guess." Isadora ignores the spectres as they begin to gather, their silvery shapes floating and bobbing serenely in a wide, spreading sea that slowly fills the foyer. Whatever loneliness Isadora has felt dissipates at once and her skin prickles uncomfortably.

"Well, an interesting turn of events while you were gone." Will steers Isadora into the cavernous dining room, throws a quick glance around them and lowers his voice to a murmur. "There's a new club member hanging around."

Isadora raises an eyebrow. "Why are you concerned? I thought they didn't bother you?"

"I don't like this one."

"O-kay …," Isadora drags the sound out and surveys the foyer where the crowd of curious spectres continue to hover – a bit like bees in a field filled with clover. "Where are they? If anyone could sense them it would be me."

Will shakes his head. "I only saw them for a split second. They were standing on the lawn out the front." He gestures as inconspicuously as he can, Isadora following with her eyes. Out on the pleasantly shaded lawn, which is now speckled with freshly fallen leaves stirred by a gentle breeze that shakes the branches of the towering oaks and springy ash, there is nothing. No person, no indication of anyone. Just an empty expanse of sun-soaked grass. Isadora wrinkles her nose.

"Of course they're not there," she mutters. "And of course it looks positively delightful. Not suspicious at all." She runs a hand through her hair and turns back to Will. "What did they look like, at least?"

Will considers, scrunches his face and thinks again, his dark eyes squinting. "Male, I think," he responds slowly. "Dark hair, kinda tall – like 5'11". Not an athlete. Way too skinny."

"Okay, subjective thinking aside, did they seem dangerous? Or lonely? Or vengeful? Most ghosts initially fall into the vengeful category then gradually segue into lonely. Usually, that makes them less dangerous."

"Why bother asking if you've already come to your own conclusions?" Will says evenly, the tiniest hint of a grin plucking at his cheeks.

"Okay, so answer me this then, smarty pants, why did they appear for you and not for me? *I'm* meant to be the magnet in the spectral world." Hands on hips, Isadora arches her eyebrows expectantly. Will leans forward.

"Probably something to do with this." He flicks at her Amethyst pendant, which sways and bumps lightly against Isadora's shirt. She slaps his hand away and clutches at the gemstone, face at once drooping into morose longing, heart suddenly so heavy it threatens to force itself right out of her chest and land on the floor with a wet, meaty slap. She is acutely aware of each painful throb beating against the walls of her ribs and finds herself focusing desperately on that when the prickling sensation of tears clogs up her throat.

"Don't," she rasps at her brother, looking down at the floor. She hadn't thought of her mum and dad since this morning when she left for town, and even then she hadn't been fully aware of the hurt that was festering away, tucked behind the myriad thoughts swirling in her mind like a kaleidoscope.

Will softens immediately and apologises gently. "I didn't mean to do that." And Isadora feels sick with herself. Hadn't he lost just as much, if not even more than she? At least her parents know she's alive, can see and interact with her if she were to give up and go home, which she'd be tempted to do if not for the threat of looping them into her circus of freakishness. She pushes back the tears, refuses to allow the hurt to continue stinging, and faces her brother.

"No apologies. Not for this." She wraps her arms around her stomach and turns to face the window, feeling a phantom sun shining on her skin. It's just as warm as the real thing. "And you're right. About this. It does protect me. To some extent." She releases her grip on the Amethyst and allows it to swing back and forth. She turns and fake gags at him. "I hate that you just conned me into saying you're right." It has the desired effect, as Will brightens.

"And it's never sounded so sweet."

X | THE WHEEL OF FORTUNE

Isadora doesn't see the new visitor, so her conversation with Will slips easily from her mind as she begins structuring a new routine. Life is decidedly strange in the old estate house. Time follows no rules and falls into a category Isadora has labelled 'too confusing to really understand'. No strict construct equals no rules – which, therefore equals complete freedom, a chaotic kind of freedom in which the ghosts seem to thrive.

After the first couple of 'days' (as Isadora is a human of tight routine, she still sleeps when she feels it should be night-time, despite the sun still shining), the ghosts appear to separate from their coalescent mess of silvery, moaning mournfulness into distinct and easily recognisable people, each of whom has a complete and enriching personality. At first, Isadora is hesitant. She wasn't fond of them en masse so she isn't so sure she'll be fond of them as individuals, either. She might even be scared to know them as people. And perhaps even more terrifying is the thought that she might *like* some of them (this, naturally, excludes Iris who has made it her mission to annoy Isadora into begrudgingly allowing her company). If this happens it will make her continual rebuttal of their needs and desires worse and threaten to trip her guilt in a manner that will send her sprawling face first onto the polished floorboards. She will be at their beck and call. For when you actually start to like people, it unfortunately progresses into a genuine desire to help them.

As avoidance is her accomplice, she steers clear of most, choosing to watch them from afar as they settle into their new home. Each spirit drifts to a different part of the building. Some see the library as a sanctuary and, shockingly, find they can touch and interact with the books. Isadora feels inexplicable tingles break out all over her skin when this happens, meaning she is in a constant state of feeling like a live wire. It makes her twitchy. Other ghosts find the main living room enchanting and choose to hover around the piano, or lounge in the chairs or on the luxurious sofa. Or they opt to wander around observing the paintings with startling intensity. Isadora has even seen a few break out into squabbles over the paintings' artistry and enter into heated debates as to whether or not they would have chosen that specific artist for their own portraits.

It feels very much like being trapped in a boarding school or an orphanage. A halfway house, if you like, for spirits once lost and now found. Isadora's psychic hackles are constantly raised, so she eventually finds solace in the walled garden at the back. It's peaceful, quiet and, even better, mostly empty. The spectres that do find their way out there tend to wander further afield and end up at the large stone barn some distance away towards the river.

Isadora sits contently now on a small wrought-iron bench beneath a healthily blossoming cherry tree. Petals of soft piglet-pink float down in the ever-present breeze and settle delicately in her lap. Once a small pile has collected, she brushes them away gently and watches as they sprawl prettily over the neatly paved walkway. The path leads back through the garden, wandering sedately up to the house's wide back steps.

A couple of ghosts linger sedately on steps, chatting away to each other, creating a sight so foreign Isadora sputters a disbelieving laugh and shakes her head. One of them, a rather foppishly dressed young man, is leaning casually against the stone railing, his heeled shoes crossed and shining in the late afternoon sun. His companion is standing tall, hands clasped in the rest position at the small of his back as he nods and smiles along with the conversation. It's so ridiculously domestic.

Isadora is so enraptured by the scene she quite forgets about the falling petals, until upon unconsciously brushing some away she discovers foreign moisture on her fingers. She blinks and peers down. A small dark stain is smeared across her index and ring fingers. She rubs the fingers against her thumb and watches the stain transfer smoothly, gliding thinly along her cool skin. Something drops into her lap with a wet splat. Then another, and another. Isadora moves her hands away and peers at her jean-clad legs now splattered with gleaming red droplets. Rich, dark and unmistakeable. Her stomach churning wildly, Isadora tries to stand only to find her legs are stuck fast. She vaguely realises that her legs are no longer in jeans but encased, instead, in flowing white satin. The gleaming pearlescent skirt is tainted by droplets of garnet blood, glistening like tiny rubies in the low light.

Dimly, Isadora realises the red is not only dropping delicately onto her skirt but seeping into the bodice as well. It appears to be originating from somewhere up high. Isadora's blurry gaze travels slowly to her stomach, the tight bodice of white muddied by a large, spreading patch of blood so dark it appears black. A trembling palm settles tenderly over the mess. She flexes her hand and winces as it squelches thickly, rivulets of blood squishing up between lily-white fingers. Isadora doesn't recognise the hand, although it may very well be her own; the size and shape are the same, but it doesn't feel like hers. It feels like a glove, tailored to perfection but somehow still ill-fitting enough to be clumsy.

The eyes Isadora is peering through travel up, blurring with either tears or loss of blood. They settle on the back of the magnificent house, which is now swathed in a thick blanket of snow. Bare tree limbs sway gracefully overhead and a trail of dark footprints stagger their way over to her slumped position, where she rests against the iron bench. Her knees are aching from both the cold and the awkward position she has fallen into. One ankle is pressing against the frigid stone path, small bits of gravel biting into her exposed skin.

A dark figure looms at the end of the path, having just exited the back door. Something in Isadora's body (*but not her body*) shrivels in terror, while at the same time another part of her fights back with fire. Fury unlike anything she has ever experienced swarms up her throat and her terrified mask splits, twisting grotesquely as words spill sharp and poisonous across the whistling wind. The figure walks closer, revealing itself to be a woman. Her dress trails in the snow, and a tangled mess of dark hair whips chaotically around her lined and age-spotted neck. Not quite geriatric, more of a matronly figure, Isadora thinks, but one without any semblance of maternal warmth.

There is a gun cocked and ready in her weathered hands. A shotgun.

Isadora feels something warm trail down her chin.

A scream rings out. It's not hers – it's far too masculine.

She stares down the empty shotgun barrels and sees nothing but encroaching darkness. She doesn't blink. Doesn't flinch. Just stares down death as it wraps her softly in coal-feathered wings, sweeping her up and away into the flurrying snowflakes, each as individual as the next.

☙

Something echoing in the darkness pulls her forward in a swirl of colour, the kind you see if you press your fingers to your closed eyelids for too long.

"Isadora!"

She doesn't come around quickly. She can still feel the sticky molasses mess of blood soaking into her clothes. Can still smell the stink of copper and feel the soft wetness of snow on her cheeks. Or perhaps it's tears. Eventually, Will's face swims into focus. His hands are on her elbows, and she can vaguely feel him struggling as he tries to heft her to her feet. She's fallen off the bench at some point. Her ankle hurts from where it has been pressed to the stone path.

"Dora?" Will shakes her shoulders, and she abruptly shoves him away. She staggers and collapses back onto the wrought-iron bench, which is now smothered with scattered petals. "You awake now?"

"Obviously," Isadora groans, leaning forward to put her head between her knees as the dizziness persists.

"Where'd you go?" She feels the shift in air beside her as Will 'sits' as best he can, the action unaccompanied by any bench creaking. Isadora shakes her head a couple of times, swiping her hair behind her ears and moving shakily to clutch her Amethyst necklace – only to find her neck bare. She had forgotten to put it on this morning. Her hand tightens into a fist and drops into her lap.

"I don't know," she whispers hoarsely. "But it was like that first time, remember?" She tips her face up to the ever-shining sun, frowning when a cloud drifts across the sky, blotting out the warmth. Turning back to her brother, she sees that Will doesn't really remember what she's referring to. Isadora sighs. "When you were still alive and you followed me out here …" she gestures at the house. "Is it ringing any ancient bells yet?" And there it is. Will's face clears in understanding.

"Yeah, I do remember that now. What'd you see?"

Isadora hums thoughtfully, now completely aware of the not-so-conspicuous spirits drifting nearby, their ears cocked and waiting. No real use in trying to hide anything; it's not like they could do much if they heard, anyway.

"I was here in the back garden. Wearing a wedding dress. And there was a woman with a shotgun. Nothing of your mystery man spirit," she adds quickly, anticipating what Will might be wanting to ask when he opens his mouth. Instead, he goes in a different direction.

"You were wearing a wedding dress?"

Isadora elaborates. "Not me, exactly. I was in a different body. Like I'd possessed the ghost instead of the other way around." She thinks on it a second. "Actually …" Isadora peers down at her hands, at the shape, the colour. She squeezes them into fists then flattens them out on her thighs. "Maybe it was the other way around. They only hijacked my mind."

"That's probably what happened to you before," Will acquiesces. "Was there a wedding dress involved when this happened last time?"

Isadora nods, then pauses. An idea has just popped into her head while thinking about the wedding dress – and what else happens at weddings. And that wild-haired woman with the shotgun …

She surges to her feet, shaking away the petals gathered in her lap, and makes a speed run for the back door. Will is left far behind.

"What are you doing?" he yells, legs scrambling to keep up. Isadora bursts through the back door and beelines towards the main living room. Her eyes immediately jump to the portrait-laden walls, scanning each face intently before moving to the next. She may not have the clearest idea of facial features, but there's no forgetting that mane of tangled dark hair.

Isadora does a fast round of the living room, jumping into the dining room when none of the portraits bear any likeness to the figure in her vision. But the dining room yields no results, either. Neither does a thorough inspection of the upstairs hallway or the bedrooms. Nothing. Isadora slows to a halt as she rounds the last bedroom.

"She's not here." Defeated, she spins in a slow circle and faces Will, who has only just managed to catch up with her. Iris has managed to find her way to the end of the hunt and is peering at Isadora curiously. "There's no pictures of her."

"What has that got to do with anything?" Will is confused. Isadora brings him up to speed.

"I was thinking about the wedding dress, then just weddings in general, and then photographs! I thought maybe there'd be a photo or painting of the shotgun lady here. And that if there was, maybe there'd be a name or something. I thought it might give me a lead."

Will snorts. "A lead? What are you, a ghost detective now?"

"No, in order for that to make sense I'd have to be the ghost. Maybe more like a psychic detective."

"Okay, getting back on topic … why are you suddenly chasing leads?"

"What?" Isadora asks. "Are you not curious, after what I've just told you?"

Will shrugs. "Well, yeah, a bit. But that doesn't mean I'm going to pull out my pipe and play detective."

"Why not?" Isadora groans. "That's two visions, Will. Two!" She holds up two fingers. "I want to know why. And I've seen one face, so I have a lead."

"So you're willing to solve this mystery, but none of the others?"

Isadora stops short. "Well, I don't know. Maybe?"

Will shakes his head. "That's not what you were saying ten seconds ago. Let me ask you this, are you more willing to go after this one and work it out because it's directly affecting you?"

Any protest Isadora might have been going to make dies in her throat. Her silence is answer enough for Will. "Wow. That's selfish of you, Dora."

"That's not fair," she tries weakly, but Will is already cutting her off.

"You're right, it's not. What about all those other ghosts out there?" He waves at the rest of the house, behind him. "The ones who've followed you for years, hoping you'd help them? What about them?"

Isadora feels panic rise up in her chest. Does Will know he's among that group? Does he know he's the same? She can't let him go there. Not yet. She has her reasons, and she's quite sure that Iris is the only other one who knows just what his circumstances are. And what Isadora is not doing to keep it that way.

"I …" Isadora trails off, trying to collect her thoughts. She hasn't expected this conversation to crop up, not now. Maybe later, but certainly not now. She needs to reroute the topic – and quickly. "I'm working on it," she finishes meekly. "And while I'm working on it, I may as well work on this. Consider it good practice!" she says loudly, as Will scowls at her. "None of the other ghosts know what they want. What am I supposed to do for them if they don't know? But this one does! They're giving me clues and things to follow, so I can't ignore them."

"Yeah, well, so far that's all led to nothing. There's no portrait here like you said. Maybe she never lived here," Will points out. "Maybe she was only a visitor."

Isadora is already shaking her head, glad that Will has moved on to safer ground. "No. What I felt as that other person …" she trails off, thinking back to the swirl of emotions that had been raging away inside the dying woman's chest. "She knew her. She lived here. *The woman with the gun lived here.* The woman in the wedding dress lived here as well, I'm sure of it." Isadora whirls and slaps one of the walls, suddenly all fired up. The bang resonates through the empty room. "If only these stupid walls could talk."

"Well," Will rubs a hand along the back of his neck. "They kind of do. I mean, this house certainly shouldn't be as clean as it is. Or as nicely decorated. So, whoever they are, they're definitely saying something."

Isadora rolls her eyes. "I know that!" she snaps, quite forgetting the delicate ground she and Will have been treading, but unable to ignore the way her nerves are flayed almost bare from being within another skin only minutes ago. The only way she can begin to describe it is that it was akin to being peeled out of her skin like a veritable human banana, leaving her innards naked before squeezing them into another container. It's all jumbled and wrong and she's left experiencing foreign feelings that make not a whit of sense to her, but perfect sense to the other. It's disgusting. Violating.

"But if these walls are talking," she continues, still agitated, "then the talking is only mumbling, and I'm, like, that one person who just nods and awkwardly laughs, hoping it wasn't a question because I can't understand what's being said!"

"Okay, well … being angry isn't going to help anything. It's only going to make it worse." Which Isadora really doesn't want to hear. Anything but a 'damn, that sucks' is going to piss her off at the moment. Instead of answering, she stalks off into the entrance hall and out the front door, angrily kicking at stray rocks on her way down the wide front steps. It certainly isn't snowing anymore. A balmy breeze kisses her face and coaxes a small sigh from her tense lips. If she is going to have visions, the least they could do is lead to an easily solved mystery – not a confusing jumble of a hallucination that leaves her head and stomach spinning nauseatingly.

Isadora seats herself roughly on the last step, places her elbows on her knees and puts her head in her hands. Frustration pulls unrelentingly at the delicate stitching holding her together, threatening another meltdown. That seems to be all she's made of recently. Bursts of irrational hysteria that end only in exhaustion and embarrassment.

An oily, spiky body brushes against Isadora's jean-clad legs. She drags her hands briefly over her eyes as she raises her head and looks down right into Bee's pale, milky eyes. It sits calmly, lashing tail the only sign of distress. Bee is apparently very finely attuned to her emotional turmoils.

"Sorry, Bee." Isadora reaches down and trails a tentative hand along Bee's spine, skin prickling at the strange texture. Isadora doubts she will ever get used to it. Bee preens under her attention and settles back on its haunches to launch itself up onto Isadora's lap. It's like a puddle of midnight heaped against her knees, its spiny ridges pressing uncomfortably up against her stomach. Perhaps a miniature dragon is a more accurate description than a cat – minus the wings, of course, but certainly not lacking in the teeth or horns department. Bee stares, blinks once slowly and settles deeper into Isadora's lap, head resting on its razor-tipped paws. A tiny, demon dragon-cat, which Isadora finds herself fondly admiring and drawing significant comfort from.

"Never would have expected a demon to act as an emotional support animal." The clack of a familiar cane sounds near Isadora's hip. Isadora peeks up and, sure enough, there is Iris standing next to her, surprisingly staunch for an old-woman ghost.

"Didn't know you could act like such a pain in the ass, and yet here we are," Iris continues.

Isadora frowns. "You did already know that."

Iris taps her cane solidly against Isadora's hip and begins to lower herself slowly and precariously to sit on the moss-lined step beside her. "Do we really need to have another heart-to-heart or are you going to suck it up and stop grouching so much? That thundercloud is only going to get bigger."

Isadora pats carefully down Bee's spine and thinks through her response rather than allowing her heated feelings to rise to the occasion. "I'm not moping … I'm frustrated. There's a big difference." She gasps when her thumb catches on one of Bee's spines. "I just don't understand how I can see these strange things and yet find nothing to connect them to my real life." She gestures at Iris, thumb bleeding a steady trickle. "Like, you and all the others are tethered here for reasons I can't possibly know, and yet I'm expected to be able to send you off into the next world or something. If I don't know, and have no way of finding out what I'm supposed to do, how am I supposed to do it?"

Bee jostles in her lap as Isadora's emotions win the battle. Entire body now aflame with frustration, she slumps and seethes silently, her bleeding digit leaving spots of rusted red on the porous stone.

"And now there's this new whatever that's just happened. I had one earlier, before this whole mess, and they just don't make sense. I don't know why they're happening or what I'm supposed to do with them, or even if they have any real meaning at all. It's frustrating." *That blood will probably stain the stone*, she thinks belatedly, eyes still fixed on her bleeding thumb even as the end of her tirade escapes her.

"Instead of focusing on what you *don't* know, how about focusing on what you do?" Iris asks patiently.

Isadora blinks. In all her anger, all her frustration, not once has that idea crossed her chaotic mind. How stupid can she be? Iris waits as Isadora groans, then allows time for the tiny lightbulb of inspiration in Isadora's brain to warm up, grow into a spark and begin casting light over the wide plane of facts just waiting to be plucked and slotted together. It doesn't quite work out that way.

"But what do I know?" Isadora muses, brows furrowed.

"Talk me through it," Iris offers. "Put it out in the open. A second set of ears can be invaluable."

"Okay ..." Isadora focuses, trying to sort the facts in a timely order to keep it all simple and streamlined, but inevitably making it more complicated as she goes. "I know someone died here, a young woman in a wedding dress. Actually, more people have died here and one was a young guy that Will saw a few days ago, but he didn't come near the house, and then there was that vision I had months ago that I was just telling you about where I collapsed and saw a heap of people and two other young people who I think might be the young couple 'cos one was wearing a wedding dress. But then there was that older woman, and I can't find anything to do with her anywhere in the house, which means she could be anyone, but then those young people might not have lived here either. Possibly they just died here, but I'm so sure the one in the wedding dress did live here and—"

"You're getting off topic," Iris cuts in bluntly. Isadora snaps her mouth shut, throws Iris a sour look and sighs, defeated.

"All my thoughts are off topic most of the time." She runs a hand through her hair, batting at Bee who flicks a mildly interested paw at the straw-coloured coils. "It's difficult to pull it all together when there's so much there."

"So don't think about it like that. Are you a psychic, or not?"

"Barely," Isadora mutters, but she shakes out her shoulders and settles more firmly into place. She doesn't like to do this. Hasn't done it since the disaster that conjured Bee ... and look how that turned out. Even then, that experience had been different to any other times she's tried it before. She doesn't know quite how she does it, only knows that she can. As if her life could get any more confusing.

Isadora reluctantly allows herself to feel rather than simply acknowledge the stone beneath her hands in an effort to ground herself, to let her raging thoughts settle a little so she can ignore them more competently. She needs a relatively clear mind, with enough empty space for what's to enter. She feels the seeping cold in her legs and feet and the soft breaths of air trailing delicately across her face. Feels the earth and her surrounds. Hears the birds, the rustling leaves, the indistinct chatter of the ghosts in the house behind her. Senses Iris's soul perched beside her and sinks back into that place she so seldom goes, too scared of sinking so deeply she can't claw her way back out. Her mind clears, empties. It exists now like the flawless blue sky above, the one that stretches to infinity and ever ongoing. She connects carefully to her environment and feels the thread of connection supply her with something.

The words begin to flow, linear – and not of her own creation, despite the fact she is speaking them incontrovertibly into existence. "There are ghosts here, lots of them tied to the house and to the surrounds. Four stand out more than the others. Tragedy … horror … intense feelings that are keeping them tied to the grounds." Behind her closed lids Isadora's eyes begin to flick back and forth rapidly. "Three female and one male. Only one is … stuck of their own design, the others are caught." As suddenly as she has forged the connection, she feels it gently break and it all fades away. Isadora shifts and emerges with a huge intake of breath. It hadn't been long, and it hadn't been much, but it had been enough.

"So?" Iris asks expectantly, hands resting one atop the other on the head of her cane, pale eyes peering steadily from behind her thick glasses.

"It isn't much," Isadora admits, "but I think I know where to start looking." She gazes out across the grounds, through the swaying trees and across the lush green lawn towards the edges of the estate. "It's out there. Echoes exist beyond the initial sound. I guess I just have to listen closely, see if I can hear anything."

Iris smiles knowingly. "You've got potential within you, girlie. Start living up to it." She hefts herself to her feet and raps Isadora sharply over the head with her cane. "And stop doubting yourself." She tramps back inside. Isadora rubs at the knot that's surely forming on the crown of her head and glances down at Bee, whose wide, white eyes stare back.

"I really hate her, Bee. Damn her for being so helpful."

XI | JUSTICE

W ill knows something has changed. Isadora's demeanour is different, almost bordering on pleasant. Her Amethyst necklace still
swings from its chain around her neck, but now Isadora doesn't wear it
like a talisman to ward off evil spirits; rather, she wears it like a charm,
something to help and not hinder her gift. Despite her lighter mood
though, it's still very clear she isn't at all at peace with her 'gift'.

Isadora still flinches away from the mobs of ghosts swarming around
her, lurches and ducks as their hands reach out periodically to stroke
along her shoulder or through her hair. They'd gotten awfully touchy-
feely lately, and Isadora can't help but bristle, even though she knows
they mean it with the best of intentions. Their newfound happiness
makes it abundantly clear how at home they feel within the walls of this
haunted old house.

Because of the crowded confines inside, Isadora spends most of her
time either outdoors or tucked away in her room, writing avidly in a
small notebook. She'd made a special trip to town to buy it, along with
a pen and nothing else. Will tries to sneak looks whenever he can, but
Isadora is unerringly aware, snapping the book shut and glaring fiercely
at him until he backs off.

Today, Will finds his sister sitting in one of the plush wingback
chairs in the downstairs parlour, face turned to the sunlight streaming through the window and eyes closed. The Amethyst pendant glows

deeply in the warmth, the myriad differing purples bursting with light. She is surrounded by pearlescent bodies milling happily to and fro, floating calmly from space to space, chattering among themselves or reading books from the upstairs library, all of them revelling in the chance to touch things again.

Will glides between the other ghosts; sometimes it still hurts to think of himself like that. A ghost! A mere imprint on the earth that is just waiting to fade away. Barely hanging on, resisting the pull of that 'something else' that murmurs away in the back of his mind. He bears no visible injuries from the accident, and Will knows this is not just luck. There is something keeping the wounds from surfacing and that is all down to his sister. Perhaps her unconscious shielding of her mind to keep her sane? He isn't sure; all he knows is, he is grateful. Ridiculously, incredibly grateful.

"Good nap?" he asks, kicking her dangling foot. She has one leg crossed over the other and isn't wearing socks. Isadora startles awake and fixes him with a half-hearted, sleep-mussed glare.

"It *was* a good nap." She kicks him back, meeting his jean-clad leg firmly. He can empathise with the other ghosts in their delight at being able to interact with the world again. To be able to touch things gives the illusion that life isn't so far out of their grasp.

"Had any more prophetic dreams, Mystic Marge?"

Isadora stretches, yawns and shakes her head. "Nothing. No dreams at all. Not complaining though." She stands and extends her arms up above her head, wincing at the pull in her back. "Anything interesting happen while I was asleep?"

It's Will's turn to shake his head. "I think a vase got broken and a portrait was knocked off the wall. Other than that, it was peaceful … un-living the dream."

Isadora snorts. "Which one broke the vase?"

"Uh," Will scrunches his nose in thought, "I think it was the one with the popped eyes, you know the ones that dangle down his cheeks? They were kicking around a soccer ball they found in the backyard outaways and it got a little out of hand."

"Oi!" Isadora yells, so suddenly that Will flinches sharply.

"Jesus Christ, Dora!" he snaps. Isadora ignores him, stalking forcefully into the hall where a group of spectres have gathered and are communing raucously. Isadora strides up to the one making the most noise and grabs a good fistful of shirt collar. Will can see it's the ghost whose eyes are dangling like statement jewellery out of its sockets, large grisly balls slick with blood and ooze. When they rotate just right you can make out the cloudy pupil and spectacularly blue iris. Isadora gives him a shake.

"No more destruction of property, you hear me? Do it again and I'll kick your spectral arse into the ether. If anyone hears or sees anything funny, this house won't be ours anymore. Oh – and just because you can't use your eyes doesn't mean you shouldn't be able to see my point." She shoves him away. "Scram!"

They do. Hastily.

Will watches them zoom through the wall and reappear outside, shapes flickering in the beaming sunlight. He ducks his head and frowns. "Was that really necessary?"

Isadora grins, just the wrong side of sly. "Sure was. Now they won't break anything else, and they won't bother me. Win-win." And strides away. Will follows.

"Where are you going?" He nearly stumbles into Bee, who emerges and trots haughtily after his sister, spiny tail held aloft.

"To find that portrait they knocked off the wall." She mounts the stairs, taking them two at a time, hand on the banister to help pull her upwards. Will reaches the top only a step behind and far less out of breath, considering he has none to spare anymore. They stroll down the hallway, dodging phantoms left and right. Isadora pokes her head into her room to ensure no spirits have snuck in there to snoop around. They haven't, and she can sense nothing repellent. On they go until they reach the upstairs library, tucked away in the back corner of the house. It's alight with afternoon sun. Will still puzzles over the phenomenon of time; there always seems to be sun, no matter where you go, which room you're in. Time is falling around them in no particular pattern, scattered through the veins and chambers of the house. There are no rules here.

Isadora shakes her head, seeing no portrait here either. She spins and stops. Will almost bumps into her and hastily steps back wondering what it is that has brought her up short. She's staring at the next door. Will frowns, thinking back to their initial tour on the day they arrived, suddenly remembering that this was the room with nothing in it. The strangely cold one that had made them all feel uneasy.

"Dora?" he prompts quietly, jogging his sister back to the present. He sees her square her shoulders and draw a fortifying breath. She reaches out and pushes the door open to reveal the empty room beyond.

And there's the fallen portrait. Lying face down on the sleek hardwood floor.

The plain white canvas gazes up at them, mounted in a richly gilded frame. Whosever's face is painted on it is hidden, pressed into the floorboards. Isadora walks in, squats and lifts the painting over, only to freeze. Will senses a shift in the atmosphere ... something gone cold and rotten, turning the molten sunshine grey and overcast.

"What?" he ventures to ask, stepping forward hesitantly. Isadora barely reacts, but her fingers tighten imperceptibly on the edges of the canvas. "What is it?" he asks again.

Bee has bristled, thorny ridges rising, back arching sharply like a cat bottle-brushed up and expecting a fight.

"It's her," Isadora whispers hoarsely. Her skin is ashen, eyes wide and unblinking. Will peers over her shoulder, curious, gaze settling on the portrait. The woman it depicts is ghastly. Sharp, hawklike eyes stare out of a pallid, waxen face. All pointy features and sour mouth. Her hair is pulled back, but Will can see the indications of wild, tangled curls. If it weren't pulled away from her face it would resemble a lion's mane.

"The woman in your vision?" Will asks. Isadora nods sharply and sets the portrait back down on the floor, heavy golden frame clunking on the floorboards. The room is frigid, Will realises abruptly, the memory of before creeping back in.

Isadora runs a hand through her hair and looks up. Her mouth drops open. "What the hell?" She rises to her feet and runs to the window, hands clutching the frame. Her breath is fogging on the glass. There are flurries of powdery white clogging the window edges, gathering in the corners. It's snowing out there. The back garden is covered in a thick blanket, snow-capped trees quivering in the harsh, whipping wind. Flakes dance left, then sharply right, curling up and over in elongated spirals. Not ten minutes ago at the front of the house there had been sun, warmth, the house held in the heavenly throes of late spring and early summer.

"Well," Will begins, unsure himself as to the sudden change. "We knew time here is all sorts of messed up."

"Not this messed up!" Isadora responds. "At least it was consistent before. Not summer out front and winter out back at the same time." She moves one hand away from the window frame to clutch at her Amethyst. "But then again …" she stares back outside, eyes narrowing ever so slightly. Her thought trails off and she turns back to consider the portrait. Her footsteps echo as she crosses the room, bouncing off the empty walls. She bends to pick the portrait up again. The pointy woman glares through the canvas.

"Will, can you go and check the weather at the front of the house?" Isadora asks. One of Will's brows flicks up in question.

"Sure. Why?"

Isadora rolls her eyes. "I'm testing a theory, thickhead. Go!" She says it like it should have been obvious.

"Fine. Jesus …" Will ambles out, almost missing the "Not my name, but thanks anyway!' Isadora calls after him.

He wanders down the wide staircase, catching a glimpse out of the high-set window at the hairpin turn of the staircase and frowns. No snowflakes here. There is a steady stream of warm sunlight cascading through the glass.

Whatever theory Isadora is testing is certainly interesting, as the front of the house is still bathed in sunlight. The windows give way to an early summer vista, complete with lush-green swaying trees and chirping birds. Several spirits are outside playing on the lawn, another group are spread out having what looks like a picnic, minus the food. Will can hear their ghostly laughter through the open front door.

Spinning on his heels, he runs back up the stairs to that unsettling, barren room. That room that is freezing cold, snow flurrying away outside the frosty window.

Isadora peers at him expectantly as he enters. "Summer. No snow at all," he tells her in disbelief. Isadora does something strange then, something Will doesn't often see from her at all. She smiles. Genuine, open and victorious.

"What …?" he asks slowly. Isadora's grin widens. She looks like an absolute madwoman as she holds the painting aloft.

"It's a clue, a lead. Something for me to work with." Her voice is alight with triumph, warm in a way Will hasn't heard in a long, long time. Even her eyes are sparkling, sending tremors of wariness down Will's echo of a spine. "Finally, something for me to focus on. Something for me to do," Isadora continues. She holds the painting out in front of her, locking eyes with the shrew-like woman, "Bring it on, you pious bitch!"

XII | THE HANGED MAN

"**W**hat exactly are you doing this for? Like, what are you hoping to gain?" Will has been dogging her steps ever since they uncovered the everlasting winter in the upstairs room, and Isadora is almost ready to hit him.

"Fun? Why does everything have to be 'save the world' worthy? Why can't I be doing this for selfish reasons?" Isadora responds scathingly. Her feet are clad again in socks and shoes and she is skipping down the back steps and into the walled English garden. The roses are as fresh as ever, blooming prettily along the red brick walls. Splashes of pink, white, orange and red.

"As we've previously discussed, clearly you can," Will answers. "And, as covered in that previous conversation, you've never been interested in the whole ghost-mystery schtick. And I refuse to believe that you're using it as experience to help the others so, why are you now so invested?"

"Call it a change of heart if you want – if it'll make you leave me alone." Isadora carefully studies the ground as she makes a slow loop of the garden. This has to be the starting point. This and the room upstairs. But she'd scoured that from top to bottom and found zilch. Isadora doesn't see Will leave, merely feels his prickly (warm), frustrated presence disappear and senses it reappear further away.

Meanwhile, the patch of dirt where she'd had her previous vision and where she's now hovering is giving her absolutely nothing. No zing, no out-of-body experience, no visions. Nothing. Frustrated, Isadora kicks at the dirt, cursing when her toe strikes a hidden rock. Hopping unsteadily on one foot, Isadora manages to fling herself onto the wrought-iron bench. She tugs her sneaker off and peels off her sock to see the damage. There's not much to see, just a reddened spot on the tip of her big toe that will surely bruise over the next couple of days. Isadora sighs, frustrated yet again at the lack of immediate progress. She wants instant gratification, dammit!

Slipping her sock and shoe back on, Isadora wanders back over to the offending rock.

"Stupid thing," she mutters, kneeling down to dust the rest of the debris away. As soon as her fingers touch the rock, a sharp pain cleaves down the centre of her forehead, so intense it sends Isadora sprawling, one hand pressed to her brow. A starburst of fireworks crosses her inner vision. She keeps eyes firmly shut as a stunning light show flashes and dances across the centre of her forehead. At last, it recedes, but it has left something there, like a worm that begins rooting and burrowing into her mind. It feels wrong, pervasive. Isadora grunts as she feels a reactive force deep within her pushing back at it. In her mind's eye, she sees it screaming, fists raised and waving to the intruder to 'get out, get away from me!'. With a monumental effort, Isadora pulls at the metaphysical roots, rips whatever it is right out of her mind and throws it, hurling it away into the ether. Her physical body goes flying backwards, slamming into the edge of the bench seat and smashing her head.

Pain sparks through her back, but it feels like an echo. Isadora opens her eyes abruptly. She's still standing. Right where she had been when whatever it was had attacked her head. What the hell? She whips around and almost screams in shock. There is her body, lying lifelessly propped up against the wrought-iron bench with her head pressing heavily on one slim shoulder. It looks awkward and uncomfortable. But she can't feel the discomfort.

Her body is lying there, but her consciousness is still standing upright.

Shit.

Isadora can feel her heart hammering, a claustrophobic squeezing in her chest. Her vision swims and she staggers. One sweaty hand moves back to her brow. Only now, the sweat feels just like the pain in her back, nothing more than an echo. There, but not.

"What the fuck?" Isadora whimpers, blinking away tears of panic. She brushes her hair roughly from her pale face and approaches her still body. "Oh, fuck! What have I done?" She kneels, feeling but not feeling the rough pricking of the paving stones beneath her weak knees. She reaches out and tries to shake her physical body. Her fingers fall straight through it and she gasps. It's like dipping her fingers into warm water. She draws back, hands trembling.

"Okay, okay, okay …" she rambles under her breath, settling back to sit on her haunches. She bites her lip so savagely it begins to bleed. She watches in shock as her physical lip reddens, bursts open and begins dribbling an identical stream. "So, there is a connection there, that's good. I guess?" Isadora drags in a deep, ragged breath and exhales slowly. "Okay. Right. Don't focus on what you can't do … focus on what you can do. So …" she trails off. What *could* she do?

She could survey her surroundings, try and figure out where she is. Or maybe, rather than *where* … *when* she is. If this is another type of vision, she could well be in the past. She scowls. Stupid instant gratification!

Her grumbling is interrupted by the uneven patter of tiny feet.

Isadora's brows shoot up as a giggling child waddles by, dressed in what looks to be an intricately embroidered gown with matching cap. So, that at least confirms that this is definitely not in *her* time then. Isadora jumps to her feet and runs after the child, not wanting to let it get away. She needn't have worried as she catches up to it in only a couple of long strides.

"Excuse me!" She reaches down. "Can you—" But whatever she was about to ask dies on her lips as her fingers slide straight through the child's sleeve – different again to when she'd grasped her own arm earlier. This time it feels as though her hand is slicing through cloud, a barely-there sensation of airiness. The child toddles on, completely oblivious to Isadora's presence.

Isadora huffs, spins – then chokes. Her physical body is gone. It is no longer propped precariously against the bench seat, which is now far less rusty and far more evenly painted.

Isadora throws her hands in the air, a familiar helpless gesture. "Guess I've got nothing better to do then," she grumbles to herself, reluctantly retreating from the garden and following the small child, whose uneven gait has carried it to the back steps where it attempts to climb on hands and knees up to the back door, which sits ajar.

Isadora hops up the steps and passes easily through the doorway, at the same time desperately trying to avoid going through the wall or the door. Anything not to be like an actual ghost. She really does not like that idea.

The house is not all that different from how she'd left it. Old (new?) furniture scattered tastefully around, oil portraits lining the sumptuously decorated walls and assorted expensive knick-knacks adorning every surface. Isadora stops and waits in the back room that leads out to the garden, where the stray child continues gambolling about. An infant as young as this is sure to have a parent or carer not far behind.

Isadora's theory soon proves fruitful, as a round-faced young woman comes hurrying into the room. Drably dressed, hair pulled back in a simple braid, Isadora places her as likely one of the serving staff and not the child's mother. The harried expression and ruddy complexion confirm it for her as the maid spots the child and heaves a sigh of relief.

"Wilhelmina!"

The little girl giggles, reaching with chubby, spit-soaked hands as the maid lifts her carefully and settles her firmly against her body. "I turn for one minute and off you go! You mustn't be doing that anymore, young lady," she scolds. The child giggles once more, smacking a wet hand against the maid's red face.

"Laura!" The poor maid's face drops.

"Not to worry, Miss," she calls, heading to the front of the house. "I found her!"

Isadora listens as the rapid footsteps fade and wonders if she should follow. She hesitates, not wanting to move too far from where her physical body is, but also worried that if she hangs around it will be for naught. She has been presented with another lead, another clue. She can hardly wait around and miss everything. Eventually, curiosity wins out and Isadora follows the maid.

She can hear their voices echoing around the main front room, the sun-drenched one with all the chairs and settees, adjacent to the formal dining room. Isadora hovers in the doorway then, remembering that they can't see her, gathers her wits and marches right into the middle of the room.

Not one eye glances at her.

Isadora smiles, turns and nearly collapses when she sees the woman who is now holding the child (Wilhelmina, apparently), snugly on her lap. The face is just as pointed, only not as severe nor as harsh as depicted in the portrait, and the wild mane of dark hair is held back in neat, shiny coils. Dressed in a simple yet elegant day gown, her dark eyes are filled with merriment as she gazes at who Isadora assumes is her infant daughter.

"Apologies again, Ma'am," the maid, Laura, continues, wringing her hands. "She's very fast."

The sharp-faced woman simply laughs lightly. "Not to worry. As long as she is safe, all is well."

Laura's features brighten and her hands cease their wringing. "Very good, Ma'am." She gives a short curtsey and exits the room. Isadora, still rooted to the ground with shock, takes a halting step forward. Despite knowing this is undoubtedly the same woman, her brain cannot assimilate the two.

"Now, little Wilhelmina …" Her voice is different as well. Isadora remembers a reverberation of harsh, barking cruelty bouncing on the wind – not this soft, devoted crooning. It's a mother's voice. Isadora knows this well, and her metaphysical heart aches. "We must get you up to your room, settle you in for a nap. Does that sound good?" Wilhelmina squeals happily enough, although Isadora seriously doubts it's any kind of reasoned response. Babies don't know much, certainly not enough to reply rationally to a posed question. But her mother nods, smiles and rises smoothly, gliding out of the room and up the stairs. Isadora follows along. Where does the baby fit into it all? Isadora wonders. There hadn't been anything anywhere about a baby … Maybe it's not involved at all. Maybe the baby is just happenstance, a little blip in the story.

"Mother!" An excited call disrupts the still air. The sharp-faced woman smiles and settles Wilhelmina more firmly against her hip.

"Up here, dearest," she calls back, and a young woman trots joyfully up the stairs. Isadora has almost had enough shocks for one day, but what's one more to a traumatised-one-surprise-away-from-turning-catatonic medium?

It's like looking in a mirror.

Isadora is looking at herself, she's sure of it. Same grey eyes, same fair hair. Same smattering of freckles across the bridge of her button nose. "Oh, what the hell?" Isadora exclaims loudly, incredulously.

The young woman strides forward and coos at Wilhelmina. "Hello there, sweetness." She brushes a hand through the strands of fairy-floss hair escaping from the front of the toddler's lace cap.

"I was just about to settle her in for a nap." The mother rocks Wilhelmina from side to side, swaying smoothly, her plain skirts rustling rhythmically.

"Oh good, Tom and I have something to show you," the young woman smiles (Isadora's smile), "down in the yard near the blacksmith's hut."

"I'll be down momentarily." The woman indulges her daughter with a gentle smile as she moves into Wilhelmina's room to put her down for her snooze. The young woman's smile widens, and she hurries away in her dress of periwinkle blue. Isadora is torn. Does she follow the mother, watch as she tucks her child in, or does she run after her doppelganger and the mysterious something she wants to show her mother?

In the end the choice is simple. The mother will be making her way down to the blacksmith's hut anyway, and Isadora would be lying if she said she isn't desperately curious about her double.

In Isadora's time, the blacksmith's hut is no longer standing. She isn't sure if there is anything that remains there; but she's not in 'her time'. Now, she watches, fascinated, as her lookalike bounds right up to the front door and barges inside, no knock or announcement. "Rude," Isadora mutters to herself, but follows her in just the same. Inside, it is dark and almost unbearably hot. A tall, broad-shouldered man is hammering away at something over one of the fires, muscles rippling beneath his dark cotton shirt. Her lookalike creeps up behind him, her light dress glowing in the shadowed interior, and places her hands over his eyes.

"Guess who?"

The man laughs, deep and warm. "There could be no one else, Isabella."

Okay, well damn. Even their names are similar.

Isabella laughs as her man sets the hammer down and turns to hug her, only for Isabella to keep him at arm's length, smile still on full display. "If you hug me like that," she gestures to his leather apron, covered in soot and dirt, "My mother will never forgive you for staining my dress."

"Ah, of course." He grins, and Isadora has to admit he is very handsome. All dark, tousled hair and deep brown eyes, dimples that pop in his olive-skinned cheeks. Good bone structure too, sharp and square. She's so busy admiring his face she almost misses the continuing conversation. "Your dress. Not as if it couldn't be cleaned or anything."

Isabella puts on a mock offended expression. "This fabric is imported, sir. It deserves better than to be dirtied up for no reason!"

Ugh, despite the blacksmith being certified eye candy, Isadora can't help cringing at their thinly veiled flirting.

"It would take a lot of time to clean anything out of that dress." Smooth as oil, Isabella's mother stands primly at the doorway, hands clasped neatly at her front. Despite her cool demeanour, Isadora can see her amusement at the couple's interaction. Isabella flushes pink and puts a sliver of distance between the blacksmith and herself.

"I wasn't aware you were there, Mother."

Her mother smiles slyly. "A mother can hear most conversations, Isabella, regardless of the distance. Now, where is this contraption you would like to show me?"

The blacksmith smiles politely and walks to the door, where Isabella's mother moves back to allow him, along with her daughter, space enough to exit. They wander around the side of the squat stone building where Isabella and her blacksmith present a small wooden box with wheels and two poles extending from the front.

"It's a cart," Isadora realises aloud, seconds before Isabella makes her own announcement.

"A cart?" her mother asks, one slim dark eyebrow raised quizzically.

"For Wilhelmina," Isabella elaborates. "It connects to Ollie's harness."

"You've built a cart for our dog to pull around, for Wilhelmina to ride in?" Her mother sounds incredulous, as if it's an absolutely absurd idea. Isadora has to agree with her.

"I would have loved something like this when I was younger," Isabella tries, her most winning smile pulling at her full lips. The blacksmith stands firm behind her, one hand surreptitiously wrapping around her waist. Isadora rolls her eyes, especially when Isabella's mother flicks her eyes down, then back up. She locks on to the blacksmith.

"And you, Tom?"

Tom smiles politely. "I think it's a splendid idea, Miss Jane. Isabella was planning to gift it for Wilhelmina's third birthday."

So, the sharp woman's name is Jane. Isadora squints, not convinced the name suits what is to become of her. Jane is smiling, seemingly delighted and somewhat softened that Isabella and Tom would organise something like this for little Wilhelmina.

"That's very kind of you, Isabella – and of you, Tom. I'm assuming, of course, that you were the one who constructed the cart?"

Tom ducks his head bashfully. "I did, Ma'am. Made it safe and sturdy."

Jane nods imperiously as the three fall into an expectant silence. A small smile graces her face. "A spoilt child is Wilhelmina. But I'm sure she will love it." She leans forward and kisses Isabella on the cheek, patting at the spot with a tender hand. "Such kindness, Isabella."

Isabella flushes happily, winding her slim fingers with Tom's as casually as she can. "Thank you."

Jane makes an elegant turn and sets off back up the gentle slope towards the towering, sandstone house, holding her pale skirts carefully above the grass with a poised hand so they float majestically around her ankles.

Isadora watches the retreat, mind thrumming, as Isabella and Tom resume their rosy-faced flirting, hands still clasped tightly together. Isadora has a niggling feeling the blood-soaked bride from her vision is Isabella, murdered in cold blood by her own doting mother whose mind is currently one whole piece of perfect.

"*Mrreow!*" Isadora twitches in shock and turns to see a slim black cat settled on the path leading back to the house. Its bright green eyes are fixed directly on her own. Isadora blinks. The cat blinks back, inclining its head and sliding down into a languid stretch, front paws flexing to extend sharp claws. It yawns, then gets up and pads over to Isadora's feet, where it sits calmly, luminescent eyes boring into hers.

"Err, hi," Isadora says awkwardly, disorientated by the cat's intense gaze. She looks around at Tom and Isabella, half-expecting Isabella to be gesturing to the cat from behind her. But Isabella is completely enraptured by the blacksmith and is paying no attention to the cat whatsoever. "Stupid cats and their veil-breaking gaze," Isadora mutters. In many ways, she herself is like a cat, extended naps in the sun included, and this cat is like any other. It is far more attuned to different worlds than any other creature. Isadora watches as the creature delicately lifts a paw and begins bathing itself.

"Am I supposed to be doing something for you?" Isadora asks halt-ingly. The cat pauses in its ablutions, locks eyes and shakes its head in one swift, itchy-ear twitch. "Okay then," Isadora huffs. She's seen enough for today, so she heads back up the path, retracing Jane's steps and leaving the enamoured couple behind.

The cat follows along.

Isadora enters the front garden and mounts the steps two at a time. She slips easily through the front door, feet noiseless on the polished timber boards as she strides out to the walled back garden.

Her body is still nowhere to be seen. "Ugh! All I want is my damned body back!" She aims a kick into the side of the steps and shrieks when her foot follows through, carrying her entire weight over and into the garden. She pokes her head up through the patch of lilies she's landed in and scowls.

"Being a ghost sucks ass," she mutters darkly, standing and shaking herself off, noticing as she does so something bumping against her upper chest. Isadora peeks down her shirt and notices for the first time today that her Amethyst necklace is swinging from its golden chain around her neck. Wait … she had taken it off when she'd gone out to survey the garden. She's sure of it. She'd thought that perhaps the little crystal might potentially block anything from coming through and so had left it in her bedroom on the dresser next to her sage.

Isadora cups the glowing purple crystal tenderly in her hand and stares. "What on earth are you doing here?" she asks no one. The lilac crystal doesn't answer her but continues to rest comfortably in her palm.

"Meow …"

Isadora spots the black cat sitting on the top step of the back land-ing, ears upright, tail lashing from side to side. It blinks and trots down the stone stairs, tail lifting into a question mark over its sleek, coal-black hindquarters in a tantalising 'follow me' gesture. Isadora releases her pendant, drawing comfort from the heavy warmth it drew to her chest, and clambers out of the garden bed to follow the cat.

"You remind me of Bee," she says as they round the back corner of the house and into a part of the garden Isadora has not visited before. The cat doesn't reply but jumps neatly onto the edge of the red brick wall, just next to a small wooden gate that is latched lightly shut with a neat leather loop. Isadora sweeps cleanly through the wooden boards as the cat leaps smoothly back to the ground, trotting onwards. It does remind her of Bee. Strongly. Isadora doesn't say anything else as the cat clearly doesn't care much for conversation. The animal leads her into a square, enclosed yard that attaches to one wing of the house. The surrounding walls are peppered with windows facing into the courtyard and the walkway from the main house has a neat overhang of roof to keep the walkways covered and protected from potential rain. Perhaps so those who lived in this wing could wander to and fro from the house keeping their packages and laundry safe. This courtyard has a simple design, with none of the frivolous adornments of the others. Isadora surmises this is most likely the staff's quarters.

The cat continues on out through another gate, this one higher and harder to get through if you're human as it appears to be locked from the outside. Isadora steps through, shuddering as she emerges on the other side. Being a 'ghost' is not an experience she would call fun at all, yet all the spirits 'back home' seem to find it no problem at all. The cat turns its head and observes her silently, pupils blown wide amid the luminescent green. "Yes, I'm still following you, don't stress," Isadora says, tossing her hair back over her shoulders and hurrying to catch up.

On they go until Isadora sees the boundary fences appear near the sprawling bush beyond the edges of the property. Here, the cat draws to a stop just in front of the fence where the lower horizontal palings leave only a tiny width of space beneath – wide enough for a rabbit or perhaps a small dog to get through, but nothing else. Isadora kneels and examines the fence. There is nothing special here at all that Isadora can see. She isn't sure why the cat has led her here. She turns and examines the creature.

"What?" she asks. The cat sits judging her with those large green eyes, as if its shrewd assessment finds her wanting. She frowns. "I can't see anything. Why did you lead me here?" The cat almost appears to sigh and leaps up the fence post to the highest rung where it balances – an acrobat placing one elegant foot in front of the other on a perilous tightrope, but altogether more impressive than any human could ever be. And done with such casual elegance.

"What am I supposed to be looking at? There's nothing here!" Isadora exclaims, frustrated once more by all these beings who seem to think she should be able to see clues clearly, as if they are boldly written messages and not completely invisible to the normal human eye. Even for a medium like Isadora, it's akin to trying to spot one particular piece of hay in a haystack.

The cat flicks an ear and looks back towards the house. As if bidden by an invisible cue, exclamations of delight suddenly ring out through the front garden and Isadora, looking up, realises the weather and time of day have abruptly changed from afternoon to early midday on the morrow. The sun is shining brightly up in its apex, and a group of adults are gathered on the large lawn, seated calmly on a picnic blanket in the shade of their pastel parasols, enjoying the mild heat and cloudless day. The house, bathed in golden sunlight, stands grandly behind them.

A small dog is dragging a cart across the smooth grass and in the back of this cart is a madly laughing Wilhelmina, all dolled up in a tiny dress, shoes and bonnet, its blue ribbons flying as the dog pulls her along.

Isadora's necklace starts warming beneath her shirt.

The adults laugh as they watch the little girl waving her small, chubby fists up to the sky in delight. Despite herself and her situation, Isadora can't help a small smile at the child's obvious happiness.

Suddenly a rabbit breaks away from its grass cover near one of the young, springy trees not far from the house. The dog's ears perk up. The rabbit stills, poised on hind legs, ears erect. It leaps away. The dog breaks into a frenzied run after it, the cart rattling precariously along behind.

The adults are no longer laughing. Wilhelmina is screaming at the sudden change of pace, her cries piercing the balmy air.

The rabbit streaks off towards the low fence next to Isadora. The one with just enough space underneath the palings for it to escape into the bush beyond. The cat jumps off the post.

The dog doesn't change its speed. It ducks under the fence to continue the chase.

There's a solid, meaty thwack. A wet, explosive splatter.

Wilhelmina isn't screaming anymore.

Her mother is.

XIII | DEATH

If Isadora was a physical being, she would have blood and brain matter all over her shoes, and possibly on her jeans up to her knees. As it is, she has none on her at all; instead, it's dripping off the grass and plant stems, thick as treacle and stinking of iron. If Isadora had a stomach, she would have vomited by now.

The cat is hovering near Isadora's legs, tail *thwipping* back and forth. Isadora can't move. Her hands are planted over her agape mouth, eyes bulging at the horrific scene that has been playing out beneath the splendidly bright sun. The light is making the drops of gore glitter queasily along the fence paling.

Isabella is the first to reach the destroyed cart, to see her little sister's practically decapitated body slouching backwards against the cart's rudimentary seat. Her bonnet has been torn clean off, along with most of her wispy hair. Isabella sinks to her knees, dress staining brown where the blood settles into the fabric. Her pale, trembling hands reach out to clasp at Wilhelmina's tiny, battered body. They never reach it. Isabella is wrenched backwards by a desperate, violent hand clenched in her collar. Her sobs choke off into gurgling coughs as her mother tosses her aside without care, her wild dark mane falling from its usual carefully sculptured style.

She is just short of howling.

"No, Wilhelmina, not my Wilhelmina ... oh!" she cuts off in a hor-rified moan as her white hands clutch at Wilhelmina's ruined dress. She pulls the toddler's boneless body into her lap, revealing her head, caved in like a melon on the wrong side of a sledgehammer. Her delicate little skull has been smushed into a mess of red and grey. She has only one eye left.

Isadora whirls off to the side and hunches over, gagging, as her ghostly stomach clenches. She can still hear Jane murmuring madly behind her, elegant face stained red and ruddy with tears, the veins in her neck popping as she begins to scream again. She starts to rock back and forth, wailing.

Isadora breaks into a run back up towards the house. Her pendant is burning against her sternum, and she can sense rather than hear the black cat galloping alongside her. She takes the front stairs two at a time and hurls herself through the closed front door, staggering and trip-ping onto her knees. Isadora pushes herself up and keeps going until she bursts through the back door and into the redbrick-walled garden. She can still hear the tremendous 'thwack' as Wilhelmina's head hit the fence. As it burst like an overripe tomato under a wayward foot.

She gags again.

"What the fuck?!" she whispers hoarsely, doubled over with her hands on her knees, chest heaving. She locks eyes with the cat, which stares impassively back, although its ears are drooping a tad suggesting it is, perhaps, just as upset as everyone else.

"That poor little girl," Isadora continues, pushing her hands against her knees to get back to full height, tottering sideways as she does. Her head is pounding in time with her rapidly beating heart. She's so sick of seeing this messed-up stuff! Isadora had been naive enough to believe she'd seen the worst, what with all those ghosts routinely hanging around and joining the club. Not even close.

"But that must be where it starts, right?" Isadora realises, phrasing the last part to the cat as if the animal will respond the way Bee does, with a cock of its head or a small chirrup. The cat flattens its ears to its silky black head and bares its teeth. "Yeah, that's what I thought," Isadora replies sickly.

An abrupt bang shatters the uneasy silence. Isadora watches as Jane stumbles down the back stairs, feet slipping and leaving grisly dark stains on the grey stone. Her front is a mess of dirt, blood and some chunky maroon bits that Isadora does not want to know about but can't stop staring at. She watches as one gelatinous blob wobbles and falls to the ground. Jane's hands are curled claws stained with blood, fingernails caked with it, tacky and dark as it begins to coagulate. But it's her eyes that terrify Isadora more than anything. Dark pits of emptiness, hollowed out and left gaping.

And they're focused directly on her.

At first Isadora doesn't move when Jane staggers towards her, then she flinches violently as Jane hurls herself forward, grabs the front of her shirt and tugs her forward. Isadora shrieks and tries to pull away, wrenching herself from the bloodstained grip and tripping backwards until her feet catch on the uneven pavement and send her sprawling.

"YOU, YOUR FAULT!" Jane is unhinged, jaw straining, eyes popping, face whiter than snow but lit with ugly patches of scarlet. "You wicked girl! You killed your sister!"

Isadora's mouth moves without her permission, forming words that aren't hers. "No, I would never! It was an accident, a horrible accident, please!" Her arms lift to protect her face and she sees they are suddenly clothed in plain linen, artfully stitched with tiny, delicate decorations. Her mother raises her fists and begins to beat her, grief fuelling her fury. Isadora hunkers into herself and takes every hit, feels every stinging punch, as distressed tears gather in the corners of her tightly shut eyes. It all comes to an abrupt halt as Jane is ripped away by a pair of strong, tanned arms that move forward to encircle Isadora tightly, drawing her into a suffocating embrace that she welcomes fervently.

Through the gap between Tom's arms – for it can only be her brave, strong Tom – Isadora can see Jane. She's sunk to her knees, slipping over to rest on one leg, face turned up to the magnificent sky of azure blue. Her mouth opens into a howl so loud, so tormented, so filled with loss that Isadora's own heart breaks.

The keening continues, deep and mournful. Jane's fists tear at her dark hair and Isadora can see it now – can see exactly where it all went wrong, the madness that was seeded from such overwhelming grief.

She now has a starting point.

As she thinks it, her world begins to spin. Something tugs in her navel, and she goes with it, spinning away from Tom's warm embrace, dragged along the dirty paving up to that old iron bench, to the figure again lying sprawled haphazardly against it, head lolling on her chest. She feels the separate parts connect as her consciousness reunites with her body. It all snaps together.

Her head bobs up sharply and her chest heaves a desperate gasp as the world converges into one picture.

The small, torn family is gone. As is the blood on the back steps.

She's back.

Isadora sinks against the scratchy, rusted bench and buries her face in her arms, breathing deeply to regain some grounding. She focuses on the feeling of her butt on the cold, hard ground. Of her feet planted firmly to the earth and the ache in her back as it rests uncomfortably against that godforsaken bench. The rapid burn gathering in her eyes as she remembers (or is intrusively reminded of) poor little Wilhelmina …

Something sharp taps at her exposed ankle, eliciting a shocked gasp as Isadora raises her head sharply. She is greeted by milky-white eyes set in a black, oily face. Bee sits casually by her feet, barbed tail lashing languidly back and forth, slicing some stray fallen leaves in half as it goes. Realisation comes in a jerky flash.

"You little asshole!" Isadora jumps up. Bee is unmoved, smug white eyes peering up at her knowingly. "You've known this whole time, huh? Haven't you?" Isadora gestures around. "Knew all about that poor little girl, this tragic wreck of a house, because you were there!"

Bee nods once.

"Ugh." Isadora sinks back onto the bench and huffs, blowing hair out of her face and, despite it all, managing to smile wryly. "Come here." She gestures to her lap and Bee immediately leaps onto it and curls up in a contented ball. Isadora traces her fingers lightly over the inky black skin and thinks. Bee knew about Wilhelmina. Bee knew about the house. Bee was summoned to her backyard on a random day while Isadora was meditating. Bee is probably a demon. All these things she now knows, or at the very least suspects.

Bee is most definitely the black cat who used to live here.

"I guess we're really connected then, aren't we?" Isadora quietly directs the last few words to Bee, who raises its head and nods sharply. "That's … good? I guess, anyway." Isadora trails off. She and Bee sit in companionable silence until Isadora breaks the spell. "Alright then. At least now I have somewhere to go. Knowledge is power … blah-blah. Let's get to solving the mystery of what the hell this house wants from me."

Bee shakes out its body and whips its tail, following along as Isadora heads inside, fingers playing idly with her necklace and her mind whirring. The searing warmth is new, and the idea that the necklace might be able to do more than one thing is something Isadora previously had not considered. There is a chance she can use it for something far better than warding off irritating spirits – which, while still very handy, will do nothing to further the untangling of the house's demands.

What I really need, Isadora thinks, is to find Wilhelmina's body. Remains have a special significance on the 'other side'; of this, Isadora is positive. So many ghosts frequent the places their physical body spent the most time, others still the place where their physical body met its end. And then there are the others – those who choose to stay where their physical body resided. Graveyards have a reputation for a reason, after all.

Clearly Jane is hanging around where she has spent the most amount of time in her life and, consequently, has suffered the most. Why any ghost would choose to do this is beyond Isadora's understanding, but enough of them do. Ghosts are incredibly strange … And she hasn't yet seen Isabella in any form other than in her visions. Isadora cringes at the word vision; it makes her seem entirely too qualified to deal with it all.

Perhaps, she surmises, if she can locate Wilhelmina, she'll be able to contact the little girl's spirit and ascertain just what it is her deranged mother wants her to do. That is, if Wilhelmina's spirit is capable of communication – and there's a significant chance it isn't. But she is the catalyst, and Isadora is sure she is the root of it all. That her death was the harbinger for all the resulting doom. Yes, Wilhelmina is definitely the key here.

"Ugh, all this time spent trying to live my life, trying to make it clear I wouldn't succumb to the whims of any ghosts, and here I am, spending my free time trying to do just that," Isadora mutters darkly to herself. She might owe Iris an apology after all this and have to spend the foreseeable future hiring out her talents to all the lonely, trapped souls who desperately want to move into the next realm. If this isn't a showcase of her talents and an audition for the job of 'ghostly problem-solver', Isadora isn't sure what it is. Perhaps a fool's errand would be more accurate. She certainly feels like a fool.

"Oh, great and mighty Amethyst," Isadora intones mockingly, slipping the pendant from her neck and holding it with the cord entwined around her small hand, dangling it like a pendulum. The stone swings hypnotically as Isadora walks through the packed house, neatly dodging spectres left and right. It's like a frat house, filled to the brim and getting no quieter as the days drag on.

She wanders out and around to the boundary fencing, eyes moving keenly back and forth as she tries to remember the path that Bee showed her, back when it was an actual cat and not a demon. The fence where poor little Wilhelmina had met her end is almost completely engulfed by vegetation, making it very difficult to spot. But she manages. Long, tangling arms of ivy grapple and snare at Isadora's arms as she attempts to clear some of it away. She swears viciously when a blackberry is uncovered, razor-sharp thorns bared and ready to cut her open at the smallest movement.

Bee sits back watching her efforts imperiously, not raising a paw to help. Typical, thinks Isadora sourly.

Eventually, she manages to clear the earth's grasp from the rotting remains of the timber fence, in doing so unearthing a somewhat disturbing discovery. A huge, faded stain. Brown, but dark enough and irregular enough in shape to distinguish it from the woodgrain. Roughly the size of a volleyball and surrounded by tiny spatters and drops.

Isadora kneels, presses her hand tenderly against the stain and focuses. Images come to mind, flashing rapidly behind her closed eyes. A cart, a dog, a rabbit. A shocking turn of speed, a bright flash of white, excruciating pain, and then … nothing. Rudimentary memories at best, but she can't expect more than that from a being who was literally a child. Children don't give meaning to memory the way adults do. There is no rational thought process, there are no clear details or nuanced emotions to link memories together, to give them definition. Everything, instead, is raw.

Isadora sits back on her heels and presses her lips together thoughtfully. If she is going to be successful in summoning Wilhelmina, she will need something that will appeal to her basic essence. Words aren't going to cut it here; the child won't understand them enough to respond adequately to tug her through the veil.

"I need her mother first," Isadora says to herself, turning her head to catch Bee's eye, as if seeking something akin to approval from the demon. Bee tilts its head and nods in a 'What do you mean?' type of way. 'Aren't we trying to get Wilhelmina to get the mother?'

Bee has a point. Isadora elaborates. "I need Wilhelmina to help the mother and the daughter. To help Isabella, I need to get to the mother in order to get to Wilhelmina, and then I should be able to get Wilhelmina to help start unravelling it all. It's like a giant loop, see?"

Bee shakes its head. Isadora sighs. "I don't need to help the mother first. I need to help the daughter first. She's the one that's asking for me by sending these visions. To help her, I need Wilhelmina – but I can't reach her here. I need something with a stronger connection. The mother will have that. Hence, I need to speak to the mother first, not to help her … just to talk to her. I can always go back to Jane to help her after I've contacted Wilhelmina and Isabella." She waves off Bee when it continues to look confused. "Trust me. I think I have it sorted."

"Yeah, sure you do."

"Alright, thanks for the vote of confidence." Crouched in the dirt, Isadora lowers her Amethyst necklace and buries her fingers in the earth, eyes fixed firmly on the faded bloodstain. "It's séance time."

XIV | TEMPERANCE

"You need a Ouija board to run a séance. You know that, right?"

"Yes, Will, thank you for that amazing observation." Isadora is sitting, legs slung over the arm of an opulently upholstered wingback chair, fingers flying across her phone screen. Will crosses his arms and slouches.

"You don't have one of those."

"Yet." Isadora switches her phone off and looks up at her older brother, smiling thinly. "Luckily for me I have a phone with an internet connection to the world of online shopping." She waves her phone in Will's face. "Even paid for Express so it should be here in a few days."

"Didn't we have this argument when you needed food and we decided not to get it delivered? And besides, will the postman even deliver out here?" he asks incredulously, dark brows all scrunched up. Isadora visibly deflates.

"No, they wouldn't, actually. I had to get it delivered to home."

Will jerks back, unsure he's heard her correctly. Isadora can see the hope beneath the veneer of shock in his eyes. "Home? You mean like home-home?"

Isadora pushes herself up in the chair, sliding her legs off the arm and curling up tightly instead. "Yep." She pops the 'P'. "Home-home."

Tense silence permeates the room. For once they are alone; no roaming spirits to be seen, although the noise filtering in from the front yard indicates several are milling around outside enjoying the golden midday warmth. Some are even laughing uproariously.

"Would it be so bad if you saw them?" Will finally ventures softly. Isadora ducks her head behind a curtain of blonde and doesn't answer. "You miss them."

"And we've already had this conversation. The outcome won't have changed, Will. I'm not doing that to them," Isadora replies flatly, a steely line of authority woven beneath the words. Her grey eyes have hardened into flints. She can feel it and Will can clearly see it, so when he opens his mouth to reply, Isadora is surprised.

"Outcomes always change. Nothing is set in life. Why won't you even entertain the thought of seeing them?"

Isadora surges to her feet. "I'm not talking about this," she mutters, marching to the door. Will steps in front to stop her, only for Isadora to plough straight through his suddenly transparent body. Will gasps and clutches a hand to his stomach, the smoky tendrils that Isadora tugged away slowly spiralling back into place. He whips around. Isadora is gone. He can hear her receding footsteps echoing up to the high ceilings and bouncing from each wall. After all that time of convincing Will he might still have some life left, with her gift of allowing him to touch, to interact, to feel in a way ghosts seldom can, she has never made him feel more like a shadow passing along the earth than in that moment. Reduced him to shadow, all because she's too stubborn to change her mind.

Well, if she's going to treat him like a ghost, he's going to act like one. He glares up at the ceiling, listening to her furious footsteps, and realises he knows exactly where she is heading. Like any classic introvert when challenged with confrontation, she is retreating to her nest. Otherwise known as her bedroom.

Will scrunches up his face and concentrates furiously. He has never attempted this before. He visualises his destination and allows himself to truly feel his transparency, the disconnection from the earth that all ghosts instinctually know … and pushes. He stumbles forward, feeling incredibly dizzy for someone who no longer has a body, so to speak, and peers around just in time for Isadora to fling open her door and utter a shrill scream. She grabs a small ornamental box from the dresser near the door and pegs it directly at his head. Will winces as it sails straight through and hits the wall harshly, leaving a sizeable hole in the plaster.

"Mature," he sneers past the shock at actually having teleported for the first time. Isadora snarls wordlessly, hand gripping the door with white-knuckled fingers.

Will sees the bunching in her arm and feels the door slam before she even makes the motion. The crash echoes down the stairs and out the front door. Through the bedroom's open window Will hears the jovial ghosts stutter their way into silence.

"What the hell?!" Isadora yells, face steadily flooding with red. The vein in her temple is beginning to show. Always a bad sign.

"You weren't going to act like an adult. I had to step up."

"By invading my privacy?" she fires back. Will huffs.

"Hardly. This house doesn't belong to you, and this isn't really your room."

"*Now* who isn't acting like an adult?" Isadora spits out through tightly clenched teeth. "Get out!"

"Not until you tell me why you don't want to see our parents. They're our family!" Will shouts back. "And they're probably worried sick about you! Can't you get past your own self-importance to see how this might be affecting them?" His hands tighten into fists. Isadora throws her head back, barking a laugh that couldn't possibly be any more sardonic.

"Being in the ground so long must have rotted your brains. I've already told you why!"

"No, you haven't, you've deflected the conversation every time!" Will advances. "What are you so scared of? And don't tell me you're scared of them being run out of town, that isn't it."

"Says who?" Isadora stalks forward. "If that's what I say it is, that's what it is. Case closed. Fuck off!" She shoves at Will's shoulder roughly, connecting this time. Will stumbles back and bumps into the window-sill, a tsunami of hot, suffocating fury rising up.

"Why do you do that?" he hisses. "Treat me like I'm alive when it suits you, then strip it all away in the next second?" His voice trembles precariously on the last word before he can swallow it back. For a split second his deep-rooted, ever-widening gulf of sorrow makes itself known, simultaneously making him vulnerable. It is all Isadora needs.

"You think you don't deserve it?" Cold. Cruel. Spoken with little to none of the emotion she had been so clearly drowning in earlier. Eyes a flat marble-grey. Isadora watches Will, watches as her blow lands and he freezes, burning anger turning to ice.

"So it's punishment then?" he asks baldly. "You're punishing me?" It's a standoff now. Isadora feels the hairs on her arms stand on end, but she won't back down. At this point she isn't sure she knows how to.

"I guess it is, Will," she replies, back ramrod-straight and head held almost arrogantly high.

"What's changed then?" he presses on. "I thought we'd moved past this."

"… I thought we had, too."

Will chews on his lip and puffs a tiny laugh. He meets his sister's flat gaze and shakes his head, dark curls flopping against his forehead. "Nice." And with that last word he sinks straight down through the floor and vanishes from sight.

A veil lifts, is whipped away, leaving the room feeling bereft, feeling … off-kilter. As with many things relating to the house, something has shifted sideways leaving Isadora uncomfortable, as if she is wearing her skin incorrectly. Just a size too small.

Isadora shudders, a cold shiver running frigid fingers down her spine. The feeling dissipates, now nothing more than dust motes in the wind, decreasing further when her eyes light upon a desolate figure skulking along the tree line, periodically glancing up at the house in what Isadora supposes is meant to be in a covert manner. Tall, dark hair, male. She can see this despite his figure being mostly hidden in shadow. The man Will mentioned what feels like years ago.

"Tom," Isadora murmurs wondrously to herself. The fight with Will packs itself away into a neat little box to be unearthed at a later date. The guilt goes with it. Instead, she focuses on this new avenue to be explored, knowing as little as she does about Tom and his eventual demise. A picture floats blurrily across her mind. White. Lots of white. Cold. Wet. Dirty. An age-old vision from many days ago.

She pushes this fresh thought away behind a wall with no door. One thing at a time. This man is quite likely a veritable mine of information, an angle she has not thought of investigating until now. She briefly wonders at her own stupidity before turning and bolting out of the room, anxious that now she has sighted him he may vanish before she can ask him anything at all.

Bee appears at her ankles as she flies down the stairs, gripping tightly to the banister as she swings, the momentum sending her tripping over the last few stairs and tumbling to her knees. She swears colourfully under her breath as she picks herself up. Her jeans have burned through at the knees, and she can feel the smarting of ruined skin with every step. Bee releases what may have been a chuckle in whatever language it speaks, which Isadora chooses to ignore in favour of hunting down Tom's undoubtedly attractive ghost, interrogation already building in her head.

Unfortunately, the first word out of her mouth when she catches him up is, "Oi!"

Not surprisingly, Tom's ghost spooks and vanishes from sight. Isadora could have smacked herself. She has unwittingly directed her anger with Will at Tom, a phantom already reluctant to approach and more skittish than a bird when you have no crumbs to offer.

Bee swipes at her leg, drawing blood in a series of long, thin scratches. Isadora gasps as she clamps a hand over the wound, glaring at Bee reproachfully. "I know it was a bad move, okay? Damn!" She draws her hand back, wincing at the watery stains now streaked across her palm. She checks her leg and notes that the bleeding is slow enough to stem itself, but grimaces as she walks over to where Tom had been before she inadvertently scared him off.

She stops on a patch of grass, the haunted house half hidden by the thatch of trees, and peers around spinning in a slow, graceful circle. Isadora thinks carefully. Her years of being surrounded by the dead and, subsequently, excluded from any kind of meaningful social interaction, have severely inhibited her ability to act in any way 'naturally' – and despite Tom being one of the dead, she has a lingering feeling he is far more attuned to the interactions of the living. His skulking, nervous demeanour certainly does not scream 'burdened soul desperate for release, revenge or redemption'. Maybe she needs … yeah … well … If she looks so much like Isabella, it's worth a try, right?

Isadora runs a hand through her hair, eyes darting, brows furrowed. She peers through the trees and spots a dark, overgrown patch further along, right about where the old blacksmith's hut would have been. She needs to do this on his terms, or Tom is never going to let her approach. Isadora squares her shoulders and wanders over, painfully aware of a pair of eyes fixed intently on her back. Tom has not left her completely. Isadora slows her pace and tries to make it look as though she is familiar with the path, as if she has been here more than once.

Her footsteps lighten, and she sways a little, attempting to make herself appear dreamy, floaty. Effervescent. Like a memory tracking back through time, searching reverently for answers.

She arrives at the ruined blacksmith's hut. The wooden roof and rafters are long gone, leaving only the bare stone walls to stand in skeletal prominence against the wooded backdrop. Ivy has sprouted and is creeping upwards reaching for the sun, leaving only a sparse expanse of uninhibited stonework to be seen.

Isadora hovers around what would have been the front door, one hand placed delicately on the wall. The stone prickles coldly against her faintly trembling fingers. Despite her outwardly dream-struck appearance, she is awash with anxious jitters. Her plan might not work; it might crumble and fall in flames. Much like the roof, she surmises, noting the scorched black streaks on the walls. Someone had wanted this place gone.

Something crunches behind her. A whisper of cold breathes across her neck.

"It looks so different," Isadora muses aloud, the baby hairs on the back of her neck rising slowly.

"So do you …" His voice is exactly as she remembers from her sojourn to the past. Although on second thoughts, the warmth is lacking, replaced instead with an emptiness so bleak Isadora's mind is flooded with images of darkness, a well that travels so deeply into the earth you would sooner reach the moon than the bottom.

"Do I?" Isadora laughs breathily, absently. Her hand trails down and off the wall, carrying her into a half-turn so she can see his face. Sharp, shadowed. A far cry from the man she had seen standing within the confines of his shop. She inhales and tastes the acrid burn of smoke, smells the sharp odour so clearly that the entire forest could be alight and she wouldn't be surprised. The back of her throat burns.

Tom examines her intently, dark eyes roving carefully across the planes and slopes of her face. "You're not right," he murmurs, moving closer. Isadora's heart goes up a notch, and she fights to stay still beneath his scrutiny. She must play this to perfection. She is, quite suddenly, remembering one time during summer when she and Will had spotted a small skink sunbathing on the edges of the pool; the way they had ceased all movement and watched with bated breath, sure the tiniest hint of movement would send it skittering away into the grass. Her heart had been leaping so quickly that she was sure the lizard would sense it, lock its beady eyes with her own and vanish with a quick whip of its metallic tail.

Tom was her cautious lizard, being drawn into the sun of his dearly beloved Isabella. Even the tiniest hint of her being a different person would send him flying back to safety.

"You're dressed differently," he says, voice croaking. Isadora looks down at her modern sweater-and-jeans combo and pretends to look surprised.

"I didn't even notice," she says softly, adding just a touch of *Am I dreaming or am I really here?* to her tone. She looks up, her expression dazed and confused, fingers scrunching in the hem of her dusty pink sweater. "I don't know how I got here." Maybe that was laying it on a bit thick, Isadora thinks.

Tom closes the gap and places a trembling hand on her arm, so carefully Isadora can barely feel the weight. His fingers twist into the fabric, cementing his grip. Their eyes meet, stony grey to deep chocolate-brown. Isadora feels something inside her twist painfully at the recognition swimming beneath his irises, watches it scrawling across the rest of his face, tugging at the corners of his mouth and tightening his jaw.

"Isabella?" he breathes, a prayer whispered, so loaded with love, with care, adoration, that the pain in Isadora's stomach is replaced by nausea. She allows Tom to tug her forward into his strong, waiting arms. She allows him to press his face into her hair, to inhale and press his lips to her temple. She can feel his lips moving, releasing silent words into the still air.

"I'm here," she murmurs into his chest, swallowing the lump bulging at the back of her throat, relieved he can't see the scrunch of guilt on her face.

"Where did you go?" Tom's voice is gruff, thick with tears. It reverberates down Isadora's spine, sending vibrations humming through her bones right down into her feet. She can feel every baritone, every hitch in breath. Ugh. Who knew lying to a grieving lover could be so difficult?

"I don't know," Isadora replies hesitantly, careful to keep the quiver in her voice. "I woke up in the back courtyard. On the ground." She tests the waters, unsure if Tom was alive at the time Isabella was callously shot to death by her own mother, of how much he knew about his fiancé's death.

"And it took you this long to find me?" Oh, no! He's definitely crying now. Isadora can feel the ghostly tears falling onto her head, soaking into her scalp. She fights not to pull away, keeping herself pressed firmly against his stuttering chest.

"I didn't know where I was." She attempts a morose sniffle and hopes it comes across convincingly. "I was scared, lost. I wasn't sure if you would still be here, waiting for me."

Tom's grip tightens. "I will always wait for you."

Isadora relaxes slightly. Tom appears convinced for the moment. Good, she can press her advantage and get him to feed her nibbles of information, morsels of perspective she doesn't yet possess but which she requires if she's going to contact Jane. Information is a goldmine, and one needs to be prepared enough to attempt an interrogation. At least that's what all the crime shows have told her and, despite some of the storylines tapering off into garbage, they're still pretty convincing.

"What do you remember, Tom?" she presses quietly, rubbing her head against his chest in a show of nestling in, drawing comfort from his proximity. One of Tom's hands clenches in her long hair and squeezes gently.

"Not much," he admits, gravelly voice so low she almost misses it. Their feet shift, crunching into the fallen leaves littered around them. The air smells wet. It's autumn in among these trees, Isadora realises. She glances at the ground. Between Tom's hardy boots is a myriad of reds, browns, and oranges. A kaleidoscope of dead and dying leaves, mulching the ground under the steady boughs of trees that have stood – and will stand – for longer than any creature.

"Tell me," Isadora murmurs, her voice as velvety as she dares, lips barely moving to shape the words. She feels Tom shake his head above her, breath huffing, muscles tensing. Isadora rubs a hand up his trembling back and soothes as best she can without speaking, until Tom sucks in a deep breath and clears his throat.

"I can't talk about it … without …" He stops and drags in another tremulous breath, still shaking his head. Isadora, frustrated, groans internally and decides she may as well take the lead on this one.

"I remember a little," she starts quietly, as if the very thought of remembering is horrific. She can do fake distress as well as the next person – perhaps not well enough to pass muster with a psychologist, but enough to trick the common person with no real knowledge of the subject. Considering Tom is very much a man of his time, Isadora is not concerned he will see through her ruse – at least for now.

"I remember Wilhelmina," she continues. Tom stiffens. "I remember my mother, in the back courtyard. I remember the gun." The large hand pressed into the small of her back stills. "I remember her shooting me."

"What?"

Isadora pulls away, taken aback by Tom's genuinely surprised exclamation. He is peering down at her, chocolate eyes wide, searching for truth where he is sure to find none. Isadora's brow crinkles.

"My mother, she shot me," she says slowly, only to be met with incredulous shock. Tom's mouth opens, closes, opens again to admit no noise at all. "You don't remember?" Isadora hedges, pulling further back until they are nearly entirely separated, Tom's large, flat hands only just ensconcing her waist, fingertips brushing at her jumper. He shakes his head, dark hair flopping over his eyes.

"I don't. Because it never happened," he says jerkily. Now it's Isadora's turn to be silent. Stunned and confused as she is, no words will form. At least, none that would be appropriate.

"B-but, what …?" Isadora shakes her own golden head. "I saw it happen!"

"Your mother never hurt you." Tom is steadfast. "She may have been distraught with the loss of …" he swallows uncomfortably, "… but she never hurt you. I would remember if she had shot you."

"But you said you didn't remember much!" Isadora points out sharply. "Could it be that you just don't want to remember how I died?" But Tom is frowning at her, muscled arms withdrawing from her waist to hang aimlessly at his sides. He cocks his head, eyes slitted.

"You're not …" he trails off. Isadora steps back.

"Not what?" she asks, mock cluelessly. But she knows it's lost. With this revelation, her poorly capered deception has been uncovered as easily as a Scooby-Doo villain.

"Not my Isabella," Tom declares, torn between hot anger and despairing sadness. A single tear tracks down his sharp cheek. Isadora rolls her eyes.

"Okay, so what? I'm not her. But I definitely saw her get shot by her crazy mother, so why are you saying differently?" It's callous, she knows. But she doesn't have the capacity to care when everything she had thought she knew about this house was being ripped out from beneath her. Being psychic was definitely not worth it if all the wires of communication kept getting hopelessly crossed. Stupid, lying house of death and decay! Who did it think it was showing her false visions?

"Because it was different!" Tom exclaims. "My Isabella met her death not at the hands of another, but—" He cuts off just as suddenly as the outburst had begun. But it is enough. Isadora's grey eyes widen.

"But what?" she asks, leaning forward, eager to hear the rest. Only Tom is already withdrawing, head once again shaking in a frenzy.

"What, Tom … what happened? What did she do?"

Tom's face crumples. "The very worst a person can do to themselves," he whispers, and Isadora can tell the memory is very painful for him. But she pushes down her empathy and focuses only on the task at hand. Collect as much relevant information as she can before the opportunity passes her by.

"She died by suicide?" Isadora presses, feet crunching in the leaves as she surges forward. She grabs Tom's arm and pulls him round to face her, only to be met with a savage shove. She falls back and lands with a muffled 'Oof!' on her butt, back arching as pain lances up her tailbone. Groaning, Isadora presses a hand to the small of her back and winces, the aftershocks of the fall tingling up her spine. She opens her eyes and whips around, ready to tear Tom a new arsehole – only to find emptiness in the space he had once occupied.

"Cowardly prick!" she yells into the silvery thatch of tree trunks, shrinking back shamefully as soon as the words escape her. She's good at that, spewing vitriol before actually thinking it through. Shame curdles in her gut before she can stop it. Her words echo along the breeze to evaporate slowly into nothingness, heard by no ears other than her own. And Bee, who chooses this moment to trot over and sit regally in front of her, milky moon eyes tracking her stilted movement as she pushes herself to her staggery feet. Isadora stumbles once, rights herself and marches right back up to the house, one half of her seething at being manhandled to the ground – and the resulting pain in her rear – the other buzzing at the knowledge she had unwittingly and clumsily gained from Tom in his moment of angered weakness.

If Isabella had committed suicide, her entire first vision was more than likely false. So that begged the question: who was sending her which vision? Was it the residual energy of the house? Jane? Or perhaps even Isabella herself, for some reason that was yet to be revealed? So many potential channels – only one radio to receive it.

She really hopes her Ouija board doesn't take too long to arrive.

XV | THE DEVIL

Walking back inside with a scraped knee, sore back and aching butt is not Isadora's idea of a grand entrance. She hears multiple snickers as she passes by a conglomeration of floating spectres. She tamps down the animosity simmering beneath her skin in favour of holding her head high and swanning past in as illustrious a fashion as she can muster. Besides, her newfound knowledge is far more important than a little teasing from ghosts. Someone had lied to her – and for a specific reason – to conceal the truth of Isabella's suicide. But who? And why? Depending on who it is that had 'sent' her the visions, their motives would be different.

Isadora heads up the staircase to her room, wondering if pacing in there would be more productive than aimlessly wandering the house mulling things over. Reaching for the door handle, she pulls up short, causing Bee to bump into the back of her legs with a disgruntled huff.

Will. She couldn't go back in there if Will had resurfaced. She doubts he had, but her brother is stubborn. He'd sought her out in the past post-argument and, if he follows his natural pattern, he could quite easily do so again in the wake of their recent dust-up.

She is tempted to knock, just in case, but decides that just opening the door and marching inside is more of a power move on the off chance he is there. When she sees he isn't, Isadora squashes down the tiny part of her that is disappointed. No time for that, no time for personal feelings when she has a mystery to solve (and yet, personal feelings keep cropping up and getting in the way).

"Okay, okay … so sh-*they* lied to me. Back when I first had that vision in the field before Will … died. Back before I met Bee. The first feel I had for this place was based on a lie. Okay then." She starts to pace, hands gesticulating as she fights to get her thoughts into some kind of rational order – rather difficult considering the thoughts themselves are quite irrational. "I run here on instinct to get away from the witch hunt, then I see Jane and I'm wearing a wedding dress … Hmmm, not sure if that has any kind of significance in Isabella's suicide. I'm not even sure the suicide happened on the same day that Isabella died – or was shown that, anyway." She turns sharply, pivoting on one tense leg to stride back to the other side of the room, head down, eyes on the floorboards but her focus totally elsewhere. "Then," she muses, "I get astral-projected into the past to see what led up to the death. I mean, I'm assuming very strongly that … what's her name? Wilhelmina! … that Wilhelmina's death had a lot to do with why this place went so sour. Nothing else makes sense!" She throws her arms in the air and, groaning in exasperation, collapses backwards onto her roughly made bed (she'd really only tugged the top cover haphazardly over the sheets so the bed didn't get filled with dust, or ectoplasm. Ghosts were nosy bastards). The mattress bounces beneath her weight as Isadora peers up at the canopy, mind whirring. Maybe she needs to meditate – although the last time she'd done that, she'd ended up with a demon cat from the ether, so … perhaps not. But then there'd been that other time with Iris that had proved somewhat helpful …

She takes a deep breath, then another, followed by another.

"Excuse me?"

Isadora jolts upright, one hand raised ready to assault if need be. On fixing her gaze on the intruder, Isadora pauses, her demeanour outwardly calm despite her racing heart. A young man is standing in front of her. Quite dead if the deeply gouged garrotte-line in his throat is to be believed. Is it Halloween yet? Makeup could never look so believable.

He quirks an immaculately groomed brow at Isadora's still-raised hand and smiles crookedly.

"Going to hit me?"

Isadora flushes and lowers her hand slowly. "Only if you give me a reason to." She shifts her weight so she is sitting on the edge of the mattress, legs crossed and back straight, as she surveys the newcomer. She hasn't seen him before; or, more likely, she has and completely ignored his existence until his countenance faded (or was forcibly ejected?) from her memory. Among the dead he was forgettable; among the living he is equally inconsequential. "What do you want?" Isadora asks him bluntly. The ghost settles himself on the floor, mirroring Isadora's posture, and regards her closely from crystal-blue eyes.

"Not very nice, are you?" he replies calmly, navy-painted nails tapping on the worn floorboards. Isadora smirks and shakes her head.

"No. I'm not. WHAT DO YOU WANT?" she asks again, leaning forward and peering down at him, grey eyes glinting. She isn't in the mood for games or for lost little spirits looking for guidance. She's already had enough of those plaguing her every waking moment. The boy's smile widens, and he leans back, planting his hands on the floor and looking more relaxed by the minute.

"I heard you know how to read Tarot cards," he says brightly. Clearly her attempts to scare him off or intimidate him into leaving aren't working. She groans in response to his question and looks up to the ceiling.

"Heard or saw?" she asks, glancing down to meet his crystalline gaze. "If it was *saw* then you know how incpt I am and that this is a waste of time."

"I was hoping you could do a reading for me." He isn't to be dissuaded, it seems.

"It's outside of my business hours at the moment, and I don't do mates' rates. Try again some other time." She flops back down to stare at the canopy, prepared to lie there until she gets hungry enough to venture downstairs (possibly bumping into Will on the way and giving him an absolute beat-down. Or apologising. She hasn't quite decided yet. She needs to vent her frustrations on someone, at any rate) and scavenge through the rapidly emptying cupboards. The only good thing about being surrounded by spirits is that none of them want to eat, despite their newly regained ability to interact with the living world. Despite this, however, one of the ghosts has stolen some of her iced doughnuts and Hell will freeze over before Isadora forgets or forgives that one.

"I have all the time in the world. So do you. I'm not going to leave you alone until I get what I want." His voice, soft and lilting, drifts to her ears.

"Is that how you almost got your head ripped off?" Isadora asks nastily, to which the boy shocks her by laughing gaily. She sits up. His painted fingers are toying with the edges of his fatal wound.

"Probably," he answers, still smiling widely. *God, it's always the persistent ones that are at peace enough to bother her consistently,* Isadora reflects. *Even worse, they do it effectively. Case in point, Iris the cane-wielding grandma.*

"Bit chipper about that, aren't we?" Isadora prods, now curious. He shrugs, raising his hand to sift through his blond hair.

"Better than being angry about it for the rest of eternity."

Isadora groans again. "I hate optimism."

"So, will you do it?" he presses. Isadora chews the inside of her lip, contemplating whether it's worth it to waste her time with this. On the other hand, she could spend her time wallowing until her Ouija board arrives in the mail.

"What's your name?"

He beams up at her. "Eric."

Isadora snorts before she can stop herself then waves her hand at him in apology.

"I'm sorry. I promise I wasn't laughing at your name." It sounds like a lie. It is a lie. His name is for an old man, not a scrawny teenager with chipped nail polish and a questionable eye for fashion. But Eric is already shaking his head, broad smile only getting broader.

"It's okay. I hate my name, too."

Isadora nods. "We have that in common." She looks around and realises something rather imperative to Eric's request. "Only thing is, I don't have a deck of cards. I left them in the mall during the witch hunt." She hasn't even thought about it until now. And she'd spent good money on her Tarot deck, which now nettles her. Yet another thing for her to complain about later on when no one wants to listen.

"Oh, don't worry about that!" Eric reaches into the pocket of his extremely skinny jeans, produces a complete deck, and uses his other hand to spread it out a little. Edged in gold and smattered with colourful, non-traditional artworks, the pack is simultaneously an eyesore and a wonder. Each picture appears to be rendered in a stained-glass design, reminiscent of church windows only minus the streaming sun and cold, dusty atmosphere. Isadora stares at the pack hesitantly.

"Shouldn't I be using a deck that calls to me? That I connect with?" She raises an eyebrow at Eric's ever cheery expression. He shakes the deck in her direction.

"Maybe that's how it's supposed to be. But you're also traditionally meant to use a deck that's been given, not bought."

"Touché." Isadora reaches out and accepts the proffered deck carefully. Despite the cards being a figment, a part of Eric's astral existence, they feel substantial in her hands, weighty. Isadora chooses to ignore this strange fact and shuffles the cards carefully. They don't cut into her fingers the way her own deck had done; they feel far more natural, almost instinctual as they fly through her fingers. After a few shuffles one card flies out, plucked from the deck by fingers that no one will ever see. Another round of shuffling discharges another card, then another, until five cards lie on the bedspread, mysteriously chosen from the pack by a divine hand.

Isadora sets the deck aside and flips the cards carefully. "Okay, so past, present and future," she murmurs, sorting through them. Suddenly, a pale hand settles over her own. She flicks steely eyes up. Eric is standing right in front of her. She hadn't seen him or heard him move. He clasps her hand and speaks.

"You really have no idea how to read a Tarot deck, do you?"

Irrational anger floods Isadora, filling her face with heat. She knows Eric will be able to see the ruddy evidence of her embarrassment all over her features.

"Excuse me?"

He isn't apologetic; in fact, he appears rather eager to help. "There are several different ways to read a deck, to read a spread of cards," he starts, shifting so he is sitting next to her on the bed, the mattress dipping with only the suggestion of another body. "First we have to understand the cards that make up a full deck."

"I know that," Isadora snaps. "I have done some research into this. I wouldn't dream of scamming people on the street otherwise."

Eric chuckles. "The everyday person has only the barest understanding of Tarot cards. It's an easy scam to do." His thin fingers glide over the upturned cards, his touch bordering on reverence. "There's the Major Arcana, the picture cards that everyone knows. The Emperor, Death, The Fool, and so on." His fingers dance over to the next card. "Then there's the Minor Arcana. The Pentacles, the Swords, the Wands and the Cups. Each one is numbered, and each number means something in correspondence with the suit." His voice is a stream, steady and babbling, weaving this way and that, riding over every stone and trickling away into a deep pool. Hypnotic.

"You've obviously run this scam yourself." Isadora says quietly. "Although you'd have done it better than me."

"Oh, I was never a scammer, but each to their own," Eric replies easily. "There's a myriad of fortune tellers and card readers out there. No one person is necessarily better than another. Some just know and understand more."

"And you appear to be an absolute wealth of knowledge," Isadora exclaims bitterly. "And you're not even a medium."

Eric bobs his head up and peers at her curiously. "You can tell?" he asks, gazing searchingly at her. Isadora considers. She'd said it flippantly, but it's true. There is nothing about Eric that would suggest he is imbued with any more power than the next person. Humanity exists on a baseline of energy; some have more than others, some have less. Eric is one of the average. Given he is one of the most pleasant spirits she has ever interacted with, Isadora explains this carefully, haltingly, not wishing to offend him and send him running, upset by her own particular brand of blunt honesty. Eric drinks it all in calmly, thirsty for any knowledge pertaining to his own personal circumstances.

"Wow," he breathes, once she's trailed off. Isadora hastens to clarify.

"That doesn't mean you don't know your stuff. Clearly you understand Tarot better than I do, and that has to say something about your connection to this kind of thing. Just because you aren't a medium doesn't mean you can't believe or have an affinity for understanding all the intricacies of a Tarot deck."

Eric listens to her well-intentioned word vomit without interrupting. They fall into silence. Isadora's hands twist awkwardly in the duvet cover as she waits. The blankness on Eric's elfin face morphs into a genuine grin.

"And here I thought you couldn't ever admit to a shortcoming."

Isadora baulks a little at his short response then laughs gratefully. "You've clearly never met me properly," she jokes.

"You always looked a tad too stressed to be dealing with the likes of me," he replies teasingly. "Now, back to the deck."

Isadora welcomes the shift in subject gratefully. "Each card has its own meaning, but in conjunction with the other cards pulled it can have many different interpretations," Eric continues. "The most important thing to remember is that Tarot is an ancient tool meant to aid in introspection. Some people believe that true Tarot is designed to show you the tools you need to utilise to reach your ideal destination. How you can achieve your goals. It opens eyes."

"Manifestation?" Isadora asks, to which Eric nods in the affirmative.

"In some cases, yes. But not all." His voice has trailed off into something deeper. More troubled.

Isadora turns to look at him. His face is still downturned, and his eyes are focused solely on the cards. There is a pinch between his brows and a troubled, nervous twitch in his jaw is jumping, pulling at the muscles and keeping them taut. Isadora reaches out and lays a cautious hand over his slim fingers. She wraps her hand around them and squeezes gently.

"You aren't just here to teach me how to read Tarot cards," she says softly. "And I'll bet you aren't here to get a reading either. What's wrong?" Normally, she wouldn't ask, wouldn't even care. But Eric is … well, different. "What do you need from me?"

Eric's head twitches away from her, cobalt eyes fixed on the far wall. He swallows, sharp Adam's apple dipping. He opens his mouth. Closes it. Opens it again. "I just …" He half-turns to face her, his expression now far removed from its previous façade of carefree happiness. A false face, a mask, to hide the sinking depths within. "I wanted to know … if they looked for me." His voice falters painfully on the last phrase, cracking and twisting, no longer an easy river but a fracturing dam. One more leak and it will all fall apart. Isadora cocks her head and doesn't relinquish her grip.

"You think I know who 'they' are?" she asks. Eric swivels stiffly to face her full on, no longer hiding. His eyes are shimmering beneath a veil of tears.

"You're the medium, aren't you?" he asks desperately, leaning forward. His hand clenches hers tightly. A small part of Isadora wants to pull away, swing the curtains back over the windows and shut him out, send him packing as she had to all the others. The thought flickers behind her eyes, and Eric sees it, flinches and pulls away, extricating his hand and placing it along with the other one demurely in his lap. "I'm sorry. To have bothered you." He slides off the bed and stands, the picture of dejection. A veritable beanpole echo of a human. The deep, red smile carved into his neck grins sadistically at her. "I'll go."

Isadora opens her mouth.

"Wait." She doesn't shout, doesn't exclaim loudly in a panic. She says it plainly, assuredly. She inhales. "Tell me who 'they' are, and I'll do what I can. No miracles, though," she adds clearly. Never let it be said that Isadora isn't honest when she needs to be. There can never be miracles in a world such as this.

Eric brightens immediately, hands clenching into fists that he knocks erratically against his lean legs. "Really?"

Isadora allows her lips to pull into a thin smile. "Sure. I have time before my mail gets here. Not like I have anything better to do." She pats the mattress next to her. Eric sits. "Who are they?"

Eric ducks his head again. "My parents."

Isadora frowns. "You want to know if your parents looked for you?" she clarifies slowly, spelling it out as if Eric were a child just on the brink of learning to speak. Eric nods. Isadora falters, unsure if her next row of questions is likely to offend or upset him. Eric grins.

"You aren't going to offend me," he says calmly. Isadora exhales through her nose.

"Maybe I was wrong about your level of universal energy because you definitely just read my mind. Okay, why do you think they wouldn't have looked for you?"

"We weren't on the best terms. Ever." He struggles over the words, physically and emotionally. This conversation is going to be a landmine, Isadora thinks.

"Just because you weren't on the best of terms when you died, doesn't mean they didn't love you. Doesn't mean they didn't look for you." One wrong step and, despite his assurance that she wouldn't offend him, her legs were on the line to be blown off. "I'm sure they looked for you. I'm sure they found you. I'm certain they put you to rest the best way they knew."

Eric sniffles. "I don't know about that," he manages to get out through an oncoming bout of tears. "I never saw any of that."

"You didn't go to your funeral?" Isadora asks, a little bewildered. Nearly every spirit she knew or had spoken to had been to their own funeral. It was one of the only good parts about being a ghost. Surely almost everybody has imagined their own funeral to some degree. Those who said otherwise were lying. But Eric was shaking his head forlornly.

"I didn't know I was dead for a long time. Longer than I want to admit." His nimble fingers fiddle with the rips in his jeans. "I kept trying to talk to people. For the longest time I thought they were just ignoring me. Parents included." He sniffles again. "So I left. Walked away and didn't see them again."

"What eventually tipped you off?" Isadora asks, simultaneously intrigued and sympathetic. Eric looks up at her, eyes brimming with tears, a wobbly, lopsided grin tugging at the corner of his thin lips.

"You did," he replies, with the barest hint of a laugh. Isadora shudders, a flood of cold rushing from head to toe through her nervous system.

"I was probably a bitch to you, wasn't I?" she asks sourly, her fingers tracing along the prancing 'Fool' depiction on the Tarot card sitting innocently on her bed. Its iridescent lines flash with every tiny movement.

"The biggest," Eric snorts. "Wouldn't even look at me when I first approached you. Then I saw the rest of them." He gestures widely. "The ghosts. Saw the wounds and realised we were all the same kind of see-through." His hands flop back to the mattress. "And I realised I was dead. And that you could see me. Us."

Isadora can feel him looking at her, feel the laser focus burning into her flushed cheeks. She can't look up. "You got your hopes up too high, didn't you? Expected me to do something to help you?" It tastes bitter rolling off her tongue, sets the air around them stinking with the guilt of it. She feels rather than sees the nod next to her.

"I did."

The mattress creaks as Eric shifts towards her. She flinches as his hand rests on her knee. Cold, so cold, so empty, so insignificant. His hand slips right into her flesh, reappearing on the other side as if it has moved through water, and come to rest on the ocean floor.

"You're still doing it. Even now," Isadora intones, so softly the words almost don't make it to his ears. But Eric smiles brokenly.

"I'm still doing it. Because I have hope. And faith."

"Hope and faith build you up until you fall. And it always hurts so much more than if you'd never hoped at all."

Silence reigns. Not even the rambunctious happenings below in the drawing room, the library or the garden can penetrate the thick bubble of quietude that seems to permeate the walls.

"Will you take me to my grave?"

Isadora blinks. "I thought you didn't think you had a grave."

"If you believe that my parents buried me, then I have something to hope for."

Isadora huffs and shakes her head, blonde hair swinging across her shoulders in a thick swathe. She spins the Tarot card on its point, The Fool flashing at her on every pass. "Where would they have buried you?"

Their journey doesn't take long. Eric had lived in the neighbourhood not far from Isadora's home. To think she had never known of his existence until he was dead. Such is the way of life. Mind your own business until someone dies and then you can mind theirs as much as you like.

On the way, she had pilfered a hoodie from some unsuspecting homeowner's washing line and jumped the fence before they could have a hope of catching her. Luckily, they hadn't appeared to be home at the time, but Isadora insists that if they had they wouldn't have caught her.

"Being a good thief is not something to be proud of," Eric admonishes, skipping over the cracks in the concrete path. Isadora refutes this statement under her breath so no one can see her talking to thin air.

"I beg to differ."

"You don't strike me as someone who begs for anything."

"Fair enough."

It's late afternoon before the churchyard hedging emerges in the gathering violet dusk. A magnificent sandstone church sits beyond, its square tower reaching powerfully into the heavens, topped by a magnificent black clock face. Dappled, jewel-bright shadows cast fractured light onto the grass as the late sun shines through the stained-glass windows. The Fool card comes to Isadora's mind, face drawn into a wide, cheeky grin among his myriad colours.

They wander around the church to the graveyard, sited on the grounds behind the church and shielded by its imposing mass. Cars stream past, headlights glowing softly as evening settles its calm blanket over the town. None of them slow at the sight of a lone young woman wandering the church grounds, especially not since she has had the foresight to grab a bunch of daffodils that had been springing in a bright, yellow swathe behind the hedges. Regarded as weeds, most likely, considering the immaculate state of the lawns. To the average citizen, Isadora looks like any grieving family member.

"Where do we start?" Eric asks, peering towards the sprouting headstones. "We'll be here until midnight trying to read all of them."

"So, we don't read all of them," Isadora answers, brushing a lock of hair from her eyes. "If your parents were going to bury you somewhere, they wouldn't have been able to get a plot here." She gestures to the moss-smothered marble stones clustered closest to the back of the church. "They're far too old. If you were going to be anywhere, you'd be …" she scans the graveyard with careful eyes, alighting on a patch of brighter, shinier marble headstones, "… there." She points and walks off, weaving around and between the tombstones, some black and inscribed with gold, others grey and rough with lichen. The stones become better, cleaner, the further she goes until Isadora pulls to a stop in front of a very new looking, very big white marker. It glows in the gathering dusk, magnificent in its opulence. A tall, impeccably sculptured angel is peering up into the sky, its perfect face the epitome of serenity. The angel is perched upon a simple square base, tendrils of marble ivy snaking elegantly up from the earth and curling gently around its ankles. Isadora leans forward to read the inscription, eyebrows shooting up as she realises Eric has been way off in his assumption of just how much his parents love him.

"Hey, Eric!" she calls over her shoulder. "I think we have a winner."

She feels him scramble over, gangly legs staggering to a stop at her side. He stares up at the angel, eyes wide. "No way," he breathes. Isadora grins.

"Think they didn't care about you?" She points to the inscription, an elegantly looped script etched lovingly into the white marble. Eric stoops to read.

Held above in the arms of the stars
Cradled forever in the beating of our hearts
We love you, we miss you

Eric glances only briefly at his name and subsequent dates, his gaze instantly moving back to trace over the epitaph once, twice, three times over. With each pass his eyes get mistier. Isadora straightens and backs up, daffodils clenched tightly in her fist. She looks out towards the sunset, now nothing more than a pale pink streak being steadily swallowed by the night. A lone star shines brightly overhead, a pinprick of diamond burning away.

Dead. Just like everything else Isadora can see.

Eric clears his throat thickly and Isadora turns back to him. Identical tear tracks streak his cheeks. He doesn't bother trying to clear them away, smiling faintly at her amidst the snot and gluey swallows. Isadora steps up and gently settles the bunched daffodils at the foot of Eric's grave, wincing at the now slightly crooked, smushed stems. Eric doesn't appear to care.

"That's a lot of money to spend on someone, kiddo," Isadora intones softly. Eric snorts wetly.

"Kiddo? We're, like, the same age."

Logically, Isadora knows this. But there's something about Eric that just screams, "I'm young, protect me!", so she chooses to ignore his comment.

"Still think they didn't love you?" she asks, peering back up at the angel's serene face. Eric follows her gaze, his breath hitching, shoulders bunching then releasing.

"This does make it difficult to justify," he answers thickly. "I just wish I'd heard it from them, rather than seeing it now." He gestures weakly at the monumental headstone. "This ... feels too little too late."

"But at least they tried," Isadora argues. "At least they made the effort. They did all of this for you, knowing you weren't going to see it. What benefit do they get from spending all that money on this for you to not even know it existed?" Isadora slips her hand into Eric's. He flinches at the contact, nonetheless holding on as Isadora continues speaking in a soft, melodic voice. "It's the actions we don't see that mean the most."

Eric sucks in a breath, releasing it slowly as his eyes slip closed. More tears bead and slide down his pale cheeks, each one gleaming for a moment in the weak light of the new moon before dropping onto his collar and melting into the fabric. He's really glowing in this moonlight, Isadora thinks. Only to realise a second later that it isn't the moonlight causing him to glow at all. She steps back, hand never once breaking contact with Eric's, and stares, dumbstruck, as Eric's skin glows pearlescent against the silken night. He looks far more like a ghost now and so much more beautiful for it. Isadora can feel warmth on her skin that can only be emanating from Eric. He is glimmering as if lit from within, and the radiance is only increasing in intensity, until Isadora has to look away, eyes squinting against the brightness. Her chest is hot, the heat emanating from the centre and spreading outwards, a minuscule, magnificent sun. Her hand, still cradling Eric's, is hot now, too, as his voice intones otherworldly in her head.

"Thank you, Isadora. Thank you for showing me. You did it."

The shining light burns so brightly, so hotly, that Isadora's eyes sear beneath her tightly closed lids for only a split second – and then ...

She opens her eyes. Eric is gone. There is only her, the squashed daffodils and the resplendent marble angel staring up into the night sky with its tiny, twinkling stars.

Isadora is silent. Slowly, she brings her still warm hand up to touch her thudding heart. She closes her eyes and dips her head as Eric's voice fades from her mind. She will never hear it again, of this she is certain. He is with the stars now, just as his epitaph claims. And she could not be happier for it.

The journey back doesn't take long, and Isadora walks it silently, mind filled only with a kind of staticky buzzing. Perhaps it's the shock taking hold. Apart from that, her footsteps are the only sound to be heard and her only companion as the old, haunted house rises up from behind the trees.

You did it.

Eric's words replay in her head. She *had* done it. The very thing so many spirits seek her out to do. Eric has gone on to whatever lies beyond, whatever metaphysical plane exists on the other side and past the trappings of death. And Isadora helped him do it. Unknowingly, she helped fulfil Eric's unfinished business and unravelled the tether that had been tying him to his misery. Isadora shivers, wrapping her arms tightly around her torso as she treks up the front stairs and slips inside. For once the foyer is quiet, with only a smattering of ghosts hanging around chatting and moaning away. Isadora floats on past them with only one thing on her mind. Sleep. She doesn't want to think it through, doesn't want to mull over Eric and what happened in the graveyard. She just wants to curl up in her bed and sleep for the next nine hours at least.

As she slides beneath the covers, a smattering of cards tip and scatter onto the floor. She casts them a glance, barely taking in the sight of the Tarot spread grinning up at her with its bright colours gleaming in the moonlight. For once, the time of day is consistent with the outside world.

Isadora pulls the covers over her head and curls into a ball, knees to chest and arms wrapped securely around herself. The warmth in her chest has faded somewhat. The last remnants of the tiny sun that had been shining within her is dying to embers. One of her hands crawls up to cup the fading heat and brushes against her Amethyst. The chain clinks daintily. The stone is hot to the touch. She has neither the motivation nor the brain power to even begin unravelling that mystery, so she casts it from her mind and sinks into an exhausted slumber.

She doesn't dream of anything that night, but half-wakes at three in the morning with the echoing cadence of Eric's voice chiming in her ears.

You did it.

XVI | THE TOWER

Her phone pings brightly from somewhere across the far reaches of the bed. Isadora pops her head up sleepily, grunts and presses her face back into the pillow. Her motivation bank is as empty as her growling stomach, and the temptation to seize her phone and throw it out the window is growing stronger with every 'ting'. Eventually, she can ignore it no longer and rises from the dead like a zombie from a desecrated grave.

The Tarot cards are still spread artistically across the floorboards. Isadora avoids looking at them as she shifts the bedcovers around to locate her phone. It's a little strange they're still there considering they had been a part of Eric's spiritual energy. Then again, he had kind of gifted them to her when he'd handed them over. Interesting.

Isadora shakes the thought away and turns back to her phone. A string of messages stare back. One is from the Post Office alerting her to the fact that her parcel has arrived at her parent's house. The other messages are … unexpected, to say the least.

One is from her dad. Way too many from her mum. Isadora frowns, wondering – why now? She's been gone for weeks at this point, enough to lose count at least. Her phone unlocks, and she stares at the shining green bubbles as two words stare back at her from her dad's message.

Happy Birthday

No way. Isadora opens the app and scrolls through her mum's messages just to make sure. Checks the date on the calendar and sucks in a breath. She is one year older today. 'Happy' birthday is such a misnomer, she thinks. No one can actually be happy on their birthday, and anyone who says otherwise is lying through their cake-stained teeth.

Still, the sentiment makes something warm and fuzzy buzz beneath her sun-starved skin, and she covets the messages as she switches her phone off again and tucks it in her pocket. She slips from the bed, dances around the spilled Tarot deck (Eric's ascension far too fresh for her to move them yet) and drags some fresh clothes from the plastic shopping bag she'd accrued on her first outing. Even if the ghosts are bereft of a sense of smell, Isadora is not. She wishes belatedly that she could have grabbed her favourite perfume before fleeing into the forest. It was her last Christmas gift from her parents. Speaking of which, she really needs to go and collect her parcel.

Exiting the house after slipping between swarms of milling ghosts, Isadora can't help but notice that Will has still not made an appearance since their fight. Bee is tailing after her, an ever-loyal shadow, but it isn't enough to quell the loneliness. Even Iris has been scarce the last few days and Isadora finds herself missing the ornery old woman and her mantra of tough love. All the other ghosts have all but abandoned her in favour of exploring and enjoying their new home.

Isadora is self-aware enough to admit to herself on her walk to the old iron entry gate that she has been incredibly self-centred the last few days, more so than usual, and not much in the mood for sharing and caring. When was she ever, really? But she has become more self-absorbed than ever after her sojourn to the past and meeting the old family. Seeing Tom, hearing his account of events, brief as their meeting had been. Him dropping the suicide bombshell. It's all more than enough to keep Isadora's thoughts occupied without leaving much room for anything else.

She jumps the iron fence nimbly, tottering only once when her ankle catches on a blackberry root. Bee glides up beside her, as languid and free-flowing as water. Together they wander down the path. Isadora has decided against going through the woods and vaulting her back fence as she used to, anxious that her parents will be home and might see her. The front of the house has fewer windows than the back, and the street is a dead end – a cul-de-sac. The only people coming and going would be residents. It also gives her an excuse to check the driveway for cars, so if someone is home she can come back later and look no more conspicuous that any other ordinary person going for a walk. Hopefully, anyway. Will may think differently, but Isadora knows no matter which way she goes about it, it's risky to be so close to home.

Appearance-wise, the house looks no different. But Isadora is used to seeing the metaphysical. A gloom has cast itself over the building. The trees planted along the front edge of the garden are wilting, their trunks greying and the leaves shedding hopelessly. There is no car in the driveway; it's desolately blank. Isadora winces as she walks along the footpath, hands tucked neatly in her jumper pockets, trying to keep her footsteps relaxed and even. Bee trots along behind her, long claws scraping harshly on the asphalt. Isadora has never been so thankful to be the only one able to see and hear the racket Bee is unabashedly making.

As she approaches the house, she spots her package sitting on the doorstep. Chancing a quick glance around, Isadora tries to make herself look casual, despite the fact that her skin is breaking out into guilty goosebumps. She strides up to the front door and, in one swift movement, bends to snatch up the parcel, tucking it securely under one arm before speed-walking back the way she's come. She maintains the pace until she is safely out of the cul-de-sac and back on the main street, where she slows, jostling the parcel into a more comfortable hold while her heart beats madly in her chest. Bee bounds up beside her, tail held aloft, and rubs smoothly against her leg. Isadora yelps when Bee's spines rip through her already torn jeans and score a long scratch down her thigh. A thin trail of blood begins leaking down her leg and onto her white sock.

"Thanks," she hisses through clenched teeth. Bee chuckles and prances merrily on ahead, practically bouncing. Stupid hell-spawn, Isadora thinks.

The wind picks up as she makes her way back along the deserted forest path. Branches sway rhythmically above her, keeping in tempo with the rustling of leaves at her feet. There are barely any leaves left on the trees now, the branches barren. Their twisting limbs are stark against the bright blue sky. Isadora remembers her walk with Iris, their brief chat and how the colours had seemed too bright to be real. The reds, oranges and yellows all popping with life despite their separation from its source.

Isadora tucks her neck further into the cosy confines of her jumper and shuffles on, ignoring the way the wind snatches at the strands of hair she hasn't tied back, tangling it around her mouth, nose and eyes. Eventually, the winding path twists its way to the old iron gate. She is extra careful to avoid the brambles this time.

The house comes into view as it always has, conveying far too much drama and pomp. *Oh, here I am, huge and imposing and grander than necessary! Wait until you hear my secrets. They're quite scandalous.* Isadora takes the steps two at a time until she is sequestered away in her bedroom, Bee her only company. Will is still nowhere to be found. She stands for a few moments, gazing around the room thoughtfully. On second thoughts, perhaps the séance would work better in the other room – the empty, ever-winter room. Isadora turns on her heel and ambles down the hall, goosebumps prickling along her arms and neck as the temperature drops abruptly. Her breath puffs into the air in clouds of white mist that hang suspended in the atmosphere. Bee, of course, emits no breath.

The handle on the door is frigid, sticking to her hand as she grips it and forces her way inside. As she'd expected, the room is empty. All she can see is bare floorboards, rattling windows and the endless snowstorm beyond. Isadora shuts the door behind her and sets the Ouija board down in the centre of the room, settling herself cross-legged behind it with her back to the rattling glass. She cups her hands to her mouth and breathes into them to warm them, shaking them out so they won't tremble too much as she hastily unwraps her package.

Finally revealed, the Ouija board peers up at her. The arrogant sun and moon pictures grin smugly up at her; the planchette is set innocently to the side leaving Isadora room to study the board in its entirety. She isn't stupid. She knows that Ouija boards rely heavily on the subconscious mind and the suggestibility of the players, which is exactly why she is doing this alone. She can't afford any potential discrepancies. Not that she would have had any willing participants anyway.

Isadora tips the planchette out of its plastic bag and places it gently on the board, obscuring some of the fanciful black lettering. She sucks in a deep breath, closes her eyes and composes herself. She doesn't really know the rules. Not exactly. From her intensive internet research, she has gathered that Ouija boards come with flexible rules, ones that change depending on who is playing. Just like a pack of Tarot cards, it depends on the wielder. The only hard and fast rules are those to prevent potential hauntings – which, obviously, Isadora isn't concerned about. It's not as if she can become any more haunted than she already is. She feels Bee settle itself opposite her, moon-white eyes staring at her unflinchingly. Its presence is a sudden, heavy comfort in the face of what she is about to do.

Isadora shakes out her already trembling hands and places them tremulously on the planchette.

"I am now opening up a line of communication to the other side." She speaks clearly, voice raised over the whistling wind outside. "Specifically, to Jane, who lived here some time ago." She clears her throat. "If you are Jane, please let me know you are here and are willing to communicate with me." Her grey gaze falls to the board expectantly. Usually, of course, Isadora doesn't bother with the charade of using a board to communicate – not when she already has a direct line. But having a helping hand is never a bad thing and sometimes enhancements are necessary when dealing with particularly stubborn or gagged spirits.

Isadora watches the planchette closely, eyes peeled for any sign of movement. Bee echoes her actions, its usually twitching tail frozen in place. Several minutes pass. Nothing happens. Isadora shifts her crossed legs and tucks her Amethyst pendant beneath her jumper collar.

"Jane?" she asks the empty room. "If you're here, please let me know." Still nothing. "Jane? There's a good chance you are here but are either unwilling or unable to communicate with me. Please understand, we are alone up here. You have nothing to fear. What you say will not leave this room. No one knows you're here but me." It's a long shot. In truth, Isadora has no idea if Jane is even lingering in the house. It's likely, given the tragic circumstances, but not a certainty.

Isadora feels her hope withering away, as still nothing happens. If Jane refuses to speak, she will have to try and seek out Wilhelmina again, using the board this time … and given the girl's tender age, it's likely that will get her nowhere. She doubts a child that young will be able to understand her questions, let alone spell out any responses correctly enough for Isadora to understand and interpret. Isadora sighs, feeing defeated, and is just about to remove her hands when the planchette gives a minute, but definite, twitch beneath her fingers. Isadora's gaze snaps back instantaneously to the board. The planchette shivers, falls still, then moves clearly and smoothly over to the YES. It remains there assertively. Isadora grins thinly.

"Is that you, Jane?"

The planchette whizzes back to the centre, then gravitates back to the YES.

"Okay. My name is Isadora. I now live in your house, and I've learned some things about this place that I would like to ask you some questions about. Is that okay?"

Again, the planchette returns to centre, hesitates, then moves back to the YES.

"O-kay ..," Isadora replies again, drawing the word out slowly. She licks her lips and considers her first question carefully. Best not to lead with anything too traumatising. No use in scaring Jane off now that she has her willing to talk. Bee gazes across the board at her, milky eyes unblinking. Isadora meets the demon's gaze and scans through her questions in her mind, settling on one that isn't too inflammatory.

"Jane, you lived in this house a long time ago, didn't you? Did you die here, too?"

YES

"You had children here. What happened to their dad?" Anything to get her to open up slowly and build some kind of rapport. The planchette zooms around the lettering.

D I E D I N A F A R M I N G A C C I D E N T

"Was that on this land?"

NO

So the father was well and truly out of the picture. Good to know.

"Your children, they were both girls … correct?"

YES

"Named Isabella and … Wilhelmina."
The planchette hesitates before shifting slowly over to the YES.
"One of them died in an accident?"

YES

"Have you seen her around here since you died?" The moment of truth. Isadora subconsciously holds her breath as the planchette shudders.

YES

Isadora's breath hisses out of her as her stomach squeezes uncomfortably. She has another potential line of communication then, but she isn't so sure she wants to see the little girl's ghost again. Seeing it once was enough.

"Have you spoken to her?"

NO

Interesting. *Why?* Isadora wonders. Jane clearly appeared to be a devoted mother during Isadora's trip back to the past. Despite her proper mannerisms she doted on her daughters and was clearly distraught after her younger girl's death. Isadora clearly remembers how desperately her parents had wanted to speak to Will, see him, after he died. So distraught they had wanted to use Isadora as a conduit between the two worlds, despite her pleas for them to let it go. Jane doesn't strike her as the type of parent to not want that, too.

"Why not?" It's a little off topic, but Isadora is genuinely curious. Bee flicks a dark, spiky ear back and tilts its head as if to ask – what are you doing? Isadora meets Bee's questioning glance and responds with one of her own, careful to keep her fingers on the planchette as it glides across the board.

HURT

Isadora frowns, "It hurt? You mean it hurt you too much to talk to her?"

GUILTY

"You feel guilty? What, like it was your fault?"

YES

"What is it with your family and their guilt complexes?" Isadora murmurs to herself, hopefully not loudly enough for Jane to hear her. She changes the subject. "What about your other daughter?" The planchette pauses, almost contemplatively. It skitters back and forth.

NO

"You haven't spoken to her either?"

NOTMYDAUGHTER

"Isabella isn't your daughter?" More guilt? Or the anger that Isadora had seen when she first arrived? But Tom had sworn up and down that what Isadora had seen could not be further from the truth. That Jane had loved her daughter very much, despite the tragedy that had occurred with Wilhelmina.

YOU

Isadora scrunches her face up in confusion. "What?"

YOU

"I'm not your daughter?" Isadora is confused. Has she miscommunicated something? Before she can ask another question the planchette is moving again.

YOUDESERVEIT

"What do I deserve?" Isadora asks softly, playing along as she desperately tries to make sense of the conversation. Her confusion only deepens when the planchette continues.

EVERYTHING

Suddenly the planchette is ripped from her grasp, and Isadora is shocked when a face, a human face, appears on the other side of the board where Bee has been sitting. Bee is now on the other side of the room, back arched and baring its long, gleaming teeth.

The face connects to a body ... a tiny body. A tiny body dressed in a dirty white frock smeared with mud and long, sticky tendrils of blood. Its little hands are a sickly grey, streaked and flecked with more blood. But it's the face that has Isadora's mouth gaping – for it's a child's face, a girl's. The front is caved in, a huge, glaring dent with long, jagged splits in the skull and skin, oozing with grey mush mixed with brown sludge. One eye is bulging, the other has completely popped free and is dangling on a stringy root of pink flesh. The mouth is a trembling gash choked with spittle, leaking at both sides and drawn down in a slovenly pout. Bubbles of saliva gather in the corners. The cheeks bulge in and out rhythmically as the tiny chest heaves. Then, horrifically, the child begins to cry.

Loud, screeching cries. Wails of terror and hiccups of hurt burst forth. Each scream is punctuated by a throb in the mottled, burst apple-head. Greyish brain matter is oozing over the child's brow, dripping into its bloodshot eye and trickling down its cheeks, mixing with the rivulets of tears. The child's arms lift and reach out to Isadora, an infant seeking comfort in the most basic, raw way a human knows.

Isadora scrambles away, mouth drawn into a silent 'O' of horror, eyes wide and unblinking. Her mind simply cannot comprehend this horror. Her knees come up to her chest as her back hits the solid brick wall behind her. She scrabbles desperately to get further away, but there is no escape from the dead child, who continues to approach in her toddler stumble. Her ripped and rotten skirt sways around her swollen, chubby, grey-tinged legs. She only has one shoe on.

Isadora's hands cease their mad clawing at the wall and fly up to cover her face. She is barely aware that she is hyperventilating. Despite all the ghosts, all the death she has experienced, something within her has short-circuited at being faced by this one. Wilhelmina's tiny, dead body.

Something cold and wet touches her arm. The baby's screams have not ceased; they have only grown louder and more panicked as her torment goes on, ignored. She cannot find anyone willing to soothe the overwhelming pain she feels. Isadora flinches away from the touch, but the wet hand is now slapping against her arm and Isadora suddenly realises that, somehow, she isn't wearing her jumper anymore. She is wearing a white dress, with cap sleeves. And she is screaming. She's not aware of when she had started, all she knows is that she can't stop.

The hands intensify in their exploration. They crawl up and down her arms, soggy and fetid. Like octopi trailing their sodden, sticky tentacles along her skin, tracing and carving patterns with their greedy suckers.

Isadora screeches, recoiling when a line of piercing pain cuts through her skin. She quickly draws her hands away from her face to inspect the cause, but is sidetracked by the toddler flailing around on her knees. Wilhelmina has crawled onto her lap, still screaming, and is now trying desperately to shove her busted head against Isadora's stomach, nestling in the way any child would to their mother to seek comfort from all the hurt the world has to offer. Isadora feels her stomach twist. She can hear the squelching of Wilhelmina's mashed forehead, the grinding of the skull plates dragging together. Isadora's strange white dress is now smothered in blood. The smell of iron assaults her nose, has her breathing open-mouthed and tasting it too.

She glances back at her arms. The flesh on her arms is a twisted map of words, carved in delicate scrawl. Beads of blood bloom from every cut. They twine and twist down her forearms to her wrists, then meander along her hands to her fingertips, where the droplets hang tremulously. 'Plink'. Isabella watches in dismay as they begin to drop from her fingers and land in Wilhelmina's sparse, dirty hair. The sensation makes the child look up. One bulging blue eye stares right into Isadora's.

Ugh! If she vomits it will land on Wilhelmina's mangled head. She will degrade the poor, wailing child even further – and that feels cruel beyond belief. Instead, Isadora shoves the hurting child off her lap with almost inhuman strength, claps her hands over her ears and screws her eyes tightly shut. Wilhelmina screams with renewed vigour. Isadora can feel the pain in her cries as if it were her own.

"STOP IT!" She feels the skin in her throat shred with the force of her cry and begin to bleed.

But that isn't all.

At her scream, all the windows in the room burst outwards, glass shattering right out of the frames. The door flies open, banging violently against the wall, where a crack now appears, running right up to the ceiling. The light fixture swings crazily, then settles.

There is no more crying. Only a shocked, empty silence.

A gentle paw settles itself, feather-light, on Isadora's trembling knee. She opens her squeezed-shut eyes and squints down at Bee, but without fully registering what she sees. There's a faint ringing sound somewhere in the distance, but everything else, all other sounds, have mysteriously faded. Isadora doesn't properly process any of it.

Until …

"Dora?"

There's only one person who calls her that.

"Dora, are you okay?"

But they'd been fighting. He hasn't been around for days.

"What's going on? Can you hear me? Hey! Dora?"

Something grips her shoulder and gives her a shake. Her body jolts, then flops, bonelessly, like a life-size human marionette with no strings. She falls forward. Will's hands strengthen their grip and hold her aloft.

"I can't hold you here forever. If I let you go, you're going to break your nose on the floor and blame me. Hey!" He slaps her across the face gently … well, gently enough not to bruise, but hard enough for the sharp sting to permeate the fog clogging up her brain. Her eyes roll up and zero hazily in on her brother's worried face.

"Thought we were fighting?" she slurs, barely catching the relieved grin that breaks out on Will's face – a grin that is not quite matched by his eyes.

"Yeah, well that's the fun thing about having siblings. At the end of the day, we're still related." He shifts her so she's resting back against the wall. Her legs slump to the side, allowing Bee ample space to move onto her lap. It settles in and peers up at her.

"'S … a shame," Isadora mumbles, shaking her head and raising a trembling hand to her brow, "that we still have to be related."

"Sure," Will answers as he settles in beside her, his shoulder just touching hers. "If it means you'll talk to me again."

Isadora sniffs, squeezing her eyes shut as her senses sharpen. "You were the one avoiding *me*." She swallows and heaves in a deep breath, the last of the cobwebs drifting away to be replaced with a vivid recollection of her Ouija experience. She shudders. Her eyes drift over to the board, now sitting innocently near the far wall. Except … wait, the planchette is moving sluggishly. Isadora lurches forward on hands and knees, crawling along the glass-scattered floor until she can read whatever the spirit is spelling out,

GUILTY

Isadora winces, casts the board aside and turns her back on it. She clutches at her arms and winces again as pain lances all the way up to her elbows. She draws her arms away from her chest and stares at them, clad again in the sleeves of her thick jumper. Will is watching her, dark eyes jumping from her arms back to her face quizzically until he can no longer stand the silence.

"What is it?"

Isadora sucks in a breath and gingerly draws her sleeves back. Her arms are covered in scrawled words, each spelling out the same thing: GUILTY.

"Guilty of what?" Will quizzes. Isadora can only shrug weakly as she tugs her sleeves back down. "Don't do that." Will's strong voice prompts her to meet her brother's gaze.

"What?"

"You know, or think you know, what that means. I know I wasn't …" He cuts off and rediverts his attention to his feet until his courage returns. "I left you after. And I'm not going to pretend I'm not angry. I am. What you said and did was low and I can't forget that. But we are family. And I'm sorry for abandoning you."

Isadora stares at him. "Isabella and I look almost exactly alike," she voices hesitantly. Will's posture relaxes. "Maybe Jane sees her daughter in me … except when I spoke to Tom—"

"Who's Tom?" Will interrupts, confused. Isadora 'ahhs' quietly when she remembers she went to talk to Tom after they fought.

"He's the ghost you saw on the first day. The one who never came inside?" Will nods as he remembers. "He's Isabella's fiancé. He was there when it all went down, and we talked. He said that Jane didn't kill Isabella – the opposite, really. She never hated her daughter, never blamed her for what happened to Wilhelmina."

Will frowns, deciding not to mention that he doesn't recognise any of these names. "So what *did* happen?"

"Isabella killed herself."

Will's eyebrows shoot up to his hairline. "Seriously?" Isadora nods. Will whistles slowly, then continues frowning contemplatively. "So, what was with the visions of violence? And why this?" He gestures to the destroyed room. Bee mewls from where it's coiled around Isadora's ankles.

"I don't know. Unless …" Isadora pauses as something dawns upon her. "Unless I wasn't talking to Jane at all." Will seems to be catching on as his eyes gradually light up with recognition.

"You think it was Isabella?"

"It would make more sense. I think she killed herself out of guilt." Her eyes trail down to her arms. "It would make much more sense than Jane, at least given what Tom said. He and Isabella had a hand in making the cart Wilhelmina died in, so that would explain the direct guilt. I mean I could be wrong, and it might've been Jane, but then Wilhelmina appearing would be punishing herself, too … Or just punishing Isabella. I don't know." She pauses. "It could have been either. And she kept saying *you.*" Isadora stresses the last word. "Like she was telling me it was my fault, too."

"You just said you look alike," Will points out.

"Yeah, but what if it's more than that?" Isadora paces back and forth, her actions becoming almost feverish as her train of thought quickens. "What if we're connected on a deeper level than just looks?"

"Reincarnation?" Will asks sceptically. "Really?"

"It fits." She whirls to face him, fully aware of how crazy she looks with her wide eyes and wild hair. Will doesn't look fully convinced, but she can tell he's on the way.

"Does it?" he asks. "Or does it just fit because you want it to?"

Isadora throws her hands up. "Why can't it fit? Is it because it's too convenient?"

Will sighs. "No. I just think you need more proof to float the theory."

Isadora falls silent. She doesn't have any further proof … until something occurs to her. "I was wearing a dress."

"What?"

"I was wearing a dress." Her voice is hushed. "When Wilhelmina climbed into my lap," the image flashes queasily across her mind, "I was wearing a white dress. Isabella's dress."

"That might mean nothing at all. And if it was Jane you were talking to, it would fit. She might've thought you were Isabella, and it might've, like, projected onto you," Will points out, jumping back when Bee swipes at his leg and emits a warning hiss. Isadora stares down at it. Its white eyes stare intensely back. *Keep going,* they seem to implore. *You're so close now.*

"In that moment I wasn't just dressed like her. I *was* her. Haunted by the death of her little sister. It's like she wanted me, specifically, to feel it. That I was guilty."

The siblings fall silent. Will still isn't convinced. And despite there being no real proof as to who she had been talking to, Isadora is so convinced it had been Isabella that her brain is going a mile a minute chasing the theory down the metaphorical rabbit hole, heart pounding at the thought of what else it might lead to. This was good. This was progress.

"I still think you need more evidence," Will says firmly, ever the dev-il's advocate. His face clears abruptly. "Oh, Happy Birthday, by the way."

It's so out of left field that something in Isadora is shaken loose and a marvellous thought occurs to her. A deranged grin tugs at the corner of her mouth as the idea grows. "Hey, Will … when's Isabella's birthday, do you think?"

His head tilts to the side as he squints at her. Isadora darts from the room, leaving him to bemusedly follow, wondering just what on earth had occurred to her and what, exactly, he had unwittingly led her into.

XVII | THE STAR

Isadora barges into her room, reaches across the bed and seizes her phone. Will follows more sedately, eyes skating curiously over the scattered Tarot cards, hands thrust deep in his ghostly pockets as Isadora frantically taps away.

"I thought you didn't know the family name?" Will asks, peering over her shoulder. Isadora nods.

"You are correct, but there's more than one way to get information." She opens a maps app and searches her current location. The phone thinks for a moment before loading up the satellite view – and there it is. Isadora zooms in on the house and a name pops up.

"Archer Estate," she breathes. Isadora turns to her brother, face alight with a feverish look he has not seen before. Her slate-grey eyes are gleaming. "Wanna bet Archer is the surname?"

Will can't keep the grin spreading across his face from showing. "I'm not stupid enough to make any kind of bet with you."

Isadora smirks, then opens a search engine and begins typing. "I feel like an FBI agent or something." She laughs, honest to God laughs, and Will briefly wonders if her Ouija experience has scrambled her brain. He's always known it would happen eventually.

"Here!" Isadora pulls up a page and shows it to him eagerly. "Read that." She passes her phone over, and Will tries to hide his sudden flinch at being corporeal again. If the suspicious glint in her eye is anything to go by, he is unsuccessful. Will ignores her scrutiny, trying not to shift guiltily, and reads the offered paragraph. It's part of some kind of history blog, an official one with a National Trust banner along the top of the page. He scans the 'History of the Archers' section and skips down to the details about the residents. Under Marcus Archer is the word DECEASED, followed by 'Farming Accident'. Will reads further.

Under Jane Archer it also says DECEASED, and 'Consumption at the Ripe Old Age of 73'. She'd had a decent innings, at least. It's the other two names that spark his interest, however, and Will can feel his brow lift as he reads. By the time he gets to the end of Isabella's section, his spectral being is awash with a cold feeling of dread.

"It's Isabella's birthday today," he says softly. In his peripheral vision, he can see Isadora nod.

"Enough proof yet?"

"It was a very good hunch. But it still might be just an amazing coincidence," Will replies sagely, scrolling down to Wilhelmina's section. He blanches. "Uh, have you read Wilhelmina's details?"

Isadora frowns. "No. I didn't think it was really relevant. We already know a lot about her."

"Not everything," Will murmurs. "Her birthday is the same as mine."

Isadora clutches at her necklace as a shocking thought occurs to her. "What about her death day?"

Will reads. Pauses. Swallows thickly, then turns to stare at his sister. "It's the same as mine." He would never forget that date. It's firmly etched into his mind, leaving a scar so deep he could jump off the edge and plummet to his death. If he hadn't already … well, kind of done that already.

"Wh-wh-en's Isabella's death d-day?" Isadora asks, stammering over the beginning and very nearly tripping over her tongue at the end. Her grip tightens on her necklace, all the euphoria from her brilliantly educated guess evaporating as quickly as it had surged to the surface. Will passes her the phone in lieu of answering her. Isadora reads. "That's next week. And we're the same age now." It takes a second for that to fully register. Isadora sinks down onto the edge of her bed. Will joins her.

"At least now I have a deadline," Isadora says flatly. Will barks a startled laugh.

"Only you would make a joke like that." He jostles her shoulder and is rewarded with a faint smile. It fades away within seconds, but the victory settling in Will's chest remains.

"If I'm right …" Isadora chews on her bottom lip, "… which I might not be …"

"Shock and horror."

Isadora shoves at her brother. "I'm not infallible," she huffs, shaking out her hair before continuing from where she had been so rudely interrupted. "If I'm right, this is where I have to make it count. I need to figure out how to help her."

Will tenses. "Help her?" His voice rises to an incredulous squeak. "Why would you want to help her? Dora, if she is the one who lured you in here and has plans for you to die, why do you want to help her?"

"If I'm her reincarnation, why wouldn't I want to help her?" Isadora counters.

"You've never helped yourself before."

Isadora bites her lip and concedes, "Okay, that's fair. Call me selfish, but it's potentially the only way to get all of this," she gestures largely, "to go back to being empty. Unassuming. Not haunted."

"How do you figure?"

"Okay, when we were having our fight, and we weren't talking, I had a heart-to-heart with one of the ghosts here."

Will looks sceptical. She can't blame him.

"Just hear me out and don't interrupt, please?"

Will sighs, nods in a 'go on' fashion and sits cross-legged on the bed. Isadora sucks in a breath and explains all about Eric – how he'd come to her, how they'd gone to the graveyard, and his eventual ascension. To his credit, Will remains politely silent through it all. Once Isadora is finished, the final word gusting out of her and feeling much like a balloon emptied of its air, he speaks.

"You've come into your purpose, huh?"

Isadora points a finger at him. "Don't even start!" she snaps, then sags. "It was mostly accidental. Just because I did it for him doesn't mean I'll do it for all the others."

"But you'll do it for Isabella?"

Isadora's mind instantly responds yes, although outwardly she hesitates. "She's hurting. I want her to go away."

"And what happens after?" Will asks. "What happens when you send her away? Are you going to stay here? The only difference will be you won't have weird visions and collapse all the time."

In truth, Isadora doesn't know. She does have a vague inkling as to what may happen if she sends Isabella to the great beyond. Some deeper inclination about how it will end. Some deeply rooted part of her knows intuitively exactly what will occur. It bugs her, like an itch just begging to be scratched, only Isadora's not sure where to aim her fingers. But on a surface level – no, she doesn't know.

"I haven't thought that far ahead. It's a problem for future me."

Will can only cup a hand over his eyes and sigh. Again.

"Okay," he relents. "Where do we start with this? How do we go about sending her to the great beyond?"

Isadora feels simultaneously elated at Will being on board and weighted with worry at the task ahead. She truly doesn't know what to do. Eric had been an accident – a happy accident, admittedly, but still. She had stumbled her way through the entire process after he had given her enough information to make an educated guess as to what he needed to move on. She is good at that, it would seem. Making educated guesses. Or maybe it's just the power of her intuition. At any rate, she thinks, Isabella is going to be a much more complex case.

"We research," she starts off slowly. "We gather as much information as we can. Build a profile of who she was, what she was like." She mulls it over. "We have to know her enough to figure out what will be sufficient to provide enough peace for her soul to untether itself from whatever is keeping her here. And we already know what's doing that. Guilt."

"So we try to alleviate the guilt?" Will asks, brow crumpled. Isadora shrugs. Will forges on. "And we already have a distinct advantage here. You." Isadora's hands tighten on her jeans. "If you are a reincarnation, you might know things you don't know yet."

She snorts a laugh. "Real clear there, Will, thanks."

"You know what I mean."

She does indeed know exactly what he means, and the concept frightens her. Because she *doesn't* know. She has no real insights to offer on Isabella at all. Heck, Isadora can barely understand herself and her own gifts, let along the psyche of a damaged (quite probably unhinged) version of herself from centuries ago. And Will is wrong; she does know what she doesn't know. And hoping that information is locked away in her brain, just waiting for the right key to unlock it, is foolish. The death day deadline will come and go before Isadora even has a chance to find the door the lock belongs to. She says none of this, however, opting instead to laugh it off, play it as a joke to conceal the fear splintering in her chest.

Will notices nothing amiss. Of course. Sees only the mirage she intends him to see – and they say no more about it.

"Off to research we go then. Joy of joys." Will stands, tucks his hands back into his pockets and waits for Isadora to join him. Research she will, Isadora thinks as they amble from the room, skipping around the Tarot deck that's still spread haphazardly on the floor. The Fool glints at her as she passes. Isadora grimaces, hand brushing against the door frame. She can only hope the internet has more to offer on the family and something concrete on the phenomenon of reincarnation. This whole mess is a heap of tangles knotted up in further tangles with no promise of anything coming loose, no matter how hard she pulls.

Isadora is so caught up in her train of thought she doesn't see Bee slink between her feet, nor does she have time to save herself when her ankle abruptly catches against Bee's inky body. She shrieks as the ground comes up to meet her, and is just bracing her hands against the fall and twisting her head so she doesn't break her nose, when a steady hand hooks the back of her jumper and yanks her upright.

"Enjoy your trip?"

Isadora drags in a relieved breath, body still shaking at her near miss. Iris, her saviour, is standing there, eyes twinkling behind her wire frames, gnarled hands perched casually on the head of her walking stick. Isadora peers past her to the other end of the hall where Will is drifting down the stairs, face caught in an impish smile. His dark, curly hair disappears from sight. Isadora looks back at Iris.

"Did you catch me, just then?" she asks in amazement. Iris grins, wrinkles deepening.

"I did. You owe me another one, young lady."

"Since when have I owed you anything?"

"Was our heart-to-heart on the wooded road not deep enough for you?" Iris croaks cheekily. Isadora snorts.

"Didn't realise your fees were so high. I wouldn't have bothered otherwise."

Iris chuckles. "Well, my wizened services don't come cheap."

Isadora stuffs her hands in her jacket pockets and leans back against the wall. "Thank you, anyway," she says to Iris. "But you know how it is … things to do, ghosts to avoid." She pushes off the wall and hurries after Will. Iris doesn't call her back, although Isadora knows she wanted to talk to her about something. Isadora thinks she knows what sort of payment Iris is interested in – and it's one she can't afford at present. After all, Iris has no deadline.

When she finally catches up to her brother, Isadora slugs him in the arm, ignoring Bee who continues to skulk around behind her like a second shadow.

"Ow!" Will deadpans, then ducks when she draws her fist back again, poised and ready to strike. "What did I do?" he whines, arms raised defensively.

"Laughing at me for nearly falling over! Did you know that was going to happen?"

"Any excuse to hit me—"

"Is a good one!" Isadora finishes for him.

"Okay! Jeez!" Will clears his throat. "I saw Iris come up behind you, and I knew Bee was there. I didn't know they were conspiring to trip you over … and what does it matter, anyway?" His dark eyes gleam curiously. Isadora sighs, holsters her weapons and walks down the rest of the stairs into the foyer.

"She wanted to ask me to do something I can't afford to focus on right now."

Will understood her; she knew he did. "Another Eric situation?"

"Isabella is my priority right now. I'm not going to be made to feel guilty about it." She was, in fact, going to feel guilty about it.

"One bridge at a time," Will responds sagely, stopping at the front door. Isadora tips her head back a little to fully look at her older brother. He looks weary. Weary in a way she has become accustomed to ever since the accident. His weariness weighs heavily on her, although he probably can't tell as she hides it behind a plethora of other emotions. She wonders if it may have been better for Isabella, given she didn't have to see what had become of her sister after her untimely death. It didn't stop her from killing herself in the end, however. Perhaps she was always doomed to suffer in the wake of death. Perhaps this was her penance. Isadora shakes the thought away.

"There's a library back that way," Isadora gestures to the offices towards the back of the ground floor. "Maybe you can start there, and I can continue with my internet research?"

"I think your 'other' form of research might be more effective," Will replies. Without waiting for an answer, he salutes her lazily and wanders off towards the library, tall figure disappearing behind one of the doors.

Bee whines impatiently at Isadora's feet. "What do you want now?" she asks grumpily. Bee ignores her, sliding away and positioning itself beside the front door. A tittering group of ghosts float past, hands grazing along Isadora's shoulders as they go. Isadora shrugs them off, tottering out the front door as Bee leaps up onto the concrete banister, white eyes trained out into the garden. Isadora squints into the warm, orange sunlight. It falls in magnificent streams, cascading through the grove of ethereally swaying trees, leaves plucking free and falling in twists of sage green and caramel brown. It's so magical that Isadora pauses, breathes deeply through her nose and forgets, for just a moment, that she is on a ticking clock.

Bee trots along the banister as easily as breathing, down the stairs and out onto the soft mat of springy grass beneath the trees. Isadora follows sedately, curious as to the demon's motive. Is she about to follow Bee off on another psychic adventure? Where on earth will her consciousness end up this time? Isadora admits the past months have felt like one psychedelic trip after another, with nothing to show for it but fresh trauma. She's seen more than enough child death. It's beginning to get old.

Still, she follows the demented, spiky, catlike creature through the trees, emerging at the end of the glade by a timber fence. A silky river gurgles down a gentle embankment, leaving Isadora's internal compass bamboozled. She has not noticed the river before. It seems to have sprung out of nowhere.

"Bee …" she turns and abruptly cuts off. Tom is standing behind her, hands hanging slack at his sides, tanned face openly shocked at the sight of her. Isadora retreats a little, colour flooding her cheeks as her gaze drops to the ground. The cadence of the river keeps the awkward silence at bay. Tom clears his throat and Isadora chances a closer glance at him, at his hair that falls in dark curls across his forehead and along the nape of his neck. She focuses on that instead of the growing intensity in his chocolate eyes.

"I wasn't expecting you to be here." He doesn't need to express this in words. Isadora is already acutely aware of it. Bee has led her down here, right into some kind of trap. And now the little sneak is nowhere to be found, seemingly content with wrong-footing her for the second time today. Isadora will have words with it later.

"I know," Isadora replies. "Especially considering the success of our last meeting."

"When you lied to me?" He doesn't sound angry – more blunt, honest. Isadora meets his eyes at last. There's something swimming in those dark depths, and she'd really rather stay dry today. No diving in too deep this time.

"I omitted a truth you never asked for."

"That's still lying."

"Only because you're such an upstanding citizen. Most people lie. All the time, really."

Tom squints at her. "You never used to."

Something clenches in Isadora's chest, and she struggles to keep the wince from her face. "Yeah, well, I do now." She looks away, down towards the burbling river. She can see the stones submerged in its depths, slick and shining in the sun. *Look, Will, I'm using my alternative form of research. Aren't you proud?*

"Actually," Tom speaks softly, contemplatively. "You did eventually. At the end."

"About what?" The light is dazzling as it sparkles on the rapidly moving current. Isadora's heart picks up the pace as she hears Tom take a hesitant step closer. She wonders if Isabella was like this when they first met. Too shy to even meet his gaze head-on, content to focus elsewhere and let him lead the conversation wherever he pleased.

"Lots of things." His deep voice is much closer now. The hairs on the back of Isadora's neck slowly stand to attention, causing ripples of goosebumps to course down her arms and back. "It scared me. The things you would omit from me."

"Care to elaborate?" Isadora presses carefully, aware that if she appears too eager, Tom will clam up. She needs to prise the facts from him delicately, like pulling teeth or ingrown hairs. Slowly and methodically.

"You saw things then. The same way you see things now."

The sun abruptly vanishes behind a large grey cloud, casting Isadora in a shroud of chilling cold. Tom continues calmly. "You lied about it then. The way you lie to me now."

"I didn't want to scare you." Isadora breathes shakily, the words suddenly ambushing her from an outside source. Her mouth moves over them, tongue dexterously forming the shapes, her palate flexing to keep the words clean, finely enunciated. But her mind doesn't think them, doesn't run them through, allow them to filter down. They have been placed there, dropped neatly into her mouth to tumble out.

"You thought it would scare me to know what you see?" Tom's hand, barely there, brushes softly through her hair. The goosebumps flare along her neck.

"I didn't want to lose you, too."

The hand drifts back, curls tentative fingers to brush the hair away from her nape. "I would never leave you. You would never lose me."

Isadora bites her lip and steps away, leaving the hand to drift down into empty space. It feels wrong. This is Isabella's fiancé, not hers. He is pining for a version of her that only exists in the grounds of this house, a version that has seemingly fought shy of him all these years in between. Tom is desperate to see her, whereas she isn't keen to see him. Isadora is not Isabella. She cannot give him the closure he so urgently needs – can only act in her place. Whatever relief she may give him is a farce. It will not last, and it will not help him.

On the other hand, she needs to know more about Isabella. Tom is a conduit to this in a way she'd thought gone until now. This is the second chance she has wished for. Let him see the Isabella in her; let him try to scoop her out of Isadora's unwilling carcass and have comfort in her company.

"I did lose you in the end though, didn't I?" Isadora says. "Was it the spirits that drove me mad? That drove you away?"

Tom moves so she can see his face, drawn in sympathy. "Only one spirit. She drove you to nightmares, delusions. Drove you to take up the knife that day. I couldn't save you."

"You can't save someone who can't save themselves," Isadora says softly. "There was nothing you could do."

Tom's face twists. "If you had only told me what was happening … it didn't have to end the way it did."

"Sometimes … people just make up their minds. They know what they want to do and how much it will cost them. And they still do it, anyway." Isadora faces him head-on, resolutely, that other voice welling, reverberating in her chest with a certainty Isadora knows would have made anything Tom tried to do absolutely futile. Isabella had known what she wanted. Pushed to it by madness, perhaps. But it didn't change the course of her actions then and it wouldn't make her regret it now. "The choice was mine. I wouldn't have done it differently." Her voice is chilled, detached. Tom winces. He lifts his shaking hand back to Isadora's face and cups her cheek tenderly, brushing aside a wayward golden strand.

"And yet I still love you. Despite your choices. Despite the end. You were never weak to me."

"Who said suicide was weak?" Isadora is in control this time. The foreign presence has gone, dissipated before Tom could make his heartfelt declaration. Leaving only Isadora to hear his confession. "It takes inordinate strength to follow through on something as hard as that. It isn't weakness."

"Your strength is our strength," Tom replies quietly, dark eyes boring into her, hotly refusing to relinquish the contact. "In all the moments since, we have been weak. Inconsequential beings with barely enough to be."

He reaches out. Isadora doesn't see him grasp her hand, only feels the encompassing warmth sinking into her palm. "And then you stepped foot on the land," his eyes shine golden with fire, "and I felt your strength return. You were never weak to me. You have not been weak since. But in that moment, the moment you died, I could barely feel the brush of your strength. The fire wasn't there."

Isadora tips her head back slightly, marvelling at the sharp line of Tom's jaw, the sheer life burning behind his captivating gaze. It doesn't distract her as much as she wishes it would. "If that is how it felt, then I am stronger for what she did. What we decided to do." She leans closer, breath scraping over his dark stubble. "The suicide granted me strength in ways nothing else could. Not even you."

Tom doesn't draw back, only stiffens. "Your reaction to me is different now. You aren't the way you were in the end. In our end." His warm fingers stroke reverently across her cheek. "Do you have everything you needed to know?" So, he hasn't been as duped as she's imagined, has merely played into it, missing Isabella as he so keenly does. Tom will do anything to see any lasting vestige – even pretend with a woman who so clearly is not the same person, no matter which fragments of a soul they may share.

"Tell it to me again. Clearly." She needs to know for sure what she's dealing with.

Tom's thumb strokes along her cheek. "Isabella could see the dead. Always. She never realised quite what it was until her sister left us."

"Isabella could see ghosts. Her little sister's drove her to madness. She escaped the only way she could. It created this," Isadora gestures. "I think I understand the broad strokes. I'm sure there's more I don't understand now that will be revealed to me later.

On impulse – and later on, Isadora will never be able to pinpoint just why she did it – she leans up on her tiptoes and plants a soft kiss on Tom's jaw just near the corner of his mouth, leaving his coffee-brown eyes shining with either tears or wonder, Isadora isn't sure. She pats a hand on his chest and walks away, the river's ever-present gurgling fading into nothing as she goes.

Whatever golden glow had existed down by the river recedes drastically and clearly had not occurred near the house. Nothing of that magical hideaway is present here, except the lingering warmth of Tom's fingers on her cheekbone. Isadora wonders how on earth Isabella could have left behind a man so devoted, so shamelessly smitten with her, for an existence so barren of life and love and so hideously shrouded in horror. Why live in a repeating cycle of blood, gore and desolation when she could so easily create a world of comfort?

Inside, Isadora knows why.

It is easier to wallow in the dark than find the strength to seek the light.

XVIII | THE MOON

S he knows she paints a despondent image as she enters the house and closes the door firmly behind her. For once the foyer is almost empty, only one lone ghost swinging dreamily from the chandelier cord and humming a nonsensical tune. Its ghostly tears drop onto Isadora's shoulder as she passes by. She wipes them away absently as she continues on, looking for Will. He should, hopefully, still be sequestered away in the library reading up a storm. Isadora crosses her fingers and hopes he's found something helpful.

Her life feels like a never-ending wheel of wishing for results and seeing nothing but a snail-trail of tidbits – each one, hopefully, leading to a satisfying ending. Only it's taking so much longer than she wants it to. She sighs. Okay, so destiny can't be rushed through to the finish; it can only be tenderly 'poked' in the right direction.

Her maudlin mulling is interrupted as a Will shaped blur flies around a corner up ahead, skidding to a stop just in front of her. Isadora shrieks, hands flying up to protect her face as Will stands panting, a heavy, leather-bound book held aloft in his pale hands.

"Jesus Will!" Isadora slaps his arm. "Don't do that!"

"Ouch!" Will cringes away. "Don't hit me … especially when I've found something you're going to be interested in." He holds the tome aloft, pages crinkling under the pressure. Isadora zeroes in on the book and peers.

"What? What have you found?"

Will clears his throat importantly, opens the book and scans the pages, finally settling on one and tapping one sentence triumphantly. "Bones," he announces. Isadora doesn't follow. Her dark brows crease in the centre.

"Bones? Please elaborate for me. I'm not following your genius."

"If all else fails you can burn the bones." Will thrusts the book under his sister's nose, which scrunches up as a cloud of ancient dust shoots unpleasantly up her nostrils.

"Thanks," she gasps, accepting the heavy book to scan through herself. Clearly, succinctly sharing information without any context is one of Will's strengths. She reads quickly, skipping chunks here and there until she reaches the passage Will has so helpfully indicated. Her frown relaxes as her brows, instead, shoot up in disbelief. "Salting and burning bones?" She peeks over at Will. "That's your Plan B?"

"Do we even have a Plan A?"

"I was getting there," Isadora rebukes, chewing on her lip. "I just haven't had time to share with the class yet. We're on a time crunch."

"*And* you were too busy making lovey-dovey eyes at To~om," Will sing-songs, hands clasped under his chin, lips pursed in a soppy pucker. Isadora's fist rises fast as a rearing snake, causing Will to back away hastily.

"Didn't realise you'd been hired by the secret service to spy on me," Isadora says in a low, threatening tone.

Will snorts. "As if spying was even necessary. You're not as sneaky as you'd like to believe." It's so nostalgically Will that Isadora warms inside, annoyance slipping away like sand between her fingers. This arguing, this back-and-forth bickering … it's as if there is no great expanse separating them. Not even death can stop the endless, childish squabbling of siblings. It's comforting to know that not all things change following tragedy. It's even as though Will forgets himself sometimes, the way people forget they're having a bad day when their best friend makes them laugh, or when they sit for a second and bask in the sun and suddenly realise that not everything has to be bad.

Isadora should listen to her internal wanderings more often. The best advice to take is so often your own.

"So, are you going to share with the class?" Will prompts when Isadora remains silent just that little bit too long. Isadora nods.

"Tom was helpful. He's pretty sure we're dealing with Isabella – and I am, too. It sounds like I was right, after the séance. She's angry, upset. Guilty, above all else. She thinks what happened to her sister was her fault. Thus," she gestures around, "this is all down to Isabella and her guilt. This has all happened because of that one moment that she thinks was her fault. We need to find a way to get through to her and convince her that it wasn't. Maybe then she'll be at peace and stop punishing herself – and me – for what happened. If we don't, it will all start up again with a different version of us and then it really will be a curse. Maybe. My point still stands. We need to find a way to break the chain and send her on."

It sounds and feels right in a way Isadora can only describe as innate.

"Any idea as to what the solution might be?" Will asks. Isadora can only shake her head, disappointed.

"Not yet. I'm hoping I'll think of something. Hopefully."

"And if you don't?"

Isadora smiles thinly, "At least we have a Plan B?"

"Yeah. Okay." Will returns her smile softly.

"Right, so secret side journeys aside," Isadora reins herself back into the here and now. "You're thinking that if we somehow track down where Isabella's remains are, we can hold them as blackmail? If you don't surrender and accept that you aren't guilty of killing your little sibling, we'll burn your bones?"

Will nods, jumping back into the prior conversation. "Yeah, exactly. Maybe not said quite like that, but yeah. Also, should we really be plotting like this in her house? What if she hears us?" Will is thinking aloud now, his gaze darting around. Isadora rolls her eyes and sighs.

"She's too lost in her own grief and misery to care what we're doing at the moment."

"Right. So all your little spacey episodes are, what? Something to do with that? With her?" Will asks, genuinely curious. Isadora clutches her Amethyst.

"Probably. I think I'm tuning into whatever residual energy is hanging around. Being connected to her probably intensifies the experience. I don't know. Maybe she wants me to know how guilty we are. How much we need to suffer for our mistakes. How much our families hate us."

"Do you have any factual basis for this, or is it all bullshit?" Will arches a thin brow, a small, sly grin playing at the corner of his mouth. One of his dimples pops.

"Isabella is selfish. She doesn't care about anything but herself," Isadora says casually. "She's like me. She is me. We are one."

Will snorts. "Alright, whatever you reckon. Your family doesn't hate you, just so you're aware." He adds it as an aside, like it's of no significance for Isadora to hear it, before drawing her attention back down to the leather-bound book. "Should we go for it? Find the bones? Have some insurance in case Plan A goes to hell?"

Isadora tucks some stray hair behind her ear, deciding to ignore Will's comment about their family. Her grey eyes are serious as she nods. "Yeah. Although apparently you should never have a Plan B," she tells Will. "If you do, your Plan A is more likely to fail."

"Another one of your facts?"

"What can I say? I'm a smart gal. I love a good fact."

"Okay, well, the fact is you're an idiot."

Their bickering carries down through the empty halls of the house, threading and weaving gracefully on the air, unheard by anyone but themselves. There are no ghosts to be seen. The sky outside is darkening into velvety night, the heavens sewn with tiny, twinkling stars whose beauty is dead long before their light ever makes the journey to Earth.

XIX | THE SUN

They're going with the 'burn the bones' plan at this stage, while the other plan is on hold. At least then, if all else fails, Isadora knows she has a leg-up.

"If I were a record of burial, where would I be hiding?" Isadora mumbles to herself as she paces up and down, eyes scanning the library shelves. She knows it's a long shot that there may be pertinent information hidden among the dusty tomes, but she doesn't want to go back to Tom. He's given her enough already; indeed, he's been an informative saviour. And she doesn't think she'll be able to access Jane, as her ghost appears to be a smokescreen for Isabella's poorly hidden guilt. Perhaps Jane's ghost has been a fake all along.

Thus, books are her only hope at this stage – unless Bee can rustle up another ghost who has some knowledge. But the demon had not been at all impressed when Isadora asked it to help, bristling arrogantly as if the task was beneath its dignity. With a flash of its pearlescent eyes, it had bounded off into the night, slinky black body swallowed up by the gloom. No doubt it thinks it's already done enough to help.

This had been some time ago and nary a flicker of whiskers has been seen since. Will had also agreed to see if he could rustle up any other sources and melted away to ask around. He, too, is yet to reappear.

The leather-bound books gleam at her, their spines decorated sumptuously in golden decals. Words are swimming through her brain, but none appear to hold any of the meaning she is seeking. There is one book, however, that seems vaguely promising … *Genealogy: A Guide to the Archer Family Tree*, she reads. Isadora plucks it off the shelf and sets it on an antique lamp table for later perusal if she can't find anything else. And it seems increasingly likely that this will be the case.

Isadora sighs as she reaches the last row of books, none of which promise to be even remotely helpful to her search. Pacing back the way she has come, Isadora plops down into the musty velvet wingback chair next to the table and turns on her phone flashlight to read – then immediately wants to hit herself on the head. Being stuck in this old house has set her thought process back by a hundred years. Why bother delving into books when there's the internet? There has to be a website to search for graves or locate specific resting places, she tells herself. Isadora types away, chewing on her lip as a list of possibilities pops up. She scrolls impatiently past the ads and speed-reads the top suggestions, finally settling on one that looks reputable.

She types 'Isabella Archer' into the 'Grave' search bar.

Only a couple of hundred responses emerge. Damn her for having such a basic name.

Isadora quickly weeds out the listings that have either died recently or are not in local cemeteries. She highly doubts Isabella would be buried too far from the house; even so, there are several likely options she and Will could search through, and she doesn't have time to manually search each one. Finally, Isadora has a shortened list of a few candidates. Each name opens up to reveal a short profile of the person, their family ties and the plot numbers. Perfect. It doesn't take long to narrow the list after that.

"There you are …" Isadora murmurs softly. She memorises the cemetery name and plot number, typing them into her Notes app just in case her memory buckles under the pressure when she and Will eventually get round to the actual grave robbing part.

Jumping up excitedly, she flies to the door and hustles down the stairs calling her brother's name, mentally recalling Bee at the same time. Bee materialises almost instantly, head cocked curiously as it peers at her from atop the banister, long, spiked tail flicking back and forth.

"You seen Will?" Isadora asks hurriedly, moving on almost instantly when Bee shakes its inky head.

Bee leaps onto Isadora's shoulders as she passes, claws digging into her skin through her jumper. Isadora gasps at the sharp pierce of pain, but makes no move to dislodge the creature.

"Will!" Isadora cups her hands around her mouth and yells, sending Bee's thorny ears swivelling backwards to press flat against its head, a hiss building in the back of its throat. Isadora ignores the gleaming white fangs and continues on. In sharp contrast to last night, the house's walls are now littered with ghosts, their hazy white bodies floating and thronging casually as if they are gathered for a delightful party where all that is served is finger sandwiches and cups of weak tea. Isadora shoves her way through them, elbows jabbing and hands pushing, ignoring their grumbles of discontent and the sensation of whispery spider-webbing as she pushes past.

Finally, she spots Will's curls as he, too, barges his way through the crowd. He follows Isadora outside into the open air as she signals furiously at him.

"What's got them so happy?" Isadora asks as soon as the door shuts behind them. Will shrugs.

"Something in the air, I guess."

"Gross," Isadora mutters, reaching up and dislodging Bee from her shoulder. Bee jumps down and settles on the concrete banister, scaly skin shining in the sun. "Never mind any of that now," Isadora hurries on. "I've found her!"

Will shakes his head. "And I did all that networking for nothing." But he smiles at her regardless, happy at his sister's success, "Congrats, detective ... where is it?"

Isadora checks her phone before answering. "Highfield Cemetery." She and Will meet each other's eyes. "It's all the way across town," Isadora realises belatedly, not having considered this fact until now. It made the logistics of their travel harder, as it wasn't a distance Isadora could walk without being noticed, even in the dark. Especially in the dark.

Will gazes off into the distance, face clouded with thought. Isadora chews on her lip, fingers playing along her chin. They skitter across a sore little bump that is likely to explode into a stress pimple within the next few days. Hopefully it will hold off until this is all over. She can only deal with one awful thing at a time. While this nonsensical thought rattles around her brain, Will's thoughtful expression clears to reveal a sunny smile, along with a glint in his eye that Isadora has not seen since his death.

"How about a little grand theft auto?" Will asks slyly, dimples on full display. It takes a second for Isadora to grasp what on earth he is talking about, and once she does, she frowns.

"Is it technically grand theft auto if it's my car?"

"Lawful theft auto?"

After briefly arguing over the merits of stealing her own car, Isadora and Will devise a plan. Bee watches them idly from behind omniscient milky eyes. Eventually, they decide on doing it that night, unwilling to waste any time in acquiring Isabella's bones.

"How do you feel about playing spy?" Isadora asks as they head out the front door and down the steps, feet scraping against the concrete. Bee weaves in between her legs, tail held loftily high, clearly in good spirits at the opportunity to escape the confines of the house. Isadora can relate.

Will grins. "Get to double-o-seven it up? Can I pretend to have an earpiece in?"

Isadora heaves an exaggerated sigh. "I guess."

"Great." Will stuffs his hands into his pockets and strolls along merrily enough. Although Isadora can see the mask for what it is, she decides not to comment. On reaching the overgrown iron fence, she shifts it aside to make room for her spiritual companions, hefting it back into place once they pass. Going around to the front of their house will be safer than trying to sneak in the back way where there's too much of a chance they'll be spotted. The back doors are all glass and look right out onto the spacious back yard from the open kitchen and living room. They'd be seen approaching a mile away. And besides, Isadora doesn't want to jump the back fence; her jeans are already ripped from ducking around that stupid iron fence.

Once they've left the tranquillity of the sheltered country road, Isadora straightens her spine and walks with purpose, as if she knows exactly what she is doing and has every right to do it. Will and Bee wander along far more nonchalantly, given their invisible status.

The house comes into view. There are no lights on inside, which is promising; hopefully their parents are deeply asleep. Isadora shoos Will inside, anyway, just to make sure. He gives her a small salute as he passes seamlessly through the front door. Isadora waits casually on the sidewalk leaning against one of the power poles, eyes scanning left to right in case someone comes along. No one does. The road is silent and still. Bee keeps her company, prowling around her ankles in a comforting fashion. It's even started up a rumbling chainsaw purr.

Eventually, Will reappears with a finger to his ear. "All clear, Spooky 1," he announces in a low rasp. Isadora rolls her eyes and shifts past him.

"Did you unlock the door?" she asks quietly. Will nods, saluting once more.

"Affirmative."

"Stop acting like a child and take this seriously," Isadora hisses, her jangling nerves overcoming her.

Will's face falls into a crestfallen pout. "You *said* I could spy it up!" he protests, a distinct whine in his voice. Isadora ignores him, focusing instead on turning the front door handle as slowly and smoothly as possible, pushing the door open inch-by-inch when the latch clicks gently. There is no other noise as it swings open. Isadora breathes out slowly and enters, silent as a ghost. Luckily, she is wearing sneakers with soft, worn soles and they make little to no noise as she creeps stealthily through the front hall, moving with deliberate slowness to avoid one of her trademark stumbles.

The kitchen comes into view, and beyond it the glass doors out to the back lawn and pool. There's a tennis ball floating on the calm surface. Isadora's insides squirm uncomfortably and she sneaks a discreet look at Will, who has perched himself on the kitchen bench and is seemingly engrossed in examining the fruit bowl.

Isadora slinks over to her brother, "Where have they put the keys?" she murmurs so quietly the words are almost lost to her own ears.

Will points to the small wooden bowl next to the fruit. Inside is an assortment of car keys, including the one's belonging to Will's totalled car. Studiously ignoring those ones, Isadora fishes through the bowl, panic rising as her fingers fail to find her own personalised keyring. Her foraging becomes more desperate and distinctly louder in the thick silence. Her forehead is beading with sweat.

"Looking for these?"

Isadora jumps violently, bashing her hip on the edge of the marble kitchen counter as the living room lights blaze to life.

Her keys dangle a distance away, enamel keyring catching the light as it lazily spins from its hook over her dad's index finger. She can't meet his eye, although she feels the intensity of his gaze fixed on her burning face. She breaks her staring contest with the keyring to throw Will a dirty look. He shrugs from his perch on the counter.

"Isadora?" Her dad's voice floats across the room, quiet enough that it won't reach anywhere else in the house, yet loud enough to boom and echo like a gunshot through her own head.

"Hey," Isadora twists her hands together awkwardly, keeping her eyes on the floor. "Wasn't expecting you to be awake."

"Clearly. Or else you would have knocked," her dad replies dryly, eyes still boring holes into the top of Isadora's head with such intensity she wonders if her hair might catch fire.

He doesn't appear angry. Not nearly as angry as Isadora had supposed her parents would be if in the worst-case scenario – thanks Will! – they caught her out. Instead, he seems … Isadora can't put her finger on it. Can't decide how he seems to be feeling – and that worries her.

She begins to fidget, picking at her nails anxiously as she draws in a tremulous breath to speak. But her dad beats her to it.

"It's good to see you, Issy," he says quietly. Isadora's fidgeting stops.

"It is?" she asks hesitantly.

Her dad shifts, setting her keys down on the counter with a clatter far too loud for the cavernous silence surrounding them. He steps forward, determined now in his movements. Isadora shrinks back as he approaches, feeling distinctly trapped by the counter at her back and wondering frantically how she might be able to make a clean escape, then—

Strong, steady arms wrap securely around her, pulling her into a warm embrace. Her brain short-circuits for a second, not comprehending the warmer-than-she-ever-could-have-expected welcome. Eyes wide, Isadora simply stands encircled in her dad's hug. She spots Will shifting into view over his broad shoulder. His eyes are warm but misted over with a desperate yearning. A hunger and longing for the affection his ghostly body has all but forgotten. Isadora's face scrunches up despite herself, guilt stirring in her writhing stomach. But Will doesn't look jealous. Despite the obvious craving he's feeling, he looks surprisingly happy for her. The smile on his face reaches his eyes. Go on, it seems to say. Hug him back. It's okay to enjoy it.

So Isadora does. She throws her arms around her father, reciprocating the love she had thought long gone. She squeezes her eyes shut as a hot flush of tears spills down her cheeks. To hear and feel another human heartbeat in such close proximity is something she hadn't realised she'd been missing until now. And here it is, fierce and steadfast. She soaks it in, like a parched sponge without moisture for too long.

Neither parent nor siblings say anything for a long while, until eventually Isadora's father releases her and steps away. His eyes are suspiciously red.

"We've missed you," he admits finally after another charged moment of staring. Isadora shrugs one shoulder self-consciously.

"I'm sorry," she replies honestly. It was never her intention to hurt her parents. But the stifling atmosphere following Will's departure had been too much to bear. And the scene she had caused in the mall had been so scary, so upsetting, she had honestly thought it was in her parents' best interests for her to disappear. They were normal people with normal lives. She couldn't allow her freakishness to continue to harm their livelihoods. Not like that. Her parents did not deserve the town's ire.

"Both of you."

Isadora blinks. She looks up through her curtain of hair in shock. Her dad is meeting her gaze. It strikes her with the force of a hammer that he means it. His eyes scour the kitchen, straining as if hoping, perhaps, to spot a faded silvery outline, the barest suggestion that Will is here with them in this clean suburban kitchen.

"He's right behind you," Isadora rasps, pointing. She tries to ignore the way her arm is shaking.

Her dad's eyes widen, and he turns sharply, peering into the darkness. Will jumps, drawing back as his father's head swivels this way and that, like a searchlight seeking comfort, safety in a tumultuous emotional sea. Isadora feels her heart sink as her dad scans straight past Will, whose hopeful expression drops away resignedly. His head dips down, Adam's apple bobbing sharply while his hands slip shakily into his pants pockets. Their dad turns to face Isadora once more. Another bout of tears is threatening to slip past his defences, and his mouth is a thin, trembling line. Isadora clears her throat awkwardly.

"I'm sorry."

But her dad is already shaking his greying head. "Not—" his voice cracks and he swallows. "Not your fault," he finishes. He blinks rapidly. "Not your fault, Isadora," he repeats softly.

Isadora notices Will slipping away and out into the hall without a backwards glance, head bowed in defeat. *She should do something.* She should delve into the well inside herself, pour some of whatever it is that exists there into Will to make him real, to allow her dad to see him. To start mending wounds so deep they've become chasms.

But she doesn't.

She keeps her eyes trained on the doorway as she replies, "Can I have my keys now. Please?"

If her dad is disappointed, he doesn't show it. Simply takes a step back and fixes her with a look she can't see enough of in the gloom to decipher. She waits until the jangle of her keys splits the silence. It would be nice if, for once, her family could have moments that weren't filled with uncomfortable silences. It's been happening far too frequently recently. Still, Isadora stretches out a hand and accepts the cold, metallic weight, curling her fingers around them tightly and murmuring a 'thank you' before turning and leaving.

She doesn't look back. Just like Will. Instead, she closes the front door behind her with a snap of finality, and hustles over to her car. The white paint gleams in what little moonlight is making its way through the clouds wafting above. Will is leaning against the passenger door with Bee curling sinuous infinity signs between his legs. Its moon-white eyes pierce the gloom. Isadora ignores the stare, unlocks her car and gestures for them both to climb in.

Without waiting for all the doors to close, she inserts the key and starts the engine. "Here …" she tosses Will her phone, which he catches seamlessly while staring sightlessly into the footwell. "Pull up a map, would you? I don't know the way."

Will lets go a stutter of breath and starts pressing the buttons, pausing only to shove the screen in Isadora's face so she can unlock it. Then they're on their way. There's no chatter, only the crappy late-night radio with its unrelenting dance music to keep them company. Every so often Isadora checks the rear vision mirror, only to be met with an unrelenting white stare. Bee appears to be enjoying itself, anyway. Will is determinedly staring out the window with enough intensity to break the glass if he tried hard enough. Isadora doesn't ask any questions. What little progress they had made as a family unit had dissipated in that cold, sterile kitchen. Eventually, however, when they're fifteen minutes into their journey, Isadora can't help herself,

"You're a terrible spy."

Will snorts wetly and wipes a ghostly sleeve across his face. He surveys the map. "Make a right at the next intersection."

Isadora checks her mirrors and flicks on the indicator as they approach the T-junction. "You wouldn't last five minutes in a spy movie."

"You wouldn't last five minutes in a horror movie."

Isadora grins. "Touché." She turns right smoothly. The siblings fall back into their old habitual silence.

"Driveway should be coming up on your right," Will says eventually. Isadora surveys the road ahead, spotting a break in the hawthorn hedges. A gravel road leads up and away into the night. She flicks on her indicator and turns, car jolting and swaying on the dips and bumps worn into the gravel – rivulets now barren from months of no rain but where water surely runs during winter, carved into the ground.

The road inclines up a gentle slope and Isadora can just make out the tall, streamlined silhouette of an elegant church, a vast contrast to the blocky structure at the cemetery closer to home. Oak trees come into view as the headlights sweep across the sheltered churchyard. A second building, presumably the Vicar's house, is just off to the left surrounded by a wrought-iron fence smothered in ivy. The church itself is dark brick with a typical triangular steeple pointing up to the heavens. Isadora is certain that in daylight this churchyard would be magnificent. By night it is just as blank and deserted as the rest of the world.

Isadora squints into the darkness beyond the church and draws the car to a stop when the first pearly gleam of marble shines into view. Leaving the car radio running and the lights on, Isadora exits the car and moves off towards the cemetery. Will and Bee follow just behind. She swings open the well-maintained gate and steps aside to let Bee and Will through, leaving it propped open as she follows them into the dark graveyard, her phone torch held aloft so she can see the names inscribed on each headstone.

"I was expecting company," Will says conversationally. Isadora flicks him a quick look before returning to her search.

"Cemeteries aren't as haunted as people think."

"Why's that?" Will sounds genuinely curious. Isadora shrugs, crouching down and wiping some grime away to read the name on an impressive grey marble tombstone. It isn't Isabella's.

"Don't know. For some reason the places most commonly assumed to be haunted rarely are. You're far more likely to experience a haunting in your own home than at, say, an abandoned hospital."

Will cocks his head to the side. "Are you sure that's true? Or are you bullshitting me?"

Isadora grins. "Bullshitting, I'm afraid. I actually have no idea why there aren't more ghosts here. I hardly ever have any idea what's going on, anyway. I make it up half the time. It's not like there's a manual or guidebook for these sorts of things."

Will snorts. "You should write one then. Become a bestseller. You'd never have to go to another job interview."

Isadora shines her phone light on the next tombstone. "As appealing as that sounds, I don't have time right now. Maybe once all this stuff has been sorted, I'll think about it. Write my memoir … if I make it out alive."

She spots Bee trotting along one of the rows ahead and tracks its progress, watching as its lithe, skeletal body comes to a stop, nose sniffing at one of the graves. Bee prowls back and forth, hackles raised, until it appears to come to a decision. It stops and sits, head raised, milky-white eyes gleaming over at Isadora and Will. Isadora can almost see a little thought bubble forming above Bee's head.

This one. It's this one.

Isadora walks over with Will by her side, carefully avoiding stepping on any graves. Isadora ignores Bee's impatient head flick and examines the worn writing carefully. It's barely visible, old and crumbling as it is, but Isadora can see enough to recognise that Bee is correct.

This is, indeed, Isabella Archer's final resting place.

"Right," Isadora huffs, more to herself than anyone else, only to realise something very important is missing. "Shit." If her hands weren't full of phone and anxiety, she would hit herself. Will looks around.

"What's wrong?"

"I didn't bring anything to dig her up!"

Will stares at her, mouth dropping. "What?" He sounds incredulous, like it's so ridiculous that Isadora should forget something as crucial as a shovel for this mission. Isadora flares up angrily.

"If I hadn't been so worried about getting caught sneaking into my house I might have remembered!" she snarls. "And seeing as that ended up being an absolute disaster, is it really so shocking that it might have slipped my mind?" It's a direct jab at Will and he knows it, face flooding with colour in a way so reminiscent of his living days (and one that should not be possible now he's dead and doesn't have any blood to blush with) that Isadora is a little taken aback.

"Well, *sorryyy*! Sorry for wanting to see my dad for the first time in weeks!"

"It was the first time for me too!" Isadora fires back, becoming increasingly irate. Bee hisses at them, wide eyes peering over Isadora's shoulder as the siblings carry on squabbling, making no effort to keep their voices down.

"Oh, bully for you, you selfish cow!" Will yells right back. "You're not dead! At least people acknowledge you. At least your own parents can still see and talk to you if you ever deign to come down from your high horse and visit them!"

He's hit a sore spot. "You bitch!" Isadora shrieks, launching herself at her brother, fists clenched with fury and striking at anything within reach. Will doesn't recoil from her barrage; rather, he is incensed that she has allowed him to become corporeal so she can attack him.

"You're the bitch!" And he raises his own fists. The two get stuck in a flurry of flying limbs, shouted curses and pulled hair. Amongst the madness, Bee hisses again, back arching as a light flares inside the vicar's house, startled exclamations floating clearly across the air.

Bee leaps atop Isabella's tombstone and swipes at Isadora, missing by only centimetres as she and Will continue to tussle. It becomes increasingly violent as Will snags the upper hand and tosses his sister to the hard earth, although she doesn't go quietly and refuses to release her hold on his shirt, tugging him roughly down as she aims a nasty kick at his knee. He falls with a yelp and the fight continues on the ground. Bee glances anxiously between them and the light now bobbing ever closer across the churchyard, past the iron gate and into the cemetery.

"Oi!" A harsh bark splits the night air, bringing Isadora and Will's fight to an abrupt, shocked stop. Isadora hastily pushes herself to her feet, not bothering to offer Will a hand up as she is not sure whether anyone else can see him at this moment. Unsure whether her anger and desire to hit him has made him visible to others.

"What on earth are you doing?" the caretaker (or Vicar? Isadora isn't quite certain) growls. He peers at her, simultaneously incredulous and angry, face red and ruddy in the yellow glow of his torch.

"Um …" Isadora thinks fast. There is, in fact, no reasonable explanation for being here in the middle of the night – or for the volley of loud swearing that has been going on. She's stumped for a second. The caretaker can see this and is just in the process of pulling himself up to full height and inflating his chest importantly – to yell at her, no doubt – when his face suddenly drains until it's the colour of spoiled milk. Isadora starts and then, realising his line of sight is now over her left shoulder and not on her face, twitches and turns ever so slightly. Understanding washes over her in an annoying wave of relief.

There's a glowing silver ghost standing a few rows over.

Despite her panic, Isadora gets an idea.

"I wouldn't move if I were you," she intones seriously. The caretaker's eyes snap back to her, wide and worried.

"W-why not?" he manages past trembling lips, anger all but forgotten. Isadora smirks in what she hopes is a cold and calculated manner.

"They don't like sudden movements. Neither do I."

His eyes bulge. "You can see it, too?"

Isadora chuckles. "Of course I can!" She raises one hand. "I am, after all, the one who summoned them here." This could be true – is, in fact, most likely true, even if it was accidental. It was probably her panicking that did it. Or perhaps the rush of strong emotion when she and Will were fighting.

The caretaker staggers back. "Send it back then!"

Isadora hums, tapping at her lips faux thoughtfully as Will clambers to his feet behind her. She can feel her heart thudding so rapidly she is briefly concerned it will rattle its way right up her throat and jump out of her mouth. Thankfully, it doesn't appear that the caretaker has noticed this, which Isadora is grateful for. Will definitely has, however.

Ignoring the questioning poke in the ribs from her brother, Isadora draws her lips back into a sly smile and shakes her head. "No. I don't think I will. Unless …" she lets the word trail off, drawing all the ethereal strength that she has access to underneath all the anxiety. That ever-present cold well of energy that stirs within her centre ripples in anticipation as the caretaker lurches forward.

"Unless what?" he asks, desperately clutching at his torch, eyes intermittently flicking between Isadora and the puzzled spirit lingering at the back, still glowing like a star between the tombstones.

"Leave this place," Isadora declares, clenching her fists and drawing the energy forward. She can see more spirits flickering to life, some that had been there already, albeit only weakly, nothing more than spectral imprints hovering about in the air, and others that she's pulled from God knows where.

They flare brightly, Will included, each lit with a spooky blue glow and, suddenly, they are all bearing down on the poor caretaker who very nearly faints at the horrifying sight. Each ghost is as ghastly as the next, except for Will, who, upon realising he can be seen, smiles brightly (too brightly to be genuine) and waves enthusiastically at the poor man who begins to sway in place, torch dipping haphazardly as his knees knock together.

Before any sort of moaning or tortured groaning can start up Isadora adds her final request. "Tell no one about what you have seen this night. Or I shall make you suffer, dogged by spirits until the end of your days, where I will find you and make you walk in the shadow of life for the rest of your existence."

The caretaker gapes. He closes his mouth then opens it again, but no sound comes out. Isadora rolls her eyes and gestures impatiently in the direction of his house.

"Go!" she commands.

The caretaker scrambles on the spot, feet attempting to take him in two directions at once before they come together and he runs for the safety of his house, blubbering in terror.

Isadora grins once his retreat is complete.

"Couldn't have done this back home?" Isadora turns to find Will gesturing at his incandescent body and scowls.

"Give it a rest," she replies darkly.

Will, looking furious, is just opening his mouth to reply when—

"Excuse me?"

Isadora looks over at one nervous spirit, its hand raised timidly. Isadora nods for the ghost to continue, but her hands start to clutch at the bottom of her jumper as the sheer number of visible, summoned spirits sinks in. They are everywhere. Some look confused, others distinctly annoyed. Isadora opts to ignore those ones and focuses instead on the ghost that is now lowering its silver hand,

"What have you done to us?" The ghost doesn't look accusing. Its expression is mildly twisted but polite enough that Isadora decides she can answer.

"I made you all corporeal." She gestures at the other floating spectres. "I even summoned some of you here. Sorry about that," she adds hastily as a few of the ghosts advance rather threateningly. The chill in the air intensifies as they begin to crowd closer and closer until they've formed a complete circle around Isadora and Will. Bee arches its back and snarls, tail lashing sharply in the ghosts' direction to keep them at bay.

"You would presume to command us? Us!" one of the ghosts shouts. "We who defy death by remaining on her lands? We who defy the laws of earth of our own choosing? I think not!"

Others take up the protest, adding their own voices and reasonings. Isadora falters, having never been met with this amount of rebellion by the spirits before. Then again, she had never willingly summoned them before (with one exception).

"You pulled me from my rest!"

"I was bossed around enough in my life. I won't have it in death!"

"I wanted to be left in peace!"

"I was conscripted to the army once. I will not do it again! No man nor woman owns me!"

A chilling howl starts up, joined gradually by more and more grating voices answering the call. Some gurgle while others screech, and they join together in a discordant harmony that ripples up and into the night air. Isadora fights the urge to clap her hands over her ears as her age-old coping mechanism fights for dominance.

Show them no weakness.

"I can send you back!" Isadora tries to shout over the cacophony. She may as well have been yelling into a vacuum for all the good it does. The ghosts get closer still, increasingly wound up by the ruckus. Isadora feels a hand snatch at her hair, long nails scraping against her scalp. She leaps back, disgusted, hands flying to her head. She spins, seeking an escape, only to be met with an unstoppable wall of glowing white. Another ghost reaches out and snags her sleeve, tugging her off balance and into the melee. Isadora shrieks as she falls, panic beginning to pulse in her stomach. It only makes things worse. The spirits glow brighter, their luminescence swelling into an almost neon shine. Isadora vaguely hears Will's voice calling out for her amid the screaming.

Isadora is forced to her knees beneath the mountain of spirits. She draws her limbs in and curls into a ball as their furious fists pound her and nails rake down her back and around her head, tearing and ripping into her clothes, pulling at her hair and grasping at her neck. Her chest feels like it's shrinking. There is no air for her to breathe. She is being crushed beneath a pressure so heavy it feels as though it's going to force her into the ground and put her six feet below so she can join them in their misery.

All other sound fades away as her mind retreats into the panic of the moment. The pain recedes and everything becomes muffled, as if she has fallen into a crashing wave and is being kept pinned underneath by the current. Isadora holds her breath and waits with her eyes scrunched closed, completely ready to surrender to the spirits and allow them to wash her away.

Then a searing rush of pain splinters across her arm. A deep, ripping sensation followed by a cascade of warmth and wetness she vaguely recognises. One of the ghosts has torn at her arm so badly she is bleeding – and rather heavily at that.

No, she thinks suddenly. Clarity sweeps back in, pushing aside the calm acceptance of fate she had become so accustomed to.

No, not this time.

Isadora allows the heat in her injured arm to spread up into her shoulder, down her chest and right into her centre where that ever-present well of repressed rage resides. The door yawns open, exposing the dark depths that lie within and pulling them forth as anger surges and pulses within her. A blinding flash of light illuminates the cemetery. The weight pushing down on her body vanishes as, in a burst of super-human energy she hurls the spirits off her. Now they are lying, sprawled in the dirt, no longer ethereal beings feeding on the remnants of life the world had left behind for them. They are no longer as scary or impervious to hurt as they had been before. And Isadora is not about to let this opportunity go. Not when there are so many of them at her disposal.

The frustration and hopeless anger that had been mounting ever since that day in the mall is now ready to boil up and brim over – and Isadora is letting it. She deserves this. This cathartic release of all her dark, unwelcome emotions. She wants to give in, let it overcome her and devour her completely.

Isadora unfurls from her foetal position, pushes herself to her feet and stares down at them. She is awash with power … pure energy howls within her. Her measly ability to see what others can't has been transformed into something else, something far more dangerous. Something, she knows, is deeply rooted in the creation of all things. And in this moment, it is hers to command.

The ghosts sense this instinctually and begin drawing into themselves, shrinking away from her and the halo of light that now surrounds her body – a stark contrast to mere moments ago when they had heralded their own power and wielded it against her. *They are pathetic*, Isadora thinks.

"Touch me again and I'll send you so far into the unknown your family will forget you ever existed!" she hisses, focusing particularly on the ghost who had scratched her. She can actually see her blood dripping from its gnarled, overgrown fingernails. It cringes, begging wordlessly with wide, dark eyes. Isadora clenches a fist, and the ghost shrieks, tumbling backwards and scuttling away in palpable fright. Isadora inhales its fear. It smells delicious, intoxicating. She is just raising both her hands, cresting on a wave of indestructibility, when—

"Dora, don't." A hand clamps down on her shoulder, ripping her away from the heights her soul had ascended too and bringing her tumbling back to earth. She whirls around, hand raised in fury, to meet Will's dark eyes. They are stern and serious but also – Isadora sees as she squints – flickering with apprehension, with uncertainty.

With fear.

Her stomach sinks.

No. No.

She closes her eyes and inhales deeply, willing that irresistible, unquenchable power licking at her insides back up to the surface. It's no good. She winces as she pushes it back down into the bottomless pit from which it had spilled. Her face is glazed with sweat, and when she opens her eyes, her vision is swimming from the effort. She staggers, supported by Will's glowing arm, and grimaces as a spiky tail grazes her leg, slicing right through her jeans and drawing her attention to the warmth of the blood as it trickles down her ankles and pools in her socks. She focuses on the dulled pain and the coppery tang, the fading warmth and tacky, wet pull on her skin as she flexes her ankle.

Slowly, the neon glow cloaking the graveyard fades into a pastel luminescence. The ghosts are still there but they are now subdued, cowed into stillness by the threat of banishment, of Isadora and the power she had wielded.

She doesn't look the picture of a fearless medium any longer. Whereas only seconds ago she had been as radiant as a full moon she is now a ragged, sweaty mess. Strands of her hair are plastered to her forehead, and her eyes are hazy and unfocused; she is being held aloft only by her brother and the faithful demon cat whose slinky body is wrapped completely around her legs.

But she knows that well is still there and always will be, ready to rise and swell like a tsunami should the need arise. The ghosts keep well clear of her for this fact alone.

Isadora realises belatedly that she is now too weak to help Will dig up Isabella's casket. "Damn," she mutters, pulling away from him and wavering as her knees threaten to buckle beneath her.

"What?" Will asks, keeping a stray hand out in case she falls over. Isadora throws him a look.

"I'm so stupid."

"That doesn't help me," Will retorts. Isadora grumbles.

"Do I look like I'm in any state right now to be grave robbing?"

Will shrugs. "Anything is possible if you're desperate enough."

"Will!"

"What?" His voice pitches on a small laugh. "It's true!"

"Help me with some suggestions, please." Isadora whines, settling herself atop a gravestone and breathing deeply. Every bone in her body is heavy, laden down with exhaustion. Who knew first-time real medium shenanigans could be so tiresome?

"Look around you," Will gestures. "You have plenty of helping hands."

He's right. All the ghosts are still there, milling around hesitantly and eyeing her suspiciously – but they're there. And they are able-bodied enough. Most of them.

"Nice one, Will," she admits and waves them over. They answer her call immediately. From her perilous spot on Isabella's tombstone, Isadora addresses the ghosts breathlessly.

"Help him dig. Don't stop until you hit something solid." And to her surprise they leap to it immediately. Digging on hands and knees, fingers scraping rapidly through the layers of dirt and mud, steadily sinking as the pile of displaced earth behind them grows bigger and bigger. Bee settles in behind Isadora, helping to keep her sagging body upright so she can watch their progress. Will doesn't complain once, nor does he rib Isadora for not helping them.

"Lazing around now, girlie?" Isadora nearly flings herself off the headstone as a voice directly behind her rasps in her ear. "Is that any way to achieve a goal?"

Iris is standing there, leaning sedately on her cane and smirking far too mischievously for a woman her age.

Once Isadora's racing heart has slowed to an acceptable non-life-threatening level, she aims a glare at the shrivelled old woman while also trying to conceal just how happy she is to see Iris there. It's like having a particularly wise conscience that pops up just when you desperately need to hear from it. And that you miss dreadfully when it refuses to speak at all. She sneaks a glance at Will whose head is now only just visible above the edge of the grave (and who is definitely also smirking. Iris and Will are too similar for Isadora's tastes. Perhaps that's why she has grown so fond of the old woman).

"How did *you* get here, with your pruney old legs?" Isadora asks mockingly. "Stole some poor old duck's mobility scooter?" Iris's smug grin widens.

"You called. I answered. It would be rude to do otherwise." Iris shuttles forward and pokes Isadora in the side to make her move over and make space. Isadora does so, carefully keeping one hand on the cool marble of the headstone lest her jelly legs falter and send her careening into the dirt.

"Not sure I remember putting out the call for a senile old sultana with sticks for legs," Isadora responds. Bee sniffles and leaps onto Isadora's shoulders, tail curling around her neck to join her Amethyst, which is glowing warmly between her collarbones. Isadora jerks when she realises this, having forgotten all about it in the rush of the past few days.

"Well, I showed up anyway," Iris replies dryly. She shifts around, grimacing, "This headstone is far too harsh for my bony old arse."

Isadora snorts and immediately screws her eyes shut as a rush of lightheadedness veils her vision in a blanket of spotty black. A wizened, papery hand clutches at her exposed wrist.

"That was some light show." Isadora can hear the smile in the old lady's reedy voice. "A far more impressive show of strength than when I first met you."

Isadora chuckles mirthlessly, listening to the rhythmic scrape and *flump* of the excavated earth as Will and his companions continue their dig. "I was an awkward, angsty teenager when we first met."

Iris arches a brow. "And obviously you've changed drastically since then."

"Only on the inside."

"Very deep down."

Isadora fleetingly considers pushing Iris off the tombstone. Let's see the old crone laugh when her hip dislocates, she thinks meanly. The thought clears almost as soon as it occurs as Will clambers out of the grave, face annoyingly dirt-free. He waves frantically for his sister, his countenance lit with an enthusiasm almost alarming for an occupation such as grave desecration. Bee snuggles in tighter as Isadora heaves herself up and staggers over, peering over the edge of the grave and down into the depths of the soil to see a plain pine box. It's streaked with dirt and age but surprisingly – and frustratingly – intact.

"Don't suppose anybody brought pliers? Or a crowbar?" Isadora asks without much hope, levering herself down to sit on the edge of the grave with her legs dangling in the air. Will snorts, lifting himself out easily and settling across from her.

"There are other ways to open a box."

"Brute force?" Isadora suggests. "Iris has a mean swing with that cane."

"I'm only here for moral support," Iris sniffs from behind her. Isadora rolls her eyes.

"Of course you are," she murmurs absently, eyes roving the cemetery for ideas. Maybe she can frighten the caretaker into lending her a pickaxe or something. Or maybe …

"You there!" Isadora calls to the ghost whose nails are still stained red from her blood. "Come here!" It hastens to comply, scrambling over while simultaneously attempting to keep a fair distance away. Isadora smirks as the ghost wrestles mind against body, the push and pull of realising it will hurt if it doesn't come closer versus knowing it will risk being hurt if it does. Its long-drawn-out quandary finally ends when it falls ragged at Isadora's feet.

"How do you feel about climbing into a coffin?"

The ghost whimpers and claws at the ground, face screwed up in anguish.

"Not keen then?"

It shakes its ratty head of hair. Isadora tuts softly, leaning over (ignoring the shooting pain thrumming up her arm from her open wound) so their faces are on a more even keel and smiles mirthlessly.

"Too bad I don't care." She concentrates and carefully prods at her energy well. There's a little more there to give. Her hands glow and the ghost's body echoes the phenomenon, shining dimly in the darkness. Isadora plants her foot in the centre of the ghost's now corporeal chest. "It won't be for long." She gives it a forceful kick. The ghost howls as it topples over the edge of the grave, landing heavily on the wooden box below, hands scrabbling desperately in the dirt as it pulls itself to its knees. Isadora grins down at it and releases the energy. Her hands cease to glow, and the ghost sinks right through the casket, its dark eyes gleaming with fear. Isadora reinstates the ghost's corporeality and, just like that, the casket has two bodies trapped inside.

"What are you doing?" Will asks from just over her left shoulder. Iris is watching too, far more contemplatively than Will, whose thick brows are furrowed in confusion. Isadora shrugs.

"You can only fit so many sardines in a can before it explodes, right?"

His frown smooths out. "You're going to stuff the coffin so full of ghosts it falls apart?"

Isadora nods. "Maybe not the best plan, but it's the one I'm running with." She peers around, gaze roving over the multitude of silvery spectres floating about, then waves an arm at a nearby pack. They flock together like startled sheep when she calls to them, then make their way over, almost as reluctantly as the first ghost. Isadora nods down at the casket. "In you get." They hesitate. Isadora rolls her eyes, wincing as another throb of pain radiates from her arm. "I won't ask again," she hisses this time, half from the pain and half from sheer impatience. The ghosts don't hesitate again.

And so it goes. Isadora directs more and more trembling ghosts into the casket until she can hear the wood groaning in protest against the strain.

"It's like some kind of crazy clown car," Will comments casually, as he stares down into the gaping hole. "Only more morbid."

Isadora nods then sways with fatigue. "Shouldn't take too much more, I can see the nails starting to pop." It's true; the nails along the side of the coffin are beginning to dislodge as the wood bulges from the mass of ghosts crammed inside. "Care to do the honours?"

Will shudders. "I'd rather not."

Isadora concedes with a nod. "Fair enough," she answers. She points at a lingering spirit that is gingerly trying to sneak away into the night. It won't get far. Thank god for wrought-iron fences. "Get over here," Isadora instructs, voice stern despite her bone-aching tiredness. God, she needs a sleep-in after this. "Get in."

The ghost slumps in defeat and reluctantly drops into the grave, forcing its opaque body into the coffin, one shining limb at a time. Only this time it's too much of a squeeze for the ghost to get its head in. It simply sits there, head shining in the moonlight as the casket groans ominously, a trickle of light spilling from the splits in the wood. The trickle becomes a flood as the wood suddenly bursts apart with a shockingly loud CRACK! Ghosts of all shapes and sizes come tumbling out in a rush of silvery light in various states of disgruntle.

"Now clear out!" Isadora barks with what feels like the last vestiges of her energy. The ghosts don't need to be told twice. They scramble up the sides of the grave like ants attempting to escape a rainstorm, leaving only the busted remains of the coffin in the bottom of the hole.

And there it is. Plan B in all its glory.

Filthy, yellowed with age and splintering at the ends, what remains of Isabella Archer sits innocently in the dirt.

Isadora strips off her blood-soaked hoodie and clambers down into the grave, setting the fabric down to create a makeshift carry bag. She reaches her exposed arms out, hands hovering over the dulled set of bones. If this is going to work, she needs all of them, even if it does come down to having to burn them into dust. Thankfully, Isabella's death had taken place so long ago only a few of the major bones remain – the pelvis, two thigh bones, a couple of ribs and, finally, a grinning skull with all its teeth still in place.

Trying not to feel nauseous, Isadora reaches the rest of the way and places her fingers carefully on the skull. It's slightly roughened beneath her finger pads, dimpled with age but not as filthy as might have been expected. Clearly old-school coffins were made to do their job admirably. One hand clasps the skull, and she lifts, eyes sliding away from the bones as she places it on her hoodie, her other hand already searching for the next piece. Eventually, Isadora pulls the fabric of her hoodie up and twists it at the top, wrapping the arms around the bundle and tying them securely so she has a money-bag type situation going on, but with bones as her currency.

She hefts the parcel up and sets it at the edge of the grave, gesturing to her brother. Will comes over and lends a hand to get her out. Isadora gasps as he pulls on her injured arm. Whatever drying blood had been protecting the tender wound rips away, allowing fresh streams of warmth to run down her chilled skin. Now her T-shirt is just as ruined as her hoodie.

Landing on the cool, clean grass, Isadora flips onto her back and breathes deeply, ignoring the cold sweat beading along her forehead and dampening her armpits. She shivers in the night air, eyes swivelling to meet Will's concerned gaze. Bee pops its head over and mewls. Iris simply pokes her impatiently with her cane.

"Going to laze about all night or are we getting back to the house?"

Isadora groans, shoving her uninjured arm behind her to heft herself up from the ground. "I have to fix this first."

The wayward ghosts surrounding them nod eagerly, keen to get as far away from the crazy medium as possible.

"And that." Isadora points waveringly at the desecrated grave.

"I'll take care of that," Will responds easily, already dropping to his knees to start shovelling the dirt back into place. Isadora murmurs her thanks and allows herself another few deep breaths, reaching once more for that impossibly deep well at her centre. Now that she knows where it is, and that it's possible to unplug it and let it flow unheeded, it's much easier to call forth that everlasting energy.

Send them back!

Isadora thinks this with everything she has, feeling the energy pool in her hands and lighting them up so they are incandescent once more. The fabric of the world shifts and ripples at her command, sucking eagerly at the ghosts she has called forth. She feels their energy, connects it to the places it feels strongest, allows those grappling roots to untwine and stretch, wrapping and weaving around the spirits to whom they belong.

Go!

The vines tug. Ethereal light sets the cemetery aflame. Isadora vaguely hears Iris gasp. Then it is all fading away, fading away ... The energy retreats into the well, back into the black void. The blue warmth fades along her arms until all that's left are the goosebumps prickling on her skin. She's sweatier now. She can feel great, big droplets of it trailing down her face and onto her collarbones. Onto the pendant that burns brightly against her chest.

"You're getting better at that," Will comments, unperturbed, as he continues to shovel huge handfuls of earth back into the hole.

"You know what they say about practice," Isadora groans, clutching at her slashed arm. Will bites back a grin.

"What?"

"It's bullshit." Isabella examines her blood-slathered hand and swallows back a grimace. "That was a complete fluke. Everything I'm *doing* is a complete fluke."

"Well, you're covering it really well." Will sits back on his heels to take a brief break. "You okay?"

If looks could kill … well, it wouldn't matter because Will's already dead. But the sentiment remains.

"Not particularly. The quicker you finish up here the quicker I can get back and rip up another of my nice jumpers to make a sling. Or a tourniquet."

Iris scoffs. "Stop making a meal out it."

"Jab me with that cane and I'll break your twiggy legs, mouldy oldie."

XX | JUDGEMENT

The journey back is anticlimactic. Isadora still manages to drive (one-handed, thank goodness her car is an automatic) out to the old Archer Estate, parking by the rusting iron gate and hoping no one sees her car. She triple-checks that it's locked before awkwardly squeezing through the gate, still bleeding profusely. Bee ducks out from under the bloodstream, slinky body twisting and twining to avoid each drop. Isadora can't help thinking a demon cat should be better equipped to deal with gore, but apparently they are just as fussy as regular cats when it comes to personal hygiene.

Sitting at the oversized dining table with a far-too-fancy tea towel pressed to her shoulder, Isadora mulls over the bag of bones sitting on the table next to her hip. A shudder runs up her spine. It's one thing to see ghosts. Quite another entirely to have someone's physical remains sitting in a neat pile right next to her.

"Still hurting?" Will interrupts her queasy thoughts, handing her a glass of water. Isadora shrugs with her opposite shoulder.

"Yep. Not much I can do about it, unless you can find some old-fashioned drugs in the bathroom. Chloroform even, if they have it."

Will chuckles. "Sorry, nothing doing at the moment." He swaps out the tea towel for a clean one, this time dampened with cool water. Isadora bites back a groan as the cold seeps into her overheated skin.

"Did you get the antiseptic from my car?" Bless her forgetfulness and the bottomless pit that is her car console. When she had first bought the vehicle, her mum had given her a first-aid kit as a gift. She's never had to use it until now. Will nods, tossing her a blue-and-white tube, which she fumbles and drops onto Bee's head. "Pick that up for me, please," she bites out as her shoulder throbs viciously. Will scoffs and shakes his head at her butterfingers.

"Unbelievable. You grow up with me and dad and our amazing ball-handling skills and you pull that performance out of the hat?" Will passes her the small tube more carefully this time. Isadora snorts and uncaps it.

"I've been told my ball-handling skills are more than adequate, thanks." Leaving Will giggling like a cheeky teenager. It's nice. Almost domestic.

Once the blood has mostly been stemmed and the antiseptic applied, to much muffled swearing, Iris clears her throat croakily from her loitering position in the doorway and sets her cane firmly to the floorboards, looking more like a sergeant major than a little old lady.

"I'm assuming there's a method to all this bone-collecting madness?" she asks, one wiry eyebrow raised. "Or are you two desecrating graves for the fun of it?"

"I don't remember any of our plans requiring a cranky old goat," Isadora replies dryly. "Do you?" She turns to Will, whose expression has morphed into exasperation.

"Respect your elders," he scolds her.

"Pussy," Isadora mutters, feeling only slightly betrayed. Sensing no way to throw Iris off track or send her back into the large, ever-threatening cloud of silvery spectres, Isadora relents. "We're going to have a confrontation with Isabella, the big kahuna … you know the one I'm talking about?" Iris nods to indicate she does indeed know the one Isadora is talking about. "And we felt we needed a failsafe in case she turns out to be more difficult to deal with than we anticipated."

Iris is frowning. "Confrontation, you say? And why is there going to be a confrontation?"

"Because there always is? Because her death day is coming up and it might be mine, too? Because we're linked intrinsically through the astral planes of resurrection, and there's a pattern developing that I don't want to be a part of, but she does? Because she's a bitch and wants me off her lawn? Because all stories have to have a final confrontation, no matter their calibre? Take your pick."

Iris is still frowning. "And you can't talk to her and sort this out like civilised people?"

Isadora groans, tipping her head back so she's looking up at the impressively decorated ceiling. "You think I haven't already tried that? What do you think the séance was for? Or why I went to find her dead fiancé? All lines of communication to her are shut off now. I've tried talking to her mother, but she won't answer the phone – and Wilhelmina is …" she waves a hand in the air, "… either not here or somewhere out there, being backed by whatever energy Isabella is putting out. I've tried communication. It's a two-way street and the others aren't playing along. Hence, confrontation."

Iris considers this. She smacks her gums, the noise making Isadora cringe. "And when is this confrontation? Will I need to bring popcorn or a hanky?"

"Is the hanky going to be for me?" Isadora drawls dully, aware that Iris is not in the slightest a fan of her plan and that this is her acerbic way of protesting. Iris shrugs.

"I'm hardly going to burst into tears of anguish if you die. I'll be stuck seeing your woebegone face for all eternity. Actually, the hanky might be for me." Iris reconsiders. "If I'm stuck with you for eternity, I'll definitely cry."

"Love the vote of confidence," Isadora replies. "Do you want to hear the plan or not?"

"I thought I already had."

"You heard the reasoning, not the logistics. I can leave you out of it if you like." Isadora really couldn't care less. Although, if Iris has this effect on Isadora, perhaps she can annoy Isabella into braining herself on the front steps or shoving her suicide knife into her eye socket like an ice pick. Maybe Iris could be useful here.

"Fine, deal me in, kiddo." Iris taps her cane on the floorboards. "Leave nothing out."

"Call me kiddo again and I'll toss your false teeth into the river."

"Children!" Will claps his hands. "Back to the point we abandoned five arguments ago."

"I only have a vague outline at the moment. All good plans are at least ninety per cent improvisation," Isadora admits, tucking a strand of bedraggled hair behind her ear. Iris 'harrumphs'.

"Are you that good under pressure?"

"We'll find out either way," Isadora replies. Will shakes his head.

"You do have an outline though, so share with the class."

She does, hesitantly, and with so many holes Will pictures the scheme like a slice of Swiss cheese in his head. It's the one they'd brainstormed earlier (it feels like so long ago it can't possibly have been this year), about Isadora trying to save Isabella, make her see reason and find her peace. Send her to the great beyond. Their Plan B is the bones. Neither plan fills himself, or Iris, with confidence.

Isadora is fiddling with the hem of her jumper. Will's eyes narrow unconsciously. She's holding something back, something that no amount of pushing or prodding will uncover. He knows his sister; she's as stubborn as they come, and if she has a plan with intimate details only she knows, it's going to stay that way.

Isadora finishes speaking and eyes both Will and Iris carefully. Bee settles in against her ankles, wrapping its tail firmly around them to keep her steady. Bee probably knows she's holding things back. Cats and demons are bound to be similar in that respect. But if Will or Iris suspect she is being less than forthcoming they don't show it – apart from Will's narrowed eyes, but he does that when he's concentrating on something, anyway.

Silence reigns between them. Only the occasional moan or scream of anguish from one or other of the other tenants echoes along the edges of their little team bubble.

"Do you take constructive criticism?" Iris asks finally, leaning on her cane, wiry brows tugged downwards over her magnified eyes gleaming away behind her coke-bottle spectacles.

"Nope."

Iris nods. "Thought so."

There isn't much to be said after that. Will can only fret internally about his sister's cards being held way too close to her chest, and waves Iris away as Isadora slips surreptitiously out into the foyer, Bee trailing closely behind. She's taken the bag of bones with her, and Will has only a moment to wonder how she did it without creating a macabre rattle before he, too, is following in her footsteps.

Isadora knows Will is behind her. She hefts the bag up closer to her chest and skips down the back steps, slipping briefly on some stubbornly green moss but managing to right herself in time.

Once she reaches the seclusion of the walled garden, Isadora seats herself on the godforsaken iron bench and ponders the weather. It appears to be spring. All new buds and perfumed air, new beginnings in a time she considers to be closing in on the end. They have their game plan; they even have a date for the battle. Isabella's death date will continue to creep closer whether they like it or not, and all the clandestine timing in these horrific events is pulling together neatly, like a violent tapestry in some cracked-out museum for the weird and decidedly unwonderful. It's hopelessness in its purest form. Inescapable hopelessness. For despite her plan and their failsafe, destiny is against her. And not much can defeat destiny.

"Do we get to relax now we've done the study?"

Isadora's head jerks up. "This isn't an exam, Will."

"Feels just as intense as an exam. It even comes with a life and death caveat."

"Not everyone felt that exams were life and death."

"That's because you never took yours seriously."

Isadora snorts derisively. "I was a write-off before ever taking my exams. What was the point?" She scrapes one sneakered foot along the ground, drawing large, despondent circles. Despair is rising up inside her, cresting into waves that make everything feel tight inside her chest.

"It's going to work."

She raises her head, tears beginning to pool in her glazed eyes. Will scrutinises her closely, brows drawn in determination.

"Whatever it is you're planning to do. It's going to work, Dora. Trust me. Trust yourself even."

Isadora chuckles then, chuckles instead of sobbing as she so desperately wants to. Her head bobs in a jerky nod. "Yes, it'll work. I believe it, Will. I do." Perhaps if she says it often enough, it just might become true.

Tomorrow is the day. Isadora's nerves are jangling so badly she can almost hear their uncoordinated melody screeching in her ears. After all their planning she, Will, Bee and, to a lesser extent, Iris had spent the remaining time procrastinating. They'd enjoyed the seemingly never-ending sunshine until a horde of grey clouds had scudded in from the horizon – connected, Isadora is certain, to the coming anniversary of Isabella's death. Things around the house have been changing as well. Previously well-painted and decorated rooms have been sinking slowly into a state of disrepair. What once was golden and gleaming is turning brassy and rusted with age. Dust has been appearing in large piles on the mantles and is now coating the polished floors. Cracks have begun splintering through the plaster, sending spiderwebs of black up to the ceiling.

The ghosts have been getting odder as well. What had once been a group of rather loud and boisterous spirits following Isadora's flee from society, has now become colder, quieter and increasingly scarce. No longer do they form in jubilant groups enjoying their afterlife (as much as one can, anyway, as a floating spectral being tied to earth by reasons both private and unknown in their very own haunted house). Now, they tend to vanish as soon as Isadora draws near. They cry, shriek and moan, sending shivers careening down Isadora's spine. Her assembly of spirits is beginning to act like the textbook ghosts that one reads about in horror novels and are portrayed on the silver screen.

Even Will is paler and less 'human' than usual. He is trying to keep up some semblance of normality while he's around her, but Isadora can tell. Whatever influence Isabella holds over the Archer Estate is slowly but surely infecting all the spirits in the house. The only being not affected by any of this is Bee, who is as uppity and unpredictable as ever. A constant, spiky companion that Isadora is leaning on more than ever as the sky grows darker.

Isadora watches as clouds gather overhead. She listens to the wind as it begins to whip through the beech trees, sending leaves cascading across the iron sky. It is freezing. There is nothing of the warmth of the last few days remaining in the air. She's managed to get a small fire burning in the hearth in the main living room, which is now lit by several guttering candles. But no matter how close she dares to creep to the fire, it never seems to warm her. Bee is curled in her lap, milky eyes reflecting the sputtering flames. Will is seated in the other wingback chair, grumbling because the stuffing inside it has, along with the rest of the house, degraded down to nothing more than stiff lumps of mouldering feathers.

They sit in mostly companionable silence, serenaded by the howling ghosts, wind and crackling flame. There is nothing much to do now but wait anxiously as the clock inches closer and closer to game time. Isadora shudders. Being so close to her 'death date' is unsettling in the extreme, and no matter how she tries to frame it in her mind, it still feels like a full stop drawing closer and closer in the sentence of her life. If Will notices her involuntary movement, he says nothing. Silence continues to reign oppressively over the siblings, a significant depart from their usual comfortable state.

Suddenly, Bee's ear twitches violently. Isadora startles a little, wondering what's wrong as she stares down at the inky body coiled tightly on her knees. She is just opening her mouth to ask, when—

"Mama!" A shrill cry shatters the relative peace. Isadora shoots out of her chair, sending a hissing Bee to the floor where its sharp claws gouge into the already ruined floorboards.

Isadora whips around to face the doorway, white-knuckled hands gripping the threadbare wingback chair. A shadow elongates along the hall floor followed by a steady thudding that works its way closer to the door. Then, horribly, whatever it is begins to cry … the awful, ear-piercing wail of a profoundly distraught child.

Isadora groans low in her throat as understanding washes over her. Nausea swirls in her stomach as she realises at once who it is. Last time they'd met had been traumatising enough. She remembers the weight of the little girl on her lap, the smell of iron and brain matter as she settled in against her chest, crooning. She remembers it so clearly, so viscerally, her nausea swells sharply. Her knees begin to tremble as one tiny, blood-speckled hand throws itself into view, followed by a chubby arm clad in mouldering lace.

Wilhelmina crawls into plain sight, mashed head swaying and sending chunks of blood and wispy, matted hair in all directions. One eye bulges out, swinging from side to side as she searches despairingly for her dear, dead mama. She continues to cry, choking on gurgles and clots of black blood as she casts about for her mother. A broken tooth falls free and is lost beneath the toddler's body as she drags herself along.

Isadora distantly hears a string of muttered "No's", and it takes her an embarrassingly long time to realise it's her.

Wilhelmina's head swings around to face the living room. Isadora can hear the brain matter sloshing and sagging with the movement, bumping up against the fractured walls of her tiny skull. She ducks behind the chair like a coward, praying that the poor child has not seen or heard her. Or, heaven forbid, recognised her as her older sister.

"Isa!" the child cries. She is too late. Isadora hears the toddler drag herself into the room. Hears the swish of her ruined clothing, the wet gargling sounds and the meaty slapping of her baby hands as she claws her way towards the wingback. Isadora swallows down the vomit in her throat and shoots Will a frantic look as he, too, attempts to hide from the poor, monstrous child. Will offers her nothing but a shrug, face taut with helpless horror.

Isadora screams when a wet hand slaps weakly against her knee. Wilhelmina is there, right next to her, wobbling unsteadily as she pulls herself to her feet by the arm of the chair while simultaneously attempting to heave herself into Isadora's lap. Oh god, the smell of iron and taste of decay on the tip of her tongue is almost too much to bear.

"Itha …" Wilhelmina lisps, burying her caved-in head into Isadora's stomach, while her lumpy arms clumsily attempt to enfold her in some sick parody of a hug.

"She's too young to know what blame is."

Isadora shrieks, heart vaulting into her mouth as both she and Will turn violently towards the direction of the voice, and Isadora ends up spitting Wilhelmina's wispy hair from her mouth as the portrait of Jane Archer, hanging innocently on the water-stained wall, surveys them drowsily.

The woman in the portrait is looking at them, watching them. Isadora would have fainted if she wasn't already so used to batshit crazy happenings going on in this house. Although her nerves are certainly taking a serious beating today, and she is certain her anxiety will never drop below 'constantly alert and ready to throw hands up in the air' from this point onward.

"She will always love you, despite what happened," Jane continues, blinking placidly in Isadora's direction. Isadora's mouth gapes as she gathers her racing thoughts. Is she seriously about to reply to a talking, living painting? For goodness sake! Pulling herself together as best she can, Isadora responds as reasonably and calmly as the situation dictates.

"I'm not Isabella." Her voice is only mildly squeaky. "Not your version, anyway," she amends as Jane raises her dark eyebrows.

"No, I suppose you are not." Jane's head bobs in a tiny nod. "But you understand what I am saying, nonetheless."

In her fright, Isadora has unwittingly clasped her arms tightly around Wilhelmina, and now the child is squirming in her grasp. Realising this, Isadora hurriedly relinquishes her hold so that Wilhelmina nearly falls out of her lap – which, of course, brings about another onslaught of whiny tears.

"Um…" is all Isadora can muster in response, gaze darting between baby and painted mother. Jane saves her from having to come up with another unintelligible response.

"I nearly died of grief myself." She peers off into the corner of her marvellously gilded frame, dark coils of hair sliding over her shoulder. "Losing both my babies, and both so young. It was torture I would never wish upon anyone. Simply horrific." Her dark eyes move back to Isadora, pinning her to the spot as they begin to mist over with tears. "And you see the worst version of me. Through your eyes, your twisted memories. Guilt is a poisonous thing. It kills all that might flourish, smothers every good thing you might feel about yourself. Turns your beloved mother into a monster so foul, so reprehensible, you would believe she pulled the trigger. The falseness of the vision you hold permeates the world around you."

Wilhelmina whines again. Isadora unconsciously clutches her tighter, enthralled by Jane, quite forgetting how revolted she has been by the tiny, unfortunate girl.

"I know what you've seen. I know what you are going to do." Jane speaks softly, painted tears sliding like crystals down her oil-rendered cheeks. "I wish you wouldn't force the suffering to continue, allow the grief to spiral onwards. I could not bear to lose another daughter, any more than you were able to bear losing another sibling."

Will flinches, not expecting to have been roped into the conversation. Jane surveys him now, slowly shaking her dark head.

"Love is tragedy. The world's greatest tragedy. We all fall so neatly into its lap. We quite forget the inevitable pain."

Her eyes drift back to Isadora. "Don't let *this* end in tragedy."

And suddenly the harsh, haggard woman in the portrait is transformed into a loving mother. Lined by age and wisdom, yet young enough to retain the rich darkness of her hair and eyes. Isadora sees none of the monster she proclaims to have been turned into – only the mother Wilhelmina remembers.

The first few drops of rain begin to spatter on the slate roof, drawing her eyes to the large windows and the grey gardenscape beyond. Isadora blinks, then glances back at Jane's portrait. It is empty. Nothing but a sea of green silk surrounded by a gilded frame. Isadora's lap is now similarly bereft of Wilhelmina's squelching weight, leaving her hands clasping nothing but a scrap of dirty, mouldering lace. There is no blood, no squashed scalp, no other sign that moments ago her lap had been filled with squalling, rotting baby. Which should be a huge relief. Yet something within her feels strangely empty at the loss.

A cold draught flows through the room, almost guttering the small fire.

"And so it begins."

The words spill from Isadora's lips on a whisper, uncontrolled and placed there by another's will. Her hands touch her trembling mouth, and she bites back any other words that may be on their way. Nothing comes.

"We've still got hours before midnight." Will hovers over her, face still a little pale but determinedly set. Bee slinks up to take Wilhelmina's place, tail curling possessively around Isadora's right arm. The biting spines don't bother her as much as they should. The stinging pain keeps her grounded and shielded from the intruder's thoughts, which curl ominously in the corners of her mind like a cloud of insidious smoke.

Will settles himself down next to her, hands braced behind him on the floor as he leans back and stares out, along with his sister, at the rain dribbling down the dirty windowpanes.

"Bet my raindrop will reach the bottom before yours." Will points out a fat bead of water that is already racing in a jagged line down towards the windowsill. Isadora allows a smile to touch her tense, milk-pale face.

"You're on."

They race raindrops as night creeps steadily in, as the scenery around them darkens far more quickly than on any of the other days they've spent there. An evening of anxious hearts hidden beneath calm facades, with Bee a comforting weight on Isadora's legs. Isadora sits in the cold living room, fearing the moment the large, still-ticking grandfather clock will chime to mark the stroke of midnight. The beginning of a new day. Perhaps her last. She is determined to see it in and show Isabella she isn't afraid. She isn't!

She falls asleep ten minutes before the bells toll.

Isabella clutches at the ripped fabric and feels it slip through her fingers. The lace is rough and scratchy. Her fingers pass over the dark stains and crumbs of dirt that still cling and refuse to let go. The floorboards bite into her knees and the cold leaches right up into the very heart of her – into an open, gaping chasm right in the centre of her body. She remembers when it tore open, rent away from her being, and how it felt as it allowed all the dark, hopeless things in.

Every day, the screams ring in her ears when she awakes. When she opens her eyes and remembers.

Warmth seeps down her face and drips from her jaw, from the tip of her nose. Some of it falls and soaks into the fabric clutched between her shaking fingers. A sob wrenches free and echoes off the hard surfaces around her. The walls breathe it in and throw it back to her, again and again, each one louder than the last. In her heart of hearts, all she wants is another chance. Not for her. Never for her. But for the other, she wants it all back.

She was a child! A tiny, fragile child whose eyes were bright and alive with all the wonder of the world, not yet overtaken by sense and reality. She wishes she did not have to face reality. Reality is cold and empty and worthless.

Her sobs become cries … and then screams. She rocks back and forth as the grief rises and crests with nowhere else to go. She feels that she might explode; surely, she cannot contain it all. It must go *somewhere*. Must be channelled away into something else, somewhere else. The chasm within cracks anew and it all spills forth. Her heart-wrenching grief, her loss, her deep desire. Her one wish.

Exhausted, she slumps over and presses her forehead to the floor. It provides a cool point of clarity, something for her to anchor onto.

"Isa?" The ghost of a whisper plays along her ears. It sounds like music. It sounds like death itself has come to visit.

"Isa …"

"Isa …"

"Isa!"

She cannot bear it and raises her head. Two pairs of eyes lock together. Her mind is surely fractured in two. She is delusional. Lost and wanting in her grief, she is creating images and projecting them clearly into her mind's eye. Surely …

She screams without knowing. Her mother enters without her seeing. She is lost in it all.

SLAP!

Clarity bursts like fireworks across her mind. Her cheek is stinging with heat and there is her mother, standing wild-eyed above her. She sees not the fear nor the anxiety. She sees only the anger. Feels only the force of the slap. She understands nothing but the ire.

She deserves it. This is her punishment, and it settles something in her, while at the same time rattling something else loose. To be at fault and understand it is the sanest she has ever been and will ever be.

Blame is a language she understands fluently and will undoubtedly hear again.

There is always someone to blame.

In this it is me.

And it always will be.

XXI | THE WORLD

It is drizzling. A faint patter drumming on the roof, a steady drip-drip on the window glass. Steely grey light streams gently through the gaps between the thick curtains attempting to keep it at bay.

Isabella groans, rolling over as the gauzy, syrupy call of sleep sings sweetly in the corner of her mind. She could drop off again, she really could. If not for the myriad of brisk footsteps thudding up the hall. Today was the day. A day for merriment, for joyous unions and the promise of a bright new future. The feeling dimmed only by the great black mark still scored deeply into the fabric of the Archer family. Once four ... cut down to three ... and now only two. The two held together by a volatile web of grief and shared suffering.

Her wedding is going to feel far more like a funeral. She will even be wearing a shroud.

The bedroom door opens to admit a tiny slip of a woman whose arms are filled with fabric and who wears a rather forced smile on her face.

"Up you get, Ma'am. Big day today."

Isabella floats through her morning routine, for the most part ignoring her maid's idle attempt at chatter. Her hair is combed and arranged into a twisted knot at the back of her head, her skin is attended to – just a light touch of colour. She is stuffed into her undergarments then draped in a simple dress. It's not time for the shroud quite yet.

She should be happy. Here she is, a young woman of fairly impressive wealth and stature, marrying a young man whose humble background should never have allowed them to be anywhere near each other, let alone joined in marriage. Her mother is a progressive woman, and Isabella should be grateful she has allowed this wedding to take place. Yet all Isabella can feel is a pit of writhing guilt and the memory of the piercing bore of her mother's eyes at Wilhelmina's funeral. She can't feel any warmth towards her mother at the moment and that makes the guilt so much worse.

They were meant to breakfast together – speak fondly of Isabella's childhood and laugh gaily around mouthfuls of fruit and oats. She is meant to feel the steady thrum of excitement course through her as she steps into a bright new, shiny chapter of life, leaving her mother fondly reminiscent of the child she used to be. None of that feels even remotely possible now.

Tom had been insistent. Let the wedding happen as it was planned. Let it be something wondrous to look forward to. Isabella had agreed because she loved him, but now she almost wishes she hadn't. *She even almost wishes she had never come to love Tom in the first place.* For how is it possible for someone as culpable as she is to deserve the love of someone as angelic as Tom? As steadfast and honest, as guiltless as he is. *She killed her own sister* – yet Tom refuses to see how evil that has made her. How unlovable she has become. Bless him for his goodness and damn her for her selfishness. Wilhelmina will never see a day such as this, will never experience a holy union of her own. She will never feel the love Isabella feels so wholly when she is with Tom. *And she did that. Isabella caused that.* She stripped her baby sister of all those opportunities – and for what? A silly little cart ride.

God has damned her for it, she knows he has. He has bestowed on her the punishment she sees and senses so frequently now. The curse of being able to hear voices and see those that have passed.

See what you have done? See what the consequences are of a moment's foolish actions? This is what you have caused, what you have sent your innocent sister to. Suffer the sight of the dead and weep for knowing you sent your sister there.

Isabella enters the small parlour that has been set up for her wedding day breakfast, fully prepared to face an empty table and eat nothing at all. She is, therefore, shocked to see her mother seated primly on the edge of her seat with the tiniest of smiles lifting the corner of her mouth. The smile wobbles when she sees Isabella obviously hesitating, torn between running back to her room or fleeing out the back door. In the end she does neither, instead sitting herself opposite her mother with nary a peep.

Her mother stays seated despite the awkward atmosphere, keeping her smile in place. Silence reigns as they both eat through a selection of cold meats, fresh fruit and warm, crusty bread slathered with honey, all set out neatly and accompanied by shining silverware. The servants are nowhere to be seen, having set the table with everything both mother and daughter could need. When they have finished eating, her mother places a warm hand atop Isabella's own before disappearing from the room. The warmth of the touch lingers, leaching into Isabella's bones and weighing her down even further with guilt. In that moment she feels that even breathing is beyond her. That the burden of the guilt is simply too strong and too heavy to bear, and she should just allow herself to sink to the bottomless depth of it and dwell there forever.

The wedding is scheduled for midday, which allows plenty of time for joyful gathering, dancing and general merriment for all those in attendance. Everyone who is anyone from their country town and surrounds is invited and will soon be showing up in their lacquered carriages or bestride majestic glossy-coated horses.

Isabella, suddenly realising how long she has spent at the breakfast table, hustles upstairs. Climbing them, her legs feel impossibly leaden, and she finds herself staggering from time to time. Once in her room she is stripped of her plain dress and eased into a much fancier one constructed of watery pale silk and with long skirts. It rustles magnificently on the timber floors, seemingly weighted with the promise of a happy future. Isabella feels she is drowning in its beauty. When they fasten a delicate string of pearls around her throat, it feels like it's choking her, and it takes everything she has not to tear it off, scattering pearls in every direction.

Finally, she slips into her dainty bridal shoes and sits staring into her mirror. Instead of an excited bride, a tired, frail stranger stares back. A stranger, trussed up like a prize pheasant ready for roasting. On a day when she should be absolutely radiant, she feels anything but. She is pale and hollow-eyed; her blonde hair is lank with no shine or lustre to speak of. Every kind word Tom has ever said to her regarding her looks now feels like the cruellest lies ever told. Isabella wishes for tears. She wants, more than anything, for the sudden hot, stinging rise of unstoppable tears to rush forth and be released as an infected wound might spew pus. But they don't come. There is nothing but a deep, empty crater at her very centre.

Outside, the drizzle has turned to snow. How unbefitting her wedding dress is for weather such as this. It feels like an omen. Feels that the cold is here to swallow up her warm body and send her to the ground as cold as her sister must be. There is no warmth in death, whether physical or of the mind.

Isabella's maid, having been talking to a blank, vacant young woman for quite some minutes now, retreats and shuts the door with a gentle snick. Isabella blinks herself back to life, her hands running absently over the silk of her dress, its slippery texture grounding her a little. Sounds begin to filter back in ... the rapid pacing of many feet on the ground floor, the cadence of different voices chatting back and forth, some anxious, others jubilant despite the turn in the weather. Her eyes drift to the window, watching as the tiny white flakes flutter past.

The sky is leaden, heavy and swollen, the slow progression of the snowflakes belying the load held above. *It should all fall at once and send the house collapsing, taking with it the people trapped inside and smothering those foolish enough to be out amongst it.* A shiver suddenly runs up Isabella's back. She shudders and wraps her arms around her middle. A flurry of snow twists violently outside her window. It feels, abruptly, that all sound has disappeared from the world, blanketed by the snow.

Until a new noise cuts across the silence, sharp as a new blade.

"Isa!"

The squeal is all too familiar. Isabella turns in shock and falls back into her dressing table, spreading her shaking arms wide to catch herself. The empty chasm inside instantly overflows with nauseating guilt. Fear squeezes at her chest and her breath pumps out in wheezing gasps.

There is a disfigured, squalling mess in the middle of her room, recognisable only by her filthy clothing. The smell of rotting flesh permeates Isabella's senses, sending one hand flying to cover her mouth and nose. The other hand stretches out and scrabbles along the dresser until her fingers latch onto the first heavy object they can find. Isabella flings whatever it is overarm at her dead sister with frightening accuracy. The hairbrush bounces off Wilhelmina's already crushed head with an audibly wet crack. Isabella gags behind her hand, and her wobbling legs barely manage to carry her along the wall to the exit. When she gets to the door Isabella flings herself bodily from the room as the heartbroken cry of her infant sister follows her, echoing down the hall.

She staggers along drunkenly, one hand still clasped over her gaping mouth, the other clutching the wall to support her weight as her chest heaves with panic. Her gaze flicks wildly to the staircase. She knows that making it down there would take an absolute miracle, but she can't stay up here while that thing remains in her room.

The smell will probably never abate. By now it will have seeped into the floorboards and into the walls, perhaps even into her bedding where she would be forced to inhale it every night until her last. All she will be able to smell will be the sickly-sweet rot of her sister's flesh mixed with the mouldering dankness on her threadbare clothes and the iron tang of blood.

Holding onto the banister for dear life, Isabella makes it down the stairs far more quickly than she initially imagined, but her panicked, uncoordinated feet flail on the last step, and she trips, toppling forward to land on hands and knees at the bottom.

Still, she cannot cry.

"Miss?" Someone is crouching down beside her, gently gripping one trembling elbow. Isabella allows them to pull her to her feet. A pale face swims into focus. It is one of the young maids, face twisted in confused concern. "Are you alright?"

Isabella shrugs adroitly out of her grip, nodding a little unconvincingly as she plasters on a smile. "I'm quite fine, thank you." Her voice is shaking. Everything is shaking. "You can get back to your duties now."

The maid hesitates, eventually nodding in acquiescence when Isabella stares her down. "Of course, Miss." She hustles off in a bustle of rough cotton skirts, throwing a quick glance over her slim shoulder as she goes. Isabella ignores it.

The downstairs foyer is freezing – whether from the weather or the sudden gaggle of people who should not be there, Isabella is not sure. All at once there are so many of them, crushing against the walls and staggering about while moaning desolately, falling through the real, living people.

What is going on? What's happening? Why are they here? I don't understand!

Isabella turns and dashes for the back door, veering off course with a wail as another one appears. He has no eyes, yet is still somehow weeping, holding his palms out and begging for comfort. Isabella dodges his questing hands and skids into the stairwell that leads down to the basement kitchen, her skirts flying behind her and her beautifully arranged hair falling apart around her face. Several kitchen staff rear back as Isabella, eyes wide and crazed, darts frantically among them. No one moves to intercept her, too shocked at her appearance as she sights and dodges all the people who should not be there.

Isabella doesn't notice any of the living, despite the half-hearted calls of her name and the hesitant hands that reach for her. Her focus, instead, is locked on the row of shining knives fastened to the far wall. She lunges desperately and unsheathes one of the bigger blades, which she holds aloft, no longer able to tell who is what, or whether they live and breathe or exist only to torment her with their bloodied, bleak remains.

"Don't come near me!" she shrieks, now quite unhinged as she wields the knife and points it at each crowded person in turn. The tormented, strung-out part of her animalistic hindbrain is convinced that everyone thronging around her is a threat sent by God himself to punish her for her wrongdoings. The dead have come to claim her as theirs – as they should. Her sister is calling to her now, and she feels it as it echoes within the chasm in her chest.

Isabella keeps her back to the wall as she skirts back through the kitchen, knife held high as her breathing stutters in her chest. She can feel the thrum of her heart right down to the tips of her daintily slippered toes. The crowd in the kitchen move with her, each face as distorted as the next as her vision swims and wavers. Eventually, the solid brick wall gives way to an exit. She feels cool air rushing up her back, leaving her exposed and vulnerable. She turns and flees, sprinting back up the stairs and into the main hall.

It is absolutely swarming with bodies.

Choking on a panicked sob, Isabella makes for the back door and flings it open so hard it crashes off the outside wall. The glass inlay shatters, sending shards glittering along the stone steps and into the garden. A black, oily streak of spines dashes through the undergrowth of the garden, rustling the leaves and tugging on the rose stems as it rapidly retreats. Isabella ignores whatever it is in favour of slipping messily down the stairs and spilling into the walled garden. She crawls along on all fours, white-knuckled hand still gripping the knife. A mess of silky white fabric pools around her legs and she struggles to regain her footing amongst the tangle. A shard of glass has lodged itself firmly in one palm. Isabella barely feels it.

A tiny bead of red blooms vibrantly on the white silk of her dress.

She doesn't feel the chilling kiss of snow against her skin, nor hear the increasingly concerned calls of her name. She simply kneels in the garden, surrounded by growing piles of snow as her hands turn pink.

"Hiss!"

Isabella jerks her head up and flinches as she comes eye to eye with a skeletal black creature. Its wide, milky gaze pins her to the spot. Its back is arched violently, and spines quiver all along its tail. She recoils as the creature bares its long, sharp fangs again, hissing from deep within its hollow chest. Isabella pushes herself up, slipping and falling as she does so to land on her backside as whatever 'it' is darts off and disappears up and over the red brick wall ensconcing the snow-blanketed garden – an inky black slither juxtaposed against the blinding whiteness of the world.

"Isabella!" Her name is called, the voice a mixture of confusion and concern, followed by a flurry of movement. Isabella starts, blade flying up and held menacingly at chest height as her wrist trembles traitorously. She recognises her mother's dark, flyaway hair attempting to escape the neat hold of her bun. Her face is lined with worry, but her dark eyes are as piercing as ever. Isabella can feel her surveillance cutting across her flimsy knife defence.

"Isabella—"

"I'm not putting it down!" Isabella yells, brandishing the weapon near her mother's face. Jane startles back, hands held placatingly in front of her, palms up. Small flakes of snow are gathering in Jane's dark brows and on the crown of her head.

"Bella." Her nickname, coming so tenderly, so reverently from her mother's mouth, is almost enough to cut through the craziness. Almost.

"Is this what you wanted?" The poisonous inflection sends Jane rearing back, mouth dropping open in shock. Isabella can't see past the glaze of tears curtaining the world. A painful sob catches in her chest. "Is this atonement? Is this what you want from me?"

Jane draws herself together. "Isabella, what on earth are you—"

"I can't do this anymore!" Isabella's sob breaks into a shout. "You have my repentance, you always will. You think I wanted to kill her? My own sister?"

Jane's face flickers in comprehension, caught between relief in knowing what Isabella is talking about and grief that her own daughter feels so tortured by the tragedy. Isabella knows none of this though, sees none of Jane's thoughts even while they are written blatantly across her features. She sees only triumph painted there, ugly and mocking. The knife tip quivers.

"My darling …" Jane speaks ever so softly. "My sweet, darling girl. You know this is not true."

"Isa!" a voice warbles from behind Jane. A tottering form stumbles out from Jane's shadow. The blood is so rich, so jewel-bright against the snow that it is almost blinding. The red deepens into purple, into mottled bruises struck through with crimson. A true painting of tragic beauty cast on the virgin snow.

"But it is," Isabella whispers, gaze never straying from her little sister. The blade quivers again. "It *is* true." Unseeing, she presses the tip of the knife to her silk-clad forearm and feels the heft of the blade against her flesh.

"I will be forgiven. If I do this." She bites into her lip and drags in a trembling breath, ignoring Tom who has come flying out of the back door with her name poised on the edge of his lips. "I will give anything, everything, for the sin I have committed. He will forgive me. You will forgive me. I will hurt no longer. We will be free." Her eyes slip shut in the same instant she goes to dig the knife into her arm.

"*Isadora!*"

She jerks, eyes snapping open.

"That's not my name," she murmurs, so softly under her breath that only the snow can hear it. The knife twitches.

"*Isadora, stop!*"

Her vision tunnels. She's trapped underwater and everything is muffled, fuzzy. Is this it? Is this the moment she fades out into the same existence as Wilhelmina? Caught there forever to wallow, to drown in her failures, reminded every day of her mistakes? Will she open her eyes and see her hands are covered in blood, that they're see-through?

Suddenly, crystalline shards of colour break through; a face swims in front of her. It's that freakish cat-thing, wide milky gaze locked and pulling on her own, drawing her focus. She recognises it somehow, feels comforted to see the spikes and oily black spines, to see the whip-like tail caressing the air and the feline sharpness of its exposed teeth. Why is the letter 'B' coming to mind?"

"Isadora?"

There it is again, her 'not' name. A mere burble of syllables, but understandable all the same. She shakes her head and winces as her brain rattles around in her skull.

"Can you hear me now?"

"Stop," Isabella whimpers, clutching at her head. The knife handle digs into her temple. "Please, stop calling me that."

"You need to focus. This isn't you. Please, Isadora—"

"Stop! Stop calling me that!" She swings the knife out in the vague direction of the voice (familiar voice, sad voice) and chokes when the pain in her head spikes, driving a pickaxe between her eyes. She feels like she's splitting in two, being carved right down the middle where the slivered halves of her body will fall to opposite sides in the snow-covered grass.

No. She needs to end this suffering. If she ends it all there will be peace on the other side. The knife pulls back, like a magnet to her arm, the tip digs into the fragile skin, a bead of red blooms …

It goes no further.

What?

Isabella frowns, blurry gaze on her arm. Her other arm is shaking with effort, with resistance against her desire to drive the knife deep into her flesh, carve out a hole that can never be filled, carve out this rotten part of her and send it spilling into the earth. She tries again, only to be met by the same block. Her own body is betraying her.

"No," she whispers, desperately now. "No, no, no, no, NO!" Tries again. Still that part of herself she cannot control is stopping her. *Not this, it murmurs. We promised we wouldn't do this. We won't do this!*

"I promised no such thing," Isabella replies, muscles clenching as she continues to attempt to drive the knife into her arm, into the pulsing froth of blood beneath. "I want this to end!"

Well, I don't!

The world trembles. Isabella stumbles with the conviction, the tenacious force in the other voice echoing within her head. There's a snap, both physical and metaphysical, and Isabella falls. The knife goes flying, landing softly in the building snowbanks, sinking deeply until the glint of the blade is covered in powdery white.

"Isadora!"

She lifts her head jerkily, eyes fluttering with the effort of consciousness. Everything hurts like one giant bruise, a bone-deep ache that pulses annoyingly in time with her pulse. Damn, why does she hurt so much? Why is her arm stinging?

Isadora peers down, barely making out the tiny gouge in her skin along the inner forearm. There's blood there. She's bleeding. Why is her skin so cold? Her damn fingernails are turning blue! She shudders, hugging her arms close to her chest. Tiny wet spots of freezing cold needle away at her arms, head and exposed neck. She tilts her face to the sky and realises belatedly, "Oh, it's snowing."

Wait, what?

"Isadora!"

"Will?" she calls back, trying to seek him out amidst the steady flurry of white. There he is, standing over near the steps, face drawn and pale. He looks worried, scared even, if Isadora didn't know him better.

She attempts to walk over, only her feet feel as if they're trapped in mud, not snow.

"Ugh…" She grunts with the effort of lifting one foot and putting it in front of the other; the harder she tries the more impossible it becomes. She's like a fly in a glue trap.

"Will! Come over and help me, why don't you?" Isadora calls out, frustrated and panting, her face now a beacon of warmth against the cold air.

"I can't!" he calls back in a strangled voice. Isadora peers over. There's nothing physically stopping him that she can see, no barriers or wayward bouncer ghosts restraining him. It can only be one thing keeping him at bay.

Isadora feels her move before she sees her. Senses the dark shift in the atmosphere behind her and remembers (mentally slapping her forehead) that there's only one ghost here who can quite literally control the environment. Who had most likely orchestrated and controlled her acid-trip of a dream (was it a dream?) earlier today.

The woman of the hour herself.

Isabella Archer ghosts into view.

Her gaunt, bloodstained figure comes to stand directly before Isadora, grey eyes roving over her face while her black-tipped fingers twitch unpleasantly. The extent of the unhinged madness swimming within her gaze sends Isadora's stomach into uncomfortable acrobatic twists. *I really hope I never looked like that*, she thinks.

"Red really isn't your colour," Isadora remarks, pulse galloping in her chest. May as well get the ball rolling, she figures. It won't hurt to at least attempt to gain the upper hand quickly and succinctly. If she does, she might actually walk out of this hell-scape alive.

Isabella does not rise to the bait and merely remains where she is, eyes locked and boring deep holes right into Isadora's head. She shifts uncomfortably beneath the scrutiny, feet still firmly trapped in the earth. The world seems to stand still, holding its breath. Even the tumbling snow seems to halt in mid-air until its master sees fit to restart time.

Isabella eventually moves, hand twitching in the direction of the fallen blade, gleaming wickedly in the snow drift. She sweeps sideways, the train of her dress flowing majestically in an ethereal breeze and sending snowflakes arching up and dancing daintily on the current. She stops, peering down at the knife, and elegantly stoops to collect it.

Isabella holds the knife as if it is a sceptre, a precious relic to be admired rather than feared. With steely eyes and a steady hand, she glides back to Isadora. Blood glistens and oozes wetly with every elegant movement, beading up and dribbling down from the wounds on her wrists. There is no fearful, hysterical girl in her anymore, no sign of the screaming, babbling mess she had been mere moments before in Isadora's 'vision'. She truly is a phantom, born of grief and rage, hardened by all her years wandering the earth planting her seeds and growing the toxic energy needed to create the haunted Archer Estate as it stands today. Isadora's confidence in her plan falters.

"You dropped something." Isabella's voice seems to come from everywhere. It groans on the wind, whispers in the snow, even echoes sweetly among the shrivelling flowerbeds. The ground shivers as its master speaks. Isabella holds the knife aloft, an offering to Isadora.

"No thanks." Isadora goes to take a step back, only her feet are caught in that damned invisible mud trap. Isabella tilts her head to the side. Clumps of matted blonde hair follow the movement and hang in haggard strands around her gaunt face.

"No?" she echoes. Her arched brows furrow. "But we are guilty. We must carve the guilt out. It's the only way to amend our unforgivable sins."

"The only thing I'm guilty of is occasionally being a bitch – and that's definitely not worthy of death." Isadora continues to fruitlessly struggle, despite knowing she is well and truly trapped in place.

"Death …" Isabella considers this. "I am not offering death. No one is worthy of death. Especially not us." She offers the knife once more. "Take it."

"Not on your un-life."

The sky darkens. The breeze kicks up into a tugging wind which plucks away at Isadora's hair. The surrounding crowd of spirits (Isadora had not noticed them gathering) are unaffected.

Isabella straightens up. "Why are you doing this?" Her voice comes out flat and stern. Like a mother berating a naughty child.

It's as if a switch has been flicked. Isadora stares, reeling from the change in demeanour. Isabella is painted with a mournful, confused expression that is so much more her age, so much more human than whatever she was projecting before. *These goddamned personality changes are going to give me whiplash!* Isadora thinks to herself.

"Doing what?" Isadora asks.

"I've seen the suffering you go through. I've seen the hardships, the desperation within. Why are you not helping yourself?"

"You've seen, have you?" Isadora asks, as that all too familiar burning flush of anger rises visibly in her face. What does this dead bitch know about any of it? She saw one dead baby and was reduced to tears and now she has the audacity to lecture Isadora on how she's been living her life? When Isabella threw her own away at the first sign of hardship? Oh no, no, no, nah-uh. They are nothing alike.

And Isadora is going to show her.

"I have seen. I know. I know the guilt, the fear, the sadness …" Isabella creeps closer, maudlin face sharpening into focus. The downward turn of her lips looks so stupid Isadora itches to punch it off.

"We were always going to reach this point. So, take the knife and admit your faults. Begin to atone for your sins—"

"*No.*"

Isabella pauses. "No?" she queries. Her head tilts to the side. "No?" she repeats. Isadora, still attempting to pull her feet free from the mud, groans.

"I'm not playing your stupid game or feeding into this awful fantasy you've got going on. It's not happening."

"Game?" Isabella asks coldly. "This is not a game. This is what we must do to repent. What we deserve as punishment."

"Punishment for what? I haven't done anything," Isadora grunts as her leg refuses to slide free from the muck. "Actually, if anything, I think I've been punished enough, don't you think?"

"It can never be enough!" Isabella cries, waving the knife in the air. "We can never be forgiven for taking their lives. We must suffer for it."

"That's absolute bullshit."

Isabella is struck dumb. Her mouth gapes slightly, grey eyes blown wide. She looks like a proper ghost now. Isadora nods into the silence.

"Exactly, so can we please move past the self-hatred garbage and get to the actual root of the problem?"

Isabella manages to overcome her shock and frown. "Root of the problem," she repeats softly, while a small, mocking smile crawls up her face. "Very well then. Please enlighten me as to what the exact root of the problem is."

"It's not your fault."

"Excuse me?"

"It's not your fault and I think you know this." Isadora stares imploringly at her ruined reflection. "You just didn't know where to put all your emotions. You didn't know what to do with them because they were so strong ... and how often do people really *feel*, the way your sister's death made you feel? All that emotion, it had to go somewhere. So, you focused it on the misplaced guilt you felt."

"It was not misplaced—"

"Yes, it was." Isadora knows. She knows so very well what it feels like.

"And how are you so certain?" Isabella asks tightly.

"Because I've been there. I've felt guilt that was not my own and carried it around until someone else was brave enough to confront me about it. So, I know how it feels. And you focused all of it on yourself, and it changed the way you saw things. The way you felt other people saw you. Like your mother."

Isabella trembles in the silence that follows, hands drawing into fists. "Observant of you." She appears to seethe, but Isadora can see the tears building up, the way her throat is bobbing nervously. Oh, she's scared, so scared of facing anything to do with her past and her mother. "But you're wrong."

"How so?" Isadora folds her arms across her chest, her glare never lessening.

"You *are* guilty. And you're just as scared as me. *We are each other.* I understand it all, and I know what comes next."

"We are less like each other than you'd like to suppose," Isadora responds. "The only things we have in common are the exact same birthday, freakishly similar names, dead siblings and almost identical bodies. Mine is *sans* injury." She nods at Isabella's wrists.

Isabella smiles sadly.

"Not for much longer."

"So, tell me, in that delusional brain of yours, how am I guilty?" She juts her chin out as the soft negotiation tactic flees her. If Isabella is going to be obstinate, then she will rise to meet her. Isadora switches from gentle gaze to a glare, challenging Isabella to prove her words are true – that Isadora truly is guilty and worthy of Isabella's fate. Isabella shifts to the side to reveal Will, who looks just as shocked as the other ghosts at Isadora's sudden change of approach.

Isadora snorts.

"Yeah, okay. If anything, that should make you feel worse," she says.

Again with the quizzical head tilt. "How so?" Isabella asks.

"I know what happened to Will. I know that you had plenty of influence in what happened to my brother. I know it wasn't him that ran the car off the road." Isadora shifts her knee, testing the bounds that are keeping her feet cemented into place. It could be her imagination, but it feels like something almost gives way. She is careful not to allow any sign of relief to show on her face. "As if one sibling wasn't enough."

"That wasn't what I was referring to, and you know it. As much as you have tried to push it deep down inside you, you know what you've done to him, what you trapped him in," Isabella replies softly. The knife twitches in her hand. Isadora can only hope Will hasn't heard what she'd just said.

"What's she talking about? Isadora … what's she talking about?"

Damn.

Isadora ignores him. She cannot allow any of the memory of that night – of what she did to keep her brother here – to rise within her or it's all over. Isabella will latch onto it the same way a leech latches onto a warm body. She will drain her dry and keep her soul, and Isadora will take the knife to her skin to see if she, too, bleeds guilt. If she lets herself feel any of that, it will be over. So, Isadora ignores Will's beseeching eyes and continues as if he had never spoken.

Isabella continues, her eyes narrowed now and alight with victory.

"There's no retribution for people like us, people who ruin the lives of those we love. There is no saving our souls."

"It's that kind of thinking that led to all of this in the first place," Isadora says, ignoring Will's continued efforts to get her attention. "God, you're actually arrogant enough to believe that what happened to your sister was entirely your fault! What kind of selfish bullshit thinking is that? You know what I think?" Isadora leans forward, arms dropping from their crossed position on her chest and coming to rest tensely at her sides. "I think that in the end you wanted an *excuse* to kill yourself."

Isabella opens her mouth to retaliate, but Isadora doesn't give her a chance.

"I think you came up with a million reasons to hate yourself. I think you managed to convince yourself that everyone hated you and everything was your fault, so you'd have the courage, the strength, to actually go through with it."

"That's not true!" Isabella shrieks. She suddenly appears quite demented, her face distorted into a horrific expression, eyes popping and brows raised so high they may as well become part of her ragged hairline. All traces of victory have fled her.

"Isn't it?" Isadora goads, for she can feel Isabella's hold on the world beginning to weaken. Her feet are now beginning to slip in the snow-coated mud. "You made up some banshee version of your mother because you were so convinced that she hated you after what happened, when I know that's not even remotely true."

"She blamed me!" Isabella brandishes the knife. "She hated me afterwards! Wouldn't talk to me. Wouldn't acknowledge me. She barely even wanted me as a daughter anymore!"

Jane flinches in the background, one hand creeping up to grip at her neck, face twisted in anguish. Good, Isadora thinks, as the snow flurries in the air grow wilder amidst Isabella's anger. Her feet gain more movement.

"And you don't think your mother was struggling? That she was grief-stricken after her baby daughter had died? She was grieving! It had nothing to do with you," Isadora sneers, spying Will's baffled concern in her peripheral vision. He doesn't realise her plan has changed tack, or that Isadora knows herself better than anyone ever could – *and she knows the best way to get her freedom is to emotionally fuck herself up.*

"And what about Tom?" Isadora ropes him in, eyes flicking to his sturdy frame. His olive skin glows golden against the frigid backdrop. "He crafted the damn cart, and I don't see him going around making weird reincarnations," she scoffs. "Face it, you just didn't know how to deal with it all … with how deeply and tragically sad you felt. You had to go and find an outlet, a way to express everything you were feeling and not feeling. You had to find something that would give you a mechanism to express all that self-hatred – and it made this. You made this hell for yourself to cope with it all, and it trapped you here. And now me, too." Isadora pushes herself forward as far as her immobile feet will allow. "You've been lying from the start, to me and to yourself." Isadora points to Jane. "Your mother loves you. She never stopped." Isabella's reddening eyes seek out her mother and she winces when they alight upon her. "And you can't convince me otherwise."

"And what about *your* mother?" Isabella fires back, unwilling or perhaps unable to face Isadora's words. "What about *that* fraying relationship?"

Isadora controls her flinch even as she raises one of her hands to her throat and wraps it securely around her Amethyst pendant. It warms comfortingly in her palm, settling the scuttling anguish in her midriff. "I know she loves me. Nothing else matters."

"And you mentioned the word 'strength'," Isabella changes tack. "We were never strong enough to face it all! We have always been weak, too weak to stay and live this life or to exist in this world. We did not deserve to live nor to die."

"Oh, grow up!" Isadora groans. "You saw one dead baby, big deal! I see hundreds of dead people and I haven't crumbled yet." One foot comes free from the sucking mud. Isadora keeps talking to cover the squelch. "But I am weak, you're right. I could never do what you did." She sucks in a deep breath. "Suicide is not something anyone who has never been on the inside of it can ever hope to understand." She and Isabella stare at each other, grey reflecting grey. "And I know that I would never be strong enough to go all the way. You were. I kept hanging on because I was too scared of what was on the other side. Because I *know* what's on the other side." Isabella shifts her feet, white dress shimmering. "I never want to be like you," Isadora says firmly. "In fact," she lets go of the necklace and leans back, "I'm willing to burn away that part of myself if I have to, so I never end up where you are."

Isabella stiffens, latching onto the two words Isadora had hoped she would notice. "Burn away?" She breathes, her grip on the knife slackening.

Isadora smiles thinly. "You know, it was way too easy to find your grave?" Isabella blanches. "Also, it turns out my brother, Will, is one hell of an investigator. Found out everything we needed to know about how to permanently get rid of a ghost." Her smile becomes mocking. "Have you ever heard the rumours about burning bones? About what it does to ghosts like you?" She laughs a little. "We read all about it. In your family library, in fact." Isadora allows her lips to peel all the way back from her teeth, revealing the smile of a shark.

"You plan to burn my remains?" Isabella asks quietly, expression glazed. "Without knowing the harm it will do to yourself? Tied as we are through—"

"What?" Isadora snorts. "Experience? That's all we share. It's *your* remains I'll be burning, not my own. As far as I'm concerned, I don't actually care what happens to you if we can't come to a conclusion that suits us both." She shrugs. "Either way, I'll be better off."

"Will you?"

"I'm not saying it again just to humour you." Just keep her talking, Isadora thinks as she subtly begins shifting her other foot, feeling the give as she slips closer and closer to freedom. *Keep her occupied. Don't let her see.* "So either we go ahead and have ourselves a therapy session and get this all sorted out peacefully, or I set your bones up in smoke and watch as you vanish into nothing. It's your choice."

Isabella is sour about it. Isadora can tell. The mere curl of her lips is enough to indicate how little she likes either suggestion, but there really is no other alternative. Isadora is not going to budge. She is not going to hurt herself and she is certainly not going to entertain Isabella's self-flagellation fantasy.

"You are not nearly as fearful or malleable as I expected," Isabella finally murmurs, knife tilting down towards her bloodstained skirt.

"I delight in exceeding expectations," Isadora replies mildly, carefully inching her foot back just a little further, trying to find some leeway in the sticky muck. Just a little more … *there!* Her foot slides free.

"Therapy is now in session."

Isadora lunges forward and, despite her stiff, freezing fingers, manages to grab Isabella's slack wrist and snatch the knife away. She flings the knife in Will's direction with a shout of 'Heads up!' that Will only just hears over Isabella's shriek of anger. Isadora sees him clumsily make the catch and, satisfied with her control over the situation for the time being, focuses her attention on her furiously struggling counterpart.

"Let go of me!" Isabella screeches.

Isadora screws her face up as the shrill cry rips through her ears. "What are you, part-banshee? Stop screaming!"

But Isabella doesn't. Instead, her howls get higher until they sound more like an animal in pain rather than a human filled with anger. Isadora glances down at her white-knuckled hand clamped over Isabella's mangled wrist and is startled to notice that, around the oozing blood and stringy sinews showing through Isabella's skin, a strange black substance is beginning to spread outwards from the wound, visible even beneath the wedding gown's sleeve. This is most definitely not part of the plan, and Isadora has not a clue what is going on. Not that it really matters in this moment.

Rather than continue to focus on the unknown, Isadora doubles down on what she does know. She needs Isabella to see things for what they truly are and not of her own 'oh, woe is me' imagining. And there's one very useful way to show her.

Time to turn the tables.

Isadora takes a deep breath, focuses sharply, locates that deep, dark, yawning cavern within her centre and forcefully rips the lid off. Pure energy fills her like sunshine bursting through a break in thick clouds. Head-to-toe she is one with the energy. Painfully aware of how it is surging within her body, Isadora casts outward to find Isabella. She is a dark, writhing mass of grief, anguish and aching sadness. With one forceful push, using their physical contact as a guide, Isadora invades that space.

Will watches in disbelief as Isadora's body becomes as taut as a bow string, as her grey eyes fill with a colour he can't even name. Isabella is desperately trying to escape his sister's iron grip, but to no avail. Instead, her body, too, becomes taut and, mere moments later, her eyes that same unnerving colour.

The world around them tilts sideways.

Isabella's heart leaps for the first time in over a hundred years when she realises where she is. *When* she is, in fact.

"Remember this day?"

She whirls around. Her wedding dress is just as bloodied as before, yet the long slices down her arms don't ooze or ache – they just are. Everything about her just *is*.

Isadora is standing behind her, still clad in that thick jumper and plain dark jeans. Her hair is a mess, yet she appears oddly wise, oddly knowing, as she surveys Isabella.

Isabella takes another longing glance around and nods. "I do remember," she murmurs. As if this day could ever leave her mind. Not in life and certainly never in death. She has, in her own horrific way, ensured that.

People are laughing. More specifically, her mother and baby sister are laughing. She herself is giggling along. Her dead heart squeezes as her eyes alight upon herself. Not much younger, yet certainly happier.

"Come on." Isadora is suddenly at her side, hand pressing into her back and relentlessly shoving her forward. Isabella stumbles as her feet attempt to keep her in place, but Isadora grips her upper arm and tugs her along, leaving Isabella no choice but to fall into awkward step beside her. This is no longer her domain. Isabella is frighteningly aware of this as she attempts to shift free, only to find that all the usual avenues are blocked by something far stronger than she.

Isadora leads them out of the courtyard and around to the front yard. The sun-soaked grass gleams emerald. Three figures are happily gambolling about in the shade of a copse of silver birch trees, protected from the heat of the day. Isabella refuses to look at her baby sister.

"You can't avoid it. Not forever. I mean," Isadora smiles sadly at her, "Not that you haven't made a good go of it so far. But you need to see this." She pinches Isabella's arm ruthlessly. "And I mean, *actually see it*. Not create some self-deprecating, self-loathing version of events. You need to see it how it was."

"Because you so very clearly understand how it was," Isabella replies sarcastically. Isadora's sad smile morphs into something almost tender.

"Sometimes it pays to be on the outside looking in. It's all about perspective."

"Why are you being so kind all of a sudden?" Isabella hugs her bloody arms against her chest, scowling. "After all, you know now for certain that I had a hand in killing your brother."

A rush of chilling fear darts up Isabella's spine at the darkness that abruptly crosses her modern counterpart's face. "This experience is not going to be so kind in a second. And if you're smart you might want to keep quiet on the dead sibling front. Unless you want your bones to be burned to dust?"

"It might be better," Isabella retorts, just to be petulant. She doesn't like the sudden tip of the scales. To be so powerless in her own domain is frightening. As is the thought of looking back at these memories, filled with such light and love as they are.

"And here I thought you enjoyed wallowing in all your woes and worries," Isadora replies. "We can continue hating life, or un-life, if we want when we get back – but not while therapy is in session. Come on." And she grabs Isabella's wrist, fingers deliberately pressing into the open wound (although there is still no pain?) and walks on.

Isabella wants to dig her heels in so badly her ankles itch with it. But she does not. She follows along dutifully and, as they draw closer to the picnic, her gaze is drawn magnetically to Tom, who is laughing gaily along with her mother and herself. Tom, darling Tom. Her innards crumple sickeningly, and Isabella feels her chest constricting with a near-silent *whoosh*. Isadora's brow twitches and Isabella knows she has noticed.

"That was a fine man you had," Isadora says casually, still forcefully pulling Isabella along, her pace unrelenting. "Do you regret choosing him?"

"Almost," Isabella whispers. Tom had tried to be with her, even after it all when their bones were mouldering away in the earth. But she had pushed him away, kept him confined to his cottage, where his last breaths had escaped his dying body. She loved him too much to allow him to leave her completely – but obviously she had not loved him enough to allow him to stay near her. He will never forgive her for that injustice, of that Isabella is certain. It's enough to break her dead heart into two clean halves.

Finally, she and Isadora crest the hill and come into full view of the picnic. Everything is just as Isabella remembers, just as serene, as picture-perfect as her memory allows. The last golden moment God would ever allow her to experience.

"Not God," Isadora says beside her, startling Isabella into realising she had been speaking aloud. When their eyes meet, Isadora simply tips her head towards the family and moves away, leaving Isabella to stand there alone, a shadow amidst the shining patch of sun her past self is basking in.

The childish sound of Wilhelmina's laughter blows along the breeze and, although the movement of the air has no effect on Isabella, she feels a sudden rush of chills on hearing that laugh. She knows what happens next and dreads it wholly and completely. The phrase 'like watching a car crash' would not have made much sense to Isabella, given her historical context, but if she had known the meaning it would perfectly describe this moment.

She can do nothing but watch. She catches the sharp movement of the rabbit in the underbrush, the twitch of the little dog's head as it notices. The sudden, frightening moment the wheels on Wilhelmina's little carriage begin to squeak faster and faster as the dog takes off, tail held high in anticipation of the chase. The scream that Isabella will never stop hearing, even in death. A discordant strike, like a bow drawn harshly along a violin's strings.

Seeing herself start in horror is a strange experience. Seeing her mother and her betrothed react in the same way is more so. She had not even thought about them, not in that moment. She had only been aware of her own skipping heart, the cold chill on her skin and her delayed reaction to a sudden, shocking event that had no business taking place on such a warm, wondrous day.

Watching her sister's head explode into red wetness against the fence paling for a second time stings more than it ever had the first time around. There is no shock to soften the blow, no adrenaline to mask the dreadful sickness and the horror churning in her insides. There is only a terrible clarity, presented to her in appallingly bright, otherworldly colour. And although she doesn't want to watch, she does.

She cannot tear her gaze away.

Isabella watches herself fall to her knees, face expressionless, one hand tangled in her hair, the other keeping her propped up on the springy grass. Her mother is screaming, she recognises absently. Crouched and screaming at what remains of her baby's body, hands grappling at the little white dress she had so lovingly wrapped her in that morning.

Tom is still standing, one hand on the back of his head as he, too, surveys the damage, nothing but disbelief painted starkly on his handsome face.

Isabella's chin wobbles traitorously.

She watches as her past self carefully pushes herself up, staggers and takes off in a tottering run. A tortured, wrenching cry follows her as the cotton of her skirt billows out in her wake, caught on the gentle breeze.

Isabella continues to observe as her mother turns to follow the cry, her face twisted in agony, hands still rhythmically clenching around Wilhelmina's dirtied dress. Only now, her dark eyes are shining with fresh concern.

"Isabella!" she calls, hesitating for a moment, torn between clutching at her baby's body and wanting to go after her eldest child. In the end her decision is clear and Isabella watches in disbelief as her mother stands, settling Wilhelmina's body reverently back onto the grass with a muffled sob and a promise to return swiftly, before turning and running to follow. Tom goes after her.

Isabella follows them, casting a final glance back at the twisted remains of her little sister as a drop of warmth trails down her dead skin.

She chases her mother and betrothed into that godforsaken courtyard. Her other self (the modern self) shadows her, moving in an almost leisurely fashion.

Her past self is crumpled in on herself in the centre of the courtyard. This, Isabella remembers well. Far too well.

She is sobbing, her back heaving. Any moment now her mother is going to run at her and begin raining down blows, striking her wherever she can, fists flying as her fury at losing her youngest daughter overcomes her. Any second now, Isabella thinks as she watches her mother draw closer, a few torn shreds of Wilhelmina's dress still wrapped in her trembling hands. It will happen soon, she knows. She is even prepared to see the wrathful expression replace her mother's usually calm demeanour. Soon, it will happen soon. Now. It should be happening now, only—

It isn't her mother who begins to strike her.

Instead, her past self has worked itself up into such a state her hands have risen and are now beating forcefully down to strike at herself. At her head, her arms, her chest, her face. Again and again and again, growing in intensity. The blows are hard and ruthless. And she is screaming. Sobbing. Wailing.

Her mother rushes forward, hands catching at Isabella's wrists as she attempts to restrain her. Jane's cries of Isabella's name are lost to her daughter. She casts a desperate look at Tom who jumps into action, flinging himself to his knees beside his fiancé, wrapping his strong arms around her while Jane keeps a tight hold on her wrists.

Isabella watches herself collapse against Tom's chest, still sobbing. Jane moves round so she is facing her daughter and kneels as well, resting her dark head of curls atop Isabella's. Together the small family grieves.

Isabella watches on, utterly confused.

"Not quite what you were expecting?"

She barely tics her head in Isadora's direction, so caught up is she in trying to process the tableau before her.

"This must be a lie," she whispers hoarsely. "A trick."

"It's the truth." Isadora says firmly. "This is the truth. You might lie to yourself, but this house won't lie when I ask it to show past events. This isn't the house under your control. This is the house and these grounds speaking truthfully for the first time in years. Finally showing all those things you were trying to hide."

"Why would I try to hide any of this?" Isabella turns. "When this is better than before?"

Isadora is silent for a moment, contemplative. Then, "I think, sometimes, it's easier to blame someone else for the way we turn out. Rather than acknowledge that we are the cause of our own problems. I think maybe it was easier for you to blame your mother, rather than acknowledge there was something wrong with you." She looks up at Isabella. "I think you were trying to protect yourself."

"I loved my mother."

"And sometimes we hurt the people we love the most to protect ourselves." Isadora speaks with a wisdom far greater than her age. Perhaps the curse Isabella has bestowed upon her has been twisted around to become a gift under this girl's fingers.

"The shooting confused me at first," Isadora continues. Isabella stares at her.

"Shooting?"

Isadora nods carefully. "When I first came here, I had a vision. That your mother shot you."

"And what are you surmising might be the cause of that? Now that you're a therapist?" Isabella asks sourly. Isadora smiles sadly.

"I think, in some way, you *felt* that your mother had shot you. That she had abandoned you, hurt you in some irreparable way. I've heard that heartbreak can feel like a gunshot, the way it pierces straight through you. Perhaps you imagined she had hurt you that way to make it easier to do what you did next. That you wouldn't regret it, because there was no one left to love you. Except Tom, perhaps."

She shrugs. "Then again, I could be talking out of my arse. It might not have meant anything at all except to scare me. Not everything has to be a metaphor for something else."

She turns to the family, still enfolded together in the courtyard. Isabella turns, too. Together, they watch as the image melts away. Isadora reaches out and grasps Isabella's wrist. Isabella closes her eyes against the various sensations, the pulling and rushing, until they emerge on the other side.

Isadora lets her wrist go. It flops against her stained skirts.

"So, are we still doing this, or …?" Isadora folds her arms across her chest and stares herself down. Isabella almost wilts beneath it, mind clearly still stuck back in the courtyard.

"Isabella." A different, soft voice catches her attention. Isabella peers up from beneath suspiciously wet lashes. Her mother is there, dark hair sleek and shining, face lined with concern and kindness, the likes of which Isabella had thought lost to her forever. Her porcelain mask begins to crack along the edges.

"I think it's time to let go, darling," her mother says, oh-so gently.

"After all I did?"

"She still loves you. Like I said," Isadora says. Then, "You were sick, Isabella. As well as being psychic. Or maybe *because* you're psychic, I don't know … I'm not a doctor. But the only person who blames you is you. If you can let go, we can all let go."

Isadora may not show it, but her heart is galloping in her chest. She honestly doesn't know whether this little trip down memory lane has been enough. Isabella may still decide their soul needs to pay more penance. She crosses her fingers beneath her folded arms and waits. She can see Will watching from the sidelines, face grim, eyes darting back and forth between the two girls, clenched fists tucked in his pockets.

Isadora wishes Iris were here. But before all this had come to a head, Isadora had asked her, and the old lady had said she would rather not watch, adding that she wished Isadora the best and would either see her on the other side of the veil or walking out of the grounds with her head held high. Isadora almost regrets not helping Iris on her way to whatever her version of heaven was, as she had helped Eric – but dwelling on things never got anyone any further down the track.

The snow continues to tumble, dancing this way and that in a private ballet set to the sound of the howling wind that is now whipping up around them.

Isabella says nothing. Simply stands there staring hollowly at the remaining members of her family. Tom is behind her mother, dark eyes giving nothing away. Almost as if he doesn't dare hope on the outcome; to have her so close, only to see her pull away once more, would be devastating. Although Isadora can't deny that walking away would be easier than letting go.

Abruptly, the air grows colder, the skies darker, and Isadora knows even before Isabella opens her mouth that she has been unsuccessful.

"I'm sorry," Isabella says mournfully. "But I cannot forgive my wrongs so easily." She holds out a bloody, glistening hand. "We haven't earned forgiveness—"

"*Bella.*"

Isabella jolts as though electrocuted.

"*Bella.*"

She twists involuntarily, a marionette on unpractised strings.

"*Bella.*" A childish, high-pitched burble carries on the wind. There's a shuffling sound. And then another call of '*Bella!*'.

Something black and spiky emerges from the bushes, large white eyes gleaming, followed by a four-limbed, completely whole and hale child. She's smiling at Isabella, showing two pearlescent teeth in her gummy grin. Big, wide blue eyes shine warmly, alight with happiness at seeing her older sister standing above her. This Wilhelmina has never seen the business end of a fence paling, or the tortured flagellation of her big sister. This Wilhelmina is as healthy and happy as the one that had been dressed that fateful morning by her mother in her white lacy dress. She giggles and continues to crawl towards Isabella, melting a path through the thick blanket of snow.

Isabella stares dumbstruck as Wilhelmina advances, determined to get to her sister, followed gaily by the spiky black demon cat whose oily tail is quivering, held high in the crisp air.

Finally, Wilhelmina reaches Isabella. Peering up in that open, wondrous way children have, she opens her chubby arms and wraps them firmly around Isabella's stationary legs. The snow in the air freezes, just simply stops where it is and hangs, suspended, like Christmas ornaments.

Isadora watches, mouth slightly open, as the gruesome, dripping red mixed with black on Isabella's sleeves begins to disappear. It fades from the deepest, darkest maroon to a paler almost pink colour, then to a lighter, barely-there rose and, finally, dissipates completely leaving the sleeves a pure, virgin white – the whole process much like watching film in reverse.

Isabella's lip is wobbling dangerously. Wilhelmina tugs at her sister's skirt and pouts.

"Bella, up!" she commands, holding her arms up expectantly.

Isabella hesitates, then, to Wilhelmina's delight, numbly crouches down to the child's level. Wilhelmina pats a delicate hand clumsily against Isabella's cheek and giggles brightly. Wilhelmina gently puts her hands on Isabella's shoulders, then, before her big sister can do anything else, flings her arms around Isabella's neck and nuzzles her head into her tense shoulder.

"Bella ..." she mumbles contentedly.

Isabella freezes for only a moment, as suspended in space and time as the snow all around her, then she can take it no longer. Her facade crumbles. She wraps her arms tightly around the little girl and holds her close, body shaking with suppressed sobs.

Isadora sees Jane place a trembling hand against her chest, clearly overwhelmed to see her deceased daughters together again.

Isabella stands, rocking her body from side to side as a sob makes it to the surface. Wilhelmina draws back and places a concerned hand back on her sister's cheek, tiny face creased in a frown.

"Why cry?" she asks solemnly. To Isadora's shock, Isabella releases a shaky laugh.

"I'm just so happy to see you," she manages to say, as evenly as she can through a hiccupping sob.

Wilhelmina's frown deepens.

"Where go?"

Isabella simply pulls Wilhelmina back into a hug. "It doesn't matter, little one." She says it reverently, as if she is coveting some precious jewel that she can't quite believe she has found. Perhaps she honestly can't believe that she is allowed to cradle this precious gem, when she had thought herself to be permanently sullied and unfit for anything so pure.

Whatever spell had been keeping the other ghosts at bay begins to weaken. Isadora can see Will attempting to make his way over to her, but she is distracted as Jane's resolve breaks and she rushes over to her girls. She hesitates for a moment, one shaking hand stretching out to rest on Isabella's hair – a request to join, which Isabella grants after only a second. Jane encircles them both in her arms, resting her cheek on Isabella's blonde head.

"I'm so sorry, Mama."

Isadora hears Isabella's sob and can only just make out Jane hushing her tenderly in response, arms tightening around her daughter.

Tom takes a careful step forward, then hesitates. He dithers on the spot, clearly unsure whether his advance will be accepted or reciprocated. Isabella looks up and her face crumples further. She carefully unwinds one arm from her little sister and gestures frantically. Jane, ever the attentive mother, gently takes Wilhelmina from her so the couple can meet each other in the middle.

Isabella closes the remaining gap as Tom rushes in, and they meet solidly in a mess of tangled arms. Isabella presses her face against Tom's sternum as he places his head on hers, lips moving frantically as he whispers something in her ear. Isabella can only nod and sob as she clutches at his back with white fingers. Tom presses a kiss into her hair and squeezes his eyes shut.

Isadora smiles. The last vestiges of the spell break and Will sidles up to her side.

"Are you okay?"

Isadora's smile widens. "Yeah, I think so. Why? Were you worried?"

"No."

And he says it with such a straight face, Isadora almost believes it.

"Mrreow …" Isadora looks down and her smile softens as Bee, cocked head and swishing tail in full swing, peers up at her looking far too proud of itself. She rolls her eyes.

"Yes, yes … okay." She crouches down and pats a careful hand down Bee's arched spine. "Well done." She even indulges in a gentle scratch behind its horn-like ears, which has Bee squinting its eyes and almost purring (if the strange chainsaw rumble emanating from it can really be classed as a purr) in thanks.

"Isadora."

She glances back up. Isabella is standing there, her now immaculate hands wringing anxiously at waist height. Isadora stands, aware of Bee twining itself around her legs almost possessively. Isabella pays it only a quick, uncertain glance before shuffling forward. Isadora is ready to tell her that 'there's no thank you necessary', but never gets there as Isabella suddenly pulls her into a hug. Neither says anything. There is no need. The hug lasts only a moment but speaks far louder than any words ever could. When Isabella draws back, she rests her hands momentarily on Isadora's shoulders before turning back to Tom's waiting arms.

Jane glides smoothly over to the two and transfers Wilhelmina back to her sister, who takes her immediately – still a touch awestruck at being allowed this closeness. Wilhelmina has no such reservations and coos happily as she snuggles into her elder's shoulder.

The snow starts back up again as the contented family glow in their unity. Only it's falling heavier and wetter than before. And it is no longer snow.

Isadora tips her head back when she realises and closes her eyes, revelling in the heavy droplets of rain that scatter around her. When she opens them again the snow is gone, leaving the paving stones in the courtyard slick and interspersed with spreading puddles. The foliage has returned to its natural green state and is bursting with life and colour. The wind has died off to nothing, leaving the steadily falling rain the only sound to accompany them.

When she focuses once more on the small gathering – surrounded now, she notices, by her usual extensive posse of ghosts who had perhaps been there this whole time and she simply hadn't noticed them – she sees that their shape is beginning to mist at the edges. The mistiness slowly grows until it has engulfed them all, and behind the curtain of pattering rain Isadora watches as they slowly, slowly completely fade away, taken by the cleansing wash of rain to wherever it is restful ghosts go.

Thank you, Isadora, she hears Isabella's voice echo in her mind, while her rapidly fading face forms a tiny smile right in the corner of her mouth.

Thank you.

And she's gone. Between one blink and the next Isabella Archer has vanished into the sheets of rain that continue to fall in a final blessing for the earth she had cursed for so long.

There's a moment of stillness. Isadora feels the air shift once more as that off-centre tilt that has been present for the weeks she has stayed in the house – from the time Isabella died and cursed the earth – finally begins to dissipate. She sighs and tilts her face to the sky, feeling the rain patter and kiss her skin, wiping it clean. It's as if she's being doused by the holiest water in the world.

Is this freedom? she wonders.

"We did it," she says to the sky, feeling the tiniest hint of a smile catch at her lips and refuse to let go.

"I'm still not sure how, though," Will admits from a few metres away. "I really thought we hadn't for a second there."

Isadora allows her grin to widen. "Yeah, Bee came through in the clutch at the end, didn't it?"

"How did it even know that would work, though? I thought Bee was in charge of the bones?"

Isadora's grin turns sly. "It was."

Will looks surprised. "So what happened?"

"Well," Isadora bends down and scoops Bee up. The creature's slinky body had been slithering nearer and nearer, and she holds it like a baby against her chest. "I asked Bee to do something special for me. And you might get mad, but ..." she pauses, then, "I was never going to burn those bones."

"You weren't?" Will does look shocked – and maybe a *little* mad.

Isadora shakes her head. "I asked Bee to bury them."

Will frowns, evidently confused. "Why would you do that?"

"I asked for the bones to be buried with Wilhelmina."

A long pause ensues. "And what was the expected outcome?"

"What happened," Isadora answers, then on seeing the expression on Will's face, elaborates. "I thought that maybe if she were buried next to her sister's remains, some part of her would feel at peace. They could be reunited in the earth, and it would come through in spirit? I don't know, I suppose it was a very uneducated guess, but I think it paid off. In the end."

"You're very lucky that it did!" Will, exasperated, exclaims loudly. "And after all that research I did for you!"

"Yeah," Isadora softens considerably, setting off alarm bells in Will's brain. "You did do that for me."

"You had nothing to base that guess on, either!" Will presses. "It was just a shot in the dark, admit it."

Isadora considers this, setting Bee back on solid ground. "I think maybe I knew deep down that some part of her had forgiven herself, but she was still too scared to let it all go. She needed to see Wilhelmina for herself and see how much she meant to her little sister. As soon as that tiny part of her forgave herself, Wilhelmina recognised this. Perhaps the bones solidified the tie between them and gave Wilhelmina the strength to reach out."

Will shakes his head. "I still think you're spitballing, but okay."

Isadora ignores her brother's scepticism and allows herself to bask in victory and in the cool freshness of the rain spattering against her face. The glow will not last; Isadora knows this. She can already sense that deep and powerful well residing in her centre filling up. She no longer has one foot in the grave and consequently has no right to speak to them. She has no more dominion here. And time, she realises, is running out. Isadora chews at her lip as guilt floods her stomach. She owes Will this.

Bee paws at her leg, white eyes as inscrutable as ever. Its head tips to the side. It's now or never, it seems to say. With a final writhing twitch, Bee rubs against her leg, gives her a gentle lick with its flickering red tongue, then saunters off into the bushes next to the stairs. Isadora grimaces as she watches it disappear. With a sudden pang she knows that that is the last time she will see the demon cat. That Bee isn't coming back. It hurts more than she thought it would. As will what comes next.

"Will?"

Her brother cocks his head. "Yeah?"

Isadora inhales shakily. "I need to tell you something."

"Ominous," he mutters. "Okay then. What?"

"Promise you won't get mad?"

He rolls his eyes. "That's so childish Isadora. What is it?"

She swallows nervously. "Isabella was right … when she said I was guilty. I am. And …" Isadora's throat constricts painfully. She changes tack, hoping it might make things easier. "You know how I always said you were different? To the other ghosts?"

Will frowns. "Yep. You said I was more like Iris – that 'unfinished business' type of spirit."

Isadora feels sick. "I lied. You were never like that."

The rain continues to fall even as Will freezes, staring at her so sharply with his dark eyes that Isadora finds herself squirming, hands jumping to fiddle with the hem of her jumper. Isadora waits, as her hair steadily soaks and starts sticking to her cheeks. Her prior sense of calm, of the cleanliness that came with the falling rain evaporates as her guilt spreads through her like an infection. It is clearly visible all over her face.

"Wha-what do you mean?" Will steps forward. "What does that mean? You lied?"

"It was me." Isadora shrinks into her shoulders, shuddering slightly. "It wasn't unfinished business that kept you here. It was me."

Will's mouth gapes as he struggles to comprehend and to find the words to respond to the weight of his sister's confession. Isadora twists anxiously on the hem of her jumper as the all-too-familiar hot sting of tears pricks her eyes. Before she can stop herself, she is blurting, "I couldn't do it, Will!"

Will shakes his head, backing off. Isadora chases after him. "I couldn't do it! I couldn't let you go. Will, please! You have to hear me out."

"Why?" Will shouts, then lets out a sardonic, humourless laugh. "Why should I even listen to you after you lied to me! And for so long, about so much. I was *suffering!*" He jabs a finger into his chest. "And you knew it! You saw it!"

"I did, I know. But please, Will, if you don't hear me out, I'll never get a chance to explain!"

"What do you mean 'never get a chance'? I'll always be here! It's not like I haven't got time! It's the only thing I do have!" Will yells back, furious. Isadora cringes, unused to seeing him like this. His eyes are dark, burning holes, and his upper lip is pulled into a wobbly sneer as he tries to keep his own tears at bay. Isadora gathers the fading remnants of her gift and throws it into her brother, watching as his skin lights up with that wondrous, luminescent glow.

Before he can retreat any further, Isadora snatches at his balled fist, catching him around the wrist. "Look!" she shouts, shaking his fist.

"Look at what? How generous you are to make me corporeal? I don't care Isadora, I don't—" He cuts off abruptly as he actually looks. His fingertips have disappeared. Shocked, Will allows his sister to speak.

"I knew it was a possibility," she waves his hand about weakly. "I need to tell you before I can't see you anymore, before you can't talk to me anymore."

Will looks as if he is seriously considering ignoring her and taking off, but Isadora stands her ground, summoning all the endurance she possesses to keep him corporeal.

"When I saw the accident … when I realised you were … dead," she swallows thickly. "I don't know how I did it. I've never done it before, but …" she licks her lips, valiantly fighting off tears, "I stopped you from going on. I stopped you—" she cuts off the protest she can see emerging, "because I was afraid. Afraid that my only friend was leaving me here. Alone." The tears quiver on her lower lids. "That there would be no one left who fully believed me without question. That I would be left here with no one to talk to. It was more than losing a brother. I would have lost the only person I knew who would never judge me for the things I'm able to see and who didn't think I was crazy. It was more than I could take without doing precisely what Isabella did. And I'm still scared." Her tears mingle with the rain streaking her face. "It was selfish of me, but I knew that if you left, I'd have nothing."

It takes a long time for Will to respond. So long that while she waits, Isadora allows the sobs burbling in her chest to break free and burst their banks, escaping in embarrassing hiccups. She has released Will's dematerialising arm at some point and has cupped her hands over her face. What should have been a time for celebrating a triumph has turned, instead, to the moment Isadora has been dreading. Indeed, she has been in complete denial that it would happen.

The rain, so comforting mere moments ago, has made her cold. She feels as if she is smothered in a wet, suffocating blanket that has chilled her right down to the bone.

But suddenly ...

Arms. Warm, solid and comforting. Enveloping her.

Her sobs only increase. The arms tighten and draw her in.

Will breathes in shakily and they remain that way for a long moment, then he speaks over the top of her saturated head.

Words that seem impossible.

Words she will never forget.

"I forgive you."

She doesn't hesitate. Isadora's flings her arms out and wraps them tightly around her brother's ribs. The siblings stay there until Isadora finds the strength to step back and swipe a jumper-clad arm across her face. "I wouldn't have survived today without you."

Will musters a wobbly grin, snorts wetly, then clears his throat awkwardly to disguise the fact he's been crying. "I know."

"Thank you." Isadora twists her hands together. "For everything."

There is so much more that remains unsaid.

Will shrugs, hands (one still clearly visible, the other barely there) sliding into his pockets – such a familiar habit it makes her feel a little warmer seeing it. "You don't have to thank me, Dora. 'S what family is for."

Isadora nods, sniffling. Unabashedly still crying, she swipes a hand across her forehead to push back her hair. She knows what she has to do now. But knowing doesn't make it a lesser feat, nor any less gut-wrenching.

"So is what I'm about to do next." Taking a deep breath, Isadora looks her brother dead in the eye and, with the very last remnants of her departing gift, says, "You can go now."

Will gasps, understanding flooding his young face. "Dora?" His voice trembles.

Isadora digs deep.

And lets go.

Her hold on Will's spirit releases. She feels it, like the rebound of a taut rubber band, stinging in the now nearly non-existent well within. A pressure she had barely been aware of lifting from her shoulders and leaving her lightheaded.

The pearly glow encapsulating Will's body increases, burning brighter and hotter with every passing second. Isadora feels the heat, can see it burning away the new rain droplets on her jumper and jeans. Just like Eric all those days ago, Will is a shining star, ready to depart for the next great place.

Isadora chokes on her tears and tries to smile as Will seeks her out, face alight with shock and – Isadora's heart twangs – fear.

Impulsively she reaches out and grabs his hand, feels his burning skin. "It's okay." She squeezes so tightly it hurts. Will returns the squeeze. "It's okay ..."

A final bright pulse of light and—

Isadora's hand closes on empty air.

She makes no sound as she sinks to her knees on the muddy paving stones and rests her hands on the cold slickness, clenching, knuckles white. Around her the ghosts who have occupied the various tracks she walked in her young life slowly begin to fade, memories and imprints of who they used to be becoming lost to the human eye once more. Skirts and canes, hats and gory injuries ... it all fades away into the falling rain, along with their mingling voices, their laughs and cries, until, for the first time in her life ...

Isadora is alone.

Well and truly alone.

She remains in the same spot. The rain hasn't stopped; it's all she can hear. There's no talking, no wailing, no crying (well, except for herself). Her ears are ringing in what feels to her to be real, total silence. Her head is now tucked into her drawn-up knees. Every inch of her is wet and cold, yet she can't bring herself to move.

This house, these grounds and all that they held ... how can she leave?

Thinking about it hurts. Thinking about Will is agony. Now there is nothing. No one.

She's alone.

Meow ...

She starts violently and lifts her head. Through swollen eyes, Isadora peers around. The broken remains of the Archer Estate stand sentinel behind her, empty windows keeping watch.

Meow ...

It's coming from the bushes next to the crumbling back steps. Isadora levers herself up slowly, wincing at the stiffness in her frozen limbs. She sloshes over to the shrubs, tucking her wet hair behind her ears. The bushes rustle as she draws close.

Isadora kneels tentatively on the soggy ground and reaches out to carefully part the branches. Tucked inside the thicket, bundled up into a fluffy ball, is a tiny black kitten. It peers mournfully at her with big, vibrant green eyes and curls itself into an even tighter ball of black fluff.

Isadora chuckles wetly, even as Bee's face swims forth in her mind. "Hello there." She gently stretches an arm out for the kitten to sniff. "Poor little thing."

The kitten appears hesitant at first but grows more confident when Isadora doesn't move. It pokes its head out and gives her hand a testing sniff. Isadora laughs lightly as its delicate white whiskers tickle her hand. The kitten purrs. Apparently, she has passed the test.

"You happy for me to pick you up?" Isadora asks sweetly and somewhat tearfully. She opens her hand and strokes a soft finger along the kitten's velvety brow. The kitten stretches and rubs its cheek happily along her finger. Isadora takes this as a clear yes and tenderly scoops the kitten up, lifting it from the bushes and cradling it to her chest.

She and the kitten lock eyes, and it's almost love at first sight.

"Do you want to come home with me?" Isadora asks, even as the kitten snuggles in and huffs contentedly. "Yeah," Isadora murmurs quietly, patting the velvety soft fur. "Home."

She hasn't thought about home in so long. Home used to be wherever her family was. Then, just wherever she felt safe. Maybe …

She nods to herself. Mind made up, Isadora shifts the kitten carefully so she can hold her arm comfortably enough to walk. And she walks. Back up the stairs and through the busted back door.

The house echoes emptily around her. Feet scuffing in the thick layer of dust coating the floor, Isadora walks. Past the grand staircase that leads up to her temporary and past bedroom. Past the dining room with its once magnificent dining table and chandelier, now no more. Past the sitting room with its elegant portraits and decorative furniture, empty now save for the smattering of broken glass littering the buckling floorboards.

She exits the front door, clambering awkwardly past the boards keeping the entrance sealed off. Down the concrete steps and to the circular driveway at the front of the house. She glances up at the dripping grove of silver-birch trees, and the fence nearby where both Wilhelmina and Isabella are buried.

Isadora turns and looks at the grand Archer house one final time.

"Goodbye."

And with that, she walks down the puddle-strewn driveway to the rusted iron fence. With no ghost parade following, she slips easily past the gate, only stumbling once and earning a startled hiss from the huddled kitten, to which she apologises immediately.

Once past the gate, Isadora doesn't look back.

The road ahead is littered with fallen leaves, all slick and stuck together with moisture, and the fence lining the pothole-riddled road is overgrown with greenery. She walks. Down the road, past the trees and fields, feeling simultaneously lighter and heavier with each step. The kitten is a beacon of warmth against her chest. Her Amethyst – probably powerless now save for her belief in it – bumps comfortingly in rhythm with each step.

"I'm going to call you Bee," Isadora tells the kitten. It yawns, little pink mouth opening wide to reveal a set of needle-sharp white teeth. Isadora smiles. "Yeah. I like it, too."

And she walks on down the road, quietly keen to see her parents and feel what it is to be family again.

For what we are will always be, and what we are, is a memory.

ABOUT THE AUTHOR

Kate Dakin is a 25-year-old author who lives in Western Junction, central Tasmania, with her mother, father and (before they left home to begin their own life journeys) her brothers, Aaron and Jared.

Kate's love for literature and storytelling began at a young age, and she passed many hours of her childhood and teenage years writing, in her own words, 'short stories, lengthy stories, absolute gibberish and, occasionally, something more'.

Kate's fascination for old-fashioned haunted houses, as well as her love of classic horror stories, inspired her to write this, her debut novel.

When she's not writing, Kate studies Education at the University of Tasmania, works part-time as a receptionist in the dental and veterinary industries and loves spending quality time with her expert writing partner and loyal companion, Columbus the cat, whose quirky personality provided inspiration for one particular character in the book. No prizes for guessing who!